ANALOG
6

is an anthology of original
and provocative science-
fiction short stories chosen
by *Analog* Magazine's
editor-in-chief,
John W. Campbell.

Since 1929, when it was first
published under the name
*Astounding Tales of Super
Science, Analog* has come
to be recognized as a leader
in the science-fiction field—
as a glance at the list of
distinguished writers
included in this volume
will show.

ANALOG 6
was originally
published by
Doubleday & Company, Inc.

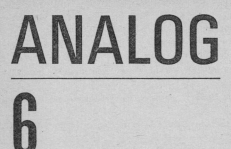

ANALOG
6

Edited by
John W. Campbell

PUBLISHED BY POCKET BOOKS NEW YORK

ANALOG 6

Doubleday edition published May, 1968
A Pocket Book edition
1st printing .... April, 1969

"Prototaph" by Keith Laumer, "Call Him Lord" by Gordon R. Dickson, and "CWACC Strikes Again" by Hank Dempsey, reprinted by permission of the authors' agent, Robert P. Mills Literary Agent.

"The Easy Way Out" by Lee Correy, reprinted by permission of the author and the author's agent, Lurton Blassingame.

"Stranglehold" by Christopher Anvil, reprinted by permission of the author and the author's agent, Scott Meredith Literary Agency, Inc.

"Bookworm, Run!" by Vernor Vinge, reprinted by permission of the author.

"Giant Meteor Impact" by J. E. Enever, reprinted by permission of the author.

"Early Warning" by Robin S. Scott, reprinted by permission of the author.

"The Message" by Piers Anthony and Frances Hall, reprinted by permission of the authors.

"Light of Other Days" by Bob Shaw, reprinted by permission of the author and the author's agent, Ted White.

"Something to Say" by John Berryman, reprinted by permission of the author.

"Letter from a Higher Critic" by Stewart Robb, reprinted by permission of the author.

". . . Not a Prison Make" by Joseph P. Martino, reprinted by permission of the author.

"10:01 A.M." by Alexander B. Malec, reprinted by permission of the author.

Standard Book Number: 671-75357-6.
Library of Congress Catalog Card Number: 63-7719.
Copyright, ©, 1966, 1968, by the Conde Nast Publications, Inc.
All rights reserved. This **Pocket Book** edition is published
by arrangement with Doubleday & Company, Inc.
Printed in the U.S.A.

To Peg
For 6257 reasons . . .
                    so far

CONTENTS

INTRODUCTION

John W. Campbell

These stories in ANALOG 6 are selected from the pages of the Condé-Nast science-fiction magazine, *Analog,* from issues that appeared during its thirty-sixth year of publication.

I am, myself, starting on my thirty-first year as editor of the magazine, and my own thirty-sixth year of working in the field of science fiction—my first story was published in January, 1930.

By this time, you'd think I'd know pretty definitely exactly what that field of "science fiction" was, and would be able to give a clear, succinct definition of precisely what it is I'm doing, and what "science fiction" is.

However it turns out that defining "science fiction" is, to a science-fictioneer, about as *un*simple as defining "life" is for a biologist. As any good trial lawyer can assure you, a lawyer can make any expert biologist witness on the stand seem foolish by simply asking him to define what this thing, "life," is that he says he's an expert witness on. Any field of great scope, involving great adaptability and flexibility, is extremely difficult to define, because it has no clear-cut, sharply definable edges, and the more you study and work with it, the more you find there are exceptions to any definitions that you knew before.

We think of life as being some organization that can grow, reproduce itself, react to stimuli, can repair itself if damaged, and can adapt to changed environmental conditions. Yes . . . but all these things are also true of inorganic crystals—and some forms of life (viruses) can be crystallized from solution, just as salt or sugar can. A crystal of copper sulfate, growing in a "nutrient medium" (a saturated solution of copper sulfate) will, if it's broken, heal its wound, and restore itself to the perfect, very complex symmetry unique to copper sulfate crystals.

Nickel sulfate, grown in a solution at room temperature, forms long, rectangular bars of nickel sulfate heptahydrate; heat the solution to a Death Valley daytime temperature, however, and the crystals adapt—they change into a completely different form, a sort of barrel-shaped crystal of many facets, called nickel sulfate hexahydrate.

Crystals of Rochelle Salt, or of quartz, or many other substances react to pressure stimulus by generating electricity —which makes them very useful in phonograph pickup cartridges.

The fact that many bacteria have one form at room temperature, and change into an entirely different form—"encysted"—in hot solutions does not of course mean that they are non-living. And of course a seed, *as a seed,* doesn't fulfill the usual definitions of "living"; it has to stop being a seed and become a "sprout" before it shows growth, etc.

The very adaptability of life makes definition enormously difficult; the boundary between "living" and "non-living" is so extremely broad, and so constantly shifting as we learn more and more about what living things can do.

Science fiction is equally difficult to define, for very similar reasons. The two major boundaries to be considered are the boundaries between science and science fiction, and that between science fiction and fantasy.

If a group of NASA scientists gets together today, and writes up a program of expected developments in space exploration today—are they writing science fiction?

When the authors of twenty-five to thirty-five years ago wrote up discussions of expected developments in space exploration, they were writing science fiction, of course—although I well recall that my MIT professors, who knew of my writing in the field, called it "science fantasy" and "nonsensical pseudoscience."

But notice that all the science-fiction writers of the thirties were doing was extrapolating—predicting—from known scientific facts to probable future consequences and achievements.

And isn't that precisely what today's NASA scientists are trying to do?

Incidentally, while the professors of the time called it "science fantasies," we did a more accurate job of prediction and basic design studies of the future, than they did. The basic design concepts of modern space probes—both robotic and manned—were worked out in pretty fair detail by 1940.

Back in the early thirties, Willy Ley and Werner Von Braun were "science-fiction fans"; the pieces Willy Ley wrote then were "science-fiction stories." Now he writes very similar material which is called "articles on rocket science." And Dr. Von Braun, of course, didn't *write* science fiction; he *did* it.

The boundary between "science" and "science fiction" quite evidently shifts quite largely because of the beliefs and viewpoints of others—not because of any inherent difference in the material discussed.

Whether you call a crystalline material "living" or "nonliving" also changes with time—if you didn't know that a virus can be crystallized from solution, it might be easy to say "this is a crystalline material; therefore it must be nonliving." But when you know about the work done on crystalline Tobacco Mosaic Virus—it gets harder to tell living from non-living. But that's solely a matter of how much you know, of what your opinion-belief is—not a matter of truth-in-reality.

Oh, it's true that some pieces can be very clearly, definitely distinguished as science fiction, not science. Edgar Rice Burroughs' books about John Carter of Mars, and his friends such as Tars Tarkas, the gigantic six-limbed green warrior of Mars . . . pure fiction. Mars, after all, has practically no atmosphere; there are no verdant canals, but only bleak scars of gigantic meteor impacts, and geological fault-lines.

Yet . . . Burroughs' stories were based on the descriptions of Mars produced by the researches of one of America's foremost astronomers of the day—Dr. Percival Lowell, at his Flagstaff Observatory that he had set up for the primary purpose of studying Mars.

So again . . . was the scientist, Lowell, writing science fiction in his reports? They turned out not to be truth-in-reality . . .

Speculation is speculation because it's a structure based on some facts, but not sufficient for a solid structure. Like a painting of a Tyrannosaurus Rex, showing him with a green-gray scaly hide. These are based on facts; the skeleton fossils show that Tyrannosaurus existed—that he was that big, had teeth like that, tiny forelimbs and gargantuan haunches and a huge tail—but his color and the nature of his hide are pure imagining.

Science fiction tries to take the skeleton of scientific facts and build around it a body of a living future. Sometimes we go pretty wildly wrong—as wrong as scientists have gone in their speculations. When those gigantic fossil bones were first found, for instance, the scientist-philosophers of the time reported that they had found parts of the skeletons of the Giants of biblical days, and drew pictures of men forty feet tall. (Nobody had ever seen a giant saurian, of course, and these bones were clearly the thigh-bones of bipedal animals, so necessarily that meant gigantic men!)

The other boundary of science fiction is the pure-fantasy division. *Dracula* we can surely and safely put in the fantasy category, just as we can surely and safely put pig-iron ingots in the "non-living" category.

"Call Him Lord," on the other hand—Gordon Dickson's story in this volume—is just as definitely and clearly science fiction. Oh, it contains no super-scientific gadgetry, save as a vague, off-stage background, but it represents a type of science fiction of real importance—the sociological science fiction. The broad freedom science fiction permits allows the author to set up a clearer picture of the real and complex problems of societies. Read the story, and you'll realize Dickson is right; there are many sins and flaws that a galactic emperor might be forgiven—but there is one, not so obvious, that is absolutely intolerable, because it will inevitably generate all others!

But that is simply the extreme, and simplified case of any ruler—that flaw cannot exist in a tolerable ruler at any level.

"Light of Other Days" also is clearly pure science fiction; it presents one and only one new postulate—the existence of "slow glass," and all the story stems from the probable human problems involved in such a simple proposition.

The difficult separation of fantasy from science fiction comes in those areas where there is data, observational facts, which Science stubbornly rejects, and labels as "folklore" or "hoax" or "fantastic nonsense" and refuses to examine. There always is such data—and such data is fair game for a science-fictioneer. He has a perfect right to accept the data, propose an integrated explanation of the observational material, and use that as a basis for a story.

For nearly three centuries now, Science has been stubbornly maintaining that there was *no* value whatever in astrological ideas—that it was totally, completely, and absolutely nonsense. That statements such as "With Saturn in quadrature to Jupiter, and Venus in triune and Earth in opposition . . ." were absolute hokum statements.

NASA scientists are now boning up on such statements; it's been found that the angular relationships between the planets *do* affect human life—particularly and most directly it determines the length of life of astronauts. Certain specific angular relationships of the shifting masses of the planets, it is now known, affect the sun—produce intense sunspots and "flares." Any astronaut caught outside earth's 1000-mile deep atmosphere during a flare would be riddled by so much high-energy radiation from the "solar wind," that he'd get a lethal dose of radiation long before he could duck back into safety.

It's long been known that solar flares cause magnetic storms on earth; it's now being discovered that the solar wind has a marked effect on the uppermost layers of earth's atmosphere. And this in turn affects the lower levels. Inescapable conclusion: Since the positions of the planets *do* affect the sun's magnetic fields, and produce sunspots and flares, which do affect earth's atmosphere—the positions of the planets is a key factor in our weather.

Precisely as astrologers claimed centuries ago!

Again, dowsing is an ancient folk art—the business of using forked twigs for locating water for wells. And ever since Science has been capitalized, Science has utterly denied the reality of dowsing.

The ability to dowse for well water seems to be a rare human talent—like the possession of "perfect pitch," or perfect memory for exact color shades. (Some women can look at a piece of material, and go shopping a week later half a continent away, and pick out an exactly matching thread by pure color memory; it's a rare talent.)

But the ability to dowse for underground pipes—gas pipes, electric cables, water pipes, etc.—seems to be about as common as the ability to play "Chopsticks" on the piano. Ten minutes' practice, and practically anyone who isn't totally tone-deaf can do it. So—and five minutes' instruction and practice with the dowsing rods, and almost anyone can start locating buried pipes. That, for some reason, is enormously easier than locating natural well water.

This is a phenomenon that is widely used, today, in towns and cities all over the country. Utility company field crews use it; plumbers use the technique to find where pipes are located.

But despite the constant, widespread, actual engineering application of this technique—Science-with-a-capital-S denies that any such thing exists at all!

Now when a writer does a story involving such a technique —the professors will, of course, call it "science fantasy" or just plain "fantasy."

Sorry—but they are wrong. Any technique that is routinely used by working engineers in the field is an absolutely valid ground for speculation; the mere fact that Science won't acknowledge that it exists has nothing whatever to do with its truth-in-reality. If it works—and it does, or engineers with a job to do wouldn't bother carrying the rods on their trucks— it *must* represent some truth-in-reality.

It's clearly some form of extrasensory perception; it isn't the rods that do the job—it's the man holding them.

Discussions of, and speculations about, extrasensory talents are, then, a perfectly legitimate basis for a science-fiction story, and it does *not* have to be a fantasy.

The major distinction between fantasy and science fiction is, simply, that science fiction uses one, or a very, very few new postulates, and develops the rigidly consistent logical consequences of those limited postulates.

Fantasy makes up its rules as it goes along; if the hero gets stuck in an impossible situation, why—*zut* he waves his magic wand, introduces a totally new proposition into the story, and wipes out the opposition. If he's trapped under water, why that's easy—he says the Magic Words, and *blurble!* Now he can breathe water instead of air, and he need only say The Word backward to breathe air when he gets out. The basic nature of fantasy is "The only rule is, make up a new rule any time you need one!"

The basic rule of science fiction is "Set up a basic proposition—then develop its consistent, logical consequences."

Now for one thing, that's a great way to study social concepts—to consider the logical human consequences of various cultural propositions, from absolute dictatorship to absolute anarchy.

Which is, of course, why so many utopian, and negative-utopian novels, ranging from Plato's *Republic,* through *Utopia* itself, to Orwell's *1984,* have been science fiction.

Science fiction gives the author freedom to explore new concepts—but it's a disciplined freedom; it demands of him honesty of thought and consistency.

Fantasy gives him the absolute and undisciplined freedom of an LSD "trip"—he can get away with anything. No honesty of thought, no discipline, no consistency is imposed. Anything goes with a flick of his magic wand, and the explanation of anything whatever is simply "Because I want it that way!"

One of the reasons that science fiction is a favorite literature of many scientists—they read it and write it—is that it is one of the few places in the modern world where a scientist is permitted to publish his speculations on what might be done with present scientific knowledge.

That's why the first published discussions of rocket ships, life-support systems, and interplanetary orbit calculations were published in science-fiction magazines—why the first general discussions of atomic power and atomic weapons appeared in science fiction.

And so accurate were some of the descriptions that, during WWII, my magazine had some trouble with one of our stories. One author had published a story describing a U-235 atomic bomb with startlingly accurate detail—so much so that the Pentagon feared someone on the Manhattan Project had gotten loose-mouthed in a bar, or at a party, and spilled beans that weren't for sprouting just yet!

No one had; it was just that the author, working from data published before the war, had come to the same conclusions the Manhattan Project scientists did—simply that, working from the same basic data, the story predicted the same mechanism that the Los Alamos scientists did.

Of course—it's a lot easier to predict and speculate than it is to build and do. It's a lot quicker, too.

Which is why science fiction can lead the parade as consistently as it does!

John W. Campbell

Mountainside, N.J.
September 1967

PROTOTAPH

Keith Laumer

I was already sweating bullets when I got to the Manhattan Life Concourse; then I had to get behind an old dame that spent a good half hour in the Policy Vending Booth, looking at little pieces of paper and punching the keys like they were fifty-credit bet levers at the National Lottery.

When I got in, I was almost scared to code my order into the Vendor; but I was scareder not to. I still thought maybe what happened over at Prudential and Gibraltar was some kind of fluke, even though I knew all the companies worked out of the Federal Actuarial Table Extrapolator; and Fate never makes a mistake.

But this had to be a mistake.

I punched the keys for a hundred thousand C's of Straight Life; nothing fancy, just a normal working-man's coverage. Then I shoved my ID in the slot and waited. I could feel sweat come out on my scalp and run down by my ear while I waited. I could hear the humming sound all around me like some kind of bees bottled up back of the big gray panel; then the strip popped out of the slot, and I knew what it said before I looked at it:

UNINSURABLE.

I got the door open and shoved some guy out of my way and it was like I couldn't breathe. I mean, think about it: Twenty-one years old, out in the city to take my chances all alone, with no policy behind me. It was like the sidewalk under your feet turned to cracked ice, and no shore in sight.

A big expensive-looking bird in executive coveralls came out of a door across the lobby; I guess I yelled. Everybody was looking at me. When I grabbed his arm, he got that mad

1

look and started to reach for his lapel button—the kind that
goes with a Million Cee Top Crust policy.

"You got to listen," I told him. "I tried to buy my in-
surance—and all I got was this!" I shoved the paper in his
face. "Look at me," I told him. "I'm healthy, I'm single, I
finished Class Five Subtek school yesterday, I'm employed!
What do you mean, uninsurable?"

"Take your hands off me," he said in kind of a choky
voice. He was looking at the paper, though. He took it and
gave me a look like he was memorizing my face for picking
out of a line-up later.

"Your ID," he held out his hand and I gave it to him. He
looked at it and frowned an important-looking frown.

"Hm-m-m. Seems in order. Possibly some, er . . ." He
pushed his mouth in and out and changed his mind about
saying it; he knew as well as I did that the big actuarial
computer doesn't make mistakes. "Come along," he turned
his back and headed for the lift bank.

"What have I got, some kind of incurable disease or something?" I was asking them; they just looked at me and gog-
gled their eyes. More of them kept coming in, whispering
together; then they'd hurry away and here would come a new
bunch. And none of them told me anything.

"The old crock in front of me, she was ninety if she was
a day!" I told them. "She got her policy! Why not me?"

They didn't pay any attention. Nobody cared about me;
how I felt. I got up and went over to the first guy that had
brought me up here.

"Look," I said. I was trying to sound reasonable. "What
I mean is, even a guy dying in the hospital can get a policy
for *some* premium. It's the law; everybody's got a right to be
insured. And—"

"I know the laws governing the issuance of policies by this
company," the man barked at me. He was sweating, too.
He got out a big tissue and patted himself with it. He looked
at a short fat man with a stack of papers in his hand.

"I don't care what kind of analysis you ran," he told him.
"Run another one. Go all the way back to Primary if you
have to, but get to the bottom of this! I want to know why
this"—he gave me a look—"this individual is unique in the
annals of actuarial history!"

"But, Mr. Tablish—I even coded in a trial run based on a one hundred per cent premium, with the same result: No settlement of such a claim is possible—"

"I'm not interested in details; just get me results! The computer has available to it every fact in the known universe; see that it divulges the reasoning behind this . . . this anomaly!"

The fat man went away. They took me to another room and a doctor ran me through the biggest med machine I ever saw. When he finished I heard him tell the big man I was as sound as a Manhattan Term Policy.

That made me feel a little better—but not much.

Then the fat man came back, and his face was a funny white color—like some raw bread I saw once on a field trip through Westside Rationing. He said something to the others, and they all started to talk at once, and some of them were yelling now. But do you think any of them told me anything? I had to wait another hour, and then a tall man with white hair came in and everybody got quiet and he looked at papers and they all got their heads together and muttered; and then they looked at me, and I felt my heart pounding up under my ribs and I was feeling sick then, med machine or no med machine.

Then they told me.

That was two days ago. They got me in this room now, a fancy room up high in some building. There're guys around to do whatever I want—servants, I guess you'd call 'em. They gave me new clothes, and the food—West Rat never put out anything like this. No liquor, though—and no smokes. And when I said I wanted to go out, all I got was a lot of talk. They treat me—careful. Not like they like me, you know, but like I was a bomb about to go off. It's a funny feeling. I guess I got more power than anybody that ever lived —more power than you can even get your mind around the thought of. But a lot of good it does me. There's only the one way I can use it—and when I think about that I get that sick feeling again.

And meanwhile, I can't even go for a walk in the park.

The president was here just now. He came in, looking just like the Tri-D, only older, and he came over and looked at me kind of like I looked at him. I guess it figures: There's only one of each of us.

"Are you certain there's not some . . . some error, George?" he said to the wrinkly-faced man that walked just behind him.

"The Actuarial Computer is the highest achievement of a thousand years of science, Mr. President," he said in a deep voice like the mud on the bottom of the ocean. "Our society is based on the concept of its infallibility within the physical laws of the Universe. Its circuits are capable of analyses and perceptions that range into realms of knowledge as far beyond human awareness as is ours beyond that of a protozoan. An error? No, Mr. President."

He nodded. "I see." That's all he said. Then he left.

Now I'm just sitting here. I don't know what to do next—what to say. There's a lot to this—and in a way, there's nothing. I got to think about it, dope it out. There's got to be something I can do—but what?

The machine didn't say much. They took me down to the sub-vault where the big voice panel is located and where the primary data goes in, and let me hear for myself. It didn't give any explanations; it just told me.

Funny; in a way it was like something I've always known, but when you hear Fate come right out and say it, it's different.

When I die, the world ends.

BOOKWORM, RUN!

Vernor Vinge

They knew what he'd done.

Norman Simmons cringed, his calloused black fingers grasped "Tarzan of the Apes" so tightly that several pages ripped. Seeing what he had done, Norman shut the book and placed it gently on his desk. Then, almost shaking with fear, he tried to roll himself into a ball small enough to escape detection. Gradually he relaxed, panting; Kimball Kinnison would never refuse to face danger. There must be a way out. He knew several routes to the surface. If no one saw him . . .

They'd be hunting for him; and when they caught him, he would die.

He was suddenly anxious to leave the prefab green aluminum walls of his room and school—but what should he take? He pulled the sheet off his bed and spread it on the floor. Norman laid five or six of his favorite books on the sheet, scuttled across the room to his closet, pulled out an extra pair of red and orange Bermuda shorts, and tossed them on top of the books. He paused, then added a blanket, his portable typewriter, his notebook, and a pencil. Now he was equipped for any contingency.

Norman wrapped the sheet tightly about his belongings and dragged the makeshift sack to the door. He opened the door a crack, and peeked out. The passageway was empty. He cautiously opened the door wide and stepped down onto the bedrock floor of the tunnel. Then he dragged the sheet and its contents over the doorsill. The bag dropped the ten inches which separated the aluminum floor of his room from the tunnel. The typewriter landed with a muffled clank. Norman glanced anxiously around the corner of the room, up the tunnel. The lights were off in the Little School. It was Saturday and his teachers' day off. The Lab was closed, too, which was unforeseen good luck, since the aloof Dr. Dunbar was usually there at this time.

He warily circled about a nearby transport vehicle. *Model D-49 Food Cargo Carrier, Army Transport Mark XIXe. Development Contract D-49f1086-1979. First deliveries, January, 1982 . . . RESTRICTED Unauthorized use of RE-STRICTED materials is punishable by up to 10 years imprisonment, $10,000 fine, or both: Maintenance Manual: Chapter I, Description . . . The Mark XIXe is a medium speed transport designed to carry loads of less than fifteen tons through constricted areas, such as mine tunnels or storage depots. The "e" modification of the Mark XIX indicates the substitution of a 500-hp Bender fusion power source for the Wankel engine originally intended for use with the XIX. As the Bender pack needs only the natural water vapor in the air for fuel, it is an immense improvement over any other power source. This economy combined with the tape programmed autopilot, make the XIXe one of . . .* Norman shook his head, trying to cut off the endless flow of irrelevant information that came to mind. With practice, he was sure that he would eventually be able to pick out just the data he needed to solve problems, but in the meantime the situation was often very confusing.

The passage he was looking for was between the 345th and 346th fluorescent tube—counting from his room; it was on the left side of the tunnel. Norman began running, at the same time pulling the sack behind him. This was an awkward position for him and he was soon forced to a walk. He concentrated on counting the lighting tubes that were hung from the roof of the tunnel. Each fluorescent cast harsh white light upon the walls of the tunnel, but between the tubes slight shadows lingered. The walls of the passage were streaky with whorls almost like wood or marble, but much darker and grayish-green. As he walked a slight draft of fresh air from faraway air regenerators ruffled the hair on his back.

Norman finally turned to face the left wall of the passage and stopped—343-344-345. The liquid streaks of pyrobole and feldspar appeared the same here as in any other section of the tunnel. Taking another step, Norman stood at the darkest point between the two lights. He carefully counted five hand-widths from the point where the wall blended into the floor. At this spot he cupped his hands and shouted into the wall: "Why does the goodwife like Dutch Elm disease for tea?"

The wall replied, "I don't know, I just work here."

Norman searched his memory, looking for one piece of information among the billions. "Well, find out before her husband does."

There was no reply. Instead, a massive section of bedrock swung noiselessly out of the wall, revealing another tunnel at right-angles to Norman's.

He hurried into it, then paused and glanced back. The huge door had already shut. As he continued up the new tunnel, Norman was careful to count the lights. When he came to number 48, he again selected a place on the wall and shouted some opening commands. The new tunnel was slanted steeply upward as were the next three passages which Norman switched to. At last he reached the spot in the sixth tunnel which contained the opening to the surface. He paused, feeling both relief and fear: Relief because there weren't any secret codes and distances to remember after this; fear because he didn't know what or who might be waiting for him on the other side of this last door. What if they were just hiding there to shoot him?

Norman took a deep breath and shouted: "There are only 3,456,628 more shopping days till Christmas."

"So?" came the muffled reply.

Norman thought: *NSA (National Security Agency) cryptographic (code) analysis organization. Report Number 36390-201. MOST SECRET. (Unauthorized use of MOST SECRET materials is punishable by death.): "Mathematical Analysis of Voice and Electronic Pass Codes," by Melvin M. Rosseter, RAND contract 748970-1975. Paragraph 1: Consider L, an m by n matrix (rectangular array—arrangement) of (n times m) elements (items) formed by the Vrevik product . . .* Norman screamed shrilly. In his haste, he had accepted the wrong memories. The torrent of information, cross-references and explanatory notes, was almost as overwhelming as his experience the time he foolishly decided to learn all about plasma physics.

With an effort he choked off the memories. But now he

was getting desperate. He had to come up with the pass code, and fast.

Finally, "So avoid the mash. Shop December 263."

A large section of the ceiling swung down into the tunnel. Through the opening, Norman could see the sky. But it was gray, not blue like the other time! Norman had not realized that a cloudy day could be so dreary. A cold, humid mist oozed into the tunnel from the opening. He shuddered, but scrambled up the inclined plane which the lowered ceiling section formed. The massive trapdoor shut behind him.

The air seemed still, but so cold and wet. Norman looked around. He was standing atop a large stony bluff. Scrub trees and scraggly brush covered most of the ground, but here and there large sections of greenish, glacier-scoured bedrock were visible. Every surface glistened with a thin layer of water. Norman sneezed. It had been so nice and warm the last time. He peered out over the lower land and saw fog. It was just like the description in the "Adventures of the Two and the Three." The fog hung in the lower land like some tenuous sea, filling rocky fjords in the bluff. Trees and bushes and boulders seemed to lurk mysteriously within it.

This mysterious quality of the landscape gave Norman new spirit. He was a bold adventurer setting out to discover new lands.

He was also a hunted animal.

Norman found the small footpath he remembered, and set off across the bluff. The wet grass tickled his feet and his hair was already dripping. His books and typewriter were getting an awful beating as he dragged them over the rough ground.

He came to the edge of the bluff. The grass gave way to a bedrock shelf overlooking a drop of some fifty feet. Over the years, winter ice had done its work. Sections of the face of the cliff had broken off. Now the rubble reached halfway up the cliff, almost like a carelessly strewn avalanche of pebbles except that each rock weighed many tons. The fog worked in and out among the boulders and seemed to foam up the side of the cliff.

Norman crept to the edge of the cliff and peered over. Five feet below was a ledge about ten inches wide. The ledge slanted down. At its lower end it was only seven feet above the rocks. He went over, clinging to the cliff with one hand, and grasping the sack which lay on the ground above him with the other. Norman had not realized how slimy the rocks had become in the wet air. His hand slipped and he fell to the ledge below. The sack was jerked over the edge, but he kept his hold on it. The typewriter in the sack hit the side of the cliff with a loud clang.

He collected his wits and crawled to the lower part of the ledge. Here he again went over, but was very careful to keep a firm grip. He let go and landed feet first on a huge boulder directly below. The sack crashed down an instant later. Norman clambered over the rocks and soon had descended to level ground.

Nearby objects were obscured by the fog. It was even colder and damper than above. The fog seemed to enter his mouth and nose and draw away his warmth. He paused, then started in the direction that he remembered seeing the airplane hangar last time. Soon he was ankle deep in wet grass.

After about one hundred yards, Norman noticed a darkness to his left. He turned and approached it. Gradually the form of a light plane was defined. Soon he could clearly see the Piper Cub. *Four place, single-jet aircraft; maximum cargo weight, 1200 pounds; minimum runway for takeoff with full load, 90 yards; maximum speed, 250 miles per hour.* Its wings and fuselage shone dully in the weak light. Norman ran up to the Cub, clambered over the struts, and pulled himself into the cabin. He settled his sack in the copilot's seat and slammed the door. The key had been left in the ignition: someone had been extremely careless.

Norman inspected the controls of the little aircraft. Somehow his fear had departed, and specific facts now came easily to mind. He saw that there was an autopilot on the right-hand dash, but it was of a simple-minded variety and could handle only cruising flight.

He reached down and felt the rudder pedals with his feet. By bracing his back against the seat he could touch the pedals and at the same time hold the steering wheel. Of course, he would not be able to see out very easily, but there really wasn't very much *to* see.

He had to get across the border fast and this airplane was probably the only way.

He turned the starter and heard the fuel pumps and turbines begin rotating. Norman looked at the dash. What was

he supposed to do next? He pushed the button marked
FLASH and was rewarded with a loud *ffumpf* as the jet engine above the wing ignited. He twisted the throttle. The
Cub crawled across the field, picking up speed. It bounced
and jolted over the turf.

. . . *Throttle to full, keeping stick forward . . . until you
are well over stall speed (35 miles per hour for a 1980 Cub)
. . . pull back gently on the stick, being careful to remain
over . . . (35 miles per hour) . . .*

He craned his neck, trying to get a view ahead. The ride
was becoming smooth. The Cub was airborne! Still nothing
but fog ahead. For an instant the mist parted, revealing a
thirty-foot Security fence barely fifty yards away. He had to
have altitude!

. . . *Under no circumstances should high angle-of-attack
(climb) maneuvers be attempted without sufficient air
speed . . .*

Instructions are rarely the equal of actual experience, and
now Norman was going to learn the hard way. He pushed at
the throttle and pulled back hard on the stick. The little aircraft nosed sharply upward, its small jet engine screaming.
The air speed fell and with it the lifting power of the wings.
The Cub seemed to pause for an instant suspended in the
air, then fell back. Jet still whining, the nose came down
and the plane plunged earthwards.

Imagine a plate of spaghetti—no sauce or meatballs. O.K.,
now picture an entire room filled with such food. This wormy
nightmare gives you some idea of the complexity of the First
Security District, otherwise known as the Labyrinth. By
analogy each strand of spaghetti is a tunnel segment carved
through bedrock. The Labyrinth occupied four cubic miles
under the cities of Ishpeming and Negaunee in the Upper
Peninsula of Michigan. Without the power of controlled
nuclear fusion such a maze could never have been made.
Each tunnel was connected to several others by a random
system of secret hatches, controlled by voice and electronic
codes. Truly the First Security District was the most spy-
proof volume in the solar system. The Savannah plant, the
CIA, Soviet IKB, and the entire system of GM factories
could have co-existed in it without knowledge of each other.
As a matter of fact, thirty-one different Security projects,

laboratories, and military bases existed in the Labyrinth with their co-ordinates listed in a single filing computer—and there's the rub . . .

"Because he's been getting straight A's," Dr. William Dunbar finished.

Lieutenant General Alvin Pederson, Commander of the First Security District, looked up from the computer console with a harried expression on his face. The two men were alone in the chamber containing the memory bank of United States Government Files Central, usually referred to as Files Central or simply Files. Behind the console were racks of fiber glass, whose orderly columns and rows filled most of the room. At the base of each rack, small lasers emitted modulated and coherent light; as the light passed through the fibers, it was altered and channeled by subtle impurities in the glass. Volume for volume, the computer was ten thousand times better than the best cryogenic models. Files Central contained all the information, secret and otherwise, possessed by the U.S.—including the contents of the Library of Congress, which managed to fill barely ten per cent of Files' capacity. The fact that Pederson kept his office here rather than at Continental Air Defense Headquarters, which occupied another part of the Labyrinth, indicated just how important the functions of Files were.

Pederson frowned. He had better things to do than listen to every overwrought genius that wanted to talk to him, though Dunbar usually spoke out only when he had something important to say. "You'd better start at the beginning, Doctor."

The mathematician began nervously. "Look. Norman has never had any great interest in his schoolwork. We may have given the chimp high intelligence with this brain-computer combination, but he has the emotional maturity of a nine-year-old human. Norman is bright, curious—and *lazy;* he would rather read science fiction than study history. His schoolwork has always been poorly and incompletely done—until six weeks ago. Since then he has spent virtually no time on real studying. At the same time he has shown a complete mastery of the factual information in his courses. It's almost as if he had an eidetic memory of *facts that were never presented to him.* As if . . ."

Dunbar started on a different tack. "General, you know how much trouble we had co-ordinating the chimp's brain with his computer in the first place. On the one hand you have an African chimpanzee, and on the other an advanced optical computer which theoretically is superior even to Files here. We wanted the chimp's brain to co-operate with the computer as closely as the different parts of a human brain work together. This meant that the computer had to be programmed to operate the way the chimp's mind did. We also had to make time-lapse corrections, because the chimp and the computer are not physically together. All in all, it was a terrifically complicated job. It makes the Economic Planning Programs look like setting up Fox and Geese on a kid's Brain Truster kit." Seeing the other's look of impatience, Dunbar hurried on. "Anyway, you remember that we needed to use the Files computer, just to program *our* computer. And the two machines had to be electronically connected."

The scientist came abruptly to the point. "If by some accident or mechanical failure, the link between Files and Norman *were never cut,* then . . . then the chimp would have complete access to U.S. Files."

Pederson's preoccupation with other matters disappeared. "If that's so, we've got one hell of a problem. And it would explain a lot of other things. Look." He shoved a sheet of paper at Dunbar. "As a matter of routine, Files announces how much information it has supplied to queries during every twenty-four-hour period. Actually it's sort of a slick gimmick to impress visitors with how efficient and useful Files is, supplying information to twenty or thirty different agencies at once. Up until six weeks ago the daily reading hung around ten to the tenth bits per day. During the next ten days it climbed to over ten to the twelfth—then to ten to the fourteenth. We couldn't hunt down the source of the queries and most of the techs thought the high readings were due to mechanical error.

"Altogether, Files has supplied almost ten to the fifteenth bits to—someone. And that, Doctor, is equal to the total amount of information contained in Files. It looks as if your monkey has programmed himself with all the information the U.S. possesses."

Pederson turned to the query panel, typed two questions. A tape reel by the desk spun briefly, stopped. Pederson pointed to it. "Those are the co-ordinates of your lab. I'm sending a couple men down to pick up your simian friend. Then I'm sending some more men to wherever his computer is."

Pederson looked at the tape reel expectantly, then noticed the words gleaming on a readout screen above the console:

The co-ordinates you request are not On File.

Pederson lunged forward and typed the question again, carefully. The message on the screen didn't even flicker:

The co-ordinates you request are not On File.

Dunbar leaned over the panel. "It's true, then," he said hoarsely, for the first time believing his fears. "Probably Norman thought we would punish him if we found out he was using Files."

"We would," Pederson interrupted harshly.

"And since Norman could use information On File, he could also *erase* information there. We hardly ever visit the tunnel where his computer was built, so we haven't noticed until now that he had erased its co-ordinates."

Now that he knew an emergency really existed, Dunbar seemed calm. He continued inexorably, "And if Norman was this fearful of discovery, then he probably had Files advise him when you tried to find the location of his computer. My lab is only a couple hundred feet below the surface—and he surely knows how to get out."

The general nodded grimly. "This chimp seems to be one step ahead of us all the way." He switched on a comm, and spoke into it. "Smith, send a couple men over to Dunbar's lab . . . Yeah, I've got the co-ordinates right here." He pressed another switch and the reel of tape spun, transmitting its magnetic impressions to a similar reel at the other end of the hookup. "Have them grab the experimental chimp and bring him down here to Files Central. Don't hurt him, but be careful—you know how bright he is." He cut the circuit and turned back to Dunbar.

"If he's still there, we'll get him; but if he's already made a break for the surface, there's no way we can stop him now. This place is just too decentralized." He thought for a second, then turned back to the comm and gave more instructions to his aide.

"I've put in a call to Sawyer AFB to send some airborne infantry over here. Other than that, we can only watch."

A TV panel brightened, revealing a view from one of the hidden surface cameras. The scene was misty, and silent except for an occasional dripping sound.

Several minutes passed; then a superbly camouflaged and counter-balanced piece of bedrock in the center of their view swung down, and a black form in orange Bermuda shorts struggled out of the ground, dragging a large white sack. The chimp shivered, then moved off, disappearing over the crest of the bluff.

Pederson's hands were pale white, clenched in frustration about the arms of his chair. Although the First Security District was built under Ishpeming, its main entrances were fifteen miles away at Sawyer Armed Forces Base. There were only three small and barely accessible entrances in the area where Norman had escaped. Fortunately for the chimpanzee, his quarters had been located near one of them. The area which contained these entrances, belonged to the Ore REclamation Service, a government agency charged with finding more efficient methods of low-grade ore refining. (With the present economic situation, it was a rather superfluous job since the current problem was to get *rid* of the ore on hand rather than increase production.) All this indirection was designed to hide the location of the First Security District from the enemy. But at the same time it made direct control of the surface difficult.

A shrill sound came from the speaker by the TV panel. Dunbar puzzled, "Sounds almost like a light jet."

Pederson replied, "It probably is. The ORES people maintain a small office up there for appearances' sake, and they have a Piper Cub . . . *Could that chimp fly one!*"

"I doubt it, but I suppose if he were desperate enough he would try anything."

Smith's voice interrupted them, "General, our local infiltration radar has picked up an aircraft at an altitude of fifteen feet. Its present course will take it into the Security fence." The buzzing became louder. "The pilot is going to stall it out! It's in a steep climb . . . eighty feet, one hundred. It's stalled!"

The buzzing whine continued for a second and then abruptly ceased.

The typewriter departed through the front windshield at great speed. Norman Simmons came to in time to see his dog-eared copy of "Galatic Patrol" disappear into the murky water below. He made a wild grab for the book, missed it, and received a painful scratch from shards of broken windshield. All that remained of his belongings was the second volume of the Foundation series and the blanket which somehow had been draped half in and half out of the shattered window. The bottom edge of the blanket swung gently back and forth just a couple of inches above the water. The books he could do without; they really had only sentimental value. Since he had learned the Trick, there was no need to physically possess any books. But in the cold weather he was sure to need the blanket; he carefully retrieved it.

Norman pushed open a door, and climbed onto the struts of the Cub for a look around. The plane had crashed nose first into a shallow pond. The jet had been silenced in the impact, and the loudest sound to be heard now was his own breathing. Norman peered into the fog. How far was he from "dry" land? A few yards away he could see swamp vegetation above the still surface of the water; beyond that, nothing but mist. A slight air current eased the gloom. There! For an instant he glimpsed dark trees and brush about thirty yards away.

Thirty yards, through cold and slimy water. Norman's lips curled back in revulsion as he stared at the oily liquid. Maybe there was an aerial route, like Tarzan used. He glanced anxiously up, looking for some overhanging tree branch or vine. No luck. He would have to go *through* the water. Norman almost cried in despair at the thought. Suffocating visions of death by drowning came to mind. He imagined all the creatures with pointy teeth and ferocious appetites that might be lurking in the seemingly placid water: piranhas to strip his bones and—no, they were tropical fish, but something equally deadly. If he could only pretend that it were clear, ankle-deep water.

Dal swam silently toward the moonlit palms and palely gleaming sands just five hundred yards away. Five hundred yards, he thought exultantly, to freedom, to his own kind. The enemy could never penetrate the atoll's camouflage . . . He didn't notice a slight turbulence, the swift emergence of a leathery tentacle from the water. But he fought desperately

*as he felt it tighten about his leg. Dal's screams were bubbly
gurglings inaudible above the faint drone of the surf, as he
was hauled effortlessly into the depths and sharp, unseen
teeth . . .*

For a second his control lapsed, and the fictional incident
slipped in. In the comfort of his room, the death of Dal
had been no more than the pleasantly chilling end of a villain;
here it was almost unbearable. Norman extended one foot
gingerly into the water, and quickly drew it back. He tried
again, this time with both feet. Nothing bit him and he
cautiously lowered himself into the clammy water. The
swamp weeds brushed gently against his legs. Soon he was
holding the strut with one hand and was neck deep in water.
The mass of weeds had slowly been compressed as he descended and now just barely supported his weight, even
though he had not touched bottom. He released his grip
on the strut and began moving toward shore. With one hand
he attempted to keep his blanket out of the water while with
the other he paddled. Norman glanced about for signs of
some hideous tentacle or fin, saw nothing but weeds.

He could see the trees on the shore quite clearly now, and
the weeds at his feet seemed backed by solid ground. Just
a few more yards—Norman gasped with relief as he struggled
out of the water. He noticed an itching on his legs and arms.
There had been blood-drinkers in the water after all, but
fortunately small ones. He paused to remove the slugs from
his body.

Norman sneezed violently and inspected his blanket. Although the mists had made it quite damp, he wrapped it
around himself. Only after he was more or less settled did
he notice the intermittent thrumming sound coming through
the trees on his left. It sounded like the transport vehicles
back in the tunnels, or like the automobiles that he had heard
and seen on film.

Norman scrambled through the underbrush in the direction
of the noises. Soon he came to a dilapidated four-lane asphalt
highway. Every minute or so, a car would appear out of the
mist, travel through his narrow range of vision, and disappear
into the mist again.

*MOST SECRET (Unauthorized use of MOST SECRET
materials is punishable by death.)* He had to get to Canada or
they would kill him for sure. He knew millions, *billions* of

things labeled MOST SECRET. Nearly all were unintelligible. The rest were usually boring. A very small percentage were interesting, like something out of an adventure story. And some were horrifying bits of nightmare couched in cold, matter-of-fact words. But all were labeled MOST SECRET, and his access to them was certainly unauthorized. If only he had known beforehand the consequences of Memorizing It All. It had been so easy to do, and so useful, but it was also a deadly, clinging gift.

Now that the airplane had crashed, he had to find some other way to get to Canada. Maybe one of these cars could take him some place where he would have better luck in his attempt. For some reason, the idea didn't trigger warning memories. Blissfully unaware that a talking chimpanzee is not a common sight in the United States, Norman started down the embankment to the shoulder of the highway, and in the immortal tradition of the hitchhiker in "Two for the Road," stuck out his thumb.

Three minutes passed; he clutched the blanket more tightly to himself as his teeth began to chatter. In the distance he heard the thrum of an approaching vehicle. He stared eagerly in the direction of the sound. Within fifteen seconds, a sixty-ton ore carrier emerged from the fog and lumbered toward him. Norman jumped up and down in a frenzy, waving and shouting. The blanket gave him the appearance of a little Amerind doing a particularly violent rain dance. The huge truck rolled by him at about thirty-five miles per hour. Then when it was some forty yards away, the driver slammed on the brakes and the doughy rollagon tires bit into asphalt.

Norman ran joyfully toward the cab, not noticing the uncared-for condition of the starboard ore cranes, the unpainted and dented appearance of the cab, or the wheezy putputting of the Wankel rotary engine—all signs of dilapidation which would have been unthinkable four years before.

He stopped in front of the cab door and was confronted by a pair of cynical, bloodshot eyes peering at him over a three-day growth of beard. "Who . . . Whash are you?" (The condition of the driver would have been unthinkable four years ago, too.)

"My name's Norman—Jones." Norman slyly selected an alias. He resolved to act dull, too, for he knew that most chimps were somewhat stupid, and couldn't speak clearly without the special operations he had had. (In spite of his memory and intelligence, Norman had an artificial block against ever completely realizing his uniqueness.) "I want to go to"—he searched his memory—"Marquette."

The driver squinted and moved his head from side to side as if to get a better view of Norman. "Say, you're a monkey."

"No," Norman stated proudly, forgetting his resolution, "I'm a chimpanzee."

"A talkin' monkey," the driver said almost to himself. "You could be worth plen . . . wherezhu say you wanna go . . . Marquette? Sure, hop in. That's where I'm takin' this ore."

Norman clambered up the entrance ladder into the warm cab. "Oh, thanks a lot."

The ore carrier began to pick up speed. The highway had been blasted through greenish bedrock, but it still made turns and had to climb over steep hills.

The driver was expansive, "Can't wait to finish this trip. This here is my las' run, ya know. No more drivin' ore fer the government an' its 'Public Works Projects.' I know where to get a couple black market fusion packs, see? Start my own trucking line. No one'll ever guess where I get my power." He swerved to avoid a natural abutment of greenish rock that appeared out of the mist, and decided that it was time to turn on his fog lights. His mind wandered back to prospects of future success, but along a different line. "Say, you like to talk, Monkey? You could make me a lot of money, ya know: 'Jim Traly an' His Talkin' Monkey.' Sounds good, eh?"

With a start, Norman realized that he was listening to a drunk. The driver's entire demeanor was almost identical to that of the fiend's henchman in "The Mores of the Morgue." Norman had no desire to be a "talkin' monkey" for the likes of Traly, whose picture he now remembered in Social Security Records. The man was listed as an unstable, low competence type who might become violent if frustrated.

As the ore carrier slowed for a particularly sharp turn, Norman decided that he could endure the cold of the outside for a few more minutes. He edged to the door and began to pull at its handle. "I think I better get off now, Mr. Traly."

The ore carrier slowed still more as the driver lunged

across the seat and grabbed Norman by one of the purple suspenders that kept his orange Bermuda shorts up. A full grown chimpanzee is a match for most men, but the driver weighed nearly three hundred pounds and Norman was scared stiff. "You're shtaying right here, see?" Traly shouted into Norman's face, almost suffocating the chimpanzee in alcohol vapor. The driver transferred his grip to the scruff of Norman's neck as he accelerated the carrier back to cruising speed.

"Crashed in a shallow swamp just beyond the Security fence, sir." The young Army captain held a book up to the viewer. "This copy of Asimov was all that was left in the cabin, but we dredged up some other books and a typewriter from the water. It's only about five feet deep there."

"But where did the chim . . . the pilot go?" Pederson asked.

"The pilot, sir?" The captain knew what the quarry was but was following the general's line. "We have a man here from Special Forces who's a tracker, sir. He says that the pilot left the Cub and waded ashore. From there, he tracked him through the brush to the old Ishpeming-Marquette road. He's pretty sure that the . . . um . . . pilot hitched a ride in the direction of Marquette." The captain did not mention how surprised the lieutenant from Special Forces had been by the pilot's tracks. "He probably left the area about half an hour ago, sir."

"Very well, Captain. Set up a guard around the plane; if anyone gets nosy, tell them that ORES has asked you to salvage their crashed Cub. Fly everything you found in the cabin and swamp back to Sawyer and have it sent down here to Files Central."

"Yes, sir."

Pederson cut the connection and began issuing detailed instructions to his chief aide over another circuit. Finally he turned back to Dunbar. "That chimp is not going to remain one step ahead of us for very much longer. I've alerted all the armed forces in the Upper Peninsula to start a search, with special concentration on Marquette. It's lucky that we have permission to conduct limited maneuvers there or I might have an awful time just getting permission to station airbornes over the city.

"And now we can take a little time to consider ways of catching this Norman Simmons, rather than responding spastically to *his* initiative."

Dunbar said quickly, "In the first place, you can cut whatever connection there is between Files and Norman's computer."

Pederson grinned. "Good enough. That was mixed in with the rest of the instructions I've given Smith. If I remember right, the two computers were connected by a simple copper cable, part of the general cable net that was installed interweaving with the tunnel system. It should be a simple matter to cut the circuit where the cable enters the Files room."

The general thought for a moment. "The object now is to catch the chimp, discover the location of the chimp's computer, or both. Down here we can't do anything directly about the chimp. But the computer has to be in contact with Norman Simmons. Could we trace these emanations?"

Dunbar blinked. "You know that better than I, General. The Signal Corps used our experiment to try a *quote* entirely new concept in communications *unquote*. They supplied all the comm equipment, even the surgical imbeds for Norman. And they are playing it pretty cozy with the technique. Whatever it is, it goes through almost anything, does not travel faster than light, and can handle several billion bits per second. It might even be ESP, if what I've read about telepathy is true."

Pederson looked sheepish. "I do recognize the 'new concept' you mention. I just never connected the neutri . . . this technique with your project. But I should have known; we have only one way to broadcast through solid rock as if it were vacuum. Unfortunately, with the devices we have now, there's no way of getting a directional bearing on such transmissions. With enough time and as a last resort we might be able to jam them, though."

Now it was Dunbar's turn to make a foolish suggestion. "Maybe if a thorough search of the tunnels were made, we could find the—"

Pederson grimaced. "Bill you've been here almost three years. Haven't you realized how complicated the Labyrinth is? The maze is composed of thousands of tunnel segments spread through several cubic miles of bedrock. It's simply too complex for a blind search—and there's only one set of blueprints," he jerked a thumb at the racks of fiber glass. "Even for routine trips, we have to make out tapes to plug into the transport cars down there. If we hadn't put his quarters close to ground level, so you could take him for walks on the surface, Norman would still be wandering around the Labyrinth, even though he knows what passages to take.

"About twice a day I ride over to Continental Air Defense Headquarters. It takes about half an hour and the trip is more tortuous than a swoopride at a carnival. CAD HQ could be just a hundred yards from where we're sitting, or it could be two miles—in any direction. For that matter, I don't really know where *we* are right now. But then," he added with a sly smile, "neither do the Russki or Han missilemen. I'm sorry, Doctor, but it would take years of random searching to find the computer."

And Dunbar realized that he was right. It was general policy in the First Security District to disperse experiments and other installations as far as possible through the tunnel maze. So it had been with Norman's computer. With its own power source the computer needed no outside assistance to function.

The scientist remembered its strange appearance, resting like a huge jewel in a vacant tunnel—where? It was a far different sight from the appearance of Files. Norman's computer had the facets of a cut gem, although this had been a functional rather than an aesthetic necessity. Dunbar remembered the multicolor glows that appeared near its surface; further in, the infinite reflections and subtle refractions of microcomponent flaws in the glass blended into a mysterious flickering, hinting at the cheerful though immature intelligence that was Norman Simmons. This was the object which had to be found.

Dunbar broke out of his reverie. He started on a different tack. "Really, General, I don't quite see how this situation can be quite as desperate as you say. Norman isn't going to sell secrets to the Reds; he's as loyal as a human child could be—which is a good deal more than most adults, because he can't rationalize disloyalty so easily. Besides, you know that we were eventually going to provide him with large masses of data, anyway. The goal of this whole project is to test the possibility of giving humans an encyclopedic mental grasp. He just saw how much the information could help him, and how much easier it could be obtained than by study, and he pushed the experiment into its next phase. He shouldn't be punished or hurt because of that. This situation is really no one's fault."

Pederson snapped back, "Of course, it's no one's fault; that's just the hell of it. When no one is to blame for something, it means that the situation is fundamentally beyond human control. To me, your whole project is taking control away from people and giving it to *others*. Here an experimental animal, a chimpanzee, has taken the initiative away from the U. S. Government—don't laugh, or so help me—" The general made a warning gesture. "Your chimp is more than a co-ordinator of information; he's also *smarter* than he was before. *What're the humans we try this on going to be like?*"

Pederson calmed himself with a deliberate effort. "Never mind that now. The important thing is to find Simmons, since he appears to be the only one who," Pederson groaned, "knows where his brains are. So let's get practical. Just what can we expect from him? How easy is it for him to correlate information in his memory?"

Dunbar considered. "I guess the closest analogy between his mind and a normal one is to say that he has an eidetic memory—and a *very* large one. I imagine that when he first began using the information he was just swamped with data. Everything he saw stimulated a deluge of related memories. As his subconscious became practiced, he probably remembered only information that was pertinent to a problem. Say that he saw a car, and wondered what year and make it was. His subconscious would hunt through his copy of Files—at very high speed—and within a tenth of a second Norman would 'remember' the information he had just wondered about.

"However, if for some reason he suddenly wondered what differential equations were, it would be a different matter, because he couldn't *understand* the information presented, and so would have to wade through the same preliminary material that every child must in order to arrive at high-school math. But he could do it very much faster, because of the ease with which he could pick different explanations from different texts. I imagine he could get well into calculus from where he is now in algebra with a couple hours of study."

"In other words, the longer he has this information, the more dangerous he'll be."

"Uh, yes. However, there *are* a couple things on our side. First, it's mighty cold and damp on the surface, for Norman at least. He is likely to be very sick in a few hours. Second, if he travels far enough away from the First Security District, he will become mentally disoriented. Although Norman doesn't know it—unless he has specifically considered the question—he could never get much farther than fifteen miles away and remain sane. Norman's mind is a very delicate balance between his organic brain and the hidden computer. The co-ordination is just as subtle as that of different nerve paths in the human brain. The information link between the two has to transmit more than a billion bits of information per second. If Norman gets beyond a certain point, the time lapse involved in transmission between him and the computer will upset the co-ordination. It's something like talking by radio with a spacecraft; beyond a certain distance it is difficult or impossible to maintain a meaningful conversation. When Norman goes beyond a certain point it will be impossible for him to think coherently."

Dunbar was struck by an unrelated idea. He added, "Say, I can see one reason why this could get sticky. What if Norman got picked up by foreign agents? That would be the biggest espionage coup in the history of man."

Pederson smiled briefly. "Ah, the light dawns. Yes, some of the information this Simmons has could mean the death of almost everyone on Earth, if it were known to the wrong people. Other secrets would *merely* destroy the United States.

"Fortunately, we're fairly sure that the Reds' domestic collapse has reduced their overseas enterprises to about nil. As I remember it, there are only one or two agents in all of Michigan. Thank God for small favors."

Boris Kuchenko scratched and was miserable. A few minutes before, he had been happily looking forward to receiving his weekly unemployment check and then spending the afternoon clipping articles out of the *NATO Armed Forces Digest* for transmission back to Moscow. And now this old coot with his imperious manner was trying to upset everything. Kuchenko turned to his antagonist and tried to put on a brave front. "I am sorry, Comrade, but I have my orders. As the ranking Soviet agent in the Upper Peninsu—"

The other snapped back, "Ranking agent, nothing! You were never supposed to know this, Kuchenko, but you are a cipher, a stupid dummy used to convince U. S. Intelligence that the USSR has given up massive espionage. If only I had some decent agents here in Marquette, I wouldn't have to use idiots like you."

Ivan Sliv was an honest-to-God, effective Russian spy. Behind his inconspicuous middle-aged face, lurked a subtle mind. Sliv spoke five languages and had an excellent grasp of engineering, mathematics, geography, and history—*real* history, not State-sponsored fairy tales. He could make brilliantly persuasive conversation at a cocktail party or commit a political murder with equal facility. Sliv was the one really in charge of espionage in the militarily sensitive U.P. area. He and other equally talented agents concentrated on collecting information from Sawyer AFB and from the elusive First Security District.

The introduction of Bender's fusion pack had produced world-wide depression, and the bureaucracies of Russia had responded to this challenge with all the resiliency of a waterlogged pretzel. The Soviet economic collapse had been worse than that of any other major country. While the U.S. was virtually recovered from the economic depression caused by the availability of unlimited power, counter-revolutionary armies were approaching Moscow from the West *and* the East. Only five or ten ICBM bases remained in Party hands. But the Comrades had been smart in one respect. If you can't win by brute force, it is better to be subtle. Thus the planetary spy operations were stepped up, as was a very secret project housed in a system of caves under the Urals. Sliv's mind shied away from that project—he was one of the few to know of it, and that knowledge must never be hinted at.

Sliv glared at Kuchenko. "Listen, you fat slob: I'm going to explain things once more, if possible in words of one syllable. I just got news from Sawyer that some Amie superproject has backfired. An experimental animal has escaped from their tunnel network and half the soldiers in the U.P. are searching for it. They think it's here in Marquette."

Kuchenko paled. "A war virus test? Comrade, this could be—" the fat Soviet agent boggled at the possibilities.

Sliv swore. "No, no, no! The Army's orders are to *capture*, not destroy the thing. We are the only agents that are in Marquette now, or have a chance to get in past the cordon that's sure to be dropped around the city. We'll split up and—" He stopped and took conscious notice of the buzzing sound that had been building up over the last several minutes. He walked quickly across the small room and pushed open a badly cracked window. Cold air seemed to ooze into the room. Below, the lake waters splashed against the pilings of the huge automated pier which incidentally contained this apartment. Sliv pointed into the sky and snapped at the bedraggled Kuchenko, "See? The Amie airbornes have been over the city for the last five minutes, at least. We've got to get going, man!"

But Boris Kuchenko was a man who liked his security. He miserably inspected his dirty fingernails, and began, "I really don't know if this is the right thing, Comrade. We—"

The fog had disappeared, only to be replaced by a cold drizzle. Jim Traly guided the ore carrier through Marquette to the waterfront. Even though drunk, he maintained a firm grip on Norman's neck. The carrier turned onto another street, and Norman got his first look at Lake Superior. It was so gray and cold; beyond the breakwater the lake seemed to blend with the sullen hue of the sky. The carrier turned again. They were now moving parallel to the water along a row of loading piers. In spite of the rollagons, the carrier dipped and sagged as they drove over large potholes in the substandard paving material. The rain had collected in these depressions and splashed as they drove along. Traly apparently recognized his destination. He slowed the carrier and moved it to the side of the street.

Traly opened his door and stepped down, dragging Norman behind him. With difficulty the chimpanzee kept his balance and did not land on his head. The drunk driver was muttering to himself, "Las' time I drive this trash. They can pick up the inventories themselves. Good riddance." He kicked a rollagon. "Just wait till I get some Bender fusion packs. I'll show 'em. C'mon, you." He gave Norman a jerk, and began walking across the street.

The waterfront was almost deserted. Traly was heading for what appeared to be the only operating establishment in the area: a tavern. The bar had a rundown appearance. The "aluminum" trim around the door had long since begun to rust, and the memory cell for the bar's sky sign suffered from amnesia so that it now projected into the air:

The D-unk PuT pavern

Traly entered the bar, pulling Norman in close behind. Once the fluorescents had probably lighted the place well, but now only two or three in a far corner were operating.

He pulled Norman around in front of him and seemed eager to announce his discovery of the "talkin' monkey." Then he noticed that the bar was almost empty. No one was sitting at any of the tables, although there were half empty glasses of beer left on a few of them. Four or five men and the barkeeper were engaged in an intense discussion at the far end of the room. "Where is everybody?" Traly was astonished.

The barkeeper looked up. "Jimmy! Right at lunch President Langley came on TV an' said that the government was going to let us buy as many Bender fusion boxes as we want. You could go out an' buy one right now for twenty-five bucks. When everybody heard that, why they just asked themselves what they were doin' sittin' around in a bar when they could have a job an' even be in business for themselves. Not much profit for me this afternoon, but I don't care. I know where I can get some junk copters. Fit 'em out with Bender packs and start a tourist service. You know: See the U.P. with Don Zalevsky." The bartender winked.

Traly's jaw dropped. He forgot Norman. "You really mean that there's no more black market where we can get fusion boxes?"

One of the customers, a short man with a protuberant beak and a bald pate, turned to Traly. "What do you need a black market for when you can go out an' buy a Pack for twenty-five dollars? Well, will you look at that: Traly's disappointed. Now you can do whatcher always bragging about, go out and dig up some fusion boxes and go into business." He turned back to the others.

"And we owe it all to President Langley's fizical and economic policies. Bender's Pack coulda destroyed our nation. Instead we only had a little depression, an' look at us now. Three years after the invention, the economy's on an even keel enough to let us buy as many power packs as we want."

Someone interrupted, "You got rocks in your head, buddy. The government closed down most of the mines so the oil corporations would have a market to make plastics for; we get to produce just enough ore up here so no one starves. Those 'economic measures' have kept us all hungry. If the government had only let us buy as many Packs as we wanted and not interfered with free competition, there wouldna been no depression or nothing."

From the derisive remarks of the other customers, this appeared to be a minority opinion. The Beak slammed his glass of beer down and turned to his opponent. "You know what woulda happened if there wasn't no 'interference'?" He didn't wait for an answer. "Everybody woulda gone out an' bought Packs. All the business in the U.S. woulda gone bankrupt, 'cause anyone with a Bender and some electric motors would hardly need to buy any regular goods, except food. It wouldn't been a depression, it woulda been just like a jungle. As it is, we only had a short period of adjustment," he almost seemed to be quoting, "an' now we're back on our feet. We got power to burn; those ore buckets out in the bay can fly through the air and space, and we can take the salt out of the water and—"

"Aw, you're jus' repeating what Langley said in his speech."

"Sure I am, but it's true." Another thought occurred to him. "And *now* we don't even need Public Works Projects."

"Yeah, no more Public Works Projects," Traly put in, disappointed.

"There wouldn't have been no need for PWP if it wasn't for Langley and his loony ideas. My old man said the same thing about Roosevelt." The dissenter was outnumbered but voluble.

Norman had become engrossed in the argument. In fact he was so interested that he had forgotten his danger. Back in the District he had been made to learn some economics as part of his regular course of study—and, of course, he could remember considerably more about the subject. Now

he decided to make his contribution. Traly had loosened his
grip; the chimpanzee easily broke the hold and jumped to
the top of the counter. "This man," he pointed to the Beak,
"is right, you know. The Administration's automatic stabiliz-
ers and discretionary measures prevented total catastro—"

"What is *this*, Jimmy?" The bartender broke the amazed
silence that greeted Norman's sudden action.

"That's what I've been trying to tell you guys. I picked up
this monkey back in Ishpeming. He's like a parrot, only
better. Jus' listen to him. I figure he could be worth a lot of
money."

"Thought you were going into the trucking business,
Jimmy."

Traly shrugged, "This could be a lot greener."

"That's no parrot-talk," the Beak opined. "The monkey's
really talking. He's smart like you and me."

Norman decided that he had to trust someone. "Yes I am,
yes I am! And I need to get into Canada. Otherwise—"

The door to the Drunk Pup Tavern squeaked as a young
man in brown working clothes pushed it halfway open. "Hey,
Ed, all of you guys. There's a bunch of big Army copters
circling the bay, and GI's all over. It doesn't look like any
practice maneuver." The man was panting as if he had run
several blocks.

"Say, let's see that," moved the Beak. He was informally
seconded. Even the bartender seemed ready to leave. Norman
started. *They* were still after him, and they were close. He
leaped off the counter and ran through the half-open door,
right by the knees of the young man who had made the announcement. The man stared at the chimpanzee and made a
reflex grab for him. Norman evaded the snatch and scuttled
down the street. Behind him, he heard Traly arguing with
the man about, "Letting my talking monkey escape."

He had dropped his blanket when he jumped onto the
counter. Now the chill drizzle made him regret the loss.
Soon he was damp to the skin again, and the water splashed
his forearms and legs as he ran through spots where water
had collected in the tilted and cracked sections of sidewalk.
All the shops and dives along the street were closed and
boarded up. Some owners had left in such disgust and dis-
couragement that they had not bothered even to pull in their

awnings. He stopped under one such to catch his breath and get out of the rain.

Norman glanced about for some sign of airborne infantrymen, but as far as he could see, the sky was empty of men and aircraft. He examined the awning above him. For several years the once green plastic fabric had been subjected alternately to baking sun and rotting rain. It was cheap plastic and now it hung limp, the gray sky visible through the large holes in the material. Norman looked up, got an idea. He backed away from the awning and then ran toward it. He leaped and caught its rusting metal frame. The shade sagged even more, but held. He eased himself over the frame and rested for an instant on the top; then pulled himself onto the windowsill of a second-story apartment.

Norman looked in, saw nothing but an old bed and a closet with one lonely hanger. He caught the casing above the window and swung up. It was almost like being Tarzan. (Usually, Norman tended to identify himself with Tarzan rather than with the Lord-of-the-Jungle's chimpanzee flunkies.) He caught the casing with his toes, pushed himself upwards until he could grasp the edge of the flat roof. One last heave and he was lying on the tar-and-gravel roofing material. In places where the tar had been worn away, someone had sprayed plastite, but more time had passed and that "miracle construction material" had deteriorated, too.

The roofs provided scant cover from observation. Fifty feet away, Norman saw the spidery black framework of a radio tower mounted on the roof of another building. It was in good repair; probably it was a government navigation beacon. Norman sneezed several times, violently. He crawled warily across the roof toward the tower. The buildings were separated by a two-foot alley which Norman easily swung across.

He arrived at the base of the tower. Its black plastic members gleamed waxily in the dull light. As with many structures built after 1980, Hydrocarbon Products Administration regulations dictated that it be constructed with materials deriving from the crippled petroleum and coal industries, Norman remembered. In any case, the intricate framework provided good camouflage. Norman settled himself among the girders and peered out across Marquette.

There were hundreds of them! In the distance, tiny figures in Allservice green were walking through the streets, inspecting each building. Troop carriers and airtanks hung above them. Other airtanks patrolled some arbitrary perimeter about the city and bay. Norman recognized the setup as one of the standard formations for encirclement and detection of hostile forces. With confident foreknowledge he looked up and examined the sky above him. Every few seconds a buckrogers fell out of the apparently empty grayness. After a free fall of five thousand feet, the airborne infantrymen hit their jets just two or three hundred feet above the city. Already, more than twenty of them were posted over the various intersections.

The chimpanzee squinted, trying to get a clearer view of the nearest buckrogers. Images seen through the air behind and below the soldier seemed to waver. This and a faint screaming sound were the only indications of the superheated air shot from the Bender powered thermal element in the soldier's back pack. The infantryman's shoulders seemed lopsided. On more careful inspection Norman recognized that this was due to a GE fifty-thousand line reconnaissance camera strapped to the soldier's upper arm and shoulder. The camera's eight-inch lens gaped blackly as the soldier turned (rotated?) in the chimp's direction.

Norman froze. He knew that every hyper-resolution picture was being transmitted back to Sawyer AFB where computers and photo-interp teams analyzed them. Under certain conditions just a clear footprint or the beady glint of Norman's eyes within the maze of girders would be enough to bring a most decisive—though somewhat delayed—reaction.

As the buckrogers turned away, Norman sighed with relief. But he knew that he wouldn't remain safe for long. Sooner or later—most likely sooner—they would be able to trace him. And then . . . With horror he remembered once again some of the terrible bits of information that hid in the vast pile he knew, remembered the punishments for unauthorized knowledge. *He had to escape them!* Norman considered the means, both fictional and otherwise, that had been used in the past to elude pursuers. In the first place, he recognized that some outside help was needed, or he could never escape from the country. Erik Satanssen, he remembered, always played the double agent, gaining advantages from both sides right up to the denouement. Or take Slippery Jim DiGriz . . . the point was there are always some loopholes even in the most mechanized of traps. What organization would have a secret means of getting across Lake Superior into Canada? The Reds, of course!

Norman stopped fiddling with his soaked suspenders, and looked up. That was the pat answer, in some stories: Pretend to side up with the baddies just long enough to get out of danger and expose them at the same time. Turning around, he gazed at the massive automated pier jutting out into the bay. At its root were several fourth-class apartments—and in one of them was the only Soviet agent in the Upper Peninsula! Norman remembered more about Boris Kuchenko. What sort of government would employ a slob like that as a spy? He racked his memory but could find no other evidence of espionage in the U.P. area.

Many tiny details seemed to crystallize into an idea. It was just like in some stories where the hero appears to pull his hunches out of the thin air. Norman *knew* without any specific reason, that the Soviets were not as incapacitated as they seemed. Stark, Borovsky, Ivanov were smart boys, much smarter than the so-called Bumpkinov incompetents they had replaced. If Stark had been in power in the first place, the Soviet Union might have survived Bender's invention without losing more than a few outlying SSR's. As it was the Party bosses controlled only the area immediately around Moscow and some "hardened" bases in the Urals. Somehow Norman felt that, if all the mental and physical resources of the rulers had been used against the counter-revolutionaries, the Reds' position would have to be better. Borovsky and Ivanov especially, were noted for devious, back-door victories. Something smelled about this spy business.

If Kuchenko was more than he seemed, there might be a way out even yet. If he could trick the Reds into thinking he was a stupe or a traitor, they might take him to some hideout in Canada. He knew they would be interested in him and his knowledge; that was his passport and his peril. They must never know the things *he* knew. And then later, in Canada, maybe he could expose the Russian spies and gain forgiveness.

The nearest buckrogers was now facing directly away from Norman's tower. The chimpanzee moved away from the tower, hurried to the edge of the roof, and swung himself over. Now

he was out of the line of sight of the infantryman. He reached
the ground and scampered across the empty street. Soon he
was padding along the base of the huge auto pier. Finally he
reached the point where the street was swallowed by the enclosed portion of the pier. Norman ran into the dimness; at
least he was out of the rain now. Along the side of the inner
wall was a metal grid stairway. The chimp clambered up the
stairs, found himself in the narrow corridor serving the cheap
apartments which occupied what otherwise would have been
dead space in the warehouse pier. He paused before turning
the doorknob.

". . . Move fast!" The knob was snatched from his fingers,
as someone on the other side pulled the door open. Norman
all but fell into the room. "What the hell!" The speaker
slammed the door shut behind the chimpanzee. Norman
glanced about the room, saw Boris Kuchenko frozen in the act
of wringing his hands. The other man spun Norman around,
and the chimpanzee recognized him as one Ian Sloane, civilian
employee No. 36902u at Sawyer AFB; so the hunch had been
right! The Reds *were* operating on a larger scale than the
government suspected.

Norman assumed his best conspiratorial air. "Good morning, gentlemen . . . or should I say Comrades?"

The older man, Sloane, kept a tight grip on his arm. A look
of surprise and triumph and oddly—fear, was on his face.
Norman decided to go all the way with the double-agent line.
"I'm here to offer my services, uh, Comrades. Perhaps you
don't know quite what and who I am . . ." He looked around
expectantly for some sign of curiosity. Sloane—that was the
only name Norman could remember, but it couldn't be his real
one—gazed at him attentively, but kept a tight grip on his
arm. Seeing that he was going to get no response, Norman
continued less confidently. "I . . . I know who you are. Get
me out of the country and you'll never regret it. You must
have some way of escaping—at the very least some hiding
place." He noticed Boris Kuchenko glance involuntarily at a
spot in the ceiling near one of the walls. There was an ill-
concealed trap hacked raggedly out of the ceiling. It hardly
seemed the work of a master spy.

At last Sloane spoke. "I think we can arrange your escape.
And I am sure that we will not regret it."

His tone made Norman realize how naïve his plan had

been. These agents would get the information and secrets from him or they would destroy him, and there was no real possibility that he would have any opportunity to create a third, more acceptable alternative. The fire was much hotter than the frying pan, and fiction was vaporized by reality. He was in trouble.

Pfft.

The tiny sound came simultaneously with a pinprick in his leg. The curtains drawn before the window jerked slightly. A faint greenish haze seemed to hang in the air for an instant, then disappeared. He scratched his leg with his free hand and dislodged a black pellet. Then he knew that the photo-interpretation group at Sawyer had finally found his trail. They knew exactly where he was, and now they were acting. They had just fired at least two PAX cartridges into the room, one of which had failed to go off. The little black object was a cartridge of that famous nerve gas.

During the Pittsburgh Bread Riots back in '81, screaming mobs, the type that dismember riot police, had been trans-formed into the most docile groups by a few spoken commands and a couple of grams of PAX diffused over the riot area. The stuff wasn't perfect, of course; in about half a per cent of the population there were undesirable side effects such as pseudo-epilepsy and permanent nerve damage; another half per cent weren't affected by normal dosages at all. But the great majority of people immediately lost all power to resist outside suggestion. He felt Sloane's grip loosening.

Norman pulled away and spoke to both men. "Give me a boost through that trap door."

"Yes, sir." The two men agreeably formed a stirrup and raised the chimpanzee toward the ceiling. As they did, Norman suddenly wondered why the gas had not affected him. *Because I'm not all here!* He answered himself with an almost hysterical chuckle. The gas could only affect the part of him that was physically present. And, though that was a very important part, he still retained some of his own initiative.

As Norman pushed open the trap, there was a splintering crash from the window as a buckrogers in full battle gear came hurtling feet first into the room. With a spastic heave, the chimp drew himself into the darkness above. From below he heard an almost plaintive, "Halt!" then Sloane's formerly menacing voice; "We'll go quietly, Officer."

Norman picked himself up and began running. The way was dimly lit from windows mounted far above. Now that his eyes were adjusted, he could see bulky crates around him and above him. He looked down, and gasped, for he could see crates below him, too. He seemed suspended. Then Norman remembered. In the dim light it wasn't too evident, but the floor and ceiling of this level were composed of heavy wire mesh. From a control board somewhere in the depths of the building, roller segments in the mesh could be turned on, and the bulkiest crates could be shuttled about the auto pier like toys. When in operation the pier could handle one million tons of merchandise a day; receiving products from trucks, storing them for a short time, and then sliding them into the holds of superfreighters. This single pier had been expected to bring the steel industry to Marquette, thus telescoping the mining and manufacturing complexes into one. Perhaps after the Recovery it would fulfill its promise, but at the moment it was dead and dark.

Norman zigzagged around several crates, scampered up an incline. Behind him he could hear the infantrymen, shed of their flying gear, scrambling through the trap door.

They would never believe his honesty now that he had been seen consorting with the communists. Things did indeed look dark—he complimented himself on this pun delivered in the midst of danger—but he still had some slim chance of escaping capture and the terrible punishment that would be sure to follow. He had one undetonated PAX cartridge. Apparently its relatively gentle impact with his flesh had kept it from popping. Perhaps not all the soldiers were wearing the antiPAX nose filters—in which case he might be able to commandeer a helicopter. It was a wild idea, but the time for cautious plans was past.

The pier seemed to extend forever. Norman kept moving. He had to get away; and he was beginning to feel very sick. Maybe it was some effect of the gas. He ran faster, but even so he felt a growing terror. His mind seemed to be dissolving, disintegrating. Could *this* be the effect of PAX? He groped mentally for some explanation, but somehow he was having trouble remembering the most obvious things, while at the same time extraneous memories were swamping him more completely than they had for weeks. He should know what the source of the danger was, but somehow . . . *I'm not all here!* That was the answer! But he couldn't understand what its significance was anymore. He no longer could form rational plans. Only one goal remained—to get away from the things that were stalking him. The dim gray glow far ahead now seemed to offer some kind of safety. If he could only reach it. Intelligence was deserting him, and chaos was creeping in.

Faster!

3,456,628 more shopping days until Christmas . . . Latitude 40.9234°N, Longitude 121.3018°W: Semi-hardened Isis missile warehouse; 102 megatons total . . . Latitude 95.00160°N, Longitude 87.4763°W: Cluster of three Vega class Submarine Launched Ballistic Missiles; 35 megatons total . . . depth 105.4 fathoms . . . Allserv IFF codes as follows: 1. 398547 . . . 436344 . . . 51 . . . "Hey, let me out!" *. . . Master of jungle poised, knife ready as . . . the nature of this rock formation was not realized until the plutonist theory of Bender's . . . New Zealand Harbor Defense of Wellington follows: Three antisubmarine detection rings at 10°98 miles from . . . REO factory depot Boise, Idaho contains 242,925 million-hp consumer fusion packs; inventory follows.* Cold gray light shining in the eyes. And I must escape or *. . . "die with a stake driven through his heart," the professor laughed.* STOP or you'll fall; MOVE or you'll die; escape escape escape seascape orescape3scape5scape2pecape4ea1aoop3o 689135010112131-01000101011000010101010001111110101—

The chimpanzee crouched frozen and glared madly at the soft gray light coming through the window.

The tiny black face looked up from the starched white of the pillow and stared dazedly at the ceiling. Around the bed hung the glittering instruments of the SOmatic Support unit. Short of brain tissue damage, the SOS could sustain life in the most terribly mangled bodies. At the moment it was fighting pneumonia, TB, and polio in the patient on the bed.

Dunbar sniffed. The medical ward of the Labyrinth used all the latest procedures—gone was the antiseptic stink of earlier years. The germicidals used were a very subtle sort—and only a shade different from antipersonnel gases developed in the '60's and '70's. William Dunbar turned to Pederson, the only other human in the room. "According to the doctors, he'll make it." Dunbar gestured to the unconscious chimp.

"And his reactions to those questions you asked him under truth drug indicate that no great damage has been done to his 'amplified personality.'"

"Yeah," Pederson replied, "but we won't know whether he responded truthfully until I have these co-ordinates for his computer checked out." He tapped the sheet of paper on which he had scrawled the numbers Norman had called off. "For all we know, he may be immune to truth drug in the same way he is to PAX."

"No, I think he probably told the truth, General. He is, after all, in a very confused state.

"Now that we know the location of his computer, it should be an easy matter to remove the critical information from it. When we try the invention on a man we can be much more careful with the information initially presented."

Pederson stared at him for a long moment. "I suppose you know that I've always opposed your project."

"Uh, yes," said Dunbar, startled, "though I can't understand why you do."

Pederson continued, apparently without noticing the other's answer, "I've never quite been able to convince my superiors of the dangers inherent in the things you want to do. I think I can convince them now and I intend to do everything in my power to see that your techniques are never tried on a human, or for that matter, on any creature."

Dunbar's jaw dropped. "But why? We *need* this invention! Nowadays there is so much knowledge in so many different areas that it is impossible for a man to become skilled in more than two or three of them. If we don't use this invention, most of that knowledge will sit in electronic warehouses waiting for insight and correlations that will never occur. The human-computer symbiosis can give man the jump on evolution and nature. Man's intellect can be ex—"

Pederson swore. "You and Bender make a pair, Dunbar; both of you see the effects of your inventions with narrow utopian blinders. But yours is by far the most dangerous of the two. Look what this one chimpanzee has done in under six hours—escaped from the most secure post in America, eluded a large armed force, and deduced the existence of an espionage net that we had completely overlooked. Catching him was more an *accident* than anything else. If he had had time to think about it, he probably would have deduced that

distance limit and found some way to escape us that really
would have worked. And this is what happens with an experimental *animal!* His intelligence has increased steadily as he
developed a firmer command of his information banks. We
captured him more or less by chance, and unless we act fast
while he's drugged, we won't be able to hold him.

*"And you want to try this thing on a man, who's starting
out at a much higher level of intelligence!*

"Tell me, Doctor, who are you going to give godhood to
first, hm-m-m? If your choice is wrong, the product will be
more satanic than divine. It will be a devil that we cannot
possibly beat except with the aid of some fortuitous accident,
for we can't outthink that which, by definition, is smarter than
we. The slightest instability on the part of the person you
choose would mean the death or *domestication* of the entire
human race."

Pederson relaxed, his voice becoming calmer. "There's an
old saw, Doctor, that the only truly dangerous weapon is a
man. By that standard, you have made the only advance in
weaponry in the last one hundred thousand years!" He smiled
tightly. "It may seem strange to you, but I oppose arms races
and I intend to see that you don't start one."

William Dunbar stared, pale-faced, entertaining a dream
and a nightmare at the same time. Pederson noted the scientist's expression with some satisfaction.

This tableau was interrupted by the buzzing of the comm.
Pederson accepted the call. "Yes," he said, recognizing Smith's
features on the screen.

"Sir, we just finished with those two fellows we picked up
on the auto pier," the aide spoke somewhat nervously. "One
is Boris Kuchenko, the yuk we've had spotted all along. The
other is Ivan Sliv, who's been working for the last nine months
as a code man at Sawyer under the name of Ian Sloane. We
didn't suspect him at all before. Anyway, we gave both of
them a deep-probe treatment, and then erased their memories
of what's happened today, so we could release them and
use them as tracers."

"Fine," replied Pederson.

"They've been doing the darndest things, those spies." Smith
swallowed, "But that isn't what this call is about."

"Oh?"

"Can I talk? Are you alone?"

"Never mind, say it."

"Sir, this Sliv is really a top man. Some of his memories are under blocks that I'm sure the Russkies never thought we could break. Sir—he knows of a project the Sovs are running in an artificial cave system under the Urals. They've taken a dog and wired it—wired it into a computer. Sliv has heard the dog talk, just like Dunbar's chimp. Apparently this is the big project they're pouring their resources into to the exclusion of all others. In fact, one of Sliv's main duties was to detect and obstruct any similar project here. When all the bugs have been worked out, Stark, or one of the other Red chiefs is going to use it on himself and—"

Pederson turned away from the screen, stopped listening. He half noticed Dunbar's face, even paler than before. He felt the same sinking, empty sensation he had four years before when he had heard of Bender's fusion pack. Always it was the same pattern: The invention, the analysis of the dangers, the attempt at suppression, and then the crushing knowledge that no invention can really be suppressed and that the present case is no exception. Invention came after invention, each with greater changes. Bender's Pack would ultimately mean the dissolution of central collections of power, of cities—but Dunbar's invention meant an increased *capability* for invention.

Somewhere under the Urals slept a very smart son of a bitch indeed . . .

And so he must choose between the certain disaster of having a Russian dictator with superhuman intelligence, and the probable disaster involved in beating the enemy to the punch.

He knew what the decision must be; as a practical man he must adapt to changes beyond his control, must plan for the safest possible handling of the unavoidable.

. . . For better or worse, the world would soon be unimaginably different.

THE EASY WAY OUT

Lee Correy

They came out of space armed and ready.

The alien ship skittered into the Earth's atmosphere in an easterly direction and landed surreptitiously about midnight in the Rocky Mountains of North America. The Master had chosen the approach trajectory and landing area after a long survey in far orbit.

"Whew!" Ulmnarrgh breathed with relief as the ship's sensors reported no great hubbub created by the silent landing in the meadow among the high peaks. "I don't think we were detected. There were no probing emissions in the electromagnetic spectrum and no phasing of the gravitoinertial field."

"Keep your guard detectors up," the Master directed. "We'll wait for daylight. In the meantime, run out the screens and keep all defenses on the alert."

Harmarrght fidgeted. "By the Great Overlord!" he snapped under his breath to his mentor, the exobiologist Norvallk. "The Old Boy acts as though he's scared to death."

Turning an eye toward the youngster, Norvallk gently replied, "Don't cover up your nervousness with bravado. All of us remember how we felt on our first landing as a cadet. A certain amount of caution is always indicated, particularly in the face of the fact that the previous probe ship didn't come back from this world."

"The only logical reason for that is a technical malfunction," the youngster shot back.

The exobiologist shook his head sadly. "Logical answers don't always hold true in exploration. This planet's inhabited by communicating beings. If you're going to insist on using logic, calculate the conclusion you get when you take into

39

account the loss of a ship on a planet whose inhabitants have an unknown level of technology. Mukch on that for a while!"

Harmarrght didn't. He had an immediate answer. "I've studied the history of our conquests for the Great Overlord, and nowhere on a thousand worlds has our high technology been equalled. *That,* sir, is an established fact! So now we crawl in here with pseudopods rolled up like a frightened orh. Why should we be so cautious when our technology makes conquest so simple?"

"You're here to learn why," Norvallk told him. "So shut up and observe. You've been trained; now you're about to be educated . . ." These young cubs just out of the Institute were always impetuous, he reminded himself. Such attitudes made excellent warriors for the Great Overlord, but when were the professional institutes going to learn to temper their indoctrination when training explorers?

The Master called for a confrontation in the control bay. This was a welcome relief to Norvallk who, as the chief exobiologist aboard, had nothing to do but sit and shiver until he could get out and have a look at things.

"Our position here, while secure at the moment, may be perilous," the Master pointed out to his crew. "I want to impress again on you the complete nature of the situation. You have all seen the reconnaissance images from the first orbiting probes that revealed the unmistakable sign of intelligent life: deliberate conversion of natural resources into more orderly features such as artificial waterways and geometrical groupings of artificial dwellings.

"It's unusual to find a planet inhabited by intelligent life. But this planet appears to be unique in that it seems to support more than one type of intelligent life.

"Communication is by means of electromagnetic radiation. There is no way of knowing at this time whether this is a naturally evolved trait, such as we found on Vagarragh Four, or the technically developed artificial extension of pressure wave communication such as we have. Rastharrh, tell us what you have discovered."

The information theory expert was somewhat hesitant. "I don't quite know what to make of it. There's more than one coding group involved. I've even run onto a highly unusual code group consisting completely of periodic transmissions of a carrier, and this may be highly indicative of a life form here that communicates by electromagnetic means. It's difficult to conceive of any planetwide intelligent life form that uses more than one type of communication symbol code. Here, there are many. It leads me to believe that this planet may have evolved several high life forms, each communicating differently."

"Norvallk, is this possible?" the Master asked.

Norvallk shrugged. "Anything is possible when dealing with intelligent, communicating beings. The physical arrangement of the planet's land areas suggests that Rastharrh's hypothesis may be correct. I wouldn't discount it. We have got to have a first-hand look."

"And that's what we're going to get." The Master gave his orders.

There was barely enough time to accomplish anything before the sun rose. The planet had a very short rotational period.

It was not a bad-looking world, Norvallk decided as he surveyed the landing site. He pointed out several features to Harmarrght. "Frozen water over there on those high peaks. And note the abundant inverted life forms growing stationary on the hills. If they are at all like the ones on Chinarrghk, they have their brains in the ground and their energy receptors above ground. And probably immobile as well . . ."

"No problem to overcome them if they can't move," Harmarrght stated flatly.

"That depends upon their biological operation and natural defenses, youngster. They could exude poisonous gases when disturbed, for example."

"We can handle that."

"Once we know about it."

"There is no obvious reason why we can't take over this planet for the Great Overlord."

"There may be several reasons why we can't. It all depends on the native life forms, particularly with regard to their Intelligence Index, Adaptability Index, and, most important, Ferocity Index."

"Oh, come now! If they're incapable of defending themselves against our advanced technology, they don't stand a chance!"

Norvallk did not answer his protégé. Lecturing no longer was effective.

It was nearly midday by the time the ground party was organized to leave the ship. Norvallk led it, supported by Rastharrh, the morphologist Grahhgh, three well-trained and experienced recording specialists, the three warrior techs. The whole party was armed with both energy weapons and pro-jectile hurlers. Harmarrght accompanied Norvallk as his direct assistant.

The ten aliens proceeded down the slope from the meadow into the valley. There was a stream on the valley floor and a chance of encountering advanced life forms.

"There are life forms everywhere!" Harmarrght remarked.

"And they take many shapes, but they don't bother us. We'll have to set automatic traps for those flying forms; they're much too fast," Norvallk observed.

They did not reach the stream until well after sunset, but the light shed by the world's natural satellite permitted the party to find its way and continue to record some data.

At sunrise, they found the grizzly bear.

"Let's take it back to the ship!" was Harmarrght's first excited comment.

"Not so fast!" Norvallk cautioned. "We watch first. Quietly. It's feeding. Look how it reaches down into the water and knocks those water-dwellers out onto the bank."

"By the Great Overlord! It's *fast!*"

"Let's see if the Master can find some counterpart from a known world." Norvallk instructed the date recorders to beam their images back to the ship. In a quick communication with the Master, Norvallk set up the search through the memory banks of the ship's computer. As he was waiting for the answer, he gave a little instruction to Harmarrght, "Notice the covering of organic filaments that may either be manipulators, sensors, or thermal insulation. And the grouping of sensory transducers around the food intake orifice."

"It carries no weapons," Harmarrght pointed out.

"It may not need them. But note the plurality of sharp artifacts on the end of each appendage. Are you willing to state unequivocally that they are not artificial?"

A message came from the ship. Zero readout from the memory bank. Plus the Master's direct order, "Bring the life form in for study, preferably functioning."

With obvious relish, Harmarrght hefted his energy projector and started forward. Norvallk tried to stop him, but it was too late.

Very few native life forms will bother a feeding grizzly bear. *Ursus horribilis* is not only strong, but easily provoked. But Harmarrght didn't know this. He found out quickly.

He fired an energy bolt at what should have been an area of vital control in the bear's midsection with the intent to paralyze the beast. The shot singed white-tipped hair and burned a hole through the skin. It hurt the bear and drew its attention to the young alien.

"Cover him!" Norvallk yelled to his party. One of the warrior techs burst forward to get between Harmarrght and the bear.

The bear stopped fishing and let out a bellowing roar. This panicked the warrior tech who fired a projectile toward the bear's head. Another of the warrior techs got into position. But the bear moved . . . fast.

The grizzly brought its huge forepaw down on the closest warrior alien. Armor and all, the warrior splattered.

The next swipe of the huge paw demolished Grahhgh, who had the misfortune to get within range. While trying to get to the second warrior, the bear stepped on Rastharrh, putting part of him out of commission. The bear rose on its hind legs to its full height of eight feet and started to swing again, aiming toward Harmarrght, but the second warrior fired an explosive bolt that caught the grizzly in the roof of the mouth and congealed its brain.

It took a little time for Norvallk to get things straightened out again. As the four transports came from the ship to pick up the dead and injured, he whirled on Harmarrght, managed to suppress his anger, and said sarcastically, "So. It had no weapons, eh? Evidence of a low technology, huh? I thought that you had studied bio-engineering . . . "

The young cadet could only remark, "Its Ferocity Index must be unreasonably high . . ."

Three more transports had to be sent from the ship to lift the grizzly's carcass. The party then resumed its course down the stream, minus three of its members. "Standing orders,"

Norvallk told them. "We take no further action against indigenous life forms except when attacked. We'll merely observe and record data. It seems that most of the other life forms have a very low Ferocity Index, but I am not going to take the chance of losing the rest of this party."

Harmarrght said nothing; he was now reasonably subdued.

Two sunrises later, the party discovered another silvertip grizzly. The aliens didn't repeat their first mistake; they stood well back and watched this bear carefully.

It was leisurely dining on the remains of a freshly-killed white-tail deer at the edge of a small clearing alongside the stream. Apparently wanting a bit of variety in its diet, the bear had managed to find an easy mark in an unsuspecting young deer.

"I am beginning to suspect that the Ferocity Index of this life form is a little bit too high for comfort," Norvallk observed.

"But still nothing that we can't overcome with our existing weapons," Harmarrght added.

"There are many other things yet to consider," his mentor told him. "Observe and remember."

While they were watching the second grizzly dine, a report came in from the ship. "The dead beast has been given a preliminary examination. Its colloidal control network is very complex and contains a highly organized colloidal computer near its primary sensors. It has the capability of a very high Intelligence Index," the Master told them.

Norvallk hastily briefed the Master on their current find and added, "We see no signs of artifacts associated with the beast unless those sharp instruments on its appendages are tools."

"They aren't. They are natural."

"In that event, it isn't using tools. I don't know whether or not it's communicating right now. Too bad Rastharrh was injured; we could use him. A new life form has just arrived! It's smaller but covered with the same sort of organic filaments. Same configuration. It's going right up to the larger beast. We may be witnessing our first example of symbiosis on this world where the large beast does the hunting and shares the meal with a smaller communicating form."

The bear looked up from its meal and recognized the small bearlike form with its broad ribbon of light brown fur down each side. But the bear was still young and still hungry; it decided to put up a defense of its meal. It had yet to learn that there are few animals of any size willing to tangle with *Gulo luscus,* the wolverine.

The wolverine simply attacked the bear as though it did not know the meaning of fear. Its flashing teeth and slashing claws were smaller and less strong than the bear's, but sheer meanness was on its side. It ripped in to kill, giving no quarter. After the first encounter in which the bear's huge paw missed in a roundhouse swing, the battle was very short and very one-sided.

The grizzly took the easy way out. It retreated, ambling off into the pine forest as rapidly as it could move.

Norvallk was shaken, but Harmarrght was now petrified. "Let me kill it!" the youngster urged.

"No. You may not be able to," Norvallk stayed him.

"It will be easy!" He hefted his energy projector and patted it.

"We tried that once. Three of us for one of them. And the Ferocity Index on this little animal is going to be very difficult to compute. It's high. Let's see what the Master's computer says." Norvallk fed all of the available data back to the ship.

The computer chewed up the available data regarding size, probable body mass, and other related factors of the two different animals, bear and wolverine; it then compared this with data from other worlds, considered the possibility of reducing the high Ferocity Index of the bear, found that it could not logically do so, discovered that it could not handle the Ferocity Index of the wolverine, and ended up in a stoppage. The wolverine's Ferocity Index was off-scale.

In the meantime, Norvallk and his group kept observing and reporting. "It's cleaning up what's left of the carcass, and it acts as though it hasn't eaten for days. It's simply glutting itself."

"Its Ferocity Index may diminish when its hunger drive is satiated," Harmarrght ventured to predict.

"In any case, it can't finish that carcass, and we'll be able to take it back to the ship for analysis."

"Ugh! I wonder." Harmarrght remarked, reeling from the odor that now wafted in their direction.

"It's fouling the remains of the carcass with musk!" Norvallk observed in amazement and almost gagged.

The wolverine, being unable to finish, had simply protected what was left so he could return to complete the meal at a later date. It then sat up on its haunches, shaded its eyes with a forepaw, and looked around.

The alien party worked very hard at remaining unseen and unheard, although most of them were gasping as a result of the horrible smell.

"Did you say something about technology earlier?" Norvallk managed to ask his student between stifled coughs.

The wolverine found its direction again and ambled off.

"Do we follow?" Harmarrght asked. "Or do we stay here and suffocate?"

"Let's go! Keep it in sight, but *don't* let it detect you," Norvallk ordered his party. He had no desire to tangle with this little beast. But he had to find out more about it.

As they went along, Norvallk asked Harmarrght, "Do you still think that this world would be easy to conquer?"

"Well . . . Nothing so far that our weapons couldn't cope with. It might be expensive and it might take time, but we could do it . . . if what we've seen is any indication. They're tough, but we're just as tough and just as well-armed."

"Wouldn't you say that this being has a reasonably high Ferocity Index?"

"Yes," Harmarrght admitted.

"Which means we would have to kill them all or subdue them. From the looks of them, we'd probably have to kill them. But suppose we don't get them all. Would you like to live here knowing that one of those things was on the loose?"

"If I'm armed and expecting it, why not?"

"What did you learn at the Institute?" Norvallk exploded. "Didn't they teach you anything about the economics of conquest and exploitation? Didn't they teach you how to evaluate the Indices?"

"Well, yes, but . . ."

"Did you ever stop to consider the difficulties of conquering a world whose inhabitants have low Intelligence Index, low Adaptability Index, low Technical Index, but high Ferocity Index? Under those circumstances, a takeover becomes a disaster if the natives fight to the death with no quarter given! *Successful* colonization requires that the native life not only be overcome, but also be re-trained and made suitable to work under the direction of the colonizers. You can't spend all your time fighting. Now that you're on a new planet for the first time, maybe you'll realize that a planet is a big chunk of real estate. You *can't* wipe out every dangerous animal on it, but if they're too dangerous you *must* dispatch them lest they continue to breed and remain a constant threat. Under a situation like that, you have to withdraw from the planet and write it off."

"Retreat? But we've never had to do that! We've *never* written off a world!" Harmarrght objected.

"We'd have written off a dozen of them if we'd known then what we know now. Those worlds were very expensive acquisitions," Norvallk reminded him as they moved along, keeping the wolverine in sight but not permitting their conversation to betray their presence. "You were filled with propaganda about the glorious exploits of those who did the dirty work. It looks different when you've been on the scene. Or it should. What is your evaluation of this world thus far? Apply what you've been taught. You can even use logic if you want."

"Thus far, we've discovered two life forms with high Ferocity Index," Harmarrght said by way of review and lead-in. "But they evidenced no obvious Communications Index, a moderate Intelligence Index, and a very low Technology Index . . ."

"I'm not willing to concede that point yet," Norvallk put in. "But go on."

"*Ergo,* the dominant species might not have a high Ferocity Index, being dependent upon symbiosis with other species to acquire this factor. I make the presumption that Ferocity Index would logically have to be lower in more intelligent, communicating beings than . . ."

"An assumption without adequate evidence," Norvallk pointed out.

"Well, on the other hand, the two forms already discovered might not be the dominant species on the planet. They might simply co-exist with the dominant form."

"Suppose the dominant form has a higher Ferocity Index," Norvallk said.

"Oh, quite unlikely! We've *never* encountered anything before with the fantastic Ferocity Index that would be required!"

"Harmarrght, it's a big universe."

"Yes, but very few planets exist with the physical character-

istics of this one. It seems to me that the Overlord might be
unhappy with a recommendation to abandon it now that . . ."

"Which means that we must gather as much data as we
can." Norvallk indicated the wolverine. "Watch! The animal
is hunting something new."

By climbing a tree, the wolverine finished off a squirrel.
Very shortly thereafter, a porcupine managed to get out of its
way. The wolverine then proceeded to catch a rabbit and a
chipmunk, but it befouled them and cached them instead of
eating them.

"Well, we seem to have stumbled on the beast that probably has the highest Ferocity Index in this neighborhood,"
Norvallk commented, then stopped in his tracks as the wolverine emerged into a clearing.

"A dwelling!" Harmarrght exclaimed. "If it belongs to this
beast, it indicates a much higher Intelligence Index than I
expected for it. Look: smoke comes from a vent on the roof,
indicating a mastery of the chemical combustion process
which . . ."

"Don't assume that it belongs to the animal," Norvallk cut
in and pointed out the tools scattered here and there around
the cabin and the plot of ground that was a garden. "It
couldn't possibly handle tools of that size. It's demonstrably
a hunter, and I wouldn't expect it to be a farmer, too." He
snapped orders to his exploring party. Quietly, the various
specialists ranged themselves in hiding around the clearing
so that their recorders had a view of the cabin from several
sides. The warriors were given strict orders not to use their
weapons except in defense of the party.

The wolverine prowled around the cabin for some time.
Norvallk waited patiently, but Harmarrght fidgeted nervously.
"Let me go up and see what's inside that dwelling," he finally
suggested.

"Not while I'm in charge of the party," Norvallk said.
"This is an exploration crew, not a military group. I equate
such bravery to stupidity at this point. I do not want to have
to return your remains to the ship . . . providing that the
animal left any remains or that we could get to you after-
wards."

"But one bolt from this projector . . ."

"How many others might be inside that dwelling?" Norvallk posed the rhetorical question to his student.

There was a movement behind one of the windows. Then, as Norvallk came up on the alert, two human children dashed out of the cabin with yells of delight.

With great consternation, Norvallk watched these two new life forms run fearlessly up to the wolverine.

"Glutton! You're back!" one of them cried.

They dropped to the ground in front of the little animal and began to stroke its coat. The wolverine responded playfully, for it had known these children all its life. They had found it as a cub, half-frozen and starved, somehow separated from its mother. Although these children had raised it as a pet, it often reverted to feral state and disappeared into the hills for days. But it always came back. Hunting was difficult and dangerous; it was far easier to be fed on schedule by the children. And the humans were capable of giving it something very pleasurable and desirable: love.

Glutton, the wolverine, rolled on its back and permitted great indignities to be taken. One of the children ran into the house and returned with some meat in a dish—and was disappointed when the wolverine refused it. But Glutton did not befoul this meal as it had done with others it could not eat.

The young bipeds talked to it, played with it, and fondled it for some time. The aliens recorded every movement and sound. Norvallk was very busy trying to make things add up in his mind; he was quite unhappy with the conclusions he was reaching. Harmarrght merely watched in great confusion; he was having great difficulty rationalizing what his own logic told him with what he had been taught.

A larger biped appeared in the cabin door. "Boys! Lunch time! Come in now!"

They started to go, but the wolverine wanted more play and love. It growled and tried to nip at one boy's leg.

The human child turned around and cuffed the wolverine smartly, scolding it as he did so.

The wolverine shook its fur and followed the boys into the cabin.

Norvallk wasted no time regrouping his party and getting them back to the ship.

"You've done an excellent job under most hazardous conditions," the Master told Norvallk and the rest of the party. "Your data confirms the conclusion we've already reached here. Ulmnarrgh has received radiations from life forms that are orbiting this world as well as in transit to nearby planets. The varied inhabitants of this world are already out in space and expanding with explosive speed. I will be recommending rather drastic measures to the Overlord. In the meantime, we raise ship at once and try to get out of here without being destroyed."

As the ship boosted away under maximum drive, Norvallk sat reviewing the data with his student. "It should be perfectly obvious to you at this point that the standard method of evaluating Ferocity Index and integrating the various Indices is useless for this planet. Tell me, have you ever run an exercise with data like this?"

"Well . . . no," Harmarrght admitted. "But this is a very slim amount of data taken in restricted locality. I will admit that the planet is dangerous . . ."

"It's the most dangerous planet I know of."

"Well . . . yes. Even our most difficult conquests involved life forms with Ferocity Indices that we could at least measure. But the drastic measures the Master spoke of might certainly . . ."

"Forgive me for anticipating you," Norvallk broke in, "but those drastic recommendations are likely to involve re-routing of ship lanes away from this vicinity and perhaps even abandonment of nearby outposts."

"But we could certainly overcome . . ."

"Again, my apologies. Do you think we could fight the several life forms we saw on that planet without expending millions of warriors and a great deal of equipment? Remember the universal law of living organisms: the Law of Least Effort. This is a big galaxy, and there are more comfortable and less expensive parts of it in which to operate."

"I guess you're right," Harmarrght admitted. "There are easier things to do."

Back on the planet, the wolverine, although it didn't consciously know the Law of Least Effort, responded to it, too. It curled up on the rug in front of the fireplace and snoozed while beings with a higher Ferocity Index quietly ate their lunch around a table.

GIANT METEOR IMPACT

J. E. Enever

The Federation Warning Post at Grimaldi perches on the rim of the crater. It was built with the five other Lunar posts, when power plays by member nations were still conceivable. Their radars have been kept abreast of discovery, and, though they have never tracked a hostile, are still the most sensitive in existence.

At this moment, Grimaldi is "out" for installation of an improved transmitter module. The Post Commander's desk is, therefore, adorned by his large boots in addition to the usual house phone and the hot radiophone link to Earth.

The house phone rings: Control console calling. The Commander reflects that Smittie must have balanced in the new circuit. We're operational again.

"Lo, Smittie, got it working?"

"Yes—but listen, Chiefie, I turned up an echo on my trial sweep. Unbelievably big . . ."

The Commander is very definitely interested. No interplanetary research fights are currently scheduled, and there can be no reason for normal traffic to wander out of the Lunar Commercial lanes into Grimaldi's sector.

"A ship, Smittie?"

"Not unless someone has built a ship with a square mile surface, Chief. It can't be anything except a big, big meteor—moving in the ecliptic, already across the moon's orbit. Even from our angle—it's something like 110° round from us—it's dopplering in like hell."

Chiefie has removed his boots from the desk and is hustling up to the control room.

Smith proves to be right. It can be nothing but a meteor;

the size is asteroidal. And, if it misses Earth at all, it will be a
very close shave.

The Post Commander happens to have read the form where
large meteorites are concerned. In a matter of two hours—no
more—tens of billions of tons may hurtle down upon some
unsuspecting metropolis; wherever the target may be, a crater
some scores of miles across will be blasted out. A fireball
nearly as wide as the crater will shower heat and hard
radiation on the area. The district beyond the crater rim will
be bombarded by a lighter scattering of debris. Earth tremors
more devastating than any natural 'quake will ripple out
across the continent. A Nation will be devastated, and any
human within a hundred miles of the crater will be triply
slain, first by X rays, next by blast, finally by incineration.

For ten seconds, Chiefie is paralyzed by sheer cold panic.
Why, oh why must he, of all creatures ever born, be saddled
with this load? But the Commander is made to the full
measure of a man. Forewarning is his trade. If forewarning,
plus modern transport, will save a single life, he will so
save it.

The first step is relatively easy. The Commander lifts the
hot radiophone. In two minutes he is through to the Inspector
General, Federation Arm, in New York. Five minutes later
every vital landline and radio channel on Earth is cleared
and silent, its operator poised for action. Here, Chiefie is aided
by the fact that he is following his normal chain of command, and probing past disciplined superiors who know him
and trust each other.

What comes next is harder. The Grimaldi post is admirably
equipped for detection and location. What it lacks is a computer which will draw a ballistic trajectory correct to the
tenth decimal.

He knows where there is just such an instrument—in Traffic
Control at the Copernicus City spaceport. There is now just
about one hundred minutes to go before that meteor hits, or
misses.

It takes Chiefie thirty-five of those minutes to establish a
working link with Traffic Control. You think that is slow?
Listen, brother—the speed with which Chiefie moves here is
what wins him the Star of Honor in iridium instead of in gold.
Did *you* ever try to operate one government department as
servant of another? Gross Departures from Approved Chan-

nels and Serious Deviations from Normal Procedures are involved! The Commander has to raise Signals Superintendent at the Spaceport, and disabuse him of the idea that his leg is being pulled. He must then reach and similarly disabuse the Traffic Controller. The Computer Programmer, who just dived into a cup of coffee, has to be pulled out of it and briefed. The buck must be passed at every one of these steps. This sounds comic, but Chiefie finds small joy in the hassle. But he goes through with it, and is finally able to dictate his problem to the computer, several hundred miles away. If, my friend, you consider thirty-five minutes slow for all that, you've spent your life on Easter Island.

An hour to go. The Grimaldi radars do not compute, but they locate nearly to the thickness of the proverbial bee's wing. Smittie has been making them do just this, again, and again, and again, clocking the positions on the record with nano-second accuracy.

By M-minute minus 55, the Copernicus computer is defining the meteor's path with increasing accuracy, using Smittie's data.

A first solution comes through. It is real bad news. There is no doubt about it—the meteor *will* hit Earth.

By M minus 50, plots are coming in from the big lidars and radars up on Earth. They have probed for the intruder, found it, located it. Working together, the ganged instruments are fixing the course with still more precision. The best computers on Earth are now joining in a second extrapolation of the point of impact. This comes through at about M minus 40. The news is better; the new prediction is that the meteor will fall somewhere in the South Pacific.

Perhaps it is going to splash rather than thump. If you wonder why, hold out a stiffish curved wire by one end. Try to keep it rock-steady. At every imperceptible tremor of your hand, the far end of the wire sweeps through a considerable volume of space. This is how a courier capsule which deviates a skillionth of a degree at launch from Earth misses the moon by a hundred thousand miles. This is the reason for uncertainty about the meteor's precise target.

M-minute minus 30. The bolide is much closer now. Successive fixes have become more and more exact. The errors are steadily narrowing, corrections have lined out the trajectory more exactly. The meteor's position and vector are now known with all the accuracy which can be of any practical importance.

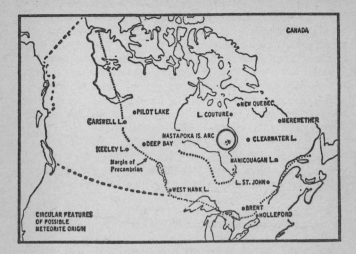

The last solution comes in. Tens of billions of tons are going to strike. They will fall at fifty kilometers per second, but will drop amost exactly midway between New Zealand and Chile —Longitude, 121° 25' West, Latitude 42° 41' South, plus or minus 9' in each case.

Not a thump, but a mid-ocean splash.

Up on Earth, a man sitting in the thorniest worry seat in all history takes his index finger off the Panic Button.

The panic is over. . . .

OR IS IT?

The piece of fiction just presented is founded on the strictest fact. Earth has been repeatedly hit by very large meteorites, their speed unchecked by virtue of their enormous size. Evidence for this has been piling up for the past sixty years. Scores of able workers in other disciplines have dug hard for the data we now hold. Soon, the seeds which they are sowing will flourish as a new exact science—the study of Meteoritics. The odd point is, however, that none of these workers has yet noticed the simple fact which is crucial to the climax of my little story. The problem here is certainly real, and is distinctly important. Something that matters has been overlooked.

I'm going to take you back to the beginning of the story. To follow its development to the present end, we are going to make a few calculations. Little more than simple arithmetic is needed for these.

That "little more" is knowledge of these easy facts:

1. That $e = \frac{1}{2} m \times v^2$. The energy of a moving body equals half its mass times the square of its velocity.
2. When the moving body is involved in a collision, the energy of movement degrades into heat. The exchange is at known rates for various materials.

The first evidence for a strike by a large meteorite was given by the Barringer brothers early this century. Here "large" means "ranging over 1,000 tons weight." The Barringers showed that the Canyon Diablo crater was formed by meteoric impact. Naturally, the demonstration met with the most pigheaded resistance from precisely those who should preserve the most open minds. Despite these people, the concept finally percolated . . . but even as late as 1930, the Barringer Crater could still provide a fresh theme for a story in the old *Amazing*.

Well over forty similar cases are now either well proven, or listed as suspect on very good grounds. Two or three more are added yearly.

Some, or all, of the following clues provide the evidence:

1. Cratering of a generally circular shape. Whatever the angle of collision, the meteorite's impact is violently explosive. Its speed, and thus the speed of the blast of superhot gases which results, vastly transcend those of chemical reactions. The power of the Barringer strike was about 2½ megatons of TNT, and it blasted a crater about 4,000 feet across.

You can model the process in miniature yourself. Spread a target of loose cement dust three inches thick on your garage floor. Shoot loose slugs of cement dust into this target from the mouth of a very small container. Getting the slugs to cohere yet hit fast will call for practice, or perhaps some ingenious contrivance. Once you get them hitting fast enough, you will produce *circular* craters in your target, whatever the angle of impact. Occasionally, material ejected from the crater will make chains of craterlets outside the crater rim, like those around the big lunar craters. Quite often you will reproduce central peaks within the craters, and, if you sprinkle a layer of limestone dust or some other distinctive powder over the target, you will now and again make replicas of the rays round the lunar craters.

2. The material of the crater floor is broken. This "breccia" grades from rock-flour at the surface to boulder-size at depth.

3. This disturbance is detectable under large craters even when all surface traces have been eroded, or covered by loess or by sedimentary rock. Gravimetric surveys show anomalously low densities beneath the crater floor.

4. Minute spherules of iron, 0.1 mm. or so across, which condense from vapors produced by the impact flare, may be distributed around the crater.

5. The unusual minerals, coesite and stishkovite, first identified near meteorite craters, are found only at these places. They are dense silicates created by the pressure of the explosion.

6. Rocks surrounding the crater are likely to be shattered in a unique fashion. Compression waves originating from the strike diffract on small irregularities within the rock. This then breaks into *shatter cones* pointing to the center of impact. This piece of evidence also outlives complete deletion of surface traces.

7. When the diameters of various types of explosion crater are graphed against their depths, the incidents group upon a quite remarkably smooth curve. This includes craters from small chemical explosions, from nuclear charges, from the terrestrial meteorite strikes, and finally the lunar craters. The curve *excludes* most volcanic craters—both the conical types, such as Vesuvius, and the Hawaiian shield craters such as Mauna Loa.

The Barringer Crater is very far from being the largest known on Earth. It could have been caused by a body weighing 10,000 tons, striking at nearly 40 kilometers per second.

The meteor which occasioned the Vredevoort Ring in South Africa was much bigger. Its volume has been estimated at a cubic mile. Blasting out the sedimentary strata, it exposed naked magma at the base of a pit scores of miles wide. At the tip of the ring, the strata were turned over to show the stratigraphic sequence in horizontal, concentric rings. The hell-pit then refilled with magma from the depths.

Larger events still have been claimed. For example, Hudson's Bay and the Japan and Weddell seas have been said to have originated in the same way. Mr. Rene Gallant, puts forward strikes by Junoesque bodies, at energies totaling more than 10^{33} ergs. This, by the way, is a quarter of the Sun's entire output of energy for an entire second! It equals the *complete* conversion to energy of a million tons of matter or the explosion of a hundred thousand million million tons— yes, seventeen zeros after the figure one—of TNT.

Very circumstantial proof should be given before these are accepted. If as little as one per cent of the energy of such an impact transferred as heat to the world's atmosphere, the air temperature everywhere would rise by about 200°C. My cal-

TEN CANADIAN CRATERS

(Not all of these are situated on the Shield)

Name	Diameter of circular feature as seen now	Estimated diameter of the original rim of crater	Upper limit of age of strike
HOLLEFORD	2.35 km	2.35 km	5 megacenturies
NEW QUEBEC	3.7 km	3.7 km	1-2 megayears
BRENT	3.0 km	3.7 km	5 megacenturies
WEST HAWK	3.3 km	3.9 km	5½ megacenturies
DEEP BAY	10	10.5 km	2½ megacenturies
LAC COUTURE	14 km	10 km	6 megacenturies
CLEARWATER EAST	21 km	18 km	4 megacenturies (Twin strike)
CLEARWATER WEST	32 km	32 km	4 megacenturies
CARSWELL LAKE	32 km	30 km	5 megacenturies
MANICOUAGAN	60 km	65 km	3 megacenturies

After M. R. Dence, Dominion Observatory, Ottawa

culation here is approximate, since it ignores the work which the heat would do in expanding the atmosphere; but my one per cent heat allowance is obviously niggardly. Strikes by major asteroids seem to be the instant recipe for pasteurized planet. They also violate the law of parsimony. Nonetheless, you must notice that even the Vredevoort event yielded *more than a million megatons of TNT.*

It is calculated that meteorites as heavy as 1,000 tons and

up are all but unchecked by the atmosphere. They strike the ground with nearly all their original speed. This ranges from about 20 kilometers per second to just over 70 k.p.s. The higher figure is the maximum which any member of the solar system can attain at the Earth's distance from the sun. The limit for a body which moves in from the galaxy with some speed to begin with is clearly much higher. A few small meteors have, in fact, been tracked by radar at over 150 k.p.s.

As the meteorite dives to the surface, there will be a formidable pressure wave. At Mach numbers 60 to 200 the sonic boom will be awesome. But it will not only be short-lived; it will be dwarfed by the blast arising from the surface impact. The relatively small Siberian shower of 1908 flattened the conifers of the Taiga to a range of 30 miles.

There are many other effects:

(a) Heat. In a large strike, the instant flare of the impact is reckoned to convert more than a quarter of the total energy into prompt heat. You should notice that in the end almost *all* the energy will degrade into heat. There is an exception, see (e) below; and for some effects, the degradation will take a considerable time.

A feature of large strikes such as Vredevoort is that the fireball must be enormous. Think of it as that from a 250,000 megaton fusion bomb. It will probably not reach the diameter of 200 miles given by a cube-root-of-power comparison with an "ordinary" Hydrogen bomb. But its measurements will *certainly* exceed the total depth of the atmosphere and stratosphere together. As a result of this, the fireball will squat upon the target area, doming up into the ionosphere, but unable to rise. It will radiate terrific energy into space. Even when the fireball has at last cooled out, the target will glow for weeks and months—again radiating a good deal of energy into space.

(b) Severe earthquakes will damage the crust.

(c) Material will be ejected beyond the crater's periphery. This will range from large crustal blocks down to microscopic powder; some of this material will travel a long way.

(d) Volatilized matter and even plasma will be thrown out to space at escape speed. Here, see Ralph Hall's fact article, "Secondary Meteorites," January and February issues, 1964.

(e) There will be some exchange of impetus between the meteorite and the spinning Earth. Substantially, this would be confined to alteration of the Earth's axial tilt and rotation period. Even an impact by Juno would affect the orbital speed by only a few centimeters per second. The reference here is to Rene Gallant's book, "Bombarded Earth," published in London by Baker.

Not merely are staggering energies released. The explosion has high "brisance," is shatteringly intense. Tremendous temperatures combine with tremendous pressures. Ralph Hall explained that nuclear reactions will occur at the heart of the flare. These, I think, may just as well *absorb* energy as release it, but either way, there will certainly be a flood of X rays and neutrons. I suspect that these might leave faint but discernible traces in the surrounding rocks.

So far, my discussion has followed precedent. I have considered a *continental* strike—one which hits a land target area. What has so far been overlooked is that three-quarters of the Earth's surface is *ocean*.

The odds are, therefore, three to one in favor of an ocean strike. For the 40+ known land craters, there must have been 120+ strikes at sea. It is *certain* that some of these marine falls equaled or exceeded the power of the Vredevoort impact. But the count does not end here.

For a start, the large majority of explored craters are in North America, just three per cent of the World's surface. There are several reasons for this: one is the comparative failure of attention to the subject elsewhere. Another is the Canadian Shield—the widest area anywhere of bare, primeval rock, where the craters of gigayears are easy to find. In any case, we must obviously multiply the number of known falls not by a factor of three, but by thirty. Hold the total down to a probable 1,000 falls in all—750 of them were at sea. There have been a sizable number of Vredevoorts in the ocean.

Your first thought will be that an ocean strike is just a damped-off edition of a fall on land. Not on your life! It's distinctly different, *and* distinctly more lethal!

Unfortunately, craters in water have a way of filling up and leaving no evidence on the surface, whatever happens to the ocean bed. We'll just have to manufacture a model by mental experiment; see where a few calculations from known facts will take us. Gauss was too lazy to reach out his arm for his log tables; to save himself trouble, he memorized the lot. We'll do the opposite and construct an asteroid whose vital statistics will make the figuring easy. Just a baby one. As we build it, we'll take a good look at it, for it won't have long to live. On then, to Vredevoort Mark II.

Four cubic kilometers will do for the size. This is just under one cubic mile: about 0.96 cubic miles to be more precise. Weight will be of the essence, so density will count. We will carve our experimental meteorite from a core fragment of planet Number Five. Pure iron, but for a trace of heavier metal which increases the density to the convenient value of eight times water. Every cubic centimeter of asteroid will weigh eight grams. I am encouraged in adopting this composition by Dr. Robert Dietz. He claims that the Sudbury nickel deposits are remnants of a slow nickel iron meteorite, which was also the origin of local deposits of heavy metals.

The shape is immaterial. Asteroids of this size are under no compulsion to be spherical, and the distribution of mass will not alter the impact energy. All the same, we'll take a good look at baby.

As carved out with tractor beams and superlasers the finished artifact is definitely a pill: a drum-shaped disk averaging a kilometer in thickness and three kilometers in diameter. The surface glints blackly evil, faceted and knobbly. Matching velocity to push it on course, we see that is spinning slowly. That notch on the rim will sight on Rigel in a few moments. We'll time the spin. Start the stop-clock now . . . 200 seconds.

Eighteen revs per hour. That's not very fast; the rim is only traveling at 100 m.p.h. But wrap that much rotation round a mass of tens of billions of tons, and you finish with quite a packet of angular momentum. Let's take a momentometer reading . . . the energy of spin comes out at 10^{23} ergs. Why, that equals about 2½ megatons of TNT! If any meteor scavenger thinks of looting this lump, he must first kill that rotation. He could do the job with his surplus Government H1 rocket engine, blasting for a month with about two million tons of propellant. It's hardly an economic proposition.

In fact, any landing whatsoever would be distinctly hazardous. At the rim, centrifugal acceleration is about a tenth Earth "G". At the pole, you might get away with a space-

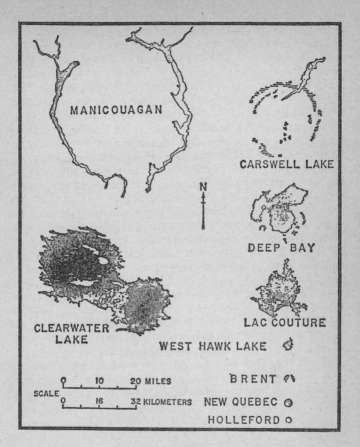

MANICOUAGAN

CARSWELL LAKE

N

DEEP BAY

CLEARWATER LAKE

LAC COUTURE

WEST HAWK LAKE

SCALE
0 10 20 MILES
0 16 32 KILOMETERS

BRENT

NEW QUEBEC

HOLLEFORD

suit landing; but even there, you must anchor a tether before going down. An electromagnet should hold, but as a confirmed belt-and-gallus man I would reinforce it with a gob of the latest plastic goo. The polar gravitation, little more than a quarter mile away from the center of gravity, is somewhat higher than one might guess. About one twelve-hundredth Earth normal. Fumble a tool as you draw it from your belt and it will only take a quarter minute to fall to the surface. Horrendous crash as spanner hits asteroid at five inches per second.

Speaking cosmically, Vredevoort II is a dust mote, but for all that we have mass with a capital M. Specific gravity 8, volume 4 cubic kilometers. The mass works out at $8 \times 4 \times (100,000)^3$ grams. 3.2×10^{16} grams. Over 35 thousand million tons.

It sounds, and is, a considerable hunk of matter, but Hermes, Eros, Icarus, all asteroids penetrating the inner Solar System as they orbit, are all distinctly larger.

We will steer the 35 billion ton missile into mid-ocean at 50 kilometers per second. Our observation eyrie will have to be well out and well to the side. There is no foretelling the speed and coherence at which the jet of plasma will gush up from the impact flare. Three or four thousand miles *may* be safety distance.

At the end of the countdown, a tremendous glare of sheer violet radiance—a color few have witnessed outside the high energy labs—lights the ocean for four hundred miles round the target, throwing the tiny clouds into vivid relief. It lasts only the space of two heartbeats, leaving us dazzled, far away as we are. That is not the impact—that is incandescent air! Air so compressed when Vredevoort II rushes through it on the last lap to the ground as to glow in the violet, and beyond. Luckily, we are not placed to hear the sonic boom which accompanies the glow; at closer range the sound is such as to pulverize bone and homogenize living tissue.

Before our eyes recover, there is another, more brilliant flare of violet. The plasma-bolt is rocketing up into space. Even at this range, it flames too brightly to be watched, brighter and hotter by far than the surface of the sun. Here is a concentration of naked energy verging into the nuclear range. We are seeing it by the lower frequencies; most of the radiation is beyond the visible spectrum. Before it disperses and cools, the jet of stripped atoms travels so fast and climbs so high, that it seems to stand upon the ocean hundreds of miles tall—an incandescent column, rainbow tipped and haloed. This is perhaps the illusion of persistence of vision, but its glare lights the entire ocean from continent to continent.

Below it, the fireball is expanding. First it is a blue-hot pinprick, then a dazzling sun-white speck, of perceptible breadth even before the plasma bolt has cooled to invisibility. It grows as a roiling, incandescent chaos, which even the eye of the imagination finds difficult to penetrate. In its lurid glare, we see a faint ripple expanding across the cloudscape. From our distance, it moves at a seeming snail's pace, though its real speed is little short of Mach 1.

Our mental experiment will take us little further; only calculation will clarify the processes which follow the flare. Since $e = \frac{1}{2}mv^2$, every gram of the meteorite's mass will carry: $\frac{1}{2} \times 1 \times (5 \times 10^6)^2$ ergs. This works out to 1.25×10^{13} ergs per gram. Now multiply this by the total weight, 3.2×10^{16} grams. The total energy comes to 4×10^{29} ergs. This is very nearly *ten teratons, or ten million megatons of TNT*. (A megaton of TNT yields "only" 4.2×10^{22} ergs.) For comparison, the largest earthquakes which have been measured since Milne invented the seismograph developed less than 10^{27} ergs; this power was spread over very great volumes of the Earth's crust and mantle.

We could express the energy as heat. A calorie is the heat needed to raise the temperature of a gram of water by $1°$ C. It equals 42 million ergs. So our experimental strike is going to produce 10^{22} calories. There is power enough, and to spare. What other effects follow those violet flares?

To begin with, the enormous heat of the impact will not only vaporize the mile or two depth of ocean at the bull's eye, it will also vaporize the crystal rocks below, clear through the Moho, and blow out the surrounding rocks as well. Beyond the area where the mantle is laid bare, rifts will expose hot magma.

The crater is as wide as Vredevoort in South Africa. Though more power is absorbed in producing plasma at the kernel of the event than in a land strike—fearful energy is needed to convert water into a plasma of hydrogen and oxygen nuclei—water *is* less dense than rock. Despite its incompressibility and high latent heat of evaporation, it is easier to shift en masse than rock. So although the seabed crater is somewhat shallower than that on land, it is just as broad. A blazing wound scores of miles wide scars the sea floor.

A ringed waterfall as high as the Alleghenies rushes in to quench it, its circumference that of a county boundary. The fiery furnace opened by this strike will *not* glow for weeks and months as it would on land; the torrents of ocean rush in, and change at once to pure steam. They stream up in a thin-walled sleeve which is as clear as air, as invisible as the gush of superheated vapor which flays the flesh from men's bones in a boiler-room catastrophe.

Here, the glass-clear gaseous water is sweeping up in volume enough to cloud a planet's atmosphere. The naked wound on the seabed glows white-hot through the wall of the frightful cylinder which encloses it. But inch by inch and foot by foot the waters sweeping in win. The column of steam still rushes up to the ionosphere, still spreads out across the heavens, but it steadily contracts. Beyond the rim of the inferno, crustal rifts are already exuding sills of lava across the ocean floor. Convulsions and seisms mount in cataclysmic fury surpassing the power of any natural quake.

All the waters of the oceans are set in oscillation. A mere volcanic eruption in the 1880s achieved this. Gigantic blast waves are ripping out far away from the crater. Dwindling in strength, they will circle the planet half a dozen times or more before they become indetectable. The turning world itself has quivered as it spins. Transfer of momentum will be small in a strike of this power. I'll neglect it.

The exact division of these different energies may not be clear. It will also fail to be of great influence on my argument. First let us consider certain thermal effects of the strike.

Remember that the meteorite delivers about 3×10^5 calories per gram: just under 10^{22} calories in all.

I take it that energy dissipated in deep Earth tremors, splashed back to space by the plasma jet, or radiated back to space from the impact flare and the fireball, is compensated by the heat gained from the magma bared by crustal damage.

The energy absorbed in massive displacement of ocean water, in tidal waves, in blast, and in local damage to the seabed, will in the end degrade to heat. This will occur soon enough for the heat to give direct backing to the impact flare; it will work immediately behind the flare in evaporating the ocean. The continuity here is, as it were, measured on a *climatic* time scale. The watch dial is calibrated in hours and days, not the split seconds appropriate to the impact.

This being so, every unit weight of the meteorite will cause the evaporation of about 600 units weight of the ocean. It takes about 600 calories to evaporate a gram of water, on average. Not merely to raise it to boiling point, but to turn the whole gram into vapor. You need over five times more heat to free the molecules from the forces which bind them together in the liquid state than to raise ice to the boiling point. But the evaporation can take place *without* raising the water's temperature at all; as when the ocean turns into rain clouds. My figure of 600 calories averages the heat transfer in the two cases, both of which will occur in our meteorite incident. The calculation runs like this: 3×10^5 calories heat available per gram of meteorite÷600 calories to evaporate one gram of water=500 grams of water evaporated.

But every cubic centimeter of our meteorite weighs as much as eight cubic centimeters of water. This means that 4,000 *volumes* of water will be evaporated by each unit volume of meteorite. *The four cubic kilometer volume of Vredevoort Mark II will evaporate 16,000 cubic kilometers of ocean.* This is about 3,800 cubic miles!

You will obviously refuse to believe these figures, so let's check the calculations by another route. The total heat equivalent of the strike energy is 10^{22} calories. Dividing this by 600 calories per cubic centimeter evaporated, we get 1.6×10^{19} cc.—16,000 cubic kilometers again. Now normal evaporation from all the oceans of the Earth by the sun's heat is just *under* a cubic kilometer per minute—rather less than a billion metric tons; sixty cubic kilometers per hour.

The meteorite equals the sun's work as a cloud maker for 16,000÷60=266 hours, just over eleven days. This is just enough to provide an average rainfall of over one and a quarter inches upon the whole Earth, oceans and land together.

By itself, this would be a foul enough stormfall. Of course, in the nature of things, the rainfall would be anything but evenly distributed. You can make your own guesses at where the peak precipitations would occur and what their value would be. But the matter would be very far from closed by a single deluge of rain spreading across the planet.

When water vapor turns into rain, all those calories which were used in evaporating it are released to go to work elsewhere. This is the energy cycle which keeps a hurricane spinning; this is the force which lifts the cu-nim thunderhead higher than Everest. *For a while* the latent heat of evaporation is employed in moving air—wind-making.

Choose your own velocities for the winds generated by meteorite rainstorms. But don't imagine they will be gentle zephyrs. They will be very fierce and will rage across the world.

However, even this is not the crucial point in this question of release of latent heat. The crux is this: though the heat of the strike will in the end radiate back to space, radiation under constant cloud cover at biological temperatures is a fairly slow business. The following cycle will continue for some time before all the excess heat leaks off the Earth:

Heat absorbed by evaporation
Condensation
Release of latent heat for further evaporation
Long range weather forecast: Very wet, very windy, very cloudy. Period of forecast indefinite.

As if this were insufficient, another factor comes into play to reinforce the overall effect of the heat cycle: let me explain it.

In the year 1883, the volcano Krakatoa blew its top. I will refer again to this event in another connection, to make another standard comparison.

"Blew its top" is an all too literal statement. The detonation pulverized several cubic miles of the volcanic cone. Where this originally peaked at a 3,000 foot summit, the ocean now rolls over part of the base. The explosion was a mere volcanic incident—two or three megatons of TNT would do as much; the energy released was only 7×10^{22} ergs.

A respectable proportion of the rock was shattered so finely that it hung twenty miles high in the stratosphere throughout the following decade. Doubtless some of it is still there.

There were noticeable effects. For the next ten years, sunsets and dawns were gaudier than usual the whole world over. It is said that over the same period, worldwide temperatures were very slightly lower than average.

Our model strike carries nearly six million times the energy released by Krakatoa.

The amount of solids thrown up by the meteorite will not be in the same ratio. They may, in fact, only be five or six thousand times as much as the pulverized volcanic cone. At first sight, the ratio of solids displaced may be thought to settle the amount of dust which is raised. This, however, is not the case. What will count is the minuteness with which the material is divided. A ridiculously small quantity of finely divided titanium oxide set free from naval smoke-floats will screen a naval task force from view.

Here the very high brisance of the meteorite explosion comes into play. Even a Barringer-size strike leaves rock-flour on the crater floor. Much of what is blasted out must be finer still. (Did you see the picture of the cloud of lunar dust raised by Lunik V?)

The fact that the strike is on the seabed will make little difference. Superheated steam blasts just as forcibly as other explosion gases. The steam jet cutting up to the ionosphere will scavenge all powder from the crater, and a great deal of ooze on the ocean bed miles from the crater will go up with it. Clearance will be more effective than in the case of the land-strike. Salt will be carried up by the steam jet, and will float as fine crystals on high. These will be joined by salt crystals which are residue of the sea water splashed across the heavens in bulk. There will also be a large contribution from microscopic particles of rock and metal which sublime from volatilized material. Even on the very moderate assumption that, erg for erg, Vredevoort II lifts only one per cent of the microscopic particles raised by Krakatoa, it will still throw up sixty thousand times as much fine powder.

Let's hack out an answer: Take a conservative ration of 100 cubic kilometers of rock powder, sublimed micro-droplets salt, and seabed ooze. Choose particles only a micron in size, or grind them down to size by blast or steam jet. Use multi-megaton blasts and steam jets and winds of tornado strength to scatter them across the stratosphere. The resultant haze teams up 200 particles thick over the entire surface. Every electron on the ground has 200 particles directly over-head. The aggregate thickness of the screen will only be a fifth of a millimeter: but did *you* ever read fine print through even one hundredth of an inch of granite?

As a result of the impact a persistent and effective dust cloud will veil the stratosphere. It will float there for a period in no wise shorter than the decade after Krakatoa. The Earth's albedo will be effectively increased. A perceptible decrease in the solar heat reaching the surface for at least ten years seems to be certain. Still speaking very literally, Vrede-voort II puts Krakatoa in the shade.

The world's weather is quite delicately balanced on the solar constant, the value of solar radiation received at the surface in clear weather. This has changed in the past. There are graphs which match the Ice Age datings of the past megayear against the cumulative effect of such astronomical changes as rotation of the axes of the Earth's orbit, precession, and so on. The resultant changes in the solar constant calculated from these effects are small; but the two graphs match with broad fidelity. Small factors, then, affect the polar ice caps and other similar matters. Our dust-veil is going to keep the Earth colder for about ten years. This is certainly time enough for the polar ice caps to grow. Even when cloud-cover has long since dispersed and the dust-shroud has settled, this growth in the polar ice will leave the planetary albedo seriously increased; more of the sun's heat will be reflected back to space.

A long, long planetary cold spell is safely predictable, despite any comparisons which are made with the cloud-cover, dust-cover, or heaven-knows-what-cover shrouding Venus. (In passing, it seems that all was not well with the estimates of surface temperature made when Mariner flew by Venus. Oh well, sailors who make brief passes at the ladies often receive equivocal replies . . .)

At first sight, the mechanical effects of the strike may seem to concern the globigerina ooze and the fish which provide an involuntary bouillabaisse. Marine quakes and seisms would not appear to concern life on land. This view neglects the matter of Tsunamis.

Commonly miscalled a tidal wave, the tsunami is normally caused by a tremor in the ocean bed: a rise or settlement of a few inches, or a jerk along a fault of a few yards or so —the type of thing which causes an earthquake on land. But on one occasion at least, the tsunami has resulted from a volcanic detonation. Right first time—Krakatoa!

Whatever the cause, an oscillation of the ocean is generated. There is no mass transference of water. Characteristically, the vibration is of low amplitude but very long wavelength. The speed of waves at sea is determined by the wavelength which in its turn is affected by the depth of the ocean. Because of its very long wavelength, the tsunami moves very fast indeed. The low amplitude may make it imperceptible when it races past a mid-ocean vessel at four hundred fifty miles per hour. This does not prevent it from raising the purest kind of hell where it breaks on shore. Here it builds into a devastating breaker which may reach miles inland. Ocean-going vessels have been stranded miles from the beach. The Krakatoa tidal wave broke upon Indonesian coasts in rollers which reached heights well over a hundred feet. It was *visible* as far off as the Cape of Good Hope. It was clearly *detectable* in the English Channel. It was still just detectable after circling the world again.

The 4×10^{29} erg punch delivered by Vredevoort II is expected to create quite a ripple. Mass displacement of the water, submarine quakes, and the pressure wave through the ocean will all contribute to the tsunami. The energy which it temporarily absorbs before restoring it as heat is conjectural. A reasonable allotment would be about one-sixth of the total power account sheet.

This will give it a force of 7×10^{28} ergs, two orders of magnitude more powerful than the largest recorded earthquakes. As already mentioned, these were continental. They spread their effects through millions of cubic miles of crust and mantle. We just do not know what tsunamis they would have raised had they been shallow disturbances under the mid-ocean.

But we *do* know what the millionfold-weaker occurrence at Krakatoa achieved. Quite obviously, the volcano did not exert its total strength in raising the tidal wave. Even if we credit the tsunami with all the 7×10^{22} ergs of the detonation, the meteorite tidal wave is a full millionfold stronger.

The tidal wave is a very efficient vehicle for transferring energy over long ranges. Frictional losses are fairly low, right up to the point where it climbs ashore to wreck the landscape. One sees it as an *area* rather than a *volume* phenomenon; roughly speaking, the third dimension is constant.

Let us, however, credit it with a decrement of distance cubed. This is conservative, being more appropriate to volume effects, like dynamite blasts in air. This decrement will make the meteoric tsunamis work at ranges the cube root of a million times those of the volcano: that is, at one hundred times the distance of the Krakatoa tidal wave. This gives it a global range in causing disaster. It will break at heights measured not in yards but in block-lengths on any shores in the middle distance, five hundred to one thousand miles away. Even at its antipodes it will wreak havoc comparable with that worked by Krakatoa at about one hundred miles range. Coastal belts all over the world—a sizable total area —will be in peril.

If the meteorite should fall within a confined ocean basin such as the Arctic, damage will recur. Before coming to rest, such a body of water will oscillate in a series of "seiches." The effect here depends on the natural frequency of the particular body of water. The series of waves would diminish in frequency—but the first few returns could all be catastrophic!

We had best abort the Vredevoort II mission while there is still time. Disintegrate that asteroid, Cadet Kinnison!

The ocean strike is clearly very different from the continental fall. The most vital distinction is this: the energy of the land strike is more violently localized and hence its destructive power is more carelessly squandered. On land, the enormous sessile fireball clings to the target surface, unable to rise because it runs out of atmosphere to rise in, even before it is fully expanded. Early in its career it is forced to spread out over the adjacent "craterscape," exposing a majority of its surface to space. So most of the heat radiates away from earth. A significant proportion of the total energy leaves the planet in this way. When the fireball has starved itself to extinction, the incandescent crater takes its turn in wasting energy in the same way over the weeks to come.

The marine fall works in a more efficient, synergic, cumulative manner. From the beginning its energy works with cruel economy. The radiation of the fireball is quenched and veiled and husbanded by steam and storm-wrack. Its heat is conveyed far and wide by the monstrous steam geyser. This also quenches and transfers the power of the ocean-floor inferno, and thus retains it on Earth. Rain follows rain, tidal waves recur, typhoons sweep again and again over a sunless world. In the districts swept by the tsunamis, the storms destroy the last chances of survival for all that grows or moves. The strike's power is transformed down to biological intensities, directed where it will harm the biosphere. When the hell-pit on the seabed is doused, and when, weeks later, the storms have died, dust and cloud veil the Earth. The long Fimbul winter begins.

My picture is unexaggerated. We consider the release of energies equal to the detonation of one megaton bombs pitched down at five-mile intervals over the entire surface of the world. True, even the ocean strike will distribute its energy less evenly than this. It is, however, precisely my case that it will come nearer to so doing than the continental impact. Most of the power of this operates to overkill an already blasted region, a district the size of a nation, but still a limited area.

Above all, remember that what I have depicted *has occurred many times*. The craters of the Canadian Shield are probably a more reliable guide to the number and timing of the past incidents than are those of North America as a whole. The Canadian Shield is a record sheet in stone; it has been ground clean, to receive the indelible and plainly legible account of more than two gigayears of meteoric history. It is about a million square miles in area, roughly one half of one per cent of the world's surface. There are craters of moderate size and upward scattered across it. One of these, Manicouagan, is in the Vredevoort size range. I leave out the larger Nastapoka Island Arc, well over one hundred miles in diameter, as well as Hudson's Bay itself. Five of these incidents seem to have occurred in the last five megacenturies, the post-Cambrian era; this is one every hundred million years on average. Multiply this by the ratio of size between the Shield area and the whole world; we then obtain the figure of two fair-sized strikes per megayear somewhere or other upon Earth. Events of Vredevoort strength will be distinctly more rare—perhaps one every five megayears—but the majority of these will happen at sea. When is the next due? Equally to the point, when did the last occur?

Here we owe a pertinent question to Mr. J. W. Campbell. It is my recollection that some years ago he posed the enigma of the Mammoths, whose frozen carcasses house undigested stomach contents. This is very puzzling indeed. The carcasses of Blue Whales are sometimes left unflensed in the cold Antarctic Ocean for just a few hours too long. When this delay occurs, the Whale's flesh is quite literally roasted within the insulating blubber by the heat of its own putrefaction.

Some whaling men acquire a taste for the gamey dish. For a distinctly smaller beast such as a Mammoth, the effect would be retarded by the operation of square/cube law. But it should still have its parallel. The well insulated stomach contents should so ferment as to become unrecognizable.

Yet Mammoth carcasses are found in both Siberia and Alaska—lying in frozen jumbles of muck and tree trunks in the permafrost—their stomach contents undigested and unfermented. I am told that on one stretch of the Alaska Highway the bulldozer drivers who cut the roadbed were forced to work in gas masks. They turned up so many carcasses of various beasties, that when these were exposed to normal day temperatures the whole area stank like an uncleared battlefield.

The situation presents other puzzles. Trees simply cannot grow in the permafrost. The vegetation with which the bodies are mixed belongs to zones several hundred miles nearer the Equator.

Nor have I ever been prepossessed with the notion that the Mammoth wore hair to keep warm. Present surviving representatives of its family run their metabolisms at only three per cent the rate of smaller Mammals. Their idea here is to avoid an unseemly, messy end in an explosion of metabolic steam. Square/cube law again. Had the Mammoth needed to keep warm, there would have been no need to evolve a coat of hair: a slight lift to the thermostat setting would suffice. Come to it, how does a beast the size of an elephant find enough browse on the tundra? Would even the Taiga sustain him? Do we know any animal bigger than a rodent which grazes pine needles? Picture the tundral Mammoth, which, having picked its daily half ton of whortleberries one by one, goes on to gather a bed of moss. He must have this if he is not to sink through the ooze to the permafrost and wake up with rheumatism.

The fact is that I will be unsurprised to learn that there *was* a calamitous change in climate that "coincided" with a catastrophe which "just happened" to arrive at the time of the demise of the Mammoths.

Our old friend Sprague de Camp has expressed great skepticism on this point. When Cosmic Catastrophe and Calamity is mooted as an easy answer to an enigma, I, too, am skeptical. Like the Missourian, I want the evidence in my hand to clinch the proof.

An ocean meteorite strike *could* be the explanation here. Two of them if you like. Asteroids sometimes "twin"; the Clearwater Lakes in Canada, one thirty and the other twenty kilometers across, resulted from a double strike. The question is not whether it *could* have been the cause but whether it *was*.

Answers to the following questions could resolve the matter:

1. What is the altitude above sea level and the proximity to the sea or otherwise of known finds of Mammoth carcasses? *Carcasses* if you please. Dry bones will be irrelevant. We know that the prototype carcass was found *at the mouth* of the River Lena in Siberia, on the shores of the Arctic Ocean.

2. *Precisely* what vegetation and what its habitat is found within the corpuses delicti? Exactly what kinds of trees were jumbled with them in the permafrost, and what type of force is required to shear or uproot such trees like jackstraws?

3. Deep borings have been made in the ice caps of the Antarctic and Greenland. Have any surprises yet been provided by the counts and analyses of particles in any limited section of the drilled cores? What should be sought here is this: concentrations of rock dust and of spherules of sublimed rock and iron. These may total a depth of only a hundredth of an inch, perhaps a little less, in a core representing a decade's accumulation of ice. The iron particles would, of course, be magnetically separable from the ice-melt. The contaminated lengths as a whole might be separable from the column of cores on a conveyor belt basis, by optical methods.

4. There are known to be circularities on otherwise level and featureless ocean floors. What are the profiles of these, and can their ages be assessed?

5. Are there any widespread anomalies in the stratigraphical record of large coastal belts which are inexplicable by normal erosive and isostatic process?

You may well add questions to the list above. Significant contributions will foster the baby science of meteoritics.

EARLY WARNING

Robin S. Scott

Lee Coulson was a big man, big in the chest and long legged, and it was difficult for him to squeeze his bulk into the narrow space under the green ducter. The ducter, with the telephone company symbol painted on its side, was a small one, the standard three quarter ton model so familiar to every citizen. It would attract absolutely no attention parked along the curb on "G" Street, SW. The fit was tight, but the parking casters were down, and once Coulson had worked his way in under the mouth of the forward duct, he had a bit more room to work. Flat on his belly like that, his cheek pressed against the damp macadam, he needed all his strength to pry up the cumbersome manhole cover over which the ducter was now parked. Coulson was a big man and none of his bigness was fat.

With the heavy cast-iron cover out of the way, Coulson dropped silently into the clammy space below. It was early evening, just dark enough to cover his movements under the ducter, and he relied somewhat on the heavy theater traffic on the street above to mask any slight noise he might make. But he didn't rely completely on it; Coulson was the sort of man who never relied very much on anything, or anyone, not under his absolute control.

By the light of a small flashlight he located the junction box mounted on the concrete wall of the wireway tunnel into which he had dropped. He broke the lead seals on the cover, removed the four screws holding it in place, and with a small induction meter began to check each pair of wires soldered into the terminal block inside. After a moment he found what he was looking for, and, working with sure swiftness, he attached jumpers to the appropriate lugs and brought an infinitely fine, nearly invisible shielded pair down through a spare knock-out in the bottom of the junction box. A few minutes with a screwdriver and the box cover was again in place, the seals forged of a dull gray thermoplastic which would withstand all but the closest inspection.

Down the wireway a few yards, Coulson found a transformer bank which furnished control voltages for the monorail running above the street under which he worked. He ran his hair-fine cable down the tunnel, stuffing it behind a convenient conduit as he went, until he reached the transformers. From one of the capacious pockets in his coveralls he drew a black metal box, twice the size of a package of cigarettes, and, after consulting the small brass plate on the nearest transformer, he inserted a fine screwdriver in the appropriate slot and set the voltage to match that of the transformer's output.

Working more rapidly now, he attached leads from the transformer secondary to the tiny pulse receiver, connected up the fine cable from the telephone terminal box, and stretched the receiver's short antenna out along the tunnel wall, carefully following a form mark in the concrete surface. With all in place, he pulled himself laboriously back up out of the tunnel, slid the ponderous manhole cover back into place, waited watchfully until the immediate area was clear of pedestrians, and slid grunting out from under the parked ducter. He drove off, then, and re-parked many miles away on a stretch of deserted country road paralleling the swampy banks of a broad stretch of the lower Potomac.

With the engine dead he waited for fifteen minutes, ears and eyes straining for any sign of activity near him. Satisfied that he was likely to remain unobserved, he pointed the ducter toward the opposite shore, a thousand yards off in the darkness, fastened a ninety-second timer to the power switch, restarted the engine, and watched the unoccupied machine, its ducted fans kicking up a faint wake in the dark river, head obediently toward the depths of mid stream. When he heard the diminishing sound of the engine cease, he listened for a moment for the faint hiss of air escaping from the sinking machine, and then set off wearily down the road to the nearest mono station.

Once again in the city center, Coulson left the mono at the cross-country flitter depot. Tool kit in hand, he entered, put a coin in a storage locker and removed a leather suitcase—not too new, not too old—went on to the men's room and dropped another coin in the lock on a booth, emerging a few moments later dressed in a conservative gray business suit, his dirty coveralls and specialized tools neatly packed in the suitcase. He waited a moment by the newsstand until a crowd of new arrivals from the Chicago flitter swept him along to the street and a rank of waiting taxicabs. After two changes of cabs sandwiching a walk of several blocks, he arrived back at the hotel room he had taken the night before. It was a little over two hundred yards from the manhole cover he had lifted four hours earlier.

The room smelled musty and unused, and after checking the traps he had set to detect intruders, Coulson threw the windows open, poured himself a stiff bourbon-and-water, and relaxed for five minutes with a cigarette. He showered then, dressed in clean clothing from the leather suitcase, and sat at the telephone for a few minutes, finishing his drink and marshaling his thoughts. At length, he dialed a number, listened to the ringer whirring away, and heard the click and change of tone when the receiver was lifted.

Knowing the man on the other end would say nothing, Coulson said: "This is Caesar. Sargasso is in place and ready to go. If I don't hear otherwise, I'll roll it tomorrow as agreed." There was no response, nothing but the soft susurrus of the man's breathing followed by an impersonal click as the connection was broken.

Coulson, too, hung up, left the hotel room, made his way through the lobby without attracting the desk clerk's attention, and took two taxicabs and the mono back to the White House parking lot on Fourteenth Street. He unlocked his battered '68 ducter, climbed in, and with a wave to the gate guard drove the tiresome thirty miles out to Manassas and his home. At 1:00 in the morning, traffic was light, and he made it in just under twenty minutes. Mary was still awake, and, as he eased his tired body under the cool sheets, she snuggled up to him and made sleepy sounds of sympathy for the fact that he had had to work so late at the office.

At 8:30 the next morning, Coulson was back at his desk

in the president's anteroom, going through the more important calls of the morning. There was one to the caterer, and Coulson was forced to spend much more time than he wished insisting that the '81 *Schloss Rheinberg* be served at the Friday night reception for the Eurofed Defense Minister. Then there was a call to the White House chef on the same matter, and a long-distance call to the Palmer House, where President and Mrs. Jacoby would be spending the weekend. At 9:15 he left his office, cautioning Miss Eckert to hold any calls for him, and after a six-block-walk down "E" Street, he took three taxis to within a block or so of the hotel room he had so briefly occupied the night before. By ten minutes before ten he had the teletape keyboard assembled and patched into the tiny transmitter in the bathroom. At ten sharp he fed the first of the tapes into the TD of the teletypewriter. Because they were in Russian, he could not read what they said. But he knew anyway. He'd helped compose the English originals.

By 10:08 the last of the tapes had been transmitted via the little impulse receiver in the manhole two hundred yards away, and Coulson busied himself at eradicating any trace of his occupancy in the room. He wiped door knobs and ashtrays free of fingerprints and dropped the single whiskey bottle and glass down the disposal chute. He packed his meager personal belongings and the teletypewriter keyboard and transmitter in a cheap suitcase, and then, suitcase in hand, he left the room for good and checked out at the desk below. By two taxis again, he traveled to Dulles International and checked his suitcase, and then by mono he returned to his office. It was nearly one o'clock, and he walked on to lunch in the cafeteria in the Briggs Building on E Street.

Two weeks later, Coulson found himself in London, in a temporary office in the American Embassy in Grosvenor Square. The London Conference between the Eurofeds and the Americas was due to start in a week, and Coulson had much to do to arrange the president's meals and accommodations in London. Friday was entirely taken up with conferences with the ambassador's staff and the embassy's Chief of Protocol. Saturday he spent talking with the staff of the embassy guest house in Knightsbridge, where the president and his party would be staying, and with the courteous gentlemen at Simpson's who would be catering the president's reception for Chancellor Elstrund at the Mayfair. Early Sunday morning, Coulson walked the damp pavements to Marble Arch and took the underground there to South Ruislip and the SAC missile base.

In the South Ruislip station, he spent a few minutes in the men's room making himself unrecognizable. He slipped a small block of wood into his left shoe, which produced a pronounced limp, pulled a black bowler low down over his forehead, reversed his jacket so that the checks showed, pushed sponge-rubber inserts into his cheeks to make his normally angular face rounder and more benign, and glued a fierce R.A.F. moustache on his upper lip. His passport, driver's license, and other personal papers he sealed into a plastic bag and dropped into the flush tank mounted high on the wall behind the toilets.

Thus disguised, and feeling a bit foolish for it, he walked the half-mile through the green April countryside to the main gate of the SAC base. There he presented his credentials— as a representative of the "British Friends of Foreign Orphans"—and was admitted to see the Duty Officer. He spoke in a high-pitched, nasal voice of his desire to enlist the support of American airmen stationed in England for his cause, and when the bored Duty Officer turned wearily for a form for his guest to fill out, Coulson triggered his gas pen and took a single quick step to catch the falling officer before he could hurt himself or crash noisily across his desk. Then a swift jerk at the red key dangling from the holder on the Duty Officer's belt and Coulson was off, walking with seemly haste back out through the main gate, the red key tucked into his vest pocket.

He was midway to the South Ruislip station before he heard alarm bells behind him, and he went to ground in a nearby wheat field until dusk had fallen and the hue and cry had clearly passed him by. Cold and weary, he abandoned the wooden block and the bowler, removed the moustache and the sponge rubber, and reversing his jacket so that it once again matched the conservative gray of his trousers, he slipped back to the tube station. There he flushed his forged credentials down the toilet, recovered his own papers, and sped back to London on the 7:15 to face a barrage of inquiries from the ambassador's staff on the president's taste for roast beef, wines, and kidney pie.

Two weeks later, back again in Washington after the London trip, Coulson was called into the president's study for one of his rare face-to-face meetings with Jacoby. As he entered the room the attorney general was just leaving.

"Sorry not to give you more time, Ed," said the president to his departing visitor, "but I have to get the arrangements for next month's Rio conference on the mono." Edward Allison nodded at Coulson as they passed. Coulson doubted that Allison was aware of his name, although he undoubtedly recognized him as one of those faceless myrmidons who handled the president's household affairs.

Jacoby waited until the door had closed behind the attorney general before he thumbed a row of buttons on his desk. Coulson knew that a vast array of human and technical agencies were now in force to protect the president's privacy. Nothing they said could be overheard.

"Good work, Lee," said the president.

"Thank you, Mr. President. How did it go?"

"Lovely. It was lovely, Lee. I wish you could have seen it. When the hot line started clacking away right in the middle of the National Security Council meeting, I thought old Allison would drop his teeth. That phony message in Russian really did the trick, and, when we got it translated and it turned out to be the old one about the traveling salesmen and the French waitress everybody knew it was a hoax, but they couldn't figure out how it had been done. I'll hand it to Allison, though. His boys found your G Street tap in less than four hours, and he's taking steps to make the whole hot line absolutely tamper-proof."

"How about the Command Circuit key? That business in London."

"Oh! That couldn't have been better. The Air Force went crazy. You should have seen the mealy-mouthed cables the Defense Secretary was getting! Still, they knew they'd goofed, and they've changed all the locks on the Command system and tightened up gate security the way it ought to have been in the first place."

"Work as well as that business with the 'For Sale' sign on the reactor down at Sandia?"

"Better. Even better."

The president got up from his desk and walked around to the window looking out on Fourteenth Street. "You know, Lee, our biggest problem is ambition: everybody all up and down the chain of command wants to get ahead, wants to show the next guy up the line just how sharp he is, what a fine state of readiness he and his unit are in. I can call for all kinds of surprise alerts, all kinds of tests and exercises, and somehow word always gets out in advance. This office is leaky as a sieve whenever more than two people are involved. As soon as I decide that SAC, or Orbit Command, or the subs ought to be given a surprise alert, someone talks too much, and all up and down the line they start humping, hoping they'll impress somebody enough to get a little gold star next to their names. Then, dammit, as soon as it's all over, they stick their feet up on their desks and go back to sleep. The only time they get a real surprise is when we—just you and I—pull something on them. And when we do, we always find something amiss, don't we? It's our only chance to keep them honest."

Coulson thought swiftly back over the previous three years, the fences he had climbed, the sewers he had navigated, the dirty little tricks he had pulled, each carefully calculated— often with broad and vulgar humor—to show up weaknesses without triggering a genuine alarm. "Yes, sir," he grinned at the president. "I guess we almost always catch them at something."

The president eyed his young assistant with some calculation. "I'm pretty generally satisfied, Lee. But the lead time between the decision to pull something on these birds and the actual test is too long. Every minute that an uncorrected situation lasts is so much more danger to the nation. I want you to sharpen up your support staff so you can get out and pull a job within hours after I get a report suggesting a soft spot."

Coulson remained silent. It looked like this was one of those days when the president was needling everybody. Sure, he might be able to work a little faster, cut the lead time somewhat, but didn't the president realize how much planning time it took? The work on false documents? The time in studying plant layouts . . . ?

The president, satisfied that he had achieved the effect

he desired, softened his tone. "So how are you feeling, Lee. Tired?"

"No, sir, ready to go again when you say."

"Well, I haven't made up my mind yet what we'll hit next. Maybe the Cape, or Vandenburg. Maybe the MOLE Command setup. I'll let you know."

Coulson knew perfectly well that the president knew exactly what his next assignment would be, but he would hold off as long as possible so he could see just how fast Coulson could work under pressure. "It would be helpful, sir, to have as much advance notice as possible. I know you want me to come up with test plans sooner, but the quality of the planning is pretty much a function of time."

"Yes, I know." The president grinned broadly at Coulson, dismissed him with a friendly wave, and returned to the mounds of papers on his desk.

Coulson rose and left the president's study, thinking of the payments on the house out in Manassas and his need to replace the '68 ducter parked in the lot outside. A promotion would come in very handy, and it looked like the best way to get one would be to impress the president with brilliant new speed in his work.

In the president's anteroom he paused a moment at Mrs. Levy's desk. She, the president's personal secretary for many years, was the only other individual who knew of Coulson's special work.

"Sarah," said Coulson, "what's the president got in mind for me next?"

Mrs. Levy looked down her long nose at Coulson, a disapproving expression on her thin old face. "If I knew, I wouldn't tell you. You know that, Lee."

"Aw, come on, Sarah. Be a sport. He's after me to speed up these tests. If I can have a few days lead time, I can really wow the old man."

"Well," sniffed Mrs. Levy, "I don't know for sure, of course, but I've heard him speak very unkindly lately of the management down at the Cape."

"Thanks a million, Sarah." Coulson swung off down the corridor whistling softly under his breath. With that much of a hint he felt sure he could study up enough on the layout, personnel, and security system at the Cape in the next few days to make a perfect attack when the order came.

Behind him, her voice far too low for him to hear, Mrs. Levy thumbed a button on her intercom. "It was just like you said, sir."

"What did you tell him?" The president's voice held laughter.

"Just what you told me to. About the Cape."

"Fine, Mrs. Levy. Fine. Now bring me the security file on the MOLE Command and cut orders for Coulson to go to San Diego."

CALL HIM LORD

Gordon R. Dickson

The sun could not fail in rising over the Kentucky hills, nor could Kyle Arnam in waking. There would be eleven hours and forty minutes of daylight. Kyle rose, dressed, and went out to saddle the gray gelding and the white stallion. He rode the stallion until the first fury was out of the arched and snowy neck; and then led both horses around to tether them outside the kitchen door. Then he went in to breakfast.

The message that had come a week before was beside his plate of bacon and eggs. Teena, his wife, was standing at the breadboard with her back to him. He sat down and began eating, rereading the letter as he ate.

". . . The Prince will be traveling incognito under one of his family titles, as Count Sirii North; and should not be addressed as 'Majesty'. *You will call him 'Lord'* . . ."

"Why does it have to be you?" Teena asked.

He looked up and saw how she stood with her back to him.

"Teena—" he said, sadly.

"Why?"

"My ancestors were bodyguards to his—back in the wars of conquest against the aliens. I've told you that," he said. "My forefathers saved the lives of his, many times when there was no warning—a Rak spaceship would suddenly appear out of nowhere to lock on, even to a flagship. And even an Emperor found himself fighting for his life, hand to hand."

"The aliens are all dead now, and the Emperor's got a hundred other worlds! Why can't his son take his Grand Tour on them? Why does he have to come here to Earth—and you?"

"There's only one Earth."

"And only one you, I suppose?"

85

He sighed internally and gave up. He had been raised by his father and his uncle after his mother died, and in an argument with Teena he always felt helpless. He got up from the table and went to her, putting his hands on her and gently trying to turn her about. But she resisted.

He sighed inside himself again and turned away to the weapons cabinet. He took out a loaded slug pistol, fitted it into the stubby holster it matched, and clipped the holster to his belt at the left of the buckle, where the hang of his leather jacket would hide it. Then he selected a dark-handled knife with a six-inch blade and bent over to slip it into the sheath inside his boot top. He dropped the cuff of his trouser leg back over the boot top and stood up.

"He's got no right to be here," said Teena fiercely to the breadboard. "Tourists are supposed to be kept to the museum areas and the tourist lodges."

"He's not a tourist. You know that," answered Kyle, patiently. "He's the Emperor's oldest son and his great-grandmother was from Earth. His wife will be, too. Every fourth generation the Imperial line has to marry back into Earth stock. That's the law—still." He put on his leather jacket, sealing it closed only at the bottom to hide the slug-gun holster, half turned to the door—then paused.

"Teena?" he asked.

She did not answer.

"Teena!" he repeated. He stepped to her, put his hands on her shoulders and tried to turn her face to him. Again, she resisted, but this time he was having none of it.

He was not a big man, being of middle height, round-faced, with sloping and unremarkable-looking, if thick, shoulders. But his strength was not ordinary. He could bring the white stallion to its knees with one fist wound in its mane—and no other man had ever been able to do that. He turned her easily to look at him.

"Now, listen to me—" he began. But, before he could finish, all the stiffness went out of her and she clung to him, trembling.

"He'll get you into trouble—I know he will!" she choked, muffledly into his chest. "Kyle, don't go! There's no law making you go!"

He stroked the soft hair of her head, his throat stiff and dry. There was nothing he could say to her. What she was asking was impossible. Ever since the sun had first risen on men and women together, wives had clung to their husbands at times like this, begging for what could not be. And always the men had held them, as Kyle was holding her now—as if understanding could somehow be pressed from one body into the other—and saying nothing, because there was nothing that could be said.

So, Kyle held her for a few moments longer, and then reached behind him to unlock her interwined fingers at his back, and loosen her arms around him. Then, he went. Looking back through the kitchen window as he rode off on the stallion, leading the gray horse, he saw her standing just where he had left her. Not even crying, but standing with her arms hanging down, her head down, not moving.

He rode away through the forest of the Kentucky hillside. It took him more than two hours to reach the lodge. As he rode down the valleyside toward it, he saw a tall, bearded man, wearing the robes they wore on some of the Younger Worlds, standing at the gateway to the interior courtyard of the rustic, wooded lodge.

When he got close, he saw that the beard was graying and the man was biting his lips. Above a straight, thin nose, the eyes were bloodshot and circled beneath as if from worry or lack of sleep.

"He's in the courtyard," said the gray-bearded man as Kyle rode up. "I'm Montlaven, his tutor. He's ready to go." The darkened eyes looked almost pleadingly up at Kyle.

"Stand clear of the stallion's head," said Kyle. "And take me in to him."

"Not that horse, for him—" said Montlaven, looking distrustfully at the stallion, as he backed away.

"No," said Kyle. "He'll ride the gelding."

"He'll want the white."

"He can't ride the white," said Kyle. "Even if I let him, he couldn't ride this stallion. I'm the only one who can ride him. Take me in."

The tutor turned and led the way into the grassy courtyard, surrounding a swimming pool and looked down upon, on three sides, by the windows of the lodge. In a lounging chair by the pool sat a tall young man in his late teens, with a mane of blond hair, a pair of stuffed saddlebags on the grass beside him. He stood up as Kyle and the tutor came toward him.

"Majesty," said the tutor, as they stopped, "this is Kyle Arnam, your bodyguard for the three days here."

"Good morning, Bodyguard . . . Kyle, I mean." The Prince smiled mischievously. "Light, then. And I'll mount."

"You ride the gelding, Lord," said Kyle.

The Prince stared at him, tilted back his handsome head, and laughed.

"I can ride, man!" he said. "I ride well."

"Not this horse, Lord," said Kyle, dispassionately. "No one rides this horse, but me."

The eyes flashed wide, the laugh faded—then returned.

"What can I do?" The wide shoulders shrugged. "I give in—always I give in. Well, almost always." He grinned up at Kyle, his lips thinned, but frank. "All right."

He turned to the gelding—and with a sudden leap was in the saddle. The gelding snorted and plunged at the shock; then steadied as the young man's long fingers tightened expertly on the reins and the fingers of the other hand patted a gray neck. The Prince raised his eyebrows, looking over at Kyle, but Kyle sat stolidly.

"I take it you're armed, good Kyle?" the Prince said slyly. "You'll protect me against the natives if they run wild?"

"Your life is in my hands, Lord," said Kyle. He unsealed the leather jacket at the bottom and let it fall open to show the slug pistol in its holster for a moment. Then he resealed the jacket again at the bottom.

"Will—" The tutor put his hand on the young man's knee. "Don't be reckless, boy. This is Earth and the people here don't have rank and custom like we do. Think before you—"

"Oh, cut it out, Monty!" snapped the Prince. "I'll be just as incognito, just as humble, as archaic and independent as the rest of them. You think I've no memory! Anyway, it's only for three days or so until my Imperial father joins me. Now, let me go!"

He jerked away, turned to lean forward in the saddle, and abruptly put the gelding into a bolt for the gate. He disappeared through it, and Kyle drew hard on the stallion's reins as the big white horse danced and tried to follow.

"Give me his saddlebags," said Kyle.

The tutor bent and passed them up. Kyle made them fast

on top of his own, across the stallion's withers. Looking down, he saw there were tears in the bearded man's eyes.

"He's a fine boy. You'll see. You'll know he is!" Montlaven's face, upturned, was mutely pleading.

"I know he comes from a fine family," said Kyle, slowly. "I'll do my best for him." And he rode off out of the gateway after the gelding.

When he came out of the gate, the Prince was nowhere in sight. But it was simple enough for Kyle to follow, by dinted brown earth and crushed grass, the marks of the gelding's path. This brought him at last through some pines to a grassy open slope where the Prince sat looking skyward through a single-lens box.

When Kyle came up, the Prince lowered the instrument and, without a word, passed it over. Kyle put it to his eye and looked skyward. There was the whir of the tracking unit and one of Earth's three orbiting power stations swam into the field of vision of the lens.

"Give it back," said the Prince.

"I couldn't get a look at it earlier," went on the young man as Kyle handed the lens to him. "And I wanted to. It's a rather expensive present, you know—it and the other two like it—from our Imperial treasury. Just to keep your planet from drifting into another ice age. And what do we get for it?"

"Earth, Lord," answered Kyle. "As it was before men went out to the stars."

"Oh, the museum areas could be maintained with one station and a half-million caretakers," said the Prince. "It's the other two stations and you billion or so free-loaders I'm talking about. I'll have to look into it when I'm Emperor. Shall we ride?"

"If you wish, Lord." Kyle picked up the reins of the stallion and the two horses with their riders moved off across the slope.

". . . And one more thing," said the Prince, as they entered the farther belt of pine trees. "I don't want you to be misled—I'm really very fond of old Monty, back there. It's just that I wasn't really planning to come here at all—*Look at me, Bodyguard!*"

Kyle turned to see the blue eyes that ran in the Imperial

family blazing at him. Then, unexpectedly, they softened. The Prince laughed.

"You don't scare easily, do you, Bodyguard . . . Kyle, I mean?" he said. "I think I like you after all. But look at me when I talk."

"Yes, Lord."

"That's my good Kyle. Now, I was explaining to you that I'd never actually planned to come here on my Grand Tour at all. I didn't see any point in visiting this dusty old museum world of yours with people still trying to live like they lived in the Dark Ages. But—my Imperial father talked me into it."

"Your father, Lord?" asked Kyle.

"Yes, he bribed me, you might say," said the Prince thoughtfully. "He was supposed to meet me here for these three days. Now, he's messaged there's been a slight delay— but that doesn't matter. The point is, he belongs to the school of old men who still think your Earth is something precious and vital. Now, I happen to like and admire my father, Kyle. You approve of that?"

"Yes, Lord."

"I thought you would. Yes, he's the one man in the human race I look up to. And to please him, I'm making this Earth trip. And to please him—only to please *him,* Kyle—I'm going to be an easy Prince for you to conduct around to your natural wonders and watering spots and whatever. Now, you understand me—and how this trip is going to go. Don't you?" He stared at Kyle.

"I understand," said Kyle.

"That's fine," said the Prince, smiling once more. "So now you can start telling me all about these trees and birds and animals so that I can memorize their names and please my father when he shows up. What are those little birds I've been seeing under the trees—brown on top and whitish underneath? Like that one—there!"

"That's a Veery, Lord," said Kyle. "A bird of the deep woods and silent places. Listen—" He reached out a hand to the gelding's bridle and brought both horses to a halt. In the sudden silence, off to their right they could hear a silver bird-voice, rising and falling, in a descending series of crescendos and diminuendos, that softened at last into silence. For a moment after the song was ended the Prince sat staring at Kyle, then seemed to shake himself back to life.

"Interesting," he said. He lifted the reins Kyle had let go and the horses moved forward again. "Tell me more."

For more than three hours, as the sun rose toward noon, they rode through the wooded hills, with Kyle identifying bird and animal, insect, tree and rock. And for three hours the Prince listened—his attention flashing and momentary, but intense. But when the sun was overhead that intensity flagged.

"That's enough," he said. "Aren't we going to stop for lunch? Kyle, aren't there any towns around here?"

"Yes, Lord," said Kyle. "We've passed several."

"Several?" The Prince stared at him. "Why haven't we come into one before now? Where are you taking me?"

"Nowhere, Lord," said Kyle. "You lead the way. I only follow."

"I?" said the Prince. For the first time he seemed to become aware that he had been keeping the gelding's head always in advance of the stallion. "Of course. But now it's time to eat."

"Yes, Lord," said Kyle. "This way."

He turned the stallion's head down the slope of the hill they were crossing and the Prince turned the gelding after him.

"And now listen," said the Prince, as he caught up. "Tell me I've got it all right." And to Kyle's astonishment he began to repeat, almost word for word, everything that Kyle had said. "Is it all there? Everything you told me?"

"Perfectly, Lord," said Kyle. The Prince looked slyly at him.

"Could you do that, Kyle?"

"Yes," said Kyle. "But these are things I've known all my life."

"You see?" The Prince smiled. "That's the difference between us, good Kyle. You spend your life learning something —I spend a few hours and I know as much about it as you do."

"Not as much, Lord," said Kyle slowly.

The Prince blinked at him, then jerked his hand dismissingly, and half-angrily, as if he were throwing something aside.

"What little else there is probably doesn't count," he said. They rode down the slope and through a winding valley and came out at a small village. As they rode clear of the surrounding trees a sound of music came to their ears.

"What's that?" The Prince stood up in his stirrups. "Why, there's dancing going on, over there."

"A beer garden, Lord. And it's Saturday—a holiday here."

"Good. We'll go there to eat."

They rode around to the beer garden and found tables back away from the dance floor. A pretty, young waitress came and they ordered, the Prince smiling sunnily at her until she smiled back—then hurried off as if in mild confusion. The Prince ate hungrily when the food came and drank a stein and a half of brown beer, while Kyle ate more lightly and drank coffee.

"That's better," said the Prince, sitting back at last. "I had an appetite . . . Look there, Kyle! Look, there are five, six . . . seven drifter platforms parked over there. Then you don't all ride horses?"

"No," said Kyle. "It's as each man wishes."

"But if you have drifter platforms, why not other civilized things?"

"Some things fit, some don't, Lord," answered Kyle. The Prince laughed.

"You mean you try to make civilization fit this old-fashioned life of yours, here?" he said. "Isn't that the wrong way around—" He broke off. "What's that they're playing now? I like that. I'll bet I could do that dance." He stood up. "In fact, I think I will."

He paused, looking down at Kyle.

"Aren't you going to warn me against it?" he asked.

"No, Lord," said Kyle. "What you do is your own affair."

The young man turned away abruptly. The waitress who had served them was passing, only a few tables away. The Prince went after her and caught up with her by the dance floor railing. Kyle could see the girl protesting—but the Prince hung over her, looking down from his tall height, smiling. Shortly, she had taken off her apron and was out on the dance floor with him, showing him the steps of the dance. It was a polka.

The Prince learned with fantastic quickness. Soon, he was swinging the waitress around with the rest of the dancers, his foot stamping on the turns, his white teeth gleaming. Finally the number ended and the members of the band put down their instruments and began to leave the stand.

The Prince, with the girl trying to hold him back, walked over to the band leader. Kyle got up quickly from his table and started toward the floor.

The band leader was shaking his head. He turned abruptly and slowly walked away. The Prince started after him, but the girl took hold of his arm, saying something urgent to him.

He brushed her aside and she stumbled a little. A busboy among the tables on the far side of the dance floor, not much older than the Prince and nearly as tall, put down his tray and vaulted the railing onto the polished hardwood. He came up behind the Prince and took hold of his arm, swinging him around.

". . . Can't do that here," Kyle heard him say, as Kyle came up. The Prince struck out like a panther—like a trained boxer—with three quick lefts in succession into the face of the busboy, the Prince's shoulder bobbing, the weight of his body in behind each blow.

The busboy went down. Kyle, reaching the Prince, herded him away through a side gap in the railing. The young man's face was white with rage. People were swarming onto the dance floor.

"Who was that? What's his name?" demanded the Prince, between his teeth. "He put his hand on me! Did you see that? *He put his hand on me!*"

"You knocked him out," said Kyle. "What more do you want?"

"He manhandled me—*me!*" snapped the Prince. "I want to find out who he is!" He caught hold of the bar to which the horses were tied, refusing to be pushed farther. "He'll learn to lay hands on a future Emperor!"

"No one will tell you his name," said Kyle. And the cold note in his voice finally seemed to reach through to the Prince and sober him. He stared at Kyle.

"Including you?" he demanded at last.

"Including me, Lord," said Kyle.

The Prince stared a moment longer, then swung away. He turned, jerked the loose reins of the gelding and swung into the saddle. He rode off. Kyle mounted and followed.

They rode in silence into the forest. After a while, the Prince spoke without turning his head.

"And you call yourself a bodyguard," he said, finally.

"Your life is in my hands, Lord," said Kyle. The Prince turned a grim face to look at him.

"Only my life?" said the Prince. "As long as they don't kill me, they can do what they want? Is that what you mean?"

Kyle met his gaze steadily.

"Pretty much so, Lord," he said.

The Prince spoke with an ugly note in his voice.

"I don't think I like you, after all, Kyle," he said. "I don't think I like you at all."

"I'm not here with you to be liked, Lord," said Kyle.

"Perhaps not," said the Prince, thickly. "But I know *your* name!"

They rode on in continued silence for perhaps another half hour. But then gradually the angry hunch went out of the young man's shoulders and the tightness out of his jaw. After a while he began to sing to himself, a song in a language Kyle did not know; and as he sang, his cheerfulness seemed to return. Shortly, he spoke to Kyle, as if there had never been anything but pleasant moments between them.

Mammoth Cave was close and the Prince asked to visit it. They went there and spent some time going through the cave. After that they rode their horses up along the left bank of the Green River. The Prince seemed to have forgotten all about the incident at the beer garden and be out to charm everyone they met. As the sun was at last westering toward the dinner hour, they came finally to a small hamlet back from the river, with a roadside inn mirrored in an artificial lake beside it, and guarded by oak and pine trees behind.

"This looks good," said the Prince. "We'll stay overnight here, Kyle."

"If you wish, Lord," said Kyle.

They halted, and Kyle took the horses around to the stable, then entered the inn to find the Prince already in the small bar off the dining room, drinking beer and charming the waitress. This waitress was younger than the one at the beer garden had been; a little girl with soft, loose hair and round brown eyes that showed their delight in the attention of the tall, good-looking young man.

"Yes," said the Prince to Kyle, looking out of the corners of the Imperial blue eyes at him, after the waitress had gone to get Kyle his coffee, "this is the very place."

"The very place?" said Kyle.

"For me to get to know the people better—what did you think, good Kyle?" said the Prince and laughed at him. "I'll observe the people here and you can explain them—won't that be good?"

Kyle gazed at him, thoughtfully.

"I'll tell you whatever I can, Lord," he said.

They drank—the Prince his beer, and Kyle his coffee—and went in a little later to the dining room for dinner. The Prince, as he had promised at the bar, was full of questions about what he saw—and what he did not see.

". . . But why go on living in the past, all of you here?" he asked Kyle. "A museum world is one thing. But a museum people—" he broke off to smile and speak to the little, soft-haired waitress, who had somehow been diverted from the bar to wait upon their dining-room table.

"Not a museum people, Lord," said Kyle. "A living people. The only way to keep a race and a culture preserved is to keep it alive. So we go on in our own way, here on Earth, as a living example for the Younger Worlds to check themselves against."

"Fascinating . . ." murmured the Prince; but his eyes had wandered off to follow the waitress, who was glowing and looking back at him from across the now-busy dining room.

"Not fascinating. Necessary, Lord," said Kyle. But he did not believe the younger man had heard him.

After dinner, they moved back to the bar. And the Prince, after questioning Kyle a little longer, moved up to continue his researches among the other people standing at the bar. Kyle watched for a little while. Then feeling it was safe to do so, slipped out to have another look at the horses and to ask the innkeeper to arrange a saddle lunch put up for them the next day.

When he returned, the Prince was not to be seen.

Kyle sat down at a table to wait; but the Prince did not return. A cold, hard knot of uneasiness began to grow below Kyle's breastbone. A sudden pang of alarm sent him swiftly back out to check the horses. But they were cropping peacefully in their stalls. The stallion whickered, low-voiced, as

Kyle looked in on him, and turned his white head to look back at Kyle.

"Easy, boy," said Kyle and returned to the inn to find the innkeeper.

But the innkeeper had no idea where the Prince might have gone.

". . . If the horses aren't taken, he's not far," the innkeeper said. "There's no trouble he can get into around here. Maybe he went for a walk in the woods. I'll leave word for the night staff to keep an eye out for him when he comes in. Where'll you be?"

"In the bar until it closes—then, my room," said Kyle.

He went back to the bar to wait, and took a booth near an open window. Time went by and gradually the number of other customers began to dwindle. Above the ranked bottles, the bar clock showed nearly midnight. Suddenly, through the window, Kyle heard a distant scream of equine fury from the stables.

He got up and went out quickly. In the darkness outside, he ran to the stables and burst in. There in the feeble illumination of the stable's night lighting, he saw the Prince, pale-faced, clumsily saddling the gelding in the center aisle between the stalls. The door to the stallion's stall was open. The Prince looked away as Kyle came in.

Kyle took three swift steps to the open door and looked in. The stallion was still tied, but his ears were back, his eyes rolling, and a saddle lay tumbled and dropped on the stable floor beside him.

"Saddle up," said the Prince thickly from the aisle. "We're leaving." Kyle turned to look at him.

"We've got rooms at the inn here," he said.

"Never mind. We're riding. I need to clear my head." The young man got the gelding's cinch tight, dropped the stirrups and swung heavily up into the saddle. Without waiting for Kyle, he rode out of the stable into the night.

"So, boy . . ." said Kyle soothingly to the stallion. Hastily he untied the big white horse, saddled him, and set out after the Prince. In the darkness, there was no way of ground-tracking the gelding; but he leaned forward and blew into the ear of the stallion. The surprised horse neighed in protest and the whinny of the gelding came back from the darkness of the slope up ahead over to Kyle's right. He rode in that direction.

He caught the Prince on the crown of the hill. The young man was walking the gelding, reins loose, and singing under his breath—the same song in an unknown language he had sung earlier. But, now as he saw Kyle, he grinned loosely and began to sing with more emphasis. For the first time Kyle caught the overtones of something mocking and lusty about the incomprehensible words. Understanding broke suddenly in him.

"The girl!" he said. "The little waitress. Where is she?"

The grin vanished from the Prince's face, then came slowly back again. The grin laughed at Kyle.

"Why, where d'you think?" The words slurred on the Prince's tongue and Kyle, riding close, smelled the beer heavy on the young man's breath. "In her room, sleeping and happy. Honored ... though she doesn't know it ... by an Emperor's son. And expecting to find me there in the morning. But I won't be. Will we, good Kyle?"

"Why did you do it, Lord?" asked Kyle, quietly.

"Why?" The Prince peered at him, a little drunkenly in the moonlight. "Kyle, my father has four sons. I've got three younger brothers. But I'm the one who's going to be Emperor; and Emperors don't answer questions."

Kyle said nothing. The Prince peered at him. They rode on together for several minutes in silence.

"All right, I'll tell you why," said the Prince, more loudly, after a while as if the pause had been only momentary. "It's because you're not *my* bodyguard, Kyle. You see, I've seen through you. I know whose bodyguard you are. You're *theirs!*"

Kyle's jaw tightened. But the darkness hid his reaction.

"All right—" The Prince gestured loosely, disturbing his balance in the saddle. "That's all right. Have it your way. I don't mind. So, we'll play points. There was that lout at the beer garden who put his hands on me. But no one would tell me his name, you said. All right, you managed to bodyguard him. One point for you. But you didn't manage to bodyguard the girl at the inn back there. One point for me. Who's going to win, good Kyle?"

Kyle took a deep breath.

"Lord," he said, "some day it'll be your duty to marry a woman from Earth—"

The Prince interrupted him with a laugh, and this time there was an ugly note in it.

"You flatter yourselves," he said. His voice thickened. "That's the trouble with you—all you Earth people—you flatter yourselves."

They rode on in silence. Kyle said nothing more, but kept the head of the stallion close to the shoulder of the gelding, watching the young man closely. For a little while the Prince seemed to doze. His head sank on his chest and he let the gelding wander. Then, after a while, his head began to come up again, his automatic horseman's fingers tightened on the reins, and he lifted his head to stare around in the moonlight.

"I want a drink," he said. His voice was no longer thick, but it was flat and uncheerful. "Take me where we can get some beer, Kyle."

Kyle took a deep breath.

"Yes, Lord," he said.

He turned the stallion's head to the right and the gelding followed. They went up over a hill and down to the edge of a lake. The dark water sparkled in the moonlight and the farther shore was lost in the night. Lights shone through the trees around the curve of the shore.

"There, Lord," said Kyle. "It's a fishing resort, with a bar."

They rode around the shore to it. It was a low, casual building, angled to face the shore; a dock ran out from it, to which fishing boats were tethered, bobbing slightly on the black water. Light gleamed through the windows as they hitched their horses and went to the door.

The barroom they stepped into was wide and bare. A long bar faced them with several planked fish on the wall behind it. Below the fish were three bartenders—the one in the center, middle-aged, and wearing an air of authority with his apron. The other two were young and muscular. The customers, mostly men, scattered at the square tables and standing at the bar wore rough working clothes, or equally casual vacationers' garb.

The Prince sat down at the table back from the bar and Kyle sat down with him. When the waitress came they ordered beer and coffee, and the Prince half-emptied his stein the moment it was brought to him. As soon as it was completely empty, he signaled the waitress again.

"Another," he said. This time, he smiled at the waitress when she brought his stein back. But she was a woman in her thirties, pleased but not overwhelmed by his attention. She smiled lightly back and moved off to return to the bar where she had been talking to two men her own age, one fairly tall, the other shorter, bullet-headed and fleshy.

The Prince drank. As he put his stein down, he seemed to become aware of Kyle, and turned to look at him.

"I suppose," said the Prince, "you think I'm drunk?"

"Not yet," said Kyle.

"No," said the Prince, "that's right. Not yet. But perhaps I'm going to be. And if I decide I am, who's going to stop me?"

"No one, Lord."

"That's right," the young man said, "that's right." He drank deliberately from his stein until it was empty, and then signaled the waitress for another. A spot of color was beginning to show over each of his high cheekbones. "When you're on a miserable little world with miserable little people . . . hello, Bright Eyes!" he interrupted himself as the waitress brought his beer. She laughed and went back to her friends. ". . . You have to amuse yourself any way you can," he wound up.

He laughed to himself.

"When I think how my father, and Monty—everybody— used to talk this planet up to me—" he glanced aside at Kyle. "Do you know at one time I was actually scared—well, not scared exactly, nothing scares me . . . say *concerned*—about maybe having to come here, some day?" He laughed again. "Concerned that I wouldn't measure up to you Earth people! Kyle, have you ever been to any of the Younger Worlds?"

"No," said Kyle.

"I thought not. Let me tell you, good Kyle, the worst of the people there are bigger, and better-looking and smarter, and everything than anyone I've seen here. And I, Kyle, I—the Emperor-to-be—am better than any of them. So, guess how all you here look to me?" He stared at Kyle, waiting. "Well, answer me, good Kyle. Tell me the truth. That's an order."

"It's not up to you to judge, Lord," said Kyle.

"Not—? Not up to me?" The blue eyes blazed. *"I'm* going to be Emperor!"

"It's not up to any one man, Lord," said Kyle. "Emperor or not. An Emperor's needed, as the symbol that can hold a hundred worlds together. But the real need of the race is to survive. It took nearly a million years to evolve a survival-type intelligence here on Earth. And out on the newer worlds people are bound to change. If something gets lost out there, some necessary element lost out of the race, there needs to be a pool of original genetic material here to replace it."

The Prince's lips grew wide in a savage grin.

"Oh, good, Kyle—good!" he said. "Very good. Only, I've heard all that before. Only, I don't believe it. You see—I've seen you people, now. And you don't outclass us, out on the Younger Worlds. *We* outclass *you*. We've gone on and got better, while you stayed still. And you know it."

The young man laughed softly, almost in Kyle's face.

"All you've been afraid of, is that we'd find out. And I have." He laughed again. "I've had a look at you; and now I know. I'm bigger, better and braver than any man in this room—and you know why? Not just because I'm the son of the Emperor, but because it's born in me! Body, brains and everything else! I can do what I want here, and no one on this planet is good enough to stop me. Watch."

He stood up, suddenly.

"Now, I want that waitress to get drunk with me," he said. "And this time I'm telling you in advance. Are you going to try and stop me?"

Kyle looked up at him. Their eyes met.

"No, Lord," he said. "It's not my job to stop you."

The Prince laughed.

"I thought so," he said. He swung away and walked between the tables toward the bar and the waitress, still in conversation with the two men. The Prince came up to the bar on the far side of the waitress and ordered a new stein of beer from the middle-aged bartender. When it was given to him, he took it, turned around, and rested his elbows on the bar, leaning back against it. He spoke to the waitress, interrupting the taller of the two men.

"I've been wanting to talk to you," Kyle heard him say. The waitress, a little surprised, looked around at him. She smiled, recognizing him—a little flattered by the directness of his approach, a little appreciative of his clean good looks, a little tolerant of his youth.

"*You* don't mind, do you?" said the Prince, looking past her to the bigger of the two men, the one who had just been talking. The other stared back, and their eyes met without shifting for several seconds. Abruptly, angrily, the man shrugged, and turned about with his back hunched against them.

"You see?" said the Prince, smiling back at the waitress. "He knows I'm the one you ought to be talking to, instead of—"

"All right, sonny. Just a minute."

It was the shorter, bullet-headed man, interrupting. The Prince turned to look down at him with a fleeting expression of surprise. But the bullet-headed man was already turning to his taller friend and putting a hand on his arm.

"Come on back, Ben," the shorter man was saying. "The kid's a little drunk, is all." He turned back to the Prince. "You shove off now," he said. "Clara's with us."

The Prince stared at him blankly. The stare was so fixed that the shorter man had started to turn away, back to his friend and the waitress, when the Prince seemed to wake.

"Just a minute—" he said, in his turn.

He reached out a hand to one of the fleshy shoulders below the bullet head. The man turned back, knocking the hand calmly away. Then, just as calmly, he picked up the Prince's full stein of beer from the bar and threw it in the young man's face.

"Get lost," he said, unexcitedly.

The Prince stood for a second, with the beer dripping from his face. Then, without even stopping to wipe his eyes clear, he threw the beautifully trained left hand he had demonstrated at the beer garden.

But the shorter man, as Kyle had known from the first moment of seeing him, was not like the busboy the Prince had decisioned so neatly. This man was thirty pounds heavier, fifteen years more experienced, and by build and nature a natural bar fighter. He had not stood there waiting to be hit, but had already ducked and gone forward to throw his thick arms around the Prince's body. The young man's punch bounced harmlessly off the round head, and both bodies hit the floor, rolling in among the chair and table legs.

Kyle was already more than halfway to the bar and the three bartenders were already leaping the wooden hurdle that walled them off. The taller friend of the bullet-headed man, hovering over the two bodies, his eyes glittering, had his boot drawn back ready to drive the point of it into the Prince's kidneys. Kyle's forearm took him economically like a bar of iron across the tanned throat.

He stumbled backwards choking. Kyle stood still, hands open and down, glancing at the middle-aged bartender.

"All right," said the bartender. "But don't do anything more." He turned to the two younger bartenders. "All right. Haul him off!"

The pair of younger, aproned men bent down and came up with the bullet-headed man expertly handlocked between them. The man made one surging effort to break loose, and then stood still.

"Let me at him," he said.

"Not in here," said the older bartender. "Take it outside."

Between the tables, the Prince staggered unsteadily to his feet. His face was streaming blood from a cut on his forehead, but what could be seen of it was white as a drowning man's. His eyes went to Kyle, standing beside him; and he opened his mouth—but what came out sounded like something between a sob and a curse.

"All right," said the middle-aged bartender again. "Outside, both of you. Settle it out there."

The men in the room had packed around the little space by the bar. The Prince looked about and for the first time seemed to see the human wall hemming him in. His gaze wobbled to meet Kyle's.

"Outside . . . ?" he said, chokingly.

"You aren't staying in here," said the older bartender, answering for Kyle. "I saw it. You started the whole thing. Now, settle it any way you want—but you're both going outside. Now! Get moving!"

He pushed at the Prince, but the Prince resisted, clutching at Kyle's leather jacket with one hand.

"Kyle—"

"I'm sorry, Lord," said Kyle. "I can't help. It's your fight."

"Let's get out of here," said the bullet-headed man.

The Prince stared around at them as if they were some strange set of beings he had never known to exist before.

"No . . ." he said.

He let go of Kyle's jacket. Unexpectedly, his hand darted in towards Kyle's belly holster and came out holding the slug pistol.

"Stand back!" he said, his voice high-toned. "Don't try to touch me!"

His voice broke on the last words. There was a strange sound, half grunt, half moan, from the crowd; and it swayed back from him. Manager, bartenders, watchers—all but Kyle and the bullet-headed man drew back.

"You dirty slob . . ." said the bullet-headed man, distinctly. "I knew you didn't have the guts."

"Shut up!" The Prince's voice was high and cracking. "Shut up! Don't any of you try to come after me!"

He began backing away toward the front door of the bar. The room watched in silence, even Kyle standing still. As he backed, the Prince's back straightened. He hefted the gun in his hand. When he reached the door he paused to wipe the blood from his eyes with his left sleeve, and his smeared face looked with a first touch of regained arrogance at them.

"Swine!" he said.

He opened the door and backed out, closing it behind him. Kyle took one step that put him facing the bullet-headed man. Their eyes met and he could see the other recognizing the fighter in him, as he had earlier recognized it in the bullet-headed man.

"Don't come after us," said Kyle.

The bullet-headed man did not answer. But no answer was needed. He stood still.

Kyle turned, ran to the door, stood on one side of it and flicked it open. Nothing happened; and he slipped through, dodging to his right at once, out of the line of any shot aimed at the opening door.

But no shot came. For a moment he was blind in the night darkness, then his eyes began to adjust. He went by sight, feel and memory toward the hitching rack. By the time he got there, he was beginning to see.

The Prince was untying the gelding and getting ready to mount.

"Lord," said Kyle.

The Prince let go of the saddle for a moment and turned to look over his shoulder at him.

"Get away from me," said the Prince, thickly.

"Lord," said Kyle, low-voiced and pleading, "you lost your head in there. Anyone might do that. But don't make it worse, now. Give me back the gun, Lord."

"Give you the gun?"

The young man stared at him—and then he laughed.

"Give *you* the gun?" he said again. "So you can let someone beat me up some more? So you can not-guard me with it?"

"Lord," said Kyle, "please. For your own sake—give me back the gun."

"Get out of here," said the Prince, thickly, turning back to mount the gelding. "Clear out before I put a slug in you."

Kyle drew a slow, sad breath. He stepped forward and tapped the Prince on the shoulder.

"Turn around, Lord," he said.

"I warned you—" shouted the Prince, turning.

He came around as Kyle stooped, and the slug pistol flashed in his hand from the light of the bar windows. Kyle, bent over, was lifting the cuff of his trouser leg and closing his fingers on the hilt of the knife in his boot sheath. He moved simply, skillfully, and with a speed nearly double that of the young man, striking up into the chest before him until the hand holding the knife jarred against the cloth covering flesh and bone.

It was a sudden, hard-driven, swiftly merciful blow. The blade struck upwards between the ribs lying open to an underhanded thrust, plunging deep into the heart. The Prince grunted with the impact driving the air from his lungs; and he was dead as Kyle caught his slumping body in leather-jacketed arms.

Kyle lifted the tall body across the saddle of the gelding and tied it there. He hunted on the dark ground for the fallen pistol and returned it to his holster. Then, he mounted the stallion and, leading the gelding with its burden, started the long ride back.

Dawn was graying the sky when at last he topped the hill overlooking the lodge where he had picked up the Prince almost twenty-four hours before. He rode down towards the courtyard gate.

A tall figure, indistinct in the predawn light, was waiting inside the courtyard as Kyle came through the gate; and it came running to meet him as he rode toward it. It was the tutor, Montlaven, and he was weeping as he ran to the gelding and began to fumble at the cords that tied the body in place.

"I'm sorry . . ." Kyle heard himself saying; and was dully shocked by the deadness and remoteness of his voice. "There was no choice. You can read it all in my report tomorrow morning—"

He broke off. Another, even taller figure had appeared in the doorway of the lodge giving on the courtyard. As Kyle turned towards it, this second figure descended the few steps to the grass and came to him.

"Lord—" said Kyle. He looked down into features like those of the Prince, but older, under graying hair. This man did not weep like the tutor, but his face was set like iron.

"What happened, Kyle?" he said.

"Lord," said Kyle, "you'll have my report in the morning . . ."

"I want to know," said the tall man. Kyle's throat was dry and stiff. He swallowed but swallowing did not ease it.

"Lord," he said, "you have three other sons. One of them will make an Emperor to hold the worlds together."

"What did he do? Whom did he hurt? Tell me!" The tall man's voice cracked almost as his son's voice had cracked in the bar.

"Nothing. No one," said Kyle, stiff-throated. "He hit a boy not much older than himself. He drank too much. He may have got a girl in trouble. It was nothing he did to anyone else. It was only a fault against himself." He swallowed. "Wait until tomorrow, Lord, and read my report."

"No!" The tall man caught at Kyle's saddle horn with a grip that checked even the white stallion from moving. "Your family and mine have been tied together by this for three hundred years. What was the flaw in my son to make him fail his test, back here on Earth? *I want to know!*"

Kyle's throat ached and was dry as ashes.

"Lord," he answered, "he was a coward."

The hand dropped from his saddle horn as if struck down

by a sudden strengthlessness. And the Emperor of a hundred worlds fell back like a beggar, spurned in the dust.

Kyle lifted his reins and rode out of the gate, into the forest away on the hillside. The dawn was breaking.

CWACC STRIKES AGAIN

Hank Dempsey

Jeff O'Hare admired himself in the hand mirror. "Yes," he said, "that's quite an Easter bonnet." The shining metal cap completely covered the top of his head, and from it sprang a porcupinelike collection of thin metal rods that projected in all directions. A thick bundle of insulated wires led from the side of the cap to a be-dialed and be-knobbed control box, out of which was clicking a squiggle-covered length of paper tape. A bell pinged dimly inside the box and the inventor, a squarish man with a thick black beard, mumbled to himself and threw a number of switches.

"There is your Electronic Phrenogram!" he announced joyously. He hurled the length of paper tape onto the desk in front of Jeff, who examined it in the dubious manner usually reserved for poisonous serpents.

"The fruit of my genius," the inventor shouted. "Product of years of exacting labor, the greatest addition to the science of phrenology since the death of the immortal F. J. Gall. The detector rods in the cap you wear are displaced vertically by the exterior convolutions of your skull. Attached to each rod is a sensitive rheostat that measures the degree of displacement, and the output of all the rheostats is recorded on the tape. What do you think? Will CWACC pay me a grant?"

Jeff took off the heavy cap and scratched his head. "Now that is a good question," he said, glancing back and forth from the cap to the tape. "Your gadget seems well designed and appears to do what it is supposed to do; the only thing that I am dubious about is your phrenology. Of all the nutsy theories to plague mankind, phrenology always seemed to me to be one of the wackiest . . ."

"Insults! I have not come to be insulted!"

"Hold on, Tiptoft, and let me finish. I said it seems wacky—and it does—but that doesn't disqualify your machine for a CWACC grant. Funds are granted by the Committee for Welfare, Administration and Consumer Control to further research of any kind, without any value judgment being involved. We have one researcher investigating acupuncture and another working spells to see if she can sour milk with them, so who are we to draw the line at a few noggin bumps . . ." The intercom buzzed and he flipped the switch. "What is it?"

"There is a gentleman here who would like to see you, a police officer by the name of Sergeant Mannheimer."

"Grrrk . . !!" Tiptoft said and reached up under his beard to clutch painfully at his throat. Jeff looked at him with raised eyebrows before he spoke into the intercom.

"In a few moments, Miss Parker, as soon as my visitor goes." He flipped off and turned to Tiptoft. "Am I to understand that you have some acquaintance with our friend, the sergeant?"

"He's . . . on the racket squad."

"Explanation enough, I can understand and sympathize with you."

He depressed one of the buttons on his desk and a square of soundproofing slid aside in the ceiling above them, disclosing a dark hole. Tiptoft gaped as a large hook descended from the hole on the end of a thin chain. The hook stopped just above the top of the desk and Jeff slipped it through the carrying handle on the phrenogram box and hung the metal cap from its point. Another button reversed the process and Tiptoft's gape widened as his invention levitated towards the ceiling and vanished; the square of soundproofing slid back into place and the only evidence that the machine had ever been present was the paper in Jeff's hand—which he dropped into a drawer and carefully locked.

"People," he said, "look for hidden objects in walls and floors, furniture and such—but no one ever thinks to search a ceiling."

"My brainchild!"

"Secure until your next visit when you will retrieve it. Please make an appointment with Miss Parker on your way out."

"Disaster! Mannheimer knows me by sight!"

"In the CWACC we brook no barriers." He slid open the

bottom drawer of his desk and drew out what appeared to be a handful of bandages and a pair of dark glasses. The bandages were sewn to a cloth base which opened at the back with a zipper. He pulled the masklike device over Tiptoft's head and managed to stuff his beard up under it then, with some difficulty, closed the zipper. Tiptoft's frightened eyes looked out from two holes in the front until Jeff slipped on the glasses.

"There, you look like your head has been run over by a truck and has been well bandaged. I defy man or Mannheimer to recognize you in that. Please return it when I see you next."

He started the dazed inventor towards the door and signaled for Mannheimer to be admitted. The two men met in the doorway and the detective's eyes bulged as they stuck there and struggled for a moment before they passed.

"What was that?" Mannheimer asked when the door had closed.

"The invisible man—don't you ever watch television?"

"No jokes today, O'Hare, please, I ain't feeling so good."

"Sorry. That was a business associate. Had a bad accident at the barber shop. The barber's razor—"

"Enough! I'm sorry I asked." The detective groaned and dropped wearily into the visitor's chair. "You gotta help me, O'Hare. If you don't help me, I'm a gone goose and maybe I'll commit suicide."

The words shocked Jeff into an unaccustomed silence. Every previous time that he had met the police officer there had been a good deal of friction between them and a certain number of mumbled threats on the detective's part. Jeff was wary; this might be a trick of some kind.

"Would you mind explaining?" he asked as he turned on the tape recorder with his knee.

"Did you ever hear of a con man by the name of Farquhar?"

"Never."

"What about a guy who calls himself Dr. Prof. Heringboot?"

"If you did your homework the way you should, or if your graft-ridden police department weren't too cheap to buy our CWACC yearbook—seven dollars *per annum*, postage included—you would know that we gave the good doctor a grant in 1957." Jeff turned and took one of the heavy, dark volumes from the shelf behind him and flipped the pages. "Yes, here it is."

"Is this Heringboot on the level?" Mannheimer asked. "I mean is he a real scientist?"

There was desperate need in the detective's voice and Jeff rejected a number of snappy answers because he knew the sergeant wasn't enough of an actor to fake this. "He is a scientist," Jeff finally said, "and a good one. He has a string of degrees as long as your arm, industrial patents that give him a nice income, an original mind, a good researcher. There is, well, only one thing wrong . . ."

"What?"

"He's as cracked as humpty-dumpty, has been for the past ten years. You'll find it all in the yearbook."

"I'll have him in the nuthouse tonight!" Mannheimer shouted, some of the old obnoxious over-confidence trickling back into his voice as he hauled himself to his feet.

"No, you won't."

"Why not?" he collapsed weakly back into the chair.

"He's harmless, that's why. You're not the first one who has tried to put him away. They took it to court and he won. Now he has a pet lawyer never more than five minutes away, a psychiatrist on twenty-four-hour call, and a bodyguard who stays with him night and day. Isn't it time you told me what this is about?"

"It's terrible! I can't even tell the lieutenant. If I tell you, will you keep it quiet? If word leaks out . . . !"

"Scout's honor," Jeff said, holding up two fingers, crossing his heart and spitting. "The CWACC is very good at keeping secrets—as you should know."

"I know, I know," he mumbled gloomily. "I gotta tell you, because I need help. Someone in City Hall, someone *very* important, has got themselves mixed up with this con man, Farquhar, who is just about the trickiest confidence man in the country. He has never been put away so all we can do is keep an eye on him when he is in town and try and pressure him to move on. The wire shop, the horse parlor, the Spanish prisoner, he's played them all and we know it—but no one has as much as laid a finger on him yet, that's how good he is.

He slipped back into town without our knowing it and has got an operation running with this Doc Heringboot and has already sucked in a mark. I just found out by accident and I can't tell anyone and if he works the mark I'm dead, finished, since I'm supposed to be running in the con men before they can pull this kind of thing."

"Who is the mark?"

"I . . . I can't tell you . . ."

"Good-bye."

Mannheimer sweated and suffered and vibrated and worked up his courage until he finally ground a name out through his chattering teeth.

"Nissing . . ."

"The new police commissioner!"

"Himself! I can't tell anyone because the commissioner is going to be very annoyed with anyone in the department who finds out he's been taken for a sucker. So . . ."

"So you've come to me to save your neck and the commissioner's. Have you thought of any way that I could do that?"

"Well . . . you know this professor, maybe you could talk to him, show him how he is mixed up in a phony deal and heading for trouble. Get him to pull out. With him gone Farquhar won't be able to work the mark by himself. Then, as soon as the prof is gone, we will put the squeeze on Farquhar and get him to leave town."

"A foolproof plan, sergeant—with just one vital piece missing. Why should I pull your chestnuts from the fire?"

Mannheimer looked uncomfortable and scratched his head.

"Go on," Jeff said with icy joviality, then nodded sagely when no reasons were forthcoming. "Very wise, not trying to appeal to my civil spirit or duty as a citizen. You know how I feel about the crooks in City Hall. Now I'm going to surprise you, sergeant—I'm going to help you. For one reason, Dr. Prof. Heringboot may be slightly around the bend, but he is as honest as the day is long and I'm sure he's not mixed up in this business of his own free will. The foundation has a certain duty towards him. Have you found out what the con game is?"

Mannheimer heaved a deep sigh and fumbled for his pack of cigarettes. "I haven't been able to get that close," he complained. "All I know is that there is some kind of invention involved so I suppose that they are trying to get Commissioner Nissing to invest in its development."

The detective groped in the cigarette package with a meaty finger, then crushed it when he found it empty. Jeff took out his own cigarette case and extended it across the desk.

"Have one of mine," he said, and pressed a button on the side of the case. A cigarette instantly appeared, projecting two inches from the case, and when Mannheimer pulled it free he saw that it was already lit.

"That's a great gadget," he said.

Jeff laid the case on the desk and nodded agreement. "It works fine, just too expensive to manufacture. Now, about this confidence man, Farquhar, I'll want his complete record as well as all the data you have on this case. The sooner the better."

"I'll type it up tonight, bring it over here myself."

"Is there any particular reason why you can't do it now?"

"Yeah, I got to go to court. We're finally pressing charges against that quack doctor, you know the one, by the name of Hampstead. He was supposed to be defended by a drunk lawyer name of Anthony J. Blackstone, but I got the word just a little while ago that the ambulance chaser is in the hospital with D.T.'s. The case will be a pushover."

"Oh, it will, will it?" A more sensitive man than the sergeant would have noticed the icy change in Jeff's tones and would have been aware of the slight narrowing of his eyes.

"Yeah. I'll get that quack put away with five to ten." He beamed with self-pride as he ground out his cigarette and reached for Jeff's case to take another.

"Would it interest you to know that Dr. Hampstead's defense is being paid for by this foundation?" Jeff said, his voice as silky as a leopard's purr before it attacks. "Also, Mr. Blackstone has been retained by the foundation as well. Since he is indisposed I will accompany you to court and conduct the defense myself." The leopard pounced. "And I'll see to it that the charges are dismissed and that you are laughed out of the courtroom, you bumbling idiot!"

"What?" Mannheimer gasped, and had the misfortune to be holding the cigarette case to his lips at the same moment— and pressing the button. The cigarette shot between his lips —and on into his mouth and vanished. He clamped his lips shut in delayed reflex and there was an explosive sound and the smoke poured out of his nose.

"I swallowed it!" he gasped.

"Good for you," Jeff murmured, relieving him of the cigarette case. "Perhaps it will do something for your digestion. Shall we go to court now?"

They rode downtown together in a cab, in silence. The detective finally dredged up enough nerve to put the question to Jeff.

"Look . . . you're not going to let this interfere? I mean, you're still going to help me get the commissioner out of the mess?"

"Naturally," Jeff said, a monument of sweet reasonableness. "My right hand always knows what my left is doing—but neither interferes with the other. But don't think the offer of later aid will stop me from eating you alive in court."

When they climbed out of the cab in front of the courthouse a seedy man wearing a stained seaman's sweater sidled up to Jeff and handed him a thick briefcase. "It was behind the bar, at the Last Chance, just like you said, Mr. O'Hare," he whispered hoarsely.

"Thanks, Arpad," Jeff said. "I've already had five bucks credited to your tab there, so you can finish the alcoholic destruction of your vocal cords."

"That's just what I'm gonna do," he rasped, and slid away.

"Until we meet in court then, sergeant," Jeff said with a cold smile. "And you go down in flames."

It was a rout, a disaster. But not for the police. Jeff sat quietly, saying nothing, while the prosecutor browbeat and intimidated the shivering Dr. Hampstead, nor did Jeff challenge or question any of the witnesses who moved through the chair in a condemning stream.

"I should have stayed in Florida," Dr. Hampstead told Jeff, cracking his knuckles in horrified apprehension. "I'll never live the winter out in the air-cooled pen this state has. I should have remained on the golden sands as you suggested—I only returned because No-cold seemed so foolproof, a boon to humanity. I am a sacrifice on the altar of injudicious civil law enforcement."

"If you mean that the crooked cops in this town have it in for you—I couldn't agree more. But you're back, and on trial, and we still have a trick or two up the old sleeve. Be strong!"

When Jeff stood to face the court there was an expectant silence.

"No witness . . ." he said.

"No witnesses?" The judge looked shocked.

"No, Your Honor, there is no need for them. The prosecution has produced enough of them and I have no intention of wasting your valuable time with more, on a case which should never have been brought to court in the first place because of insufficient evidence. The nostrum which Dr. Hampstead has had manufactured and sold under the catchy name of No-cold is exactly what he claims it to be, and I shall so prove to this court."

"I object, Your Honor," the prosecutor broke in. "A number of expert witnesses have come before us and shown, beyond the shadow of a doubt, that there is no cure for the common cold . . ."

"No cure *they* knew about," Jeff said. "None of them ever tested No-cold and I have positive proof that No-cold is exactly what it says it is."

"Objection overruled." The gavel banged.

"Thank you, Your Honor," Jeff said, and rustled the thick wad of papers in his hand. "Now, for the sake of the records: Every bottle of No-cold is labeled with its contents and directions for use, and when taken, dissolved in milk as directed, will produce the results as stated."

"I protest!" The prosecutor was on his feet again. "This quack potion contains nothing except some common vitamins and a little iron and calcium. It's worthless. Any druggist will sell you—"

"Any druggist will sell you aspirin!" Jeff interrupted. "Whether it is called that or by a fancy trade name or acetylsalicylic acid. But under *any* name it is still the drug of choice for a number of ailments all the way from headaches to rheumatism. Availability is no measure of effectiveness."

"Overruled, Mr. Prosecutor," the judge said and banged his gavel tiredly. "And don't you think you could limit these interruptions, or we'll be here until next week."

The flushed attorney dropped into his chair and Jeff gave him a smile of wonderful innocence. "I shall not be much longer," he said. "The label on each and every bottle of No-cold states clearly that when taken as directed it prevents colds in children. And it does. I offer in evidence this scientific document as exhibit A. It is a study made in 1961 by Dr. Frank E. Barnes, Jr., who is chairman of the Committee on School Health of the North Carolina Medical Society. Dr. Barnes made a study of the local high-school basketball players, both boys and girls, and found that a ridiculous diet was eaten by the majority of the children and that only *two* percent drank an adequate amount of milk daily. The doctor did his study during a period of three months and found out that those children who received vitamin supplements avoided colds and did not miss any classes during those winter months. While the control group of children, living only on their 'ridiculous' diet, missed classes and were down with the usual number of colds."

The prosecutor was on his feet again, triumphantly waving a piece of paper. "If I may interrupt, Your Honor, we already know of this so-called study. But we also know that the report was rejected for publication by the *Journal of the American Medical Association* on the grounds that high-school students do not need vitamin supplements in their diet. Did you know about *that,* Mr. O'Hare?"

"I know about that," Jeff said in just as oily and unctuous a voice. "I also happen to know that the editors of the *A.M.A. Journal* are wrong, as editors and members of established scientific authority have been, from time to time, in the past. And I think you had better withdraw your statement about Dr. Barnes' report being 'so-called.' Are you calling him a liar? Do you doubt the scientific accuracy of this carefully done work? Remember—the A.M.A. editors just gave an opinion, a wrong one in fact, that vitamins don't aid high-school children. Will you go further . . . ?"

"Perhaps my words were a little hasty," the red-faced prosecutor said. "If there could possibly be any cause to misinterpret them, I shall be happy to have them struck from the record."

"And just in time, too," Jeff added, holding out another sheet of paper. "Exhibit B. At a symposium on Nutrition in Medical Practice in 1964, three years after Dr. Barnes' study, there were a few words said on the subject by Dr. Robert W. Hillman of State University of New York, Downstate Medical Center. Dr. Hillman said, and I quote his very words, that: 'the teen-ager—and especially the teen-age girl

—is the worst-fed member of the household. . . . As a result, up to three-quarters of the population of teen-aged girls may be two-thirds deficient in such nutrients as vitamins A and C, thiamine, riboflavin, calcium and iron.' So it has been proven that most teen-agers have vitamin deficiencies, despite any official or unofficial opinions to the contrary. It has been proven that children with vitamin deficiencies suffer from colds. At a fair and competitive price for its contents and solution, No-cold, when taken with milk as directed, will make up the dietetic deficiencies—and will prevent colds. The defense rests."

"You have done it again, Jeffrey O'Hare, and I shall be in eternal debt to you." Dr. Hampstead's voice quavered with emotion as he pressed Jeff's hand between his.

"All part of the service of the foundation, Doctor. All I ask in return is that you accept a little suggestion. Florida . . ."

"I am on my way now, I was a fool to ever have returned to this evil metropolis. There are other cities that would benefit just as well by the fruits of my discoveries."

"Just remember that the next time you have an urge to save mankind." Jeff waved as they parted in front of the courthouse and flagged down a cab.

It was just five when he entered the CWACC office and his secretary, Sally Parker, was giving her nose a last dusting in the wall mirror, before hurling herself into the rush-hour battle. Jeff ran his eyes happily over her slim figure as she stood on tiptoes to look into the glass. "I must say that outfit does a lot for your natural attributes. But, are you becoming a beatnik or are the knee-length knitted stockings a desire to return to the simple, peasant days of America's youth?"

"Mr. O'Hare," she said, closing her purse and giving him one of her most disdainful sniffs. "I am wearing these awful objects in the pursuit of pure science. And money." She rolled one of the heavy stockings down to reveal another and thinner stocking beneath it, this one of a particularly horrible and mottled purple color. "For eighteen months now I have been wearing these awful stockings in the office, and they will not wear or tear in any way. You may recall I receive a grant of twenty-five dollars a month for this service. You may also remember that you have been after me for ages to give them more wear outside of work. I have now devised this plan to wear them abroad without embarrassment, for which you will raise my grant to fifty dollars a month."

"Forty," Jeff said, filling out a voucher. "As long as you have them in shrouds they can't be snagged. But it's worth the extra fifteen for the extra work. Sign here."

"You, sir, are a cheapskate, you and your cheapskate foundation." She angrily scrawled her name.

"You should know—you're the only other employee."

Jeff was alone in the office and it was a good chance to catch up on some paper work while he waited for Mannheimer. He put Sally's voucher in the *Mr. X* file and made a note of the increased testing time on the apparently indestructible stockings, in the hope that their mysterious inventor —about whom they knew nothing—would return one day and reveal the secret of their construction.

To encourage himself in his labors, Jeff had dinner sent up from the restaurant across the street—and a bottle of bourbon from the package store around the corner. By carefully dividing his attention between them and intermittently scratching through the files and taping some letters for Sally in the morning, he pleasantly passed the time until nine o'clock when an officious hammering on the hall door announced Mannheimer's arrival.

"Come in, Sergeant," Jeff said. "And from that expression of deepest gloom on your honest face I would say that this has not been one of your happiest days. Come in, have a seat, and I'm sure that you are off duty enough to join me in a drink, and if you won't mention this afternoon's trial neither will I."

The detective fell heavily into a chair, accepted the drink and handed over a thick envelope—all without a word. Jeff respected the silence and flipped through the contents of the folder while he sipped at his own drink. "Very interesting," he said when he had finished. "Your records tell me far more than I care to know about Farquhar, but absolutely nothing about the present operation except the address of Dr. Prof. Heringboot's laboratory. This operation needs more intelligence—in the military sense of knowledge, that is, no slighting reference to your undoubted, though well concealed, powers of mind."

"How you going to find out anything?" Mannheimer asked

glumly. "Bug the place? I tried that—with no results. You don't catch an old hand like Farquhar that easily."

"Of course not—I catch him a lot easier. I'm just going to walk in there and ask them what is going on."

"You're going to *what?*"

"Come now, Sergeant, don't bulge your eyes in that unattractive manner. The Doctor Professor is an old friend of this foundation and will be happy to see me. We are always interested in his work. Farquhar will have to put up with my presence and he has no legitimate complaint because this is supposed to be an aboveboard business matter." Jeff took an electric razor from the closet and began going over his face while he talked. "I'll go there tonight, you can phone me in the morning and I'll give you a complete report."

"You're looking for trouble, O'Hare—this Farquhar is a tough nut. There have been a couple of guys that disappeared that we think he had a hand in."

"I take it that your suspicions are more accurate than your grammar." He clicked off the shaver and stowed it away in the closet, emerging this time with a luxurious leather attaché case with gold fittings. "O'Hare is a tough nut, too, and can take care of himself. We'll get to the facts—and this will help." He opened the attaché case and pointed to the built-in tape recorder. "The microphone is concealed in the handle, very useful gadget." He weighed the empty case thoughtfully, then added a ream of typing paper and the bottle of bourbon for ballast.

"We'll share a taxi," Jeff said turning off the lights. "You can drop me around the corner from Heringboot's laboratory and the police department can pay the fare."

There was only silence on the trip downtown, and Jeff waited until the cab had vanished before he walked around the corner to Newby Street. This section of the city was devoted to light and heavy manufacturing and the storing of these products, and was almost deserted after dark with just an occasional car passing under the widely separated street lights. Number 32 proved to be a small and shabby four-story building almost hidden by the giant warehouses that surrounded it. Jeff climbed the short flight of crumbling, stone steps, straightened his tie, pressed the corner of the attaché case that turned on the tape recorder, and rang the bell. Almost at once a light came on inside, he could see it through the fanlight, and after a great rattling of locks the door squealed open.

"Welcome . . ." a man said, blinking out into the darkness. Then the warm tone of his voice went frigid. "Who are you?"

"Jeffrey O'Hare," he said brightly, "and I'm here to see Dr. Prof. Heringboot, if you please."

"What do you want with him?" the other snapped. He was tall and lean, with a pleasant face, well tanned, that sported a British-officer type moustache. Jeff had recognized him as Farquhar, from the pictures in the police file, but kept this fact to himself. He ignored the other man's tones of anger and answered with the voice of sweet reasonableness.

"A personal matter, I'm sure you wouldn't be interested. Now—if you would be so kind as to inform the doctor that I am here . . ."

Jeff smiled blandly while Farquhar chewed his lip in a crisis of indecision. He glanced about at the empty street and made his mind up. "All right, come in," he said.

He led the way up a musty flight of stairs and threw open a door. Jeff had just a glimpse of a large room fitted up as a laboratory of some sort, when his attention was drawn to a man in a white laboratory smock, with his back turned, who was working at one of the benches.

"Dr. Heringboot, there is someone to see you," Farquhar said. The man turned. "Yes?" he said.

Smiling warmly Jeff stepped forward. It had been years since he had last seen Heringboot, but he knew him well from their past association. "Dr. Prof. Heringboot, this is a pleasure," he said.

He had never seen this man before in his life.

"What is it you want?" the pseudo-Heringboot asked. He was a small man with sandy, thin hair and a very worried expression. Jeff smiled warmly, but did not answer until he had turned to place his attaché case on a nearby table. He was thinking rapidly.

"Dr. Heringboot, my firm has sent me here on a confidential matter. If you would be so kind—here is my card." Jeff opened his wallet and flipped through the plastic dividers until he found a business card, extracted it and handed it to the man. He, of course, had to flip through the dividers because each of them held a different kind of card.

"J. J. O'Hare," the imitation professor doctor read. "International Funds Ltd., Bern, Schweiz. But—what does this mean? What is it about?"

"Ist iss eine konfidentialische mattervotter," Jeff intoned in a thick, teutonic voice.

"Please speak English. I do not speak German here in this country."

You don't speak it any other place either—if you believe that was German, Jeff thought to himself. His smile was even broader. "Of course. I was just explaining that this was a confidential matter." He rolled his eyeballs theatrically towards the hovering Farquhar.

"That's perfectly all right, tell me what you want. Mr. Farquhar is my partner, I have no secrets from him . . ."

A distant, ringing bell interrupted him and he glanced towards Farquhar who mumbled something distinctly unpleasant under his breath as he left the room.

"Couldn't this matter wait until some other time," the mock doc said nervously. "We have an important meeting this evening and there won't be time for anything else."

Jeff mumbled as incoherent an answer as he could and kept one eye on the door. They exchanged excuses for a few moments until Farquhar returned. When Jeff saw who was with him his smile broadened until it was not unlike that of a hungry alligator.

"Mr. Nissing," he said, rushing forward, "what a happy coincidence, meeting you like this. It is because of you that I am here."

Nissing drew back, his beady eyes staring suspiciously from behind the ramparts of his fat cheeks. "And who are you, sir? I never saw you before in my life!"

"Nor I you, sir." Jeff whipped out another of the same cards and proffered it. "But you will understand when I say that you are a well known and prominent figure and I have, of course, seen your likeness in the newspapers. But more than that, my firm has recently become aware of certain investment plans of yours and I am here to see if I can be of any aid." Jeff blandly ignored the strange looks the three men were hurling back and forth at each other as he rattled on. "International Funds is a world-wide firm with investments in every part of the globe. Our operation is so successful that we, ha-ha, suffer from an *excess* of money, and you know how bad that is. Money works for you, sir, and uninvested capital is a waste. When we heard that Dr. Prof. Heringboot had an invention that needed financing I was dispatched at once. When we heard that you, Mr. Nissing, were also investing, I rushed even faster. Tell me, do not leave me in suspense—are you underwriting all the developmental costs or is there still a small spot for us? My checkbook is in my pocket and I am instantly ready to write a check for any sum."

The two con men were suffering silently, but Nissing relaxed and actually smiled as he rubbed at his fat jowls. "Very glad to hear this, O'Hare. I have been considering investing, but the sum was rather large and I'll be only too happy to have a partner in this venture."

"And what would be the size of International Funds' contribution?"

The piggy eyes were half closed. "Could you, say, see your way clear to putting in . . . one hundred thousand dollars?"

Jeff took his pen out and smiled patronizingly. "Is that all? Ahh, we had hoped this was a *big* investment. But small or big, we back them all." He reached towards his inner pocket, but stopped his hand halfway. "I'm sure you wouldn't mind my having a look at the invention before signing the check."

"I'm sure the professor wouldn't mind," Nissing said. "But —you said you knew all about it?" There was more than a touch of suspicion in his voice.

"*Knowing* about a thing and *seeing* the proof are entirely different," Jeff said, treading lightly along the edge of the precipice. He hadn't the slightest idea yet what the invention was about.

"Of course, of course, you'll have to have something to tell to your principals in Bern. How about it professor? Mr. Farquhar?"

Both these individuals smiled insincerely and wriggled inside their clothes, but there was no escape.

"Go ahead, Doctor," Farquhar finally said. "We would all enjoy seeing your incredible machine in operation."

"That's for sure," Nissing said enthusiastically. "It really has to be seen to be believed."

The substitute Heringboot turned to a large control panel and switched on the apparatus. "The destruction of matter requires a good deal of power," he said, "as does its reconstruction once it is in wave form." Jeff raised his eyebrows but said nothing. "While the transmitter apparatus is being charged up I can demonstrate the operation of the matter destroyer—"

"This is the absolute best," Nissing said, "I never get tired of watching it in operation."

"Would you please hand me one of those beer steins, Mr. O'Hare," the doctor-professor asked. "In fact, you can aid me by placing it between the polarizing plates of the matter destroyer, but be careful to take your hands away before I activate it."

There was a box on one of the tables filled with thick, cheap beer mugs. Jeff took one up and weighed it in his hands; it was solid, chunky glass and seemed completely normal in every way. He placed it on the foot square sheet of metal as he was directed. The metal plate stood on heavy ceramic insulators and there was another plate, a twin of the first, suspended a foot above it by more insulators. In this way the two plates formed the bottom and top faces of a cubic foot of space.

"Stand back!" the imitation Heringboot shouted dramatically as he threw a large knife switch on one of the panels. The dynamo changed tone as it labored under the load and there was a slight discharge of static electricity from the insulators that held up the plates. This was all that could be seen, not very exciting at all—except for the fact that the beer stein grew misty, fading away before their eyes until, with a faint crackling sound, it vanished completely.

As the dynamo moaned into silence Jeff realized that he was standing stiffly with his jaw hanging open. He closed it with a sharp clack and jumped forward, swinging his hand back and forth between the plates and encountering nothing more resistant than thin air.

"Impressive, isn't it, Mr. O'Hare," Farquhar murmured into his ear.

"Yes," Jeff said, grabbing at the cracked shards of his composure, "but no more than I expected after reading the reports."

"And exactly *what* did these reports say?" Farquhar's voice was sharper now.

"How about that, O'Hare, how about that?" Nissing boomed.

"Tremendous!" Jeff told him, escaping from the hovering Farquhar. "So tremendous that I would love to see it done again. How about you, Mr. Nissing?"

"Never get tired of it. How about it, professor?"

The pseudo professor leveled a look of smoky hatred at Jeff but silkily reassured Nissing that he was always ready to oblige. This time Jeff prowled around and examined the two plates from all sides and even from underneath and stood so close when the second beer mug vanished that there was a crackle of static electricity from the tip of his nose. He knew a lot about the various ways machines and gadgets could be rigged and he was sure that there was no chicanery here.

Whatever force flowed between those metal plates *did* make the glassware vanish.

"Your matter destroyer seems to be very efficient," he said, as calmly as he could. "Now I hope that the transmitter apparatus you mentioned is just as interesting."

"You're right as rain," Nissing agreed. "There's no future in just taking things apart, you have to put them together again if there is to be any money in it."

"Of course, the transmitter," the fake professor said surlily, and turned to the control board to conceal his anger. "In the demonstration you have just witnessed the beam of electronic vibrations has simply destroyed the object, dispersed its material into the air as a cloud of subatomic particles. However, in the sealed chamber of the transmitter, the particles are used to modulate a wave of very refined energy which is transmitted to the receiver where the object is reassembled again in its original form, uninjured and unaltered by its voyage. Of course in this case, for demonstration only, the transmitter and receiver are located in the same room, though in our field tests successful transmissions were carried on at a distance of over some fifty miles."

"And with a little capital the power can be increased to cover any distance," Nissing said. "That's what they told me and I guess you can see, commercially-wise, what that means, O'Hare." He started to unstrap the watch from his wrist. "Here, you can use my watch, just like you did last time."

Jeff caught the worried glance that the phony scientist shot at Farquhar, and it was the con man who smoothly answered the question.

"I don't see why not. Any object can be transmitted, any object at all."

He put his hand out for the watch, a thin, wide, crystal and eighteen-karat oyster with a brazenly expensive gold band. Nissing gave it to him and Farquhar turned to pass it on to the false Heringboot, turning his back to do so. Jeff smiled happily—this was more like it. And, as the professor demonstrated the machinery, the smile grew wider and wider.

"I put the watch into the transmission chamber, which in this case must be sealed off and evacuated because the presence of any air interferes with the action of the scanning wave. But a glass window has been installed in the front of the chamber so that you may watch the process."

He bent behind a bulky piece of machinery while Jeff and Nissing watched through a thick glass port set into the front. The familiar insulator-mounted plates were visible inside, then the professor's hand as he put the watch down. An air pump began to hammer and they waited a few minutes until the reading on the pressure dial was satisfactory.

"Watch this," Nissing said proudly. "Just watch this!"

The dynamo hummed, electricity crackled and the watch faded from sight until it vanished and the chamber was empty. Across the room more sparks spat on a duplicate machine, mounted as this one was with a dish-shaped aerial, near which Farquhar was standing. Nissing trundled heavily across and pointed in the window at the watch.

"Now how about that!" he chortled and spun the sealing wheels on the side of the box. Air hissed in through the seals and a moment later he held the watch in his palm, chilled with frost from the vacuum—and perhaps the treatment it had undergone.

"Still ticking and keeping good time," Nissing said, turning the watch over and pointing to the lines of engraving there. "My watch without a doubt, unharmed, the inscription just as plain as ever. What do you say O'Hare—is International Funds interested?"

"You can bet your bottom dollar that we are," Jeff said happily. "A most illuminating demonstration and—"

"Perhaps you will want to examine the machines and principles of operation, Mr. O'Hare," Farquhar broke in smoothly. "I am the business partner and know nothing about these things. Why don't you stay here for a few moments and talk to Professor Heringboot, ask him anything you like. I have matters to discuss with Mr. Nissing and we will rejoin you in a few moments."

Farquhar's trained con man's hand was already guiding the commissioner towards the door while Jeff thought quickly. As long as Nissing was around they couldn't pull any funny business with him, and this looked like a smooth ploy to separate them. But the whole business was chancy—and he certainly had nothing to fear from the scrawny little fake scientist. He flexed his muscles under his coat.

"By all means," he said heartily. "I'll have a pleasant chat with the Herr Doctor Professor."

The door closed as they left and Jeff turned. The other man was walking towards him with his hand raised as though he were going to shake hands. Jeff started to say something, but at the moment he realized the man was holding his arm and for some reason it kept bending in the wrong direction as though it were going to break off; he followed it around to ease the pain.

"Hey—!" he said, but there was a sudden crunching sound that bounced about inside his head and all the lights went out.

Consciousness returned accompanied by a number of unpleasant sensations which Jeff struggled to control before he opened his eyes. When he finally did so he saw a ceiling swinging in swift circles above him; he forced it to slow and stop only with great and painful concentration. It was dusty and cracked, decorated with ancient spiderwebs and adorned with a single dirty light bulb in a wire cage. His neck hurt, his head hurt, and his stomach heaved about like a raft on a stormy sea. When he turned to look around him, lightning shot between his eyeballs and he groaned aloud.

"About time you awoke from your drunken slumbers— overindulging at your age, *Dummkopf!*"

The voice had a rasping, familiar quality to it and Jeff forced his eyes open again and squinted at the man seated across the room from him. A thin old man with tufts of white hair behind his ears and a pair of old-fashioned, gilt frame pince-nez glasses clamped infirmly onto the bridge of his red-tipped nose.

"Doctor Professor Heringboot, I presume," Jeff said, and with each word his head pulsed as though a mighty drum were beating within it.

Heringboot turned away from the cluttered laboratory bench and blinked at Jeff over the top of the glasses. "You know my name?" he asked.

Jeff pushed himself up slowly until he could sit on the edge of the hard cot. "You know me, too, professor. Jeff O'Hare of CWACC. You relieved us of some funds for a grant once."

"Aha! I thought the face was familiar; O'Hare of course. But the years have not treated you kindly, less hair and that sort of thing. And the drinking."

"It was the boys upstairs who didn't treat me so kindly, doc. And I have *not* been drinking. What you are looking at are the results of contusion, abrasion and concussion. My head hurts."

Heringboot climbed down from his high stool, pattered over to Jeff and peeled back one of his eyelids like a fishwife skinning a flounder.

"Oww!" Jeff said as the lightning stabbed again.

"You may be correct," the scientist mused. "The pupil indicates possibility of a blow on the cranium as does the blood on the shirt collar." He began rummaging through a large cabinet filled with bottles, taking down one after another and mumbling to himself. "Chlorpromazine hydrochloride . . . Picrotoxin . . . Oxtriphylline . . . Desoxycorticosterone acetate . . ." With swift motions he began to mix a number of these chemicals together in a beaker, then reached for a bottle of distilled water. "Are you sure you weren't drinking?" he asked Jeff.

"Positive."

"Then a tincture will be more *bessere*." He slopped in a great gout of ethyl alcohol and a small amount of water and brought the beaker over to Jeff, stirring it with a glass rod. "Drink this down to the last drop and your troubles are gone, *kaputt*."

"Are you sure I won't be *kaputt*?" Jeff asked suspiciously, looking at the bubbling contents of the beaker. Where the professor pulled the rod out he expected to see it half dissolved.

Heringboot urged him forcefully to drink and his will power was at low ebb so he obeyed. Outside of some preliminary internal rumblings, like the warning of distant volcanoes, the potion went down easily enough and very quickly a happy numbness surged through his system, followed by a wave of enthusiasm and a feeling of power.

"That's great stuff," Jeff said, standing and flexing his muscles, feeling ready to tear down stone walls. "You ought to patent it. You have a fortune waiting there for a hangover cure and general pepper-upper."

"The fruits of my genius fall like rain—I have no time to waste on commercial transactions." He went back to the laboratory bench and began to clatter the glassware.

"You wouldn't happen to know a man by the name of Farquhar?" Jeff asked, running his hand through his pockets. They were empty; wallet, checkbook, everything gone. He shrugged and went over and rattled the handle on the steel door set into the concrete-block wall. It was unmoving and had a healthy solidity about it.

"Of course, I know him—he is my lawyer."

"Lawyer?" Jeff's still recuperating brain stumbled over this confusing thought. "But what happened to your old lawyer?"

"Accident. Very tragic. Both legs broken by a hit and *rennen* car, and he is still in the hospital. He sent a letter saying Farquhar was the best man for the job."

"I see," said Jeff, and what he saw was a staged accident and a forged letter, child's play for an old hand like Farquhar. "There is another man whom you may know. I don't know his name but he is a short guy, worried look, has sandy hair that is getting thin on top—"

"You are discussing Scobie, my bodyguard . . ."

"Bodyguard!"

". . . Very wise decision on my part." Heringboot ignored the interruption as he hooked more piping to the condenser. "Very efficient. Saves money, too. Two in one. He is my assistant as well, a trained laboratory technician of experience, and at the same time is an expert with the judo, what you call a Schwarzgurtel."

"A black belt, I might have known," Jeff said, rubbing the contused back of his neck. "The parts are all falling into place. I think the time has come to get out of here and make a few alterations in their plans."

"You cannot leave," Heringboot said abstractedly as he adjusted a Bunsen burner under the towering collection of glass. "The door is stuck again, they don't seem to be able to fix it. And that is the only exit from this cellar."

"Very neat," Jeff said, inspecting the walls. They were solid concrete and there were no windows. The only other opening was a circular coal-hole in one wall, but it was covered by thick metal bars that had been welded to the iron frame. It angled upwards for a few feet and he could just make out a metal lid on the other end that did not seem to be secured in any way. The coal chute was wide enough to get up and the lid could be easily removed and he could escape the cellar that way—except for the bars.

"Did Farquhar ever give you any papers to sign?" he asked the scientist.

"Of course!" the old man snapped testily. "That's what I hire a lawyer for. I have no time to read that sort of thing. He brings, I sign."

"You are being victimized and cheated, Dr. Prof. Heringboot," Jeff said dramatically. "Farquhar is a fake and your precious assistant is passing himself off as you and they are working a big con and undoubtedly using papers you have signed to verify it."

"Boys will be boys," Heringboot mumbled while he squinted at a column of rising bubbles. "I expect to be cheated. Just as long as enough money is left for my experiments I do not care. My lawyer is hired to keep me out of the *Nervenheilanstalt,* the asylum, and he will keep doing that in order to keep the money coming in for himself. I am crazy all right—crazy like a fox! Hah!"

Jeff controlled his temper. He had to get Heringboot on his side or he would never get out of this cellar. The precious pair upstairs must be ready to milk their mark tonight and blow town if they were willing to take a chance on locking him down here.

"I need your help, Professor," he explained patiently. "Your lawyer and bodyguard-assistant are finishing off their dirty business right now. They've rigged up your matter destroyer. It must be yours. They would never . . ."

"I have never heard of a matter destroyer."

"A gadget with two metal plates on insulators. You put something between them and turn on the juice and it vanishes."

"Unwissenheit!" Prof. Heringboot shrieked and knocked over a yard of glassware. "This is *lacherlich!* You are describing my Einsteinian Space-Time demonstrator. It has nothing to do with the destruction of matter. I merely built it to prove a point in the theory of spatio-temporal coordinates, then I told that *schrecklichschuft* of an assistant to dismantle it."

"Then it is not a matter destroyer?"

"Matter destroyer—what kind of nonsense is this?" the professor shouted, waving his fist angrily over his head. "You are the one should be put away, not me, saying something like that. I told you it was a demonstrator; it does not alter space, but it can be dangerous, highly dangerous to use. I must stop them!" He ran to the door and tugged angrily at the handle.

"Locked," Jeff said tolerantly. "I have a feeling they want us both down here where we can't cause any trouble. There is another way out . . ."

"Where?" Heringboot shouted, pacing the floor like a caged lion.

"There," Jeff said, pointing to the ancient coal chute. "We could get out that way if those bars weren't over the opening."

"Bars! Bars are as nothing to Heringboot, I laugh at bars! Those fools . . ." He muttered angrily to himself while he tore open the cabinet and began to quickly assemble apparatus on the table. "Something simple . . . there is not the time to waste . . . cellulose nitrate, what they call the gun-cotton, that is the answer . . ." There was a rapid gurgling as he filled a crock with nitric acid. "And then some cellulose . . . $C_6H_{10}O_5$ . . . yes, yes, that's it!"

Jeff looked on interestedly while the angry scientist threw open the door of the first-aid cabinet and ripped out lengths of absorbent cotton. He started to stuff this into the acid, then broke off to root out a bag of plaster of paris and began to make a paste from this in a large bowl. Working with both hands at the same time, muttering constantly, he produced a wicked looking wad of gun-cotton and a half-congealed sludge of plaster. Jeff held the containers while Heringboot applied the explosive to the iron ring that held the bars over the opening, then slapped on a covering of plaster. The plaster was practically hard by the time he poked a hole in it and inserted a piece of alcohol-soaked string for a fuse. Then he washed his hands, buttoned his white laboratory coat and put on an immense black fedora hat that hung on a hook next to the door.

"I am ready," he announced. "Shall we leave?"

"After you, Professor."

"*Gut.* I would suggest the back to the wall over there with the work bench for shelter. There will be noise, some flying particles, and it is best to take precautions . . ." He touched a match to the fuse and scuttled back out of the way, crouching next to Jeff.

The fuse smoked and crackled up to the plaster and the thing exploded with a thudding boom. Jeff looked on in admiration as the ring and bars flew the length of the cellar and clanged against the far wall.

"Satisfactory," Heringboot said, stepping through the cloud of smoke and dust and examining the jagged opening in the wall.

Jeff wriggled up the chute, pushed off the cover and hauled himself out. There was still plenty of ancient coal dust in the chute and Heringboot complained loudly about the condition of his white coat when Jeff pulled him up and had to be hushed into grumbling semi-silence. There was enough reflected light from the sky for them to see that they were in a junk-cluttered back yard, walled in on three sides by tall buildings and on the fourth by the shabby rear of the building they had just left. Light glimmered around the edges of the drawn curtains in the rooms above and the whining of the generator could be clearly heard in the quiet night.

"Either they're deaf or they didn't hear the explosion with all the noise they are making themselves," Jeff said, trying the handle on the rear door; it was unlocked. "Let us, therefore, make our presence known." He made his way into the building with Heringboot treading on his heels.

"Just on time," Jeff said cheerfully, throwing wide the door to the upstairs laboratory.

The three men in the room stood, frozen, like a tableau from a bad play. Nissing was in the process of handing over a large pile of cash to the conspirators who were both reaching for the loot at the same time. All three of them stared at the figures in the doorway with wide-eyed astonishment.

"Mr. O'Hare!" Nissing gasped. "What has happened to your clothes? I was told you had been called away."

"Full explanations in a moment," Jeff said, keeping a wary eye on black belt Scobie who was stalking forward in a half crouch, arms before him, hands ready to strike. "No, no," Jeff said in simulated terror, drawing back as the other came closer.

Scobie smiled, remembering his easy success upon the last occasion they had met and reached out his hand. The smile vanished as Jeff grabbed the hand, pressed, twisted, kicked the other man's legs out from under him as he fell, chopped him swiftly with the hard edge of his hand as he dropped and even had time to give him the knee before he hit the floor. Before Scobie could as much as groan he was prone and unconscious. Jeff smiled down at the silent figure.

"You took me off guard last time," he said. "For your information I'm black belt, too—and I picked up a few things in the Marines that they aren't allowed to teach in judo class."

Jeff said the last words as he raced across the room, and when Farquhar's hand went into his desk drawer Jeff's hand was right beside it. After a brief scuffle Jeff had the gun and slipped it into his pocket. "Now we can talk peacefully," he said.

"What is the meaning of this outrage?" Nissing shouted. "What have you done to Professor Heringboot?"

"Nothing," Jeff told him placidly. "The *real* Professor Heringboot is the gentleman in the black hat there; the man I slugged was an imposter."

"Then you mean—"

"The machine is a fake and there is simply no matter transmitter."

"My money—"

"Has been swindled from you. That pale individual trying to edge towards the door is a well-known confidence man who has been milking marks for years."

"But . . . I saw the matter destroyer destroy matter," Nissing said as he grabbed his money from the table and began to stuff it back into his briefcase.

"Bah!" Heringboot said, folding his arms dramatically. "You

saw my Einsteinian Space-Time demonstrator demonstrating. No matter was destroyed."

"B-but . . ." Nissing was shaking his head with bewilderment; he waved towards the bulk of the matter transmitter. "You were here, Mr. O'Hare, you saw the apparatus work. It transmitted my watch across the room."

Jeff smiled and picked up a wrench. "This fine piece of machinery contains a well-known stage illusion," he said, then broke the glass in the viewing window with the wrench. "Here, look inside—do you see that vertical piece of glass set in at a forty-five degree angle? That's the secret of the illusion. I'll explain: The first thing these boys did was buy a watch that duplicated yours—which was no big problem. I saw Farquhar make the shift, handing the duplicate to the now-unconscious Scobie. We watched Scobie put the *duplicate* into the back of this box. We saw it through the angled glass. Then the light over the watch slowly dimmed while the light here—on this side—slowly brightened. The second light illuminates a second box, an empty duplicate of the first that is set at right angles to it. So—darkness falls behind the angled glass which now acts as a mirror and we seem to see the watch fade from sight as it is replaced by the image of the empty box. Nothing to it."

Nissing looked back and forth between the machines, then pointed to the matter receiver. "I don't understand yet—we found my watch in that machine."

"Of course. Farquhar walked over and slipped it in while our backs were turned. Simple. The secret of all good illusions is simplicity."

"Tricked . . ." Nissing said to himself with dawning comprehension. "Swindled!" he shouted angrily and pointed at Farquhar. "You crook! Where is the twenty thousand dollars I paid you last week?"

"This sort of enterprise is not without its expenses," Farquhar said, smiling sincerely. "I'm afraid your original investment has been absorbed into operating costs—"

"Pay up you crook, or I'll beat it out of you!" Nissing advanced, fist raised, face flushed. Jeff grabbed him by the coat sleeve.

"No violence, please," he said. "With two exceptions we are all gentlemen here. I shall see to it that your money is reimbursed. Did these crooks at least give you any papers or agreements in return for all this hard cash?"

Nissing looked baffled. "Yes, but I don't see that that has any relevancy." He took a handsome-looking legal document from his briefcase and handed it to Jeff. "Here is a patent assignment, profit agreement and all the rest."

Jeff took and examined it quickly. "Appears to be in order," he said. "Carefully drawn up, and that is Heringboot's signature in the corner. No doubt this is one of the papers he signed without reading. This satisfies me, Mr. Nissing, and I have a small confession to make to you. I am not in the investment business as I led you to believe. I am an employee of an educational foundation that is very well endowed, the professor will assure you of the truth of that. Since my foundation has been a sponsor of much of Professor Heringboot's work we feel a certain obligation in this matter. Will you allow us to help? We will pay you the twenty thousand and see how much we can get back from these con men. But, in order to justify this transaction on our books, would you be so kind as to sign over these rights that you have purchased . . . plenty of room right here at the bottom."

"Happily, happily," Nissing said, and scribbled away at Jeff's dictation and scrawled his signature.

"My checkbook?" Jeff said to Farquhar, who shrugged and pointed wordlessly to Jeff's attaché case lying in one corner. It had been pried open and the spool of tape ripped from the recording machine, but all the things they had taken from his pockets had been thrown in there. He pulled out his checkbook and pen and wrote a check for Nissing.

"Good as gold, Mr. Nissing," he said, handing it over. "Our foundation has bags of money."

"What's going to happen to these crooks?" Nissing asked, pocketing the check. "I mean, the police . . ."

"I understand perfectly, sir. Considering your new appointment as commissioner this could be embarrassing. Would you be satisfied if they vanished? Bottom of the river, concrete on the feet and that sort of thing?"

Nissing went white. "You can't mean . . . No . . . I won't be a party to it."

"What the eye does not see the heart does not grieve," Jeff said with an evil smile, at the same time rubbing his hands together with a dry, rasping sound. "Might it not be best for

you to leave now and try to clear your mind of this whole
matter?"

"Yes . . . of course . . . fine idea . . ." Nissing quickly
clutched up his briefcase, coat and hat and swept from the
room forgetting to say good-bye. His footsteps hurried down
the stairs and they heard the front door slam. Jeff turned to
Farquhar and extended his hand, palm up.

"Pay up!" he said sternly. The con man hesitated a moment,
then took out his wallet and handed a pile of bills over to Jeff.
"Professor, see if Scobie has any money on him while I count
this," he said, flipping through the greenbacks.

Scobie's still unmoving body yielded up some more money
but when Jeff counted it all there was still over four thousand
dollars missing.

"Cough it up, Farquhar," he said, fixing the man with
glittering eye. "You can't have spent that much on this setup.
Where is it?" He raised a solid fist and blew on it.

"No violence!" the con man squealed and hurried over to
the desk and began to root in the back of the bottom drawer.
He found what he was looking for, then straightened up with
a large automatic pistol in his hand and aimed it at Jeff.
"Now," he said coldly, "give me back the money."

"Two guns," Jeff mused. "I should have thought of that."

A loud crash sounded from the other side of the room as a
glass beer stein appeared out of the thin air and fell to the
floor. Farquhar jumped and swung the gun in that direction.
Jeff plucked another beer stein out of the full box next to him
and hurled it across the room. It caught Farquhar in the
temple and he went over and down and out for the count.

"Wunderschone!" Doctor Professor Heringboot chortled and
looked at his watch. "Now with the power settings from the
demonstrator I can determine the temporal displacement. This
must be the first sample I used . . ." His words degenerated
into a mumble as he began to scratch equations on a scrap of
paper.

"As I hoped," Jeff said. "You told me your invention was a
space-time demonstrator that did not demonstrate any quali-
ties of space, which leaves us with time." There was a louder
series of crashes as a dozen more steins appeared and broke
on the floor. "I hoped your gadget was sending the glassware
through time in some fashion and I am cheered to see my

deductions so well justified. These crooks could only see the machine as a gadget to work a con game—when all the time they had an operating time machine in their hands." He patted the signed agreement in his pocket. "A portion of which now belongs to CWACC, signed, sealed and delivered. A good night's work O'Hare," he said, congratulating himself since no one else was there to do it. He picked up the phone.

"All that remains now is to ring up Mannheimer and tell him that his new commissioner is off the hook. And have him pick up this precious pair and put them in the cooler for a few months. Assault and battery, possession of illegal firearms and such, that should do it. They won't complain—and they'll leave the state quickly enough when they're finally turned loose."

A shrill screaming split the air and an outraged cat with puffed fur and extended claws appeared in midair and dropped to the floor, howling and spitting. It darted under a workbench.

"So that's where you went, my little *schatz*," Heringboot said happily, calling to the cat. "You naughty kitty—traveling through time!"

"Mannheimer speaking . . ." the voice rasped in the phone pressed to Jeff's ear.

"I have good news for you, Sergeant," Jeff said. "Come hear it—and bring two pairs of the city's best handcuffs with you. It's been a busy night."

STRANGLEHOLD

Christopher Anvil

Stellar Scout James Connely and Sector Chief of Scouts Gregory MacIntyre sat by the communicator, with the star charts spread out around them, and considered their predicament.

From the nearby communicator came a recorded voice: "Don't land. Keep off this planet. For everybody's sake as well as your own. Stay away."

MacIntyre growled, "Nice and informative, isn't it? What's wrong with the planet? Earthquakes? Plague? Carnivores? Vermin? You'd think anyone that gets in trouble and throws up a warning satellite would have the wit to say what the trouble is. But no, all we're told is, 'Don't land. For everybody's sake. Stay away.' A lot of help *that* is."

A rapid sequence of beeps came in, and Connely said, "Well, at least we know it's Barnes." Barnes was a stellar scout who'd been missing well over a year, and MacIntyre recognized his voice.

"Yeah," said MacIntyre sourly. "It's his voice, all right, and it's his recognition signal, but he doesn't seem to have been using his brain. The thing is just a little miniature warning satellite. If he'd only followed standard procedure, he'd have put a full-size signal satellite in orbit before he went down there. Then he could have got a full-length message started back through channels the same day he got in trouble. But this thing leaves us tied in knots."

Connely nodded moodily.

MacIntyre went on, "A message like this should be relayed, without delay, straight to our HQ in this sector. That's routine. The booby trap in the setup is that the Stellar Scout Department is a part of Planetary Development Administration. This

137

message will get distributed like lightning, so many copies to Planet Certification, so many to the Colonization Council, so many to Central Records, *and one copy to Space Force HQ in this sector.*"

"Yeah," said Connely. "I see what you mean."

"Good," said MacIntyre. "Then maybe you can help me figure it out. There are only two possibilities. Either what is on that planet *is* as dangerous as it sounds, or it isn't. In either case, you have to bear in mind that the Space Force and Planetary Development do not have the sweetest possible relationship with each other. If the planet *is* dangerous, it's going to look suspicious that I am out here. A sector chief hardly ever goes out on a scouting trip. I'm only here because I got tangled up with a new piece of equipment, and couldn't get loose before the ship took off. That's the truth. But it's an unlikely kind of an accident, and nobody's going to believe it. Word is going to get around that I *knew* there was trouble here, and came out to check before sending in the alarm. That's a serious offense. There will be an investigation. Regardless how the investigation turns out, the Space Force will get considerable mileage out of it."

Connely nodded. "There's no doubt about that."

"Or," said MacIntyre, "alternatively, the place may turn out *not* to be dangerous. Nevertheless, the Space Force is going to rush here all set up for a fight. Big cruisers will be roaring all over the place. Monitors will be orbiting the planet ready to knock off anything that tries to get away. They'll have the solar beam reflectors all set up ready, in case of trouble. Now, if they get all that stuff up out here, and it turns out there's nothing more dangerous on the planet than a chipmunk, Planetary Development Administration is going to be in a mess."

Connely nodded exasperatedly. In his mind, he could hear the wise commentators, and see the glaring headlines: "NO EMERGENCY" "PDA WRONG AGAIN" "SPACE FORCE CHARGES BUNGLING."

Connely could also see the newssheets that would pop out of innumerable printers in countless homes as hurried husbands bolted breakfast and read: ". . . Why was a PDA sector chief present at the scene of this latest bungling? Why does a mess like this follow right on the heels of the expensive uproar off Cygnes VI, and the disaster on Bemus III? Why must the public pay through the nose for the endless bickering and backbiting between these two monster organizations Planetary Development and the Space Force? Who is responsible? Careful analysis of the power struggle that took place at Cygnes showed without question that the local PDA official tried to mousetrap his opposite number in the Space Force. In this present instance, we actually find a high official of Planetary Development right on the spot, officiating as the misleading report was sent in . . ."

The communicator beeped again, and said:

"Don't land. Keep off this planet. For everybody's sake as well as your own. Stay away."

MacIntyre swore. "All right, Con. You see the problem. What's your solution?"

Connely shrugged. "I'm no politician, Mac. But as far as I can see, once we relay that warning, the mud hits the fan. After that business on Cygnes, everybody's a little—tense."

"Yeah," growled MacIntyre.

"On the other hand," said Connely tentatively, "regulations say we've *got* to relay that message." He looked at MacIntyre meaningfully. "As soon as we *hear* it, that is."

"Hm-m-m," said MacIntyre thoughtfully.

The two men looked at each other.

"Of course," said MacIntyre, "if we'd had the communicator . . . say . . . disassembled when we approached the planet, we wouldn't have heard the message."

"No," said Connely. "That's right. The message wasn't sent out till our approach triggered off the satellite."

"And then," said MacIntyre, "with our communicator out of order, there'd be no *need* to relay the message."

"Of course not," Connely agreed. "We couldn't relay it if we didn't hear it. That's common sense."

The communicator said loudly, "Don't land. Keep off this planet. For everybody's sake as well as your own. Stay away."

MacIntyre said tentatively, "Con, does the reception seem a little rough to you, as if something's going out of whack?"

"Hm-m-m," said Connely, "now that you mention it, it probably wouldn't do any harm if we took a glance at the inside of the thing, would it?"

"An ounce of prevention," said MacIntyre piously, "is worth a pound of cure. Now, let me help you get that inspection cover off."

Several minutes later, parts of the communicator were spread out generously over Connely's non-regulation gray rug.

"Probably," said MacIntyre, "when we land on this planet, just for safety's sake we ought to orbit an extra-powerful signal satellite. Then, at the mere touch of a button in the ship here, we could relay any warning—if, that is—any small warning satellite should happen to be up here. And meanwhile, if we didn't cancel it periodically, the satellite would send out its emergency call."

"Good idea," said Connely. He glanced at the clouded blue and green planet in the viewscreen. "Of course, it doesn't *look* dangerous."

"No," said MacIntyre. "And it probably isn't, either."

"Still, it's a good idea," said Connely. He went off to take care of it, relieved at the thought that the two monster bureaucracies were not about to come together in a head-on clash with him in the middle. Now it might be possible to get down to business.

A little later, they started down to the planet.

On their way down, they noted a number of small isolated villages on the screen, and a few fair-sized, medieval-looking cities widely scattered along the seacoast. Then Connely brought the ship down on a stretch of level grassland several dozen miles from a village built near the edge of a forest. His idea was to get a quiet look at the planet, and the natives, by sending out a few probes. Meanwhile, if there was any danger, it could hardly sneak up on the ship across that expanse of level land, and the detectors would spot anything airborne.

The ship had hardly settled down, however, when there was a noise in the corridor, and a yellow warning light began to flash. This yellow warning light told of activity by the Intru-Grab, a device designed to seize intruders, and installed in the corridor, near the inner air-lock door. So far, Connely had had nothing but trouble with the IntruGrab. Now, he looked out in the corridor to see its big globe halfway between ceiling and floor, and its metallic arms ranging far up and down the corridor.

Connely walked to the cross-corridor, saw nothing there, and decided that the IntruGrab had suffered a malfunction. He was happy to see that so far, at least, it made no effort to stuff him into the globe; but the metal arms snaking through the air around him were beginning to make him uneasy.

He was about to go back to the control room when he noticed a piece of roughly woven orange cloth on the floor of the corridor. He glanced around, wondering where that had come from, and bent to look at it.

This changed his angle of vision so that a glimpse of reflected light further up the corridor caught his attention. He stepped aside, to see, lying on the deck, a short, well-balanced dagger with no guard, and a thin double-edged blade that had been sharpened almost to a needle point. The lower third of the blade was snapped off, and lay close by. Frowning, Connely straightened. He'd had no such knife on board before, and the cloth, too, was strange. It followed that they must have come from outside. But the air lock was still shut.

Uneasily, Connely glanced around.

There was no one in sight in the corridor, but now from the direction of the control room came heavy breathing and a furious thumping sound. Connely dodged past the angled reinforcing members, and looked into the control room.

MacIntyre, a savage expression on his face, came down with both heels on a thing like a length of dull-green two-inch rope. Connely realized with a start that this was a snake, about four feet long. Just as he realized this, he felt a sensation much as if a feather pillow had been tossed lightly against his back. Something clattered to the floor. There was a scuffling behind him, and across the control room, the familiar yellow warning light began to flash. Connely turned, to see the IntruGrab's metal arms snatch up a gray-cloaked and hooded figure, which vanished in midair before it reached the globe. Just then, there was a grunt from MacIntyre, and the green snake went flying past Connely down the corridor. Three of the IntruGrab's metal arms grabbed the snake before it hit the floor, and stuffed it into the globe.

A flicker of reflected light caught Connely's attention, and he saw lying in the corridor another dagger just like the one that had hit his helmet earlier. This one, however, was not broken. Connely looked around for the thing that had caused the sensation of a pillow hitting his back, and then remembered that he was wearing a new item of equipment called "reflex clothing." This, like the IntruGrab, had been forced on him by MacIntyre, who firmly believed in new and modern equipment—the newer and more modern, the better.

Connely put his fist out, and punched himself in the stomach. His clothing stiffened as he hit it, distributing the force of the blow so that he felt only a light push over the front of his body. The fabric of his sleeve, however, also stiffened, to drag back against his arm, so that he found it impossible to strike as quickly as he intended. It occurred to Connely that it would be a good thing if he never had to move fast while wearing "reflex clothing."

MacIntyre was by now looking down the corridor, massaging his throat. "That snake," he said, "was a constrictor. Did you have any snakes or snakes' eggs in the storeroom?"

"No," said Connely. "And I didn't have any daggers or hooded men in the storeroom, either." He described what had happened, and MacIntyre scowled.

"Maybe there was something to what Barnes said, after all."

"Yes, and it explains why he didn't try to say just *what* the trouble was. How would he describe this?"

Connely went into the control room, and, just in case there should be large-scale trouble outside, he pushed down the lever that put the battle-computer in control of the ship. He was thinking as he did this that a planet as backward as this one appeared to be probably couldn't endanger the ship itself, and probably he and MacIntyre would know in time if it happened. But it was best to be on the safe side.

As soon as the lever was pushed all the way down, however, the gravitors gave a howling whine, the accelerometer needle whipped around its dial, and the scene on the outside viewscreen jumped backwards and melted into a blur. The communications screen cut into the battle-control circuit, and lit up to show the green image of the ship hurtling toward a blocky turreted structure like a medieval castle. From this structure, the battle screen showed peculiar wavy lines and ghostly whitish blurs moving out toward the ship. From the ship, in turn, a set of yellow missile tracks, and dazzling bolts from fusion guns slammed out at the massive structure. As the ship flashed past, Connely quickly reset the viewscreen. He saw walls and towers erupt in boiling clouds of dirt and masonry. The ship now flipped end-for-end, with a tortured whine from the gravitors, raced back, and hit the remains of the structure a second time on the way past. The ship then landed, in almost the same spot where they had set down originally.

Connely, dumbfounded, looked at MacIntyre. MacIntyre pulled his jaw shut, and glanced at Connely with a blank expression. Connely shook his head, studied the viewscreen, and was rewarded by the sight of an empty expanse of grassland. Thinking it might be possible to get a better view from one of the ship's upper turrets, Connely went up a ladder, and slid back the armor plating from the transparent dome.

A thing about eighty feet long, with teeth as big as elephant's tusks, sprang at the ship. A snake shaped like a boa constrictor, and about the size of a sea serpent, thrust its snout at Connely like a battering ram.

Connely almost fell down the ladder in his haste to get out of the turret. He only barely had the presence of mind to hit the switch that would throw the armor back over the turret. He sprang to the controls, and then it dawned on him that the battle-computer would long since have finished off any such things as he had seen. And if it hadn't, the sheer weight of the blows would be knocking the ship around by this time.

He glanced at the viewscreen and saw merely the empty expanse of grassland. He stared at this a moment, then went back up the ladder and pulled the armor away from the turret again. The ground outside was now acrawl with waves of spiders the size of a man's hand, that climbed up on the ship and began to spin a web of white strands from ship to ground, fastening the ship down with a thick white membrane that grew thicker and tougher as he watched.

Connely automatically reached for the hand controls of the fusion gun in the turret, and then paused. He climbed down, and readjusted the viewscreen, which showed him the same view of empty grassland. He climbed up and looked out the turret. He saw big whitish sheets and cables now covering the ship, and being drawn taut by other cables that ran off to the side. As he watched, the hull of the ship began to warp and buckle.

Connely dropped down the ladder and sprang to the viewscreen. There was nothing but empty grassland. He realized suddenly that there had been no feeling of motion, and no sound from the plates of the ship. If the ship were being squeezed like that, there would be movement, and loud creaks and groanings from the bending metal.

MacIntyre, who'd been watching with growing amazement as Connely hurtled up and down the ladder, said abruptly, "No offense, Con, but would you mind telling me what the devil you're doing?"

"Go up to the turret and take a look," said Connely.

MacIntyre grunted and went up the ladder. An instant later, his voice carried down from above, and he shot down the ladder to make a flying jump for the control board.

Connely leaned casually against a bulkhead in the control room, and watched as MacIntyre grabbed at the controls, then froze halfway, and stared at the viewscreen. He shifted views several times, then glanced at Connely, turned and went back up the ladder. While he was up there, Connely walked back into the corridor, to see if the second knife that had been thrown at him was still there. He found it lying where he had seen it before, and noted again that it was a very narrow-bladed knife, apparently balanced especially for throwing, and designed to penetrate flesh with the slightest effort.

There was a faint hum as the armor slid back over the turret, then MacIntyre was standing beside Connely, who straightened up from the knife, and said, "The more I see of this planet, Mac, the more I have to agree with Barnes."

"Yes," said MacIntyre. "Me, too. And speaking of Barnes, I wonder where he landed?"

"I don't know," said Connely, "but we ought to be able to find his ship. And we might just as well start looking now."

MacIntyre nodded. His face had an unusually thoughtful expression as they walked back into the control room, and Connely lifted ship.

Once they had a reasonable altitude, Connely released several probes that flashed away on predetermined courses. As the ship streaked north, more probes dropped out. A little over an hour had gone by when a red light lit up on a small panel, to show that Probe 6 had spotted something that matched the taped description of Barnes' ship. Connely sent out the signal to recall the others, and then studied on a small auxiliary screen the image sent back by Probe 6.

The country where Barnes' ship had set down was rolling grassland, much like the place where Connely had landed.

Here, too, there was a village a few dozen miles away, which suggested that Barnes, like Connely, had hoped to take a quiet look at the people of the planet, but didn't want to frighten them away, or make a sudden dramatic appearance that would upset their lives. Connely smiled sourly at this last thought. The native inhabitants of this planet were apparently well able to take care of themselves.

As Connely was thinking this, the gravitors whined, and another massive structure of high slit-windowed towers and walls appeared on the screen. This one was made entirely of black stone, and as it enlarged on the screen, it rapidly took on the brooding, foreboding aspect of a vulture perched on a tree limb. A sense of dread gripped Connely. The outlines of the control room seemed to waver and run around him, like a sketch drawn in washable ink and placed under water. Then abruptly the illusion was gone, and the outside viewscreen showed a towering column of dust and debris rolling skyward where the structure had stood. The sense of dread was gone as if it had never been.

MacIntyre said suddenly, "Look at this screen!"

Connely glanced at the auxiliary screen, to see a ragged scarecrow figure dancing and waving its arms by Barnes' ship.

"That," said MacIntyre, "looks like Barnes, to me."

When Connely brought his ship down, the figure was still there, and now they could see that Barnes' eyes were tightly shut. The wild waving of his arms that they had taken for happiness at the thought of being rescued turned out instead to be a violent shooing motion, as if Barnes were trying to warn them away.

Connely said, "Before we open the hatch, it might be worthwhile to see what this place looks like from the turret."

"Yes," growled MacIntyre, studying Barnes' thin worn face. "Meanwhile, I'll run out the loudspeaker and pickup and see if he can tell us anything."

Connely climbed into the turret, ran back the protecting armor, and looked at a scene out of a madman's nightmare. The rolling grassland, which showed up as an empty stretch of ground on the viewscreen, appeared to be filled with a maze of tall moss-covered stone walls cut with large rectangular holes like window-openings and doorways. In the oversize doorways lay huge snakes, big crabs with oversize claws, and semifluid horrors like giant jellyfish. The window-openings were closed by big spider webs, or partially blocked by gray cone-shaped nests of hornets and wasps. A brief glance was enough for Connely, who looked away before the scene etched itself any more sharply in his memory.

From below came MacIntyre's voice, as he spoke into the loudspeaker.

"Can you hear me all right, Barnes?"

"Go away," came a rough voice. "Get out of here before they get you, too."

"Can you get around to our air lock?"

"Are you insane? I can't go anywhere through this stuff."

"What's wrong? Why can't you get here?"

Connely said, "He can't, Mac. There's an illusion of big walls, boa constrictors, giant crabs . . . Open your eyes on that sight, and you'd be afraid to take three steps."

"It's more," came Barnes' voice. "It's not just a visual illusion. It's tactile as well. You can touch it, feel it, smell it. It can grab you, block you, flatten you. Whatever you do, don't leave your ship or open up the air lock."

"What's wrong with your ship?" said MacIntyre. "Can't you go back inside, and lock up?"

Barnes gave a short laugh. "My ship? Where is my ship? Do you see it?"

MacIntyre hesitated an instant. "It's right behind you," he said.

"You see it?"

"Yes, in the viewscreen."

"Ah, in the viewscreen," said Barnes. Then he added matter-of-factly, "Yes, I suppose the viewscreen picks up the basic physical reality, and doesn't show the rest. But to me, there's a low hut back here, and that's all. You say that's the ship?"

MacIntyre said, his voice somewhat desperate, "The ship's right behind you."

"*You* say so," said Barnes musingly, "but what's reality, anyway? Only an illusion that fits all the senses. How do I know what's true for you will be true for me?"

"Truth's truth," said MacIntyre sharply.

"It may be so on Earth," said Barnes. "It isn't so here. Truth is the image imposed by the stronger mind on unformed matter. Truth changes. It's changed several times since I've been here. Once, while it was in flux, I got up a satellite. At least, I think I did."

"You did," said MacIntyre. "Now stop this nonsense about truth, and get ready to climb into the ship. I'm going to move over closer to you."

The ship lifted and moved gradually closer to Barnes. Connely looked warily out the turret, his eyes only partly open, to see the apparently solid stone walls seem to compress and slide around the ship as it moved forward. Barnes came into view, and behind him, a low thatched hut. The ship stopped within several yards of Barnes, and MacIntyre said, "Con, are we close enough?"

"It looks so to me," said Connely.

"O.K., Barnes," said MacIntyre. "Climb in."

Barnes stepped forward with his hands outstretched and his eyes tight shut. He came in under the curve of the ship, out of Connely's range of vision. Connely heard him say wonderingly, "I feel it."

A few minutes later, there was the sound of the outer airlock door coming open. Then the sound of it going shut. MacIntyre said, "Can you hear me, Barnes?"

"Yes," said Barnes. "I hear you."

"I'm going to douse you with disinfectant. It's new stuff, and it's death on germs, but try not to swallow any of it."

"All right."

Connely slid the armor back over the turret, and dropped down to the control room. He snapped off the microphone connection to the wall speaker in the air lock.

"Are we *sure* this is Barnes?" he said. "From what I've seen of this planet, I'd hate to take a disguised native on board."

"You've got a point there," said MacIntyre. "He *looks* like Barnes. But, how—"

Connely nodded sympathetically as MacIntyre looked perplexed.

"Well," said MacIntyre, "we don't have records of fingerprints or retinal patterns handy, but I *may* be able to find out if that isn't Barnes." He snapped on the microphone, and said in an excessively cheerful voice, "You getting a good washdown in there?"

A gargling sound came back at him. A few moments later, Barnes' voice said, "Ye gods, what awful stuff!"

"It's the new disinfectant I was telling you about," said

MacIntyre. He added positively, "It's much better than what we used before."

There was a little pause. Then Barnes' voice said shortly, "Yeah."

"When we get back," said MacIntyre, "I'm going to completely refit your ship. The fact that you couldn't handle the situation here shows how out-of-date your equipment is."

There was a considerable silence, then Barnes' voice said, "Listen, Mac, I appreciate your getting me out of that mess. But before we go through that business about refitting the ship again, would you mind letting me out of this air lock? Your improved disinfectant is eating patches of skin off my feet."

"I'll give you another rinse," said MacIntyre. Then he snapped off the air-lock speaker and glanced at Connely. "I can't swear that's no native. But he sounds like an Interstellar Scout to me."

Connely nodded agreement, and went to get a fresh uniform for Barnes.

About fifteen minutes later, the lanky Barnes was slumped in Connely's control seat, his arms and legs jutting out of the too-small uniform. Barnes looked worn, thin, and somewhat out of sorts after being snatched up by the IntruGrab and put into the globe with the dead snake.

"Listen," said MacIntyre pugnaciously, "*I* spent the first part of the trip in there. If *you* can't take a few minutes of it, that's tough."

"Go on outside for a few months first," said Barnes irritatedly. "See how you like it then."

"If you'd used your equipment properly," said MacIntyre, "you probably wouldn't have got into that mess in the first place."

Barnes glanced at Connely. Connely had never met Barnes before, but in that moment they seemed to be brothers. Connely said sympathetically, "What happened?"

Barnes drew a deep breath. After a moment, he said, "Well, to begin with, I took a rough survey of the planet, and decided it was harmless. I tested the air, ran through all the usual checks, and then I was *convinced* it was harmless. I should have put a signal satellite in orbit, but I only had the new model, and for some fool reason, it wouldn't transmit.

Still, I wanted to look at the place. So, like a jackass, after I came down I got out of the ship to take a walk around."

MacIntyre growled, "Unarmed?"

"Not, not unarmed. Among other things, I had on your good-for-nothing reflex helmet and clothing. I also had on your worthless M1-X Gazelle Boots, and in addition I had your new Self-Draw Matter-Displacement gun strapped to my waist."

"Then," said MacIntyre, looking puzzled, "you were ready for anything."

"Except the weapons," said Barnes.

MacIntyre frowned. "What weapons?"

"My *own* weapons," said Barnes angrily.

There was a lengthy silence as the two men glared at each other. Connely leaned back, ready to enjoy the spectacle of somebody else fighting with MacIntyre for a change. After a brief glaring contest, Barnes said furiously, "Why don't you try all these things out first, prove them, and go slow about putting every maniacal contraption that comes along into the ships?"

"Join the Space Force," snapped MacIntyre.

Barnes turned red, sucked in a deep breath, and rose half out of the chair. MacIntyre balled his fists and leaned forward. Connely glanced around nervously at all the instruments that might get smashed up.

Apparently, the same thought occurred to Barnes and MacIntyre, who glanced pugnaciously around, and then by mutually graduated stages, that were a little hard for a bystander to follow, slowly subsided into their seats.

Connely tried to get the conversation back on its tracks. "What happened after you went out of the ship?"

Barnes blinked, and looked around as if he'd forgotten where he was.

"Oh," he said. "Well, till I got about thirty feet from the ship, *nothing* happened. Then there was a growl, I turned around, and a thing much like the Hound of the Baskervilles, was coming straight for me, from the direction of the ship."

"What did you do?"

"The first thing I did," said Barnes, "was to make the mistake of starting to reach for my gun. *Bang!* It slammed out of the holster into my hand and fired itself. The animal was almost on me by this time, and I hadn't wanted to shoot for fear I'd put a hole through the ship, which was right behind it. Rather than risk another shot, I made my second mistake, and pressed down on the toes of the Gazelle Boots, like you're supposed to if you want to get somewhere in a hurry."

Connely had never heard of Gazelle Boots before, and cast a questioning glance at MacIntyre. MacIntyre refused to meet his gaze, and looked off noncommittally at a corner of the control room. This told Connely that Gazelle Boots were one of those items on which production had been "temporarily suspended pending further study." If the boots had still been in production, MacIntyre would have looked back with stern righteousness.

Barnes said, "The left-hand boot took off in a hurry, but so did the right-hand boot. I landed flat on my back, and this animal bounded over my head. Well, I couldn't wait to get on my feet, but in my hurry, I couldn't keep from pressing down on the toes of the boots before I got up. Every time I did this, the boots went somewhere fast, and I bounced and dragged along after them. The animal's jaws were snapping shut half an inch from my face, and I was in a terrible state by the time I managed to get to my feet. I barely had the wit to press down alternately heel-and-toe, according to the directions for walking in Gazelle Boots, and then the boots really streaked out fast. But the reflex clothing froze up like cast iron every time there was any sudden stress on it, so I *couldn't* move my legs fast, and at the same time I *had* to, because of the boots."

Connely shook his head sympathetically. "Then what?"

The boots almost snapped my legs off at the ankles. I ended up on the ground again, and the monster dog was all over me. I was firing at it, and couldn't seem to hit it. Then suddenly the dog was gone, and a voice somewhere was talking some kind of foreign language. The meaning seemed to form in my head at the same time as the foreign words that I couldn't understand."

Barnes shook his head in reminiscence, and after a little silence, MacIntyre said, "What did the voice say?"

"It said, 'Why, this fellow is a mere beginner. He's got his spells crossed.'"

MacIntyre looked blank. "Did it say *'Spells'?*"

"That's what it said."

There was another silence, and then MacIntyre said, "Then what happened?"

"That was it," said Barnes. "The dog was gone. I went back to the ship and discovered that the first shot from the matter-displacement gun had taken a chunk the size of a beachball out of the outer hull and frame of the ship. Before I could repair it, everything changed to look the way it looks out there now."

Connely said, "But what happened after that? I mean, what did you do?"

"What *could* I do? Once I was stuck there, with those monstrosities staring at me from that wall, I didn't do much traveling, I can tell you that. And I couldn't work on the ship, because I couldn't see it, or feel it. Then a stream of visitors began to come, and I discovered that I was a curiosity. Some of them tried to teach me the language, which they said I had forgotten completely because of mental shock. I think they all looked over the ship while they were around, although I couldn't see the ship myself, so I couldn't be sure. Pretty soon, an argument started between a couple of factions of these visitors.

"As nearly as I could figure it out, one side claimed that I had made the ship and other devices myself, subconsciously, but didn't have the conscious skill to operate them. The other faction claimed that the whole thing was a hoax, engineered by Aloom, or someone with a similar name. They quizzed me on the subject, and when I learned enough of the language to tell them the plain truth, they had a big laugh over it.

"Then each side claimed that what I'd said proved their theory. One side claimed that it showed that I was a basically irrational sort of person who relied on intuition rather than reason, and as everyone knew this meant that I would tap the subconscious more easily. The other side that the illusion was too detailed to be the work of an irrational untrained mind. The whole illusion must have been impressed on me from outside. This argument got hotter and hotter, and the insults flew back and forth, and all I can say is, I'm glad they didn't forget to feed me now and then."

MacIntyre said, "They had a fight?"

Barnes nodded. "There was thunder and lightning—or seemed to be—earthquakes, tornadoes, and all kinds of natural disasters. The sky was black for a solid week one time. I don't know how to describe it. At any rate, now and then things would go into a state of flux, the walls would seem to run like glue, and then they would form again with a different arrangement. Not *much* different, but enough so you could notice it. I think what it meant was that one side had wrested mental control away from the other side. While this was happening, I could get a wavering view of the ship and grassland around it."

"In other words," said MacIntyre, frowning, "their illusions canceled each other out?"

"Maybe," said Barnes. "Or maybe, when they nullified each other, I was able to impress my own picture of reality on the scene."

MacIntyre shook his head violently. "It wasn't all illusion. Truth is things are as God sees them."

"Sure," said Barnes, "but can we see things that way?"

The discussion was making Connely uneasy. To try to get it back into some familiar channel, he said, "We had a few strange experiences ourselves, right after we landed, and before we put the battle-computer in control." He told Barnes about the snake and the dagger, and added, "It seems like a fair conclusion that the people on this planet have highly developed psychic powers."

"I suppose that's it," said Barnes. "Whatever they've got, it's no fun to tangle with it."

Connely looked at MacIntyre. "What do we do about a planet like this?"

"The first thing is to get off it. See if we can drag Barnes' ship up with a gravitor beam, and then put some space between the planet and us." He frowned as he said this, and it occurred to Connely that MacIntyre's problems would not be over once they got off the planet.

MacIntyre put this into words himself after they'd got Barnes' ship up, and were in orbit well out from the planet. "This," he said sourly, "is a real, first-class mess."

Connely nodded, but Barnes said, "Why? It looks like a simple 'No Landing-No Colonizing' job to me. We put the warning satellites in orbit, notify Planet Certification, and let it go at that."

"Fine," said MacIntyre. "And just what *reason* do we give?"

Barnes opened his mouth, then shut it again. "Hm-m-m," he said. "Well, that is a problem."

"The authorities," said MacIntyre, "don't believe in psychic phenomena. Here we've got a whole planet full of psychic phenomena. Now, what do we do?"

Barnes said hesitantly, "You're a sector chief, Mac. They'd believe *you*, wouldn't they?"

"They'd believe I was in need of a rest cure. I wouldn't believe this myself, if I hadn't seen it."

The three men were silent a moment, then Connely said, "Suppose we brought back proof?"

"*What* proof? The viewscreen didn't show what we saw outside. Therefore the records won't either."

"All right. But what about the snakes, the knives, and the man that appeared in the corridor out there? *They* were real. And we've got the dead snake and the knives."

"Sure, but how do we prove where they came from? Just suppose we had visual records of the whole thing. It *still* wouldn't prove anything to anyone else, because it could have been faked. And if we got a record that *couldn't* possibly be faked by present techniques, it would merely show that we'd developed a clever new technique in advance of the times. The only way that we could convince the authorities would be to bring them here. How do we do *that?*"

The minutes crept past as the three men groped for an answer to this problem. In due time they ate, and then retired to Connely's small cabin, just off the control room. MacIntyre settled in the armchair, Connely sat down at the desk and tilted back the chair, and Barnes stretched out on the bunk. Time crept past. Connely, unable to bridge the gap between unyielding authority and unblinkable fact, found himself drawing a sketch of maniacs gibbering from behind iron bars. Suddenly, as he looked at this sketch, it seemed to mean something. He pulled over another piece of paper and began to write:

TOP SECRET

To: Sector GHQ
Planetary Development Authority
Subject: Acute Infectious Insanity.
Sirs:
We enclose herewith the official logs of Stellar Scout

Ships 82 and 87. On the dates mentioned in the logs, the following events took place:

a) Scout Ship 82, after a routine planetary inspection, was landed by Stellar Scout J. R. Barnes, on the planet identified in the coded data sheet enclosed. Taking normal precautions in the absence of any visible danger, Barnes left his ship to observe the planet at first hand. Though thoroughly experienced in his work, and well armed, he experienced the following subjective phenomena: 1) attack by a large dog-like animal, which was unaffected by Barnes' weapons, and which later vanished; 2) a voice, though no visible person was present; 3) alteration of his surroundings, the ship becoming invisible; 4) visitation by mysterious local inhabitants, who became engaged in a violent controversy caused by his (Barnes') presence; 5) imprisonment by the said local inhabitants.

b) Stellar Scout Ship 87 was landed on the same planet by Stellar Scout James Connely, accompanied by Sector Chief of Scouts Gregory MacIntyre, who was on board to inspect the functioning and operation of new equipment. Although neither man left the ship at any time while on the planet, they experienced the following subjective phenomena: 1) Sector Chief MacIntyre believed himself attacked by a snake of moderate size, which attempted to choke him by constriction; 2) Stellar Scout Connely believed himself attacked twice with thrown knives; 3) both men observed, through the forward fusion turret, realistic illusions of objects, external to the ship, which did not appear on the outside viewscreen.

Full details of these occurrences are enclosed in the accompanying report.

In explanation, it is suggested that the three men were, during their landing on the planet, rendered temporarily insane by the action of some unknown highly-infectious agent or agents.

Although this condition subsided promptly upon leaving the vicinity of the planet, it is clear that the planet should not at the present time be opened to colonization and development. Warning satellites have, therefore, been put in orbit about the planet, according to the regulations concerning medically-dangerous planets.

MacIntyre read the paper carefully. "I think you've got it, Con! They can *accept* this. And, of course, once they do, they'll be bound to *investigate* it. Meanwhile, in the more complete report, we can put enough information so anyone who can understand will see what actually happened."

Barnes read the paper and nodded approval. "Better that *we* suggest we were temporarily nuts than that *they* think of it."

Connely said, "It's too bad we can't just say what actually happened."

MacIntyre nodded. "Still, it's always this way. We've got a science-based civilization, and if psychic phenomena occur, they're either rationalized away, or denied outright. It's as if science were somehow *allergic* to psychic phenomena, like a hay-fever sufferer who can't stand ragweed. Although why that should be, I don't know."

Barnes said, "I can answer that one, Mac. When I was stuck on that planet, as I said, some of the natives tried to 'reteach' me their language, which they thought I must have forgotten. I got good enough at it so that they could understand me, and I tried to explain what had actually happened. One day, they told me how they *knew* my explanation couldn't be the true one."

"How?"

"Well, they said, at the base of my argument was this thing I called 'science.' And 'science' they said, was a transparent impossibility, because it was built on an assumption that was provably false."

MacIntyre frowned. "What assumption is that?"

"That experiments can be repeated, and give the same results at different times and for different investigators."

"They don't believe that?"

"No, and what's more, to *prove* it wasn't true, they followed my instructions and got some copper wire and magnets, had a small compass made, and then passed the magnetic field through the wire, using the compass to detect the induced electric current. They carried out a series of experiments, in which the current flowed *in either direction or not at all,* as they wished."

MacIntyre whistled. Then he said, "Oh, you mean, they made that *illusion.*"

"I don't think it *was* an illusion, Mac. I think their psychic control was strong enough to reverse a weak current flow caused by a weak electromotive force. But regardless whether it was an illusion or not, the result was the same: to make a perfectly good experiment worthless. Can you imagine trying to develop science on a planet where, so far as you can tell with your senses, the same experiment gives you one result on Tuesday, and another on Wednesday, depending on your own or somebody else's attitude? On this basis, science could never even get started."

"Yes," said Connely, "but wait a minute. The whole point of science is that the experimenter is *disinterested*. He comes to Nature, and puts the question. Whatever answer Nature gives, he accepts, and then goes on from there. These natives of yours didn't have the right scientific attitude."

"I'll say they didn't," said Barnes. "They *willed* the current to go one way or the other."

"All right. Get them to suspend use of their psychic powers, hold the right mental attitude, and experiments will work for them, too."

"Sure," said Barnes. He glanced around at some inexpensive novels Connely had brought along, pulled one out, opened it, and handed it to Connely. He put his finger beside one of the lines and said, "Look at that."

Connely glanced at it:

". . . at him furiously. She cried out, 'If you do, I'll . . .'"

Connely nodded. "I see it. What of it?"

"Look at it. *But don't read any of it.*"

Connely tried it, and said, "The only way I can do that is to unfocus my eyes. Otherwise, if I see it, I've read it."

Barnes nodded and closed the book. "There's the trouble the natives have. Once you do something automatically, how do you *not* do it? They've probably been exerting psychic influence all their lives. They can no more suspend it and take up a proper scientific attitude than we can glance at a line of print without reading it."

MacIntyre said, "Speaking of a 'proper scientific attitude,' I have doubts that many of our own scientists are 'disinterested observers,' anyway. It strikes me there wouldn't be much experimenting done if they were."

"Maybe so," said Barnes. "But that doesn't matter so long as they don't have, or for whatever reason don't exert, enough psychic influence to affect the result. And the schools, with their standard experiments, would tend to screen out at the beginning those who didn't get the usual results, for psychic reasons or otherwise."

"So," said MacIntyre frowning, "what we end up with is that a scientific civilization just naturally inhibits the development of psychic phenomena, and a 'psychic' civilization just naturally inhibits the development of science. So whichever one gets a big enough lead tends to get a stranglehold on the other one."

"Right," said Barnes.

MacIntyre sat silent for a long moment, thinking it over. Finally he said, "Well, all we can do is send in that report. But first, we'd better get your ship fixed, and get started back."

Barnes got up. "The sooner we get out of here, the better, as far as I'm concerned."

They went into the control room, where Connely took a long look at the viewscreen. "Boy, whoever gets put in charge of investigating 'acute infectious insanity' has some jolts in front of him."

Barnes nodded. "But bear in mind, down there they're just as bigoted and pig-headed about science being impossible, as people are elsewhere about psychic phenomena being impossible."

Connely said, "And that will just make it all the worse when the two sets of know-alls come together."

"It will be a real mess, all right," said Barnes.

MacIntyre was beginning to smile. "Oh, I don't know about that. It strikes me as plain justice. You could even make a saying out of it."

"Such as what?" said Connely, looking doubtful.

MacIntyre smiled.

"One good bigot," he said, "deserves another."

THE MESSAGE

Piers Anthony and Frances Hall

"Manuel Ramirez, you deserve to be kicked by a mule for your stupidity!" the young man exclaimed, venting his Latin heritage upon himself.

It was his own fault. He had not survived his childhood in the savage gutters of Juarez without many times learning the lesson of appearances. Now he was caught in a trap—clean and clean shaven in his presentable clothes, black hair slicked back—and two hundred solars wadded into his back pocket.

Even without the money, never should he have left his knife at home. Fluency was all very well; but his skills with the tongue had now led him into the fatal error of overconfidence. True, one does not go armed to the University Registrar's office; neither does one present oneself there without the necessary fee. These are laws of civilization. But also, one does not cut through an unlit alley alone. This is the law of survival. Exultation is no excuse for carelessness, in Juarez.

Two men blocked the farther exit, their dark shapes silhouetted against the blinking neons of the saloons in the thoroughfare beyond. Manuel did not need to look back to know that there were two more behind him; he read it easily in the confident stance of those ahead.

"These hombres have you in the sack, Manuel," he told himself. "You stand now an excellent chance for the knife in the gut, or the brains splattered upon the pavement. Before or after they obtain your two hundred. Or perhaps during the transaction. Soon your solars and your future will be gone . . ."

There was no place to hide; the hombres were already watching him, sure of their mark. He could not run, nor could he hope to fight; there were too many, and they would know

159

*their business. Yet it seemed such a great waste. By centavo,
by peso, solar by solar, Manuel had earned the money, as
bouncer in the saloons of Juarez—where a glib tongue often
made cruder measures unnecessary—and at other odd jobs.
He had saved the solars by ruthlessly denying himself all but
basic necessities. If he did not register now, this evening, his
place would be taken by the next applicant in line and he
would not be able to move up again before he was beyond
the registration age. For space, only young men were wanted;
twenty was too old to begin the long training. There were
great numbers of applicants, all deserving; a man had to make
use of his chance when he had it, or it was lost to him forever. There was no sympathy; no excuse.*

*If he did not resist, maybe they would not kill him. Yet he
could not give up his fee. His whole meager life had been
focused on this point, this entry into the University, this
escape from the terrible squalor, this evening in the twentieth
year of his life. His money was his life. He must try to save it.*

How? There was no way. He was alone.

No way—except the unexpected. That was it.

He must put up the bluff. He must surprise them.

*Manuel quickened his pace—toward the hoods in front. He
gestured and called out, as though afraid they might not see
him.* Surprise. Put them off balance. *What he would do or say
when he reached them he did not know.*

Captain Eric Larsen of the starship *Alpha One* sat stiffly at
his desk, frowning tensely at a thin sheet of paper in his hand.
He looked up at Ramirez's entrance, and the frown was replaced by a look of chill disapproval at the brown xenologist
clad in informal whites.

Ramirez thought: *Diablo! Every inch the offended colonial,
el Capitan, here. And only yesterday I hoped he might
mellow.*

This was Larsen's first FTL command, he knew. *Alpha One*
was the first super-c ship owned by the people of Rigel,
Earth's first stellar colony. This voyage of trade was the first
one under the new ownership; it was also the first flight ever
to be scheduled from Rigel direct to the Holmen colony at
Tau Ceti. One might expect a certain reserve in a young man
carrying such responsibilities. Moreover, in mid-passage a
capsule had arrived from the Acting Executive of Rigel, and

the orders it contained the captain could only consider frivolous: The *Alpha One* must not bypass the third vertex of the stellar triangle, after all; he and his crewmen must take the *Alpha One* to Earth, there to take on a passenger for Holmen. Ramirez. All this was hardly calculated to mend the young captain's humor.

All this Ramirez had taken into account; all this he could have dealt with. But neither by tact nor diplomacy had Ramirez been able to allay the other's bitterness. He looked again at the cropped blond hair and the ice-blue eyes staring back. This rancor sprang from deeper wells than those of a disgruntled colonial whose ego had been mishandled. What had happened?

The captain shoved the paper at him. "Look this over, *Doctor* Ramirez."

The paper was very thin and dirty yellow. Both sides were filled with dots and dashes in closely packed squares. It resembled Morse code; yet the greenest com man could not have taken it for any human message. Ramirez fingered the smooth surface curiously.

This message could be, incredibly, only one thing.

"It's the Thargan code."

Captain Larsen smiled sourly. "Very good, Dr. Ramirez. *Very* good. Tell me, can you by any chance read this Thargan code? For that matter, Doctor, can you read Thargan itself?"

Ramirez ignored the baiting tone. He could not fully understand the colonial's resentment of him; but his past had schooled him in strict control. Almost unconsciously he dug a hand into his pocket. He palmed the two copper centavos and closed his hand about them until their edges bit painfully into the flesh. Until such understanding came, he must refuse to be provoked. He answered evenly: "I can make out something of both, Señor Capitan—"

"*Something* of both?" Larsen interrupted dryly. "Perhaps I misunderstood. I was under the impression that my ship had been pre-empted by the author of the first authoritative dictionary of Thargan."

Laboriously, Ramirez corrected the multiple confusion. "Getting this Earthman to Holmen at the earliest possible moment was a matter of some importance, Capitan, and no other ship could be readied in time. *Alpha One* was already en route to Tau Ceti."

"So Mother Earth commands us to make a detour—to backtrack. Earth just can't get used to not commanding the comings and goings of every piece of intersteller hardware she chooses to need at the moment, whether she owns it or not."

"It did not seem too much to ask that a small detour be made—for which Earth, I believe, paid very well."

Larsen snorted. "A *small* detour? We had to turn back to Earth when we were a third of the way to Tau. We have lost a full two weeks, Doctor."

Ramirez continued: "As for the dictionary—of course we do not know that it is authoritative. The Thargs doubtless have far superior references for their own use . . ."

Another derisive snort.

"But in any case, I did not author it. I *edited* it, using the lists and notes compiled by a Señor Kelly of Holmen."

"You know Kelly?"

"I met him when I visited Holmen three years ago—but that was before this visit from the Thargs."

Before this visit. But not before a previous encampment by intelligent aliens on Holmen. The deserted remnants of this encampment were what Ramirez had gone to Holmen to examine.

Holmen, the sole planet of Tau Ceti, almost twelve light-years from Sol, was Earth's second—and farther—extrasolar colony. The colony was minuscule—some nine hundred people —but thriving. To the Holmenians, two years before, fate had assigned the doubtful honor of first actual contact with the aliens.

The first meetings had gone well. A vast slick block of a ship came down out of a gray sky one fall day, and metallically black humanoids walked out of it. The visitors' shapes were subtly . . . wrong. At a distance they appeared oddly unsolid. This was an illusion; they were quite sturdy.

The aliens seemed more surprised at the meeting than were the people of Holmen, and eager to get acquainted. Communication of sorts was soon worked out. The aliens stayed.

And stayed.

They were neither overly friendly nor overtly hostile. A vague unease began to grow among the Holmenian colonists

—nine hundred men, women and children isolated twelve light-years from Sol.

The Thargs were adept; they quickly picked up human words, but seemed inept at conveying their own. A young colonist named Kelly, with a knack for linguistics, had labored for months compiling a long but far from adequate list of words and concepts, and had sent it to Earth at his first chance. That had been many months ago. Ramirez, on Earth, had taken over the lists and pored over them night and day.

Was it possible to derive any basic knowledge of the Thargs through a close study of their language? Ramirez thought so. As in human languages, something of their world, their history, their values—their cultural essence—must inhere in their speech. And in their artifacts.

But Thargan artifacts were absent. Even reports of them were hard come by. Someone had taken a picture of the Thargan ship. Compared to its skyscraper size and slick lines, Sol's FTL models were crude and lumbering; but no human being had stepped inside the Thargan ship. However, the Thargs displayed their gadgets freely to their hosts.

They were ingenious, the gadgets. They seemed almost to have intelligences of their own; but no human being seemed ever to have examined their working parts. Oddly, the Thargs showed an intrigued interest in the frankly inferior machines of the Holmenians. Why? In the face of such scanty information, man was left with their language as almost the sole clue to Thargan culture—or subculture. How typical were these visitors of their kind?

While the Thargs tarried on at Holmen, Ramirez had burned out months of his life assembling Kelly's definitions and conjectures into an intelligible grammar. He now knew the language as well as any human being; but it was what he did not know that disturbed him. He called for help, and got some.

While a study team of Sol's top men in many specialties attacked the information, Ramirez flew to Oslo. The only native Holmenian on Earth at that time was a girl named Lydia Farrell, who was finishing her senior year at the University there. She would not have seen any Thargs herself, but there might be information she had received in her letters from home.

Absorbed in the sinister riddle of the Thargs, trying to probe the unknown implications of Earth's first meeting with the alien, Ramirez had flown to Oslo completely unprepared for anything important to happen in his personal life. Then he met Lydia.

She had the grace of a nymph, she had the face of a sunny-ringleted madonna, and he realized—with a shock almost of recognition—that she was the One.

In time, the study team came up with a few probative conclusions. The Thargan ship had come from a star far more distant than any that solar ships had attempted to visit. The consensus was that their world was probably a planet of one of binary suns. Acrux, some three hundred seventy light-years from Sol, seemed most likely to be their home star.

The men of the study team sifted and sorted and programmed the computer; and Ramirez's unease spread to the others. Their information was shot through with ominous gaps, small discrepancies. They spoke to each other of cultural differences in, for example, the worth placed upon the individual; they must allow for this. Even so, "ngan" seemed to share more of the connotations of the human word "unit" than of "person." Why?

Machine culture? A hive society? No. These Thargs were highly independent. It occurred to Ramirez that such adverse connotations could be the result of words such as "ngan" being used in a slang sense; the argot, perhaps, of some particular group of Thargs; but this was only a hunch that he had no way of testing.

In any case, Earth could not take it for granted that the Thargs were friendly; even less could Holmen. Small incongruities persisted. Disturbing ones. What was it the madonna had said? (Even now it was hard to sort out the information objectively.) The Thargans had shown great interest in books on human anatomy, borrowing them from the settlement's new hospital, presumably to duplicate for their ship's records. Also, Thargs were always on hand to observe the colonists at their work and at their recreation. They passed out puzzles of various kinds, and taught them various games of mental skill —though the Thargs rarely played themselves, preferring to watch the colonists compete with each other. "It's as if they were running us all through a battery of intelligence tests," a friend had written Lydia from Holmen. "Why?"

Then there was the size of their ship. Earth's hyperdrive was complex—but fairly small. In theory, its size need not be greatly increased even on an intergalactic flight. So, it probably was not to house the drive that the Thargan ship was so large; and the Thargan crew was less than a hundred. Did the Thargs, then, carry cargo? If so, it was never unloaded. Or did they expect to return with cargo . . . ?

The Solar Government became convinced now that more, much more, must be found out about the Thargs—soon. Ramirez was commissioned to go to Holmen and find out all he could. This was the reason behind the commandeering of the *Alpha One*. Nine hundred colonists and more lived on Holmen, and the madonna was one of them; she was already en route back to her native planet when Ramirez, his heart thumping like a schoolboy's, had called to invite her to a concert, to any place that would serve as an occasion to be in her company again. Diablo! He should have guessed she would return on the only ship available for months. And she would return to an incalculable danger . . .

He must not be too late.

Larsen's heavy irony snapped Ramirez from his musings. "If the good Señor Doctor will condescend to share the message . . . ?"

"May I ask how this came into our hands, Capitan?"

"The net intercepted it forty minutes ago."

As Ramirez studied the sheet he could make out only bits and pieces at first; but his fingertips went cold, and for a moment the cabin seemed to lurch about his head. His spine stiffened. "May I see the capsule this came in?" he asked sharply.

Coldly, Larsen reached into his desk and produced it.

The Thargan artifact closely resembled the type of message capsule that was standard on Earthmade FTL ships. Like the Terran product it was of some paper-thin black metal and felt warm to his palm. At one end was a tiny drive mechanism— worthy of later study on Earth, for the Thargan ships seemed faster than Earth's FTL's, and capsules below a certain critical mass—and these were well below—were faster yet, in hyperspace. At the other end of this one was the signaling mechanism, tightly sealed in.

They could never have intercepted the capsule had it been moving at full velocity; it must have just started on its journey.

"You have complete data on this capsule's hypergeodesic, Capitan?"

"Naturally." The captain fished in the desk again and handed Ramirez a slip on which was scrawled a long series of numerals and letters. Ramirez studied them and performed some complex mental calculations. Some showed the capsule's course when intercepted; the others were a decimal translation of the destination instructions edge-coded into the capsule itself. Still another set showed the position, course, and velocity of the *Alpha One* at the time the capsule's signal was picked up.

Larsen said: "We now know their home planet, no doubt. Or will, as soon as you deign to tell—"

But Ramirez was beyond resenting or even noticing Larsen's manner. "If a quick reckoning is correct, we have been right about their home world. This capsule was on its way to Acrux."

"The message, *Doctor?*"

Ramirez could not be certain of every word; but he knew with fateful certainty that his rendering was roughly correct.

To: Commander Ahum, X-Cybernet Procurement.

From: Pulguth Bax, Active Procurer, Capt., *Moloch.*

Subject: Availability of X-Cybernet Units, Sector 3.

1. Unit supply discovered Sector 3 planet subject of previous communication.

2. The planet's entire unit supply was immobilized per schedule and has been transferred to ship's cargo holds.

3. Units in prime condition. Transfer has been accomplished with no functional impairment, but no further immobilization other than phase 2 will be risked.

4. Units will be delivered in phase 2 for processing.

"So, *now* we see why these Thargs travel about in such a giant ship!" Ramirez said under his breath.

Larsen took back the copy. "I was directed by the Acting Executive of Rigel—by special capsule, no less—to keep you fully informed of any alien life or communication encountered in that connection, and to consult with you on any matter in such connection. So, I herewith consult. Do we put this message back into the capsule and let it resume its journey, or do you want it for your collection, Doctor?"

Ramirez's face was gray. "Señor Capitan, it does not matter now about that! First we must think how we are—"

Larsen interrupted peremptorily: "I have consulted with you. I have fulfilled my obligation. You may go now, Dr. Ramirez."

Ramirez stared at the young captain. He didn't understand! "Capitan, I must tell you—"

"Doctor," Larsen said with controlled fury. "I am a fair man. I'm going to explain to you just once why your presence in my cabin is intolerable to me. Then you will leave—on your own or with help." Larsen put his hand in his jacket and withdrew a disk about the size of one of the antique dollar coins of North America. He handed it to Ramirez. "Look at it. What do you see?"

With no premonition Ramirez glanced at the disk; and held it, and stared at it. He clamped an iron control on his inner turmoil. He *must* have the captain's co-operation; and the captain must unburden himself of some venom before any information could get through to him.

"I see . . . a madonna," he said at last. "She is most lovely indeed."

Larsen reclaimed the picture, staring into its illusion of depth and life. His features softened. "This is . . . Lydia. I met her at Oslo. I was studying astrogation at the University there, while Rigel was negotiating for *Alpha One*. She graduated *summa cum laude* and returned to her people on Holmen a month ago. She was to be my bride—"

It must be like this, Ramirez thought hazily, to see your own arm lopped off, and know that presently you will feel the pain.

Was to be. It was not too late, then. He need not tamely accept—

But time was racing away. Even now Lydia could be beyond all help. He shook, but quickly regained self-control.

"May I congratulate you on your taste," he heard himself say to Larsen.

"You may not! I was to marry her the moment my ship . . . the *Alpha One* . . . arrived on Holmen on the anniversary of the Holmen settlement. It was to have been a glorious occasion—a new anniversary to add to the old—the date of first trade independent of Earth. And the captain of that expedition had the promise in marriage of the most beautiful and intelligent girl of new Holmen. Yes, the girl in that picture—until you broke it up."

Ramirez started violently. "I, Capitan!"

"You. You, I believe, are the one who pulled political strings to get a passenger's ticket aboard an independent ship —one not even scheduled . . . You are the one who somehow pressured the Acting Rigellian Executive to order the vessel to detour to Earth after all on an emergency basis. Why? Why, to pick up the learned Dr. Ramirez, who else? All because you couldn't wait to powwow with your Thargan friends. From this message it looks as though they've already left Holmen. Too bad, Doctor, since you managed to get the whole Solar government into the act. Earth just can't bear to be bypassed, can she? Any pretext will do to keep Rigel and Holmen tied to her apron strings. This insane caper you have forced me into has delayed the schedule two whole weeks. Do you understand? I'll arrive at Holmen *two weeks late for my wedding!*"

It was not final. It was *not* final. The wedding would not be between Lydia and Larsen. But this was like worrying about a coin lost in a holocaust. He *must* control himself if he expected to control the captain.

"But surely a message of explanation—"

"Yes, a message. A message capsule, to be precise, or do you in your wisdom know of a broadcast band that can outstrip an FTL ship? Such a message could have given notice, yes. But none was sent."

"I do not underst—"

"No, I didn't think that you did. It is too much to look for intelligence in a philosophical doctor. I'll put it into words that even you can grasp: no message was sent because *your Earth government branded your project TOP SECRET.*"

Of course. He had forgotten.

"Meanwhile," Larsen continued savagely, "I've left my bride standing at the altar without any explanation at all. She must believe that I have crashed in space. When she finds that I did not, she'll think . . . oh, God, she'll have to believe that I did not love her enough to be punctual. *Now* do you understand, Señor Doctor?"

Ramirez understood. Resolutely he looked at the situation from Larsen's point of view. No wonder the man had been upset, and angrier with every reminder. Larsen saw his passenger as the source of untold anguish to his loved one.

He could not be blamed. Nevertheless, the major shock was yet to come.

"I'm sorry, Capitan. But *you* are the one who does not understand."

Larsen jumped to his feet. "Get out!"

Ramirez saw that reason was not about to prevail; he abandoned it. In two steps he was at the captain's desk, standing a good two inches taller than Larsen's stocky frame. One experienced hand gripped the man's lapel.

"I listened to you, Larsen. Now you listen to me. This is important!"

Larsen's jaw dropped. Ramirez didn't give him a chance to speak. "I didn't come aboard as a tourist, Captain. I was sent because there was a strong suspicion that the security of the colonies and perhaps of Earth herself is in danger from these Thargan guests of the Holmenians. You'd better bless the delay this detour of yours has caused, because that delay—and blind luck—have given us confirmation."

Larsen shrugged the hand away; Ramirez could feel the solid musculature underneath the dark blue uniform. "I hope this is good enough to keep you out of irons, Doctor," he muttered. He was going to listen now.

Ramirez sat on the desk, speaking intently. "The message, Larsen, the message. The Thargan capsule we intercepted. That tells the whole story."

The captain returned a blank stare. "They've bought some machinery from the Holmenians. What has that got to do with—"

"Machinery!" Ramirez exploded. "Great God, señor, no! Not machinery."

"Cybernetic units. Computers. Same thing."

"X-cybernetic units," Ramirez corrected. "I called this term *X* because there seems no exact equivalent in any Earth language I know. But if I were to attempt to translate it, the nearest I could come might be *bio. Bio*-cybernetic units. And the other word—'ngan'—may also be translated as 'person.' *Those are human beings they're talking about!*"

Larsen's face went white. "But the only planet they've visited—"

"Precisely, Capitan. Holmen. The Thargs have requited Holmen's hospitality by abducting the entire population!"

"Holmen!" Larsen unconsciously exhibited his own intellectual capacity by quoting verbatim from Ramirez's halting translation of the Thargan message. " 'The planet's entire unit supply was immobilized per schedule and has been transferred to ship's cargo holds.' The entire planet! Nine hundred people."

"And more."

"They wiped out the entire planet?"

"That we do not know, Capitan. 'Prime condition,' the message says. Let us hope the people are unharmed as yet." Ramirez fell silent, flexed his fingers thoughtfully and studied his square nails as he waited for the second shock to hit Larsen. It came. Ramirez closed one fist.

"Lydia! Oh, no, no! They've—"

Ramirez hit him, just hard enough to shake him free from hysteria. "Be thankful you *weren't* on schedule, Señor Capitan. You, too, would have been taken. Now, at least, we have some chance—"

Larsen's features cleared. Young, emotional he was; but Ramirez had counted on the fact that a lot of man went into the making of a captain. When Larsen spoke again his voice was under tight rein. "This ship—the *Moloch*—we must be very close to it, otherwise we could never have intercepted that capsule. We have its hypergeodesic—" His hand banged down on the intercom. "Jeffry!" he snapped. "Unlimber the emergency lasers and set 'em up for action. Pronto. Change course to track the source of that capsule we picked up. Put your men on full alert—NOW!"

Ramirez said: "Capitan, this is no war vessel. We can't—"

Larsen smiled mirthlessly. "It will do, Doctor, it will do. Surprise and an accurate beam—those can blast any ship from space."

"Capitan, you *cannot* risk the *Alpha*. If they blast us back— and we don't know the range of their immobilizer—then Earth would have no warning."

Larsen hesitated only a moment. "We'll ship Earth a capsule. All right, Doctor?"

Ramirez didn't bother reminding him of the security blackout. "But, even if we succeed in blasting them—we will have lost, Capitan. Consider: the . . . units . . . were transferred to their ship!"

This halted Larsen in mid-stride. "I can't blast Lydia . . . I can't kill Holmenians. But we must do *something!* If it were some question of astrogation!" he burst out. "Some accident in space—*that* I could deal with. My God, Ramirez, her life depends—"

He seized Ramirez's shoulder and appealed to him directly. "What do we do?"

Ramirez looked down at his hands. Two old-fashioned copper coins rested in a palm. His mind was operating at full throttle. "There was a similar situation, almost, once . . ." he murmured. "The enemy is secure from our attack, one way or the other. And that message shows no mercy. If we let him go, the people of Holmen will certainly die. Or worse."

Larsen was incredulous. "A similar situation?"

"We have only one weapon: talk."

Larsen laughed harshly. "Is *that* the best idea you can come up with, Doctor? You are going to talk these murdering pirates into taking the Holmenians back to Holmen and turning them loose?"

"You have a better idea, then, Capitan?"

Slowly, Larsen shook his head. "It isn't possible," he said flatly. "Yet—you talked your way out of some spot like this, you say? It worked?"

"In Juarez, long ago. If it had not worked, Capitan, I would not be here today."

"Well, we have no choice. When do we leave?"

"We?"

"To visit this Pulguth Bax."

"We have no time to lose, Capitan. First we must send him a message that will cause him to pause and wait for us, before he accelerates faster than our power to overtake him . . ."

The alien craft loomed, a vast hole in the blue of hyperspace. The rendezvous would have been far more convenient, of course, in normal space; but the Thargs were traveling and the Earth ship, to parley, had to accommodate to the conditions prevailing. An hour later and the *Moloch* would have been unreachable.

An oblong opened in the surface; internal illumination spilled out. The two spacesuited figures hove to, slapped magnets against the hull and walked on in. The oblong closed; pressure built up. Presently they were admitted to the interior.

Ramirez set the example by removing his suit and laying it, together with an obvious sidearm concocted for the occasion, on the bench provided. Larsen reluctantly followed suit—or unsuit. They had agreed beforehand on the necessity of this little show; they had to give tangible evidence of their good faith by coming voluntarily and divesting themselves of weapons.

Only when they stood naked of armament did the Thargan escort appear. "We wish to meet with Captain Pulguth Bax of the *Moloch*," Ramirez said boldly in English.

Light flashed. He knew they were being electronically searched for concealed weapons or other suspicious devices. The silent Thargs then led the way to an austere cabin in which a single massive individual stood. Round yellow eyes stared at them out of a face that gave the illusion of being black metal. This was apparently Captain Bax. The guards withdrew to a side wall. The Tharg spoke, in guttural but precise English.

"How did you know my name, my ship?"

First mistake. Ramirez would have to play this part straight and hope that it didn't cost him the one sure advantage he clung to: his knowledge of the Thargan language. His dictionary was phonetic; he could understand the spoken language as easily as the written, if he had time to ponder it. Larsen said nothing; he looked about him grimly.

"We intercepted your message," Ramirez said.

"You speak Thargan?" This Bax was exceedingly sharp; somehow, Ramirez hadn't counted on such alertness.

"Our machines were able to decode part of it," Ramirez lied.

Bax summoned four guards. "Take these two aliens to the galley and reduce their bodies to plasma," he said in Thargan.

"Wait!" Ramirez cried in alarm. "Aren't you even going to hear what we have to say?"

Bax signaled and the guards stepped back. "One knows the language; the other does not," he said.

Second mistake. He had fallen into the trap; his alarm had

betrayed to Bax that he understood Thargan. Bax had effectively stripped him of his advantage. Except—

Except for his background. And the gamble that the psychology of the Tharg was similar to that of Juarez's hoods.

"I am assuming," Ramirez said, sparring for time to think, "that your psychology is essentially similar to ours."

"It may be," Bax said. "Proceed."

Ramirez felt Larsen, beside him, let out his breath with relief. He himself felt none. Any major conjecture he might make could be in error. Then both their lives were forfeit, and Dios knew how many more.

"The officials on my home planet of Earth tend to . . . frown on the use of, er, bio-cybernetic units. Nevertheless, an industrial society such as ours has an ever increasing need for these. We, therefore, have the anomaly of a government that refuses to acknowledge the needs of its civilization."

The Tharg made a momentary quiver which seemed to be equivalent to a nod. Ramirez had won the first round—maybe. Now, if he could avoid any further blunders—

He continued with smooth insincerity: "Frankly, after I got the content of that message of yours that we intercepted I wanted to talk with you in person."

Bax looked bored. "About what?"

"As I said in my message to you, we might be able to do each other a favor. In our sector it has become virtually impossible for the honest entrepreneur to obtain sufficient units to supply the demand without encountering . . . harrassment . . . by the authorities. For that reason I broke with the, uh organization handling these matters. But now I find you, who must have mastered your technology more efficiently than we. You are able to make do with an incredibly small number of units! We had never found it worth our time to harvest a population of Holmen's size, of less than one thousand; the cost of such a raid would hardly be recovered. Frankly, sir, I could make it worth your while for me to get back in the business once more. If you would share your secret with our technologists—show us how you are able to utilize single units where we would require two or more . . ."

Was he making sense to the Tharg, or did too much of the doubletalk show?

"Come," said the Thargan captain, and Ramirez let out his breath.

Dim corridors rang with their footsteps as Bax led the way to a balcony overlooking an extensive block of cages. There men, women and children were crowded together, prisoners. From what Ramirez could see of them at this distance they seemed unhurt except for dignity; there was a good bit of noise and a rising effluvium that spoke ill of Thargan sanitary facilities. The captives were obviously regarded as cattle. Beside him, Ramirez felt Larsen stiffen.

Ramirez worried anew about Larsen's stability. He would have preferred to come alone; but Larsen had exercised his captain's prerogative and insisted on coming. Lydia was somewhere in the depths of this hellship. Ramirez tried to put the thought aside to keep this knowledge from unnerving him. He was none too sure of his own stability should he set eyes on her in this place.

During the *Alpha One*'s feverish pursuit of the Thargan craft Ramirez had instructed Larsen carefully. He had pointed out that the aliens could be expected to subject their visitors to revolting sights in order to provoke genuine reactions; but there had been little time to go into detail. To his relief, though Larsen whitened, he did not lose his self-control.

"I'm surprised you haven't processed them yet," Ramirez said to Bax. "We find it awkward if too much time elapses."

"There is your difficulty," Bax diagnosed. "You are in too much of a hurry to reduce them—as I was, before I learned this trade. You strip out the brain itself and ship only that, am I correct?"

"I'm no technician," Ramirez said, trying to avoid another trap. "I don't know just how far they actually cut it down now. But weight is a factor, and since the, ah, torsos are useless—"

"Field reduction is wasteful," Bax insisted. "Too crude. You discard the spinal cord, the neural endings, even the ganglia. Am I right?"

Numbly, Ramirez nodded. He dared not look at Larsen.

"In consequence, you have high losses from transinstallational debilitation, especially in hookups demanding precision and intelligence; your customer demands his money back. Am I right? Other units soon malfunction and go dead; your customer complains of high mortality. On our planet such defective units naturally command low value."

Ramirez's conjecture about the purpose of the "units" had been correct, then. The compact and efficient computers that are organic brains were used in Thargan machinery for control of complex automated processes. No wonder their technology was superior. How the transplants were made; how the brains, presumably conscious, were controlled, he did not care to speculate. But such practice could hardly be condoned by the great majority of the members of a civilized race. He was dealing with an unscrupulous private operator.

Or was he? Was he committing the anthropomorphic fallacy of equating human ethical values with the ethics of an alien race? For that matter, even human ethical values had been far from uniform over the years. True, brain-transplant had always been outlawed; but only so far as the human genus was concerned. Human slavery had been the norm for more centuries than it had been proscribed. He needed more information, more time to think. Yet he must not, by remaining silent too long, give Bax any extra thinking time.

"If you have solved these problems—"

Bax was warming to his subject. "Central processing. There's your answer. Skilled technicians, proper facilities, unhurried reduction, and you can guarantee your client fully attentive and intelligent units."

—A large operator, with an organization such that it was possible for him to have central processing and send message capsules to his home base. Could he rule out the possibility that the Thargan government condoned or abetted Bax's activities?

"You have no trouble, then, with, uh, psychological resistance?"

"Shock collapse? We used to, until we found out how to maintain frontal lobe function. Cautery of the sleep centers before reduction is part of the answer. Thanks to that and to certain other pre-debilitative measures, we can now guarantee our clientele complete control of unitary awareness."

"Sounds risky."

"It works. Now, you will wish to know how we get maximum service per unit? Chemical processing of the original assembly. Takes more time, yes, to reduce the body to plasma, but our clients pay us for quality. The assembly must be removed from the vat and hung-out at precisely the right stage

of vertebral softening. A skilled surgical technician then hooks
out almost the entire central nervous system more or less
intact. Hearing is conserved, eyes remain functional. Pain centers outside the brain itself can be instrumented for per-
formance-quality control."

The room lurched and blurred. Ramirez tautened his grip
on himself. "What about training?"

"Within hours after transplant many of our units are able to
withstand instructional stimuli. At the center you have the
services of a battery of experts—adapters, conditioners, instructors, programmers, standardizers, even depersonalizers for
refractory cases—who know their jobs. The extra weight is
small when you consider the superior product you obtain by
shipping the entire assembly live."

Was the Tharg giving him his "answer," or was he leading
up to some climactic pitfall? Ramirez looked steadily into Bax's
yellow, catlike eyes; and could read nothing.

"Your claims impress me . . . if true. Even so, animate
shipment presents so many practical hazards—feeding and
cleaning and preventing loss of units through panic reactions.
A number of ours will damage themselves beyond repair in
irrational attempts at escape."

Bax led them through a short corridor into another chamber. One side was lined with what looked like drawers to
some huge wall-filing cabinet or vault. On each wall was a
small panel with a small opening. There was an acrid stench
from the several sweating Thargs. They wore only yellow
breech-clouts and were shoving a boxlike apparatus into place
at one end of the great cabin. "Here is our solution to that
problem," Bax said. "Animate shipment is impractical. That
is why we put them in phase two at our convenience."

Bax barked at three guards, who clomped out—to return
moments later with a struggling Holmenian. "Observe."

Ramirez was glad that the man, involved in his desperate
struggle, did not notice the only other human beings in the
room—himself and Larsen.

He sensed rather than felt a movement from Larsen beside
him. Dios, Larsen *must* hold now, or all was lost! He did, in
spite of the man's noisy struggle as he was hauled to the box.
Two Thargs held him while a third stripped away his shreds

of clothing. Naked and struggling, the man was thrust feet first into the box, forcibly folded into fetal position, and jammed beneath a tight lid. The black container was exactly the right size; obviously it had been tailored to human specifications.

So far there seemed little point to this demonstration, unless this were a death box and Bax's intent was to shock him into another blunder. Could the man breathe? Ramirez realized his hands were sweating. He unclenched his fists and waited, hoping that the volatile Larsen would continue to hold firm.

A technician in a gray tunic spoke gutturally into the panel beside the box. Instantly a crane swung a square brass plate over the box—with impossible precision. Ramirez glanced at the control panel, which had not been touched. He noted a rounded recess in the panel. An eye? He felt a coldness in his spine. Bax, who had followed his glance, nodded and spoke to the panel. Instantly the wall beside the panel lighted up from inside. Transparent as glass, the wall revealed every detail of the thing within—a vertebrate brain half-submerged in some nutrient fluid, atop the pulsing network of an entire nervous system stretched across a frame that resembled a small loom.

"You see what correct processing can do? Of course that is a Thargan unit, but the pith is essentially identical to that of a man."

The brass plate settled down over the box in a kind of cap. The technician stepped over to the box, ran wormlike fingers around the edge of the cap to test for tightness. He looked toward the panel and gave another order. The brain seemed to pulse. The cap lifted itself away, poised for later action.

Calmly, the Thargs in the yellow breech-clouts—slave?—lifted away the lid. A metallic hand came down, sank its flexible claws into the air in the box. The hand heaved—and the man was lifted out, perfectly visible in a solid block of—something. One of the cabinet drawers opened. The claws sought it out without further guidance and deposited the block in it. At a word from the technician to another panel the drawer closed with a decisive click. Ramirez violently suppressed an urge to retch.

"Magnificent!" he exclaimed. "Instant stasis. That's your secret?"

"We believe in efficiency," said Bax smugly. Apparently they had passed this test. "Surely you are familiar with the technique?"

"We have a deep-freeze technique somewhat similar, but we never thought of applying it to field procurement. Your ingenuity does you great credit."

"Perhaps we could make an arrangement," Bax said. Ramirez's heart leaped. Had the Tharg finally taken the bait? Now it might be possible to find out for sure which side of Thargan law Bax operated on.

"We, too," Bax went on, "are hampered by elements in the Directorate who reject the only correct and permanent solution to the over-population problem. Even though our civilization's business would collapse without bio-cybernetics, there are endless hypocritical objections to the use of Thargan-derived units."

. . . So much objection, Ramirez felt surer now, that Bax, instead of raiding the Thargan slums, had come all the way to Holmen on the lookout for units of other species. He was an outlaw.

That would simplify things. You can't cheat an honest man. He must, somehow, use this as the key to his strategy. He pricked up his ears. Bax was putting out a second feeler.

"However, there is no specific law against using alien units."

"Ah. This is exactly what I had counted on." Ramirez tried to look and sound elated.

Encouraged, Bax continued. "It might be possible for us to provide you with a certain number of Thargan-derived units in stasis that your own administrators would not object to . . ."

"I think we could match that number with our own product," Ramirez said after an appropriate pause, "provided the matter were handled with, uh, discretion." He hesitated artfully. "My superiors would of course require a, er, contract, imprinted by both parties—"

The Tharg smiled. "A formal guideline? It could not be binding."

"In the event of an unexpected change of personnel, some statement is necessary. From time to time the power structure in the organization shifts abruptly. The new . . . leader might not be privy to the details of the agreement."

Bax performed his nod. "Ah. I comprehend."

He should. Ramirez's slum experience had taught him that any criminal enterprise is governed by some variant of jungle law.

"It shall be done. But first—"

Something in the alien's manner alerted Ramirez. It was not over yet. Had he given himself away after all?

"The present shipment would not come under the agreement," Bax said. "But there may be a few additional suggestions we can make for the effective processing of units. For instance, the procedure for the two sexes is not identical. Allow me to point out the nuances."

"Very considerate," Ramirez said, smelling rat strongly now. He was very sure that the next few minutes were not going to be pleasant.

He was right. Bax had a major trump and he played it now, with the timing of a connoisseur. The demonstrator model was not a man.

The figure of the girl between the still Thargan guards seemed to brighten as his vision centered on her, while the busy work room dimmed. Every object, everything, faded from his awareness, except for her. The grim aliens, the massive blackship receded into nothing.

She was halfway to the platform, her tumbled ringlets coming barely to the chest of the Thargan guard who, at Bax's signal, now struck her forward unceremoniously. She half fell, caught herself on a stanchion. She started to rise, then froze. She was staring into the lighted Thargan unit. The guard jerked her to her feet.

Some part of him must not founder . . . One of her little green shoes was missing, he noted irrelevantly.

Some part of him knew that above all he must not betray what he felt now; it held his face blandly impassive while his mind, like a lone swimmer caught up in a black rip-tide, tried to cope. Too late, he remembered Larsen and shot out a restraining hand.

Larsen leaped toward the girl as a cry broke from him. "Lydia!"

She turned slowly, her blue eyes blinking in the light glaring overhead, as though she had just been brought out from a dark room. Her face was pallid, quite devoid of feminine retouchments, and there was a dark bruise on one side of her tender throat. Her dress, of something that had once been soft and yellow, was soiled and torn, held together at one side by a matted strand of green netting that must once have served to subdue the wayward ringlets above. A leg was gashed above the bare foot.

As her eyes found Larsen she straightened. She drew herself up like a daffodil, thought Ramirez, somewhere almost below the crystallizing black awareness that was disposing its forces for action, a daffodil sprung upright in spite of being trampled on. He knew pain—

"Eric!"

They stood together, Eric and she, his tense arms around her quivering body, no longer aware of the manner of their meeting or of the very tenuous endurance of it. Dry-eyed, they kissed, and spun together in the center of their private universe—and fell apart, strengthless, in the ebon grip that lifted and pulled them in opposite directions.

—But there was no time left now for pain. *How had Bax known?*

The picture. She would have a disk, Ramirez realized now, feverishly, or a locket, similar to Larsen's, containing his picture. Bax, covering all bets, would have ordered a roundup of such trinkets at first contact from the *Alpha One;* and so Bax had come by the bit of knowledge that voided at a single stroke Ramirez's complex stratagems. Larsen's emotional display was final evidence that the prisoners were not mere merchandise to the *Moloch*'s visitors. Ramirez had mobilized his will for action. Yet no conceivable action could retrieve Lydia's life now, or the lives of her people. Still Ramirez, desperate and empty now of stratagem, looked to Larsen for help.

But there was no help there. Larsen was fighting uselessly, while Lydia contended with two Thargs. Her ragged dress was torn open in the struggle. Larsen cried out and almost broke away from his captors, but they quickly cut him off and dragged him back; but not so quickly or so roughly as to damage his commercial value by striking his head. Larsen's voice cried out to him, this time.

"Ramirez, for God's sake, stop them! Help us!"

At these words, Lydia looked about wildly, as the Thargs

pinioned her wrists behind her. Her eyes found Ramirez; she seemed aware of his presence for the first time.

"Manuel Ramirez! Help us!"

The Thargs paused as Ramirez strode forward authoritatively. This gave him a few more instants for thinking; what he would do next he did not know—except that he must appear quite calm. With clinical detachment he looked the girl up and down; then turned to give the blond man an even colder scrutiny. Finally he turned to Bax.

"This unit is not part of your shipment," he said curtly, indicating Larsen.

Bax laughed.

"Moreover, thanks to your heavy-handed bungling, he is of no further use to me. Therefore I shall expect you to provide me with adequate compensation."

Bax—surprised?—hesitated. The silence lengthened, and lengthened again while Ramirez relaxed, a picture of expectant aplomb as he withstood Bax's speculative stare. Finally Bax quivered tentative agreement. "What do you regard as adequate?"

Ramirez looked significantly at the thing in the transparent panel.

Bax nodded thoughtfully. "There is a spare. I think we might arrange . . ."

"Ramirez, what are you saying—!" Larsen shouted. "To save yourself you'd sell us all . . ."

Larsen's words were cut off as one of the Thargs folded him with an expert jab to the solar plexus. Almost in a breath Larsen was positioned. The brass plate swung over, descended in silence. On signal, the man's still body was stacked in a drawer, beside the other. A sound came from Lydia as she watched, that was something between a moan and a sob. The Thargs turned their ministrations upon her.

She did not resist now. She seemed to have withdrawn into a world of her own as they stripped her. Only as they were about to position her did she turn her eyes to Ramirez. Her lips moved, once, but no sound came out.

Ramirez's face was ashen. He turned away. Then the sound came out.

"Traitor!" Lydia's hoarse cry echoed faintly through the metal corridors. "Traitor, traitor, trait—!"

A chill numbness pervaded Ramirez. He ignored the cry, clenched his fist about the coppers in his pocket as her cry was cut off. "Proceed," he said to Bax. The hand in his pocket was sticky with blood.

Bax proceeded.

His heart pounded like a schoolboy's as he stood in the short white corridor and knocked on the door that he knew Lydia was behind. He had wanted to be with her when she woke, but the Thargan technicians had forbidden his excited presence; had in fact, shoved him out bodily. But by now they must have her revivified. Ramirez was about to push open the door when it was opened for him by a square-faced female Thargan technician, who nodded him in without words.

"Lydia?"

She was draped in something white and close-fitting and she was seated on a sort of chair. She looked wildly after the departing technicians and rose, obviously agitated.

For several moments they eyed each other in silence. Some instinct warned him to wait for her to speak.

"Ramirez. Manuel Ramirez." She seemed unable to go on. Her throat moved once, convulsively, and then she seemed more mistress of herself. She spoke in strained, artificial tones. "It is good to see a human face, even . . . even here. I have been thinking of the last things I can remember. I sincerely hope that we misjudged you, Eric and I."

Sincerely hoped . . . we . . .

She was, at his request, the first of the Holmenians to be revivified. He looked about now at the stacked boxes with their gruesome contents. These—and the female Thargan technicians—would be the first things to meet her eyes when she had opened them. How could she, then, but believe Larsen's version of his motives? Yet, believing this, she spoke to him.

Clearly, she was stalling for time and for information.

Well, he'd give her the information, so that they could get on to the important part. Dios, she must not go on thinking . . . ! Yet she looked at him so oddly a gray doubt nibbled at him. With anyone else a few swift words would get the information out of the way; with her, he felt oddly tongue-tied and helpless. He strode to her and took her white hands in his brown ones. They were ice-cold.

"Thank you for your confidence, madon . . . Señorita Lydia."

"Where is Eric?" She spoke quietly, but Ramirez felt she was fighting down hysteria.

"Here, Señorita." At the surprise and skepticism written in her face, he added: "In this very building—in another room such as this. He, too, will be awake soon and you may then go to him. For now—you have some questions?"

Relief shone in her face—and doubt. She said coldly, "The first one is, why did Bax let you go free—if he did?"

So that was it, then. "I thought we all were lost when Bax's guards brought you out, Señorita. But I remembered the alley—"

"Alley?"

"In Juarez—back on Earth, Señorita. I was a young man, full with hope, but trapped in an alley. The hombres—it seems so long ago—were intent on robbing me and taking my life. I had no defense. Yet I escaped whole and with my solars. I had to hope that by some such scheme we might be able to carry out the bluff against Señor Bax."

Lydia looked about at the stacked boxes, five high against all four walls, of perfectly visible immobilized human beings. Her Holmenian friends, neighbors, acquaintances, relatives. The people she had grown up among. Her body shook once, violently. "So you saved yourself then," she said, "as you save yourself now."

"A trick, nothing more. The hoodlums of Juarez—I had to put them off balance. I stepped right up and—panhandled, I believe is the word? I panhandled them for a bottle of tequila."

"And—?" asked Lydia as he paused. She was, he saw, interested in spite of herself.

"They were so surprised that they didn't even bother to search me."

"They simply coughed up the money?"

Ramirez nodded, trying to appear oblivious of the derision in her tones. His hand went to his pocket to bring out the coins. "I've kept these with me since that day—as small trophies, you might say, and a lesson."

She looked at the coppers in his palm but did not touch them. "And you panhandled Bax for tequila, Señor Ramirez?"

Diablo, why should her mockery tongue-tie him?

"I'm afraid I did, Señorita, in effect. I told him that the, uh, subservient class was distinguished by its yellow hair; that his careless handling of the sexes had ruined my perfectly good valet."

"Valet? *Eric?*"

"It was a thin story, but the best I could come up with at that moment. I demanded reimbursement."

"Naturally, he believed you . . ."

"He was too surprised *not* to believe," Ramirez persisted. "He had outsmarted me at every turn. He had no respect for my intelligence. He had to assume that I was sincere. It never occurred to him that one would have the audacity, otherwise, to make such a demand. He had to assume, therefore, that my entire offer was on the level."

"Offer?"

Ramirez explained.

"But your offer wasn't on the level, of course."

Ramirez ignored her irony. "Such a deal—Earthmen for Thargs—would be most convenient in his business, you see, and Bax was carried away by his own greed. He finally signed the contract I had brought with me. If I was so easy to outsmart, the connection could be most profitable to him. I returned to the ship—"

"To the *Alpha One?* You expect me to believe that Eric's crew—"

"His crew were fanatically faithful to their captain, Señorita Lydia. I spent, as it happened, some considerable time in the *Alpha*'s air lock, explaining to them my failure to bring him back with me from the Thargan vessel. But once they became convinced—"

"Oh, you did convince them of your honorable intentions?"

"It was not easy, Señorita. The useless contract Bax had signed made no impression on them. The convincer was the Thargan unit I managed to talk Bax out of. I let them look into the transparent side . . . *Then* they listened. They raided the cargo and built for me the very biggest message capsule you could imagine!"

"A message capsule? To send to Earth?"

"To send to Tharg—"

"And the *Alpha One*'s crew were taken in by—? I mean, what did you put in such a huge capsule—a bomb?"

"Very close. I put the Thargan unit in it, and the contract document bearing Bax's seal."

She stared at him. "That fixed up everything, of course," she said tonelessly.

"But, of course, Señorita Lydia—though I confess to you that this was the hardest wait of my life—the wait for acceptance at the University was, beside this, nothing! Tharg is a civilized interstellar culture, that much is plain. It did not achieve this status by tolerating blatant lawless activity. The moment my message to them presented incontrovertible proof—"

"And so you waited all this time, Señor Ramirez? Where?"

"Why, here, Señorita. I waited here—with what apprehension you may imagine—for the Thargan Directorate's reply. Meanwhile we cleaned up the mess here on Holmen, the *Alpha One*'s crewmen . . ."

"*Holmen?* Did you say we're on *Holmen?*"

"But, of course, Señorita. I thought you underst . . . but of course!" He cursed his own ineptness—with her alone, of all persons. "You believed we were at Bax's hideout—"

He didn't quite see her come—or maybe he had moved toward her. She was there, facing him, one shoulder bare. Her hands rested softly on his shoulder and the faint aroma of her person invaded his senses. Suddenly she laughed—a laugh of sheer relief and release, which continued until her whole body shook. She kissed his face over and over, laughing and crying at once, as a child would who had expected punishment and received instead a wanted present. He steadied her with a hand to her elbow. He kissed the warm nape of her neck as the laughter began to subside. She looked at him out of starry eyes.

"Manuel Ramirez, you are without doubt the most remarkable—"

She did not have a chance to finish the sentence, because he pulled her to him. She responded, no longer as a child, but with passionate abandon as he pressed his lips on hers.

From behind him there was a coughing grunt, followed by several rapid words in Thargan. Unconsciously Ramirez tightened his grip and silently raged at the uniformed Tharg, execrating his entire tribe for this untimely interruption. Lydia instantly stiffened in his arms. She jerked back. Her eyes

opened, and opened wider as she stared, stunned, at the tall
Tharg standing there eyeing them with open curiosity. Ramirez turned on him and spoke two words. The Tharg performed a shrug reminiscent of Bax's and retired to one side
of the room; but he did not go out.

Lydia's eyes blazed with suspicion. She backed away again
as Ramirez stepped toward her. "You lied! You lied to me!"

So she still believed what she had believed at the start.

"You think I could lie—to you?"

"Why not? You lied to the hoods of Juarez to save your
skin. You yourself said that you lied to Bax. And you have
saved your skin, so far."

"I . . . I—" Ramirez was, for once, at a loss for words.

"So you sent some capsule straight to Tharg, you said, and
not only straight to Tharg—location unknown—but straight to
the top authorities of Tharg." Her eyes were blue steel. "You
must have the devil's own talent in your tongue for me to
have believed that for an instant."

"Lydia, I—"

"Just what did that alien say to you, Señor Ramirez?"

"I am to represent Earth at Tharg, Señorita Lydia. A capsule from Earth signed by the Solar President authorizes and
commands this. This . . . er, man . . . is a messenger from
the Thargan ship's captain."

"What Thargan ship? We are on Holmen—you said."

"Why, the one that has returned to Holmen with the people
Bax abducted, including yourself, Señorita. It brought also
restorative apparatus and personnel qualified to operate it.
It brought apologies from the Thargan Directorate—"

"What did this alien say to you?" Lydia demanded again.

"He asked whether the Thargan captain should prepare
quarters for two or for one."

"I see." He could not tell from her tone whether or not she
believed him. "And you told him—?"

"I told him to wait."

"I see," she said again. "Is this a proposal, Manuel?" Her
voice was flat and impersonal and her eyes were hard.

"No."

"Oh?" She looked about her at the still forms in the boxes,
at the interested Tharg stationed by the wall. A shiver passed
through her, but she spoke with cold sarcasm. "Then just
what was it that you had in mind?"

He took her defiant face between his hands.

"Lydia, I have loved you from the first instant I set eyes upon you, and I want you for my wife, yes. But I shall not propose. Not while your eyes tell me that you still half-believe that I sold out the human race!"

She studied his face. "I could never be your wife, believing that," she said quietly. Some of the anger seemed to have gone out of her. She put her hands over his as he still held her. She seemed still fighting for calmness. His fingers tightened on her face.

"And you need proof that I am *not* guilty of saving my skin at the expense of the Holmenians . . . ? You can, of course, find this proof just by stepping through that door. But you cannot accept here and now the unsupported word of Manuel Ramirez, is that it?"

As he waited in silence, Lydia's face became a curious study in embarrassment and compassion; but she spoke forthrightly. "When I think of what you've saved me from—and Eric—and all of us—if this is true, I'm ashamed to doubt. But Manuel, both of us were carried away just now. You fell in love with a pretty face and figure, but you don't really know me, nor I you. We both know, just the same, that you would not be content—"

"Don't decide now. I will stay here."

"And then, aren't you forgetting Eric?"

The hell with Eric! "But suppose we had met first, Lydia, you and I? What then?"

"But we didn't, Manuel, so we won't suppose anything of the sort."

"Dios!" he burst out. "A senseless accident of timing—blind chance—and must we tamely run our lives just so, on account of this? No! This I will not accept. I will stay."

"You have an assignment on Tharg, Manuel, remember? And all this makes more sense than we want to think. Would you be content to spend the rest of your life on Holmen?"

"If this is where you—"

"Holmen is where I was born, where I grew up. I have been educated for Holmen. I was not chosen at random; I was sent to Earth, to the University, by my own people here, at great expense, in the expectation that I would return with knowledge that can be used here. They knew perfectly well I would not fail them. Eric understands this; he also comes from a frontier planet. Holmen will be our home. Or at least we planned . . ." Her voice trailed off under Ramirez's intent gaze.

"I will stay!" he repeated.

"Was that the purpose of *your* education, your education to be contact man from Earth with the alien race we knew would be encountered—to spend your life on this remote pioneer planet? We don't even know each other, Manuel," she said again, against his silence. "If you knew me I don't think you'd like me. I'm sorry. . . . I'm ashamed. But I do need that proof you spoke of. I will believe you when I see Eric alive and well. I must see him—now!"

"You shall." He released her and nodded toward the door through which he had entered. "Lydia, wait!"

Halfway down the corridor, she stopped.

"So our meeting has changed nothing for you, Lydia?"

She stood very still. Presently she turned, slowly, and faced him as he stepped toward her. "Don't use it against me, Manuel, your talent." Her eyes were luminous—and unreadable. "I'm his mate."

Larsen caught up with Ramirez that night, at the bottom of the ramp that led into the great Thargan starship. "In all the excitement and confusion and congratulations here today I was afraid I wouldn't get to see you alone to thank you personally before you leave. . . . That capsule. I understand that you must have sent it to Acrux. I also understand that the prisoners in stasis—including Lydia and myself—were piloted back by official representatives of the Thargan Directorate for this revivification today on Holmen. What bothers me is this: That original capsule was addressed to the outlaws and would have landed in their lap; your capsule didn't. Why?"

"Capitan, our message was not addressed to them. We triggered it with an amplification system that the authorities were bound to notice and intercept. That, of course, was the finish for Bax. His ship, arriving soon after, was impounded, his base cleaned out. Bax and his cohorts were put on trial for cybernetic murder and attempted genocide. The Thargan Directorate now wishes to establish friendly relations with Earth—"

Larsen looked at him with admiration. "So, out of such an unpromising beginning you've managed to establish friendly relations between Earth and Tharg." He clapped a hand on Ramirez's shoulder and walked with him up the ramp. "Also, one fast-talking xenologist promoted to Terran ambassador to Tharg, I hear. Ramirez, what a performance!"

If you only knew, Ramirez thought, glad for the moment that the man had not known about his own involvement with Lydia. He managed a grin.

"Señor, I'm just a panhandler at heart," he said modestly.

He hoped that in the years to come he would be glad that he had not panhandled that which could never rightfully belong to him.

LIGHT OF OTHER DAYS

Bob Shaw

Leaving the village behind, we followed the heady sweeps of the road up into a land of slow glass.

I had never seen one of the farms before and at first found them slightly eerie—an effect heightened by imagination and circumstance. The car's turbine was pulling smoothly and quietly in the damp air so that we seemed to be carried over the convolutions of the road in a kind of supernatural silence. On our right the mountain sifted down into an incredibly perfect valley of timeless pine, and everywhere stood the great frames of slow glass, drinking light. An occasional flash of afternoon sunlight on their wind bracing created an illusion of movement, but in fact the frames were deserted. The rows of windows had been standing on the hillside for years, staring into the valley, and men only cleaned them in the middle of the night when their human presence would not matter to the thirsty glass.

They were fascinating, but Selina and I didn't mention the windows. I think we hated each other so much we both were reluctant to sully anything new by drawing it into the nexus of our emotions. The holiday, I had begun to realize, was a stupid idea in the first place. I had thought it would cure everything, but, of course, it didn't stop Selina being pregnant and, worse still, it didn't even stop her being angry about being pregnant.

Rationalizing our dismay over her condition, we had circulated the usual statements to the effect that we would have *liked* having children—but later on, at the proper time. Selina's pregnancy had cost us her well-paid job and with it the new house we had been negotiating and which was far beyond the reach of my income from poetry. But the real source of our

annoyance was that we were face to face with the realization
that people who say they want children later always mean
they want children never. Our nerves were thrumming with
the knowledge that we, who had thought ourselves so unique,
had fallen into the same biological trap as every mindless
rutting creature which ever existed.

The road took us along the southern slopes of Ben Cruachan
until we began to catch glimpses of the gray Atlantic far
ahead. I had just cut our speed to absorb the view better when
I noticed the sign spiked to a gatepost. It said: "SLOW GLASS
—Quality High, Prices Low—J. R. Hagan." On an impulse I
stopped the car on the verge, wincing slightly as tough grasses
whipped nosily at the bodywork.

"Why have we stopped?" Selina's neat, smoke-silver head
turned in surprise.

"Look at that sign. Let's go up and see what there is. The
stuff might be reasonably priced out here."

Selina's voice was pitched high with scorn as she refused,
but I was too taken with my idea to listen. I had an illogical
conviction that doing something extravagant and crazy would
set us right again.

"Come on," I said, "the exercise might do us some good.
We've been driving too long anyway."

She shrugged in a way that hurt me and got out of the car.
We walked up a path made of irregular, packed clay steps
nosed with short lengths of sapling. The path curved through
trees which clothed the edge of the hill and at its end we
found a low farmhouse. Beyond the little stone building tall
frames of slow glass gazed out towards the voice-stilling sight
of Cruachan's ponderous descent towards the waters of Loch
Linnhe. Most of the panes were perfectly transparent but a
few were dark, like panels of polished ebony.

As we approached the house through a neat cobbled yard
a tall middle-aged man in ash-colored tweeds arose and waved
to us. He had been sitting on the low rubble wall which
bounded the yard, smoking a pipe and staring towards the
house. At the front window of the cottage a young woman in
a tangerine dress stood with a small boy in her arms, but she
turned disinterestedly and moved out of sight as we drew
near.

"Mr. Hagan?" I guessed.

"Correct. Come to see some glass, have you? Well, you've

come to the right place." Hagan spoke crisply, with traces of the pure highland which sounds so much like Irish to the unaccustomed ear. He had one of those calmly dismayed faces one finds on elderly road-menders and philosophers.

"Yes," I said. "We're on holiday. We saw your sign."

Selina, who usually has a natural fluency with strangers, said nothing. She was looking towards the now empty window with what I thought was a slightly puzzled expression.

"Up from London, are you? Well, as I said, you've come to the right place—and at the right time, too. My wife and I don't see many people this early in the season."

I laughed. "Does that mean we might be able to buy a little glass without mortgaging our home?"

"Look at that now," Hagan said, smiling helplessly. "I've thrown away any advantage I might have had in the transaction. Rose, that's my wife, says I never learn. Still, let's sit down and talk it over." He pointed at the rubble wall then glanced doubtfully at Selina's immaculate blue skirt. "Wait till I fetch a rug from the house." Hagan limped quickly into the cottage, closing the door behind him.

"Perhaps it wasn't such a marvelous idea to come up here," I whispered to Selina, "but you might at least be pleasant to the man. I think I can smell a bargain."

"Some hope," she said with deliberate coarseness. "Surely even you must have noticed that ancient dress his wife is wearing? He won't give much away to strangers."

"Was that his wife?"

"Of course that was his wife."

"Well, well," I said, surprised. "Anyway, try to be civil with him. I don't want to be embarrassed."

Selina snorted, but she smiled whitely when Hagan reappeared and I relaxed a little. Strange how a man can love a woman and yet at the same time pray for her to fall under a train.

Hagan spread a tartan blanket on the wall and we sat down, feeling slightly self-conscious at having been translated from our city-oriented lives into a rural tableau. On the distant slate of the Loch, beyond the watchful frames of slow glass, a slow-moving steamer drew a white line towards the south. The boisterous mountain air seemed almost to invade our lungs, giving us more oxygen than we required.

"Some of the glass farmers around here," Hagan began, "give strangers, such as yourselves, a sales talk about how beautiful the autumn is in this part of Argyll. Or it might be the spring, or the winter. I don't do that—any fool knows that a place which doesn't look right in summer never looks right. What do you say?"

I nodded compliantly.

"I want you just to take a good look out towards Mull, Mr. . . ."

"Garland."

". . . Garland. That's what you're buying if you buy my glass, and it never looks better than it does at this minute. The glass is in perfect phase, none of it is less than ten years thick—and a four-foot window will cost you two hundred pounds."

"Two hundred!" Selina was shocked. "That's as much as they charge at the Scenedow shop in Bond Street."

Hagan smiled patiently, then looked closely at me to see if I knew enough about slow glass to appreciate what he had been saying. His price had been much higher than I had hoped— but *ten years thick!* The cheap glass one found in places like the Vistaplex and Pane-o-rama stores usually consisted of a quarter of an inch of ordinary glass faced with a veneer of slow glass perhaps only ten or twelve months thick.

"You don't understand, darling," I said, already determined to buy. "This glass will last ten years and it's in phase."

"Doesn't that only mean it keeps time?"

Hagan smiled at her again, realizing he had no further necessity to bother with me. "Only, you say! Pardon me, Mrs. Garland, but you don't seem to appreciate the miracle, the genuine honest-to-goodness miracle, of engineering precision needed to produce a piece of glass in phase. When I say the glass is ten years thick it means it takes light ten years to pass through it. In effect, each one of those panes is ten light-years thick—more than twice the distance to the nearest star—so a variation in actual thickness of only a millionth of an inch would . . ."

He stopped talking for a moment and sat quietly looking towards the house. I turned my head from the view of the Loch and saw the young woman standing at the window again. Hagan's eyes were filled with a kind of greedy reverence which made me feel uncomfortable and at the same time convinced me Selina had been wrong. In my experience husbands never looked at wives that way, at least, not at their own.

The girl remained in view for a few seconds, dress glowing warmly, then moved back into the room. Suddenly I received a distinct, though inexplicable, impression she was blind. My feeling was that Selina and I were perhaps blundering through an emotional interplay as violent as our own.

"I'm sorry," Hagan continued, "I thought Rose was going to call me for something. Now, where was I, Mrs. Garland? Ten light-years compressed into a quarter of an inch means . . ."

I ceased to listen, partly because I was already sold, partly because I had heard the story of slow glass many times before and had never yet understood the principles involved. An acquaintance with scientific training had once tried to be helpful by telling me to visualize a pane of slow glass as a hologram which did not need coherent light from a laser for the reconstitution of its visual information, and in which every photon of ordinary light passed through a spiral tunnel coiled outside the radius of capture of each atom in the glass. This gem of, to me, incomprehensibility not only told me nothing, it convinced me once again that a mind as non-technical as mine should concern itself less with causes than effects.

The most important effect, in the eyes of the average individual, was that light took a long time to pass through a sheet of slow glass. A new piece was always jet black because nothing had yet come through, but one could stand the glass beside, say, a woodland lake until the scene emerged, perhaps a year later. If the glass was then removed and installed in a dismal city flat, the flat would—for that year—appear to overlook the woodland lake. During the year it wouldn't be merely a very realistic but still picture—the water would ripple in sunlight, silent animals would come to drink, birds would cross the sky, night would follow day, season would follow season. Until one day, a year later, the beauty held in the subatomic pipelines would be exhausted and the familiar gray cityscape would reappear.

Apart from its stupendous novelty value, the commercial success of slow glass was founded on the fact that having a scenedow was the exact emotional equivalent of owning land. The meanest cave dweller could look out on misty parks—

and who was to say they weren't his? A man who really owns tailored gardens and estates doesn't spend his time proving his ownership by crawling on his ground, feeling, smelling, tasting it. All he receives from the land are light patterns, and with scenedows those patterns could be taken into coal mines, submarines, prison cells.

On several occasions I have tried to write short pieces about the enchanted crystal but, to me, the theme is so ineffably poetic as to be, paradoxically, beyond the reach of poetry—mine at any rate. Besides, the best songs and verse had already been written, with prescient inspiration, by men who had died long before slow glass was discovered. I had no hope of equaling, for example, Moore with his:

> *Oft in the stilly night,*
> *Ere slumber's chain has bound me,*
> *Fond Memory brings the light,*
> *Of other days around me . . .*

It took only a few years for slow glass to develop from a scientific curiosity to a sizable industry. And much to the astonishment of we poets—those of us who remain convinced that beauty lives though lilies die—the trappings of that industry were no different from those of any other. There were good scenedows which cost a lot of money, and there were inferior scenedows which cost rather less. The thickness, measured in years, was an important factor in the cost but there was also the question of *actual* thickness, or phase.

Even with the most sophisticated engineering techniques available thickness control was something of a hit-and-miss affair. A coarse discrepancy could mean that a pane intended to be five years thick might be five and a half, so that light which entered in summer emerged in winter; a fine discrepancy could mean that noon sunshine emerged at midnight. These incompatibilities had their peculiar charm—many night workers, for example, liked having their own private time zones—but, in general, it cost more to buy scenedows which kept closely in step with real time.

Selina still looked unconvinced when Hagan had finished speaking. She shook her head almost imperceptibly and I knew he had been using the wrong approach. Quite suddenly the pewter helmet of her hair was disturbed by a cool gust of wind, and huge clean tumbling drops of rain began to spang round us from an almost cloudless sky.

"I'll give you a check now," I said abruptly, and saw Selina's green eyes triangulate angrily on my face. "You can arrange delivery?"

"Aye, delivery's no problem," Hagan said, getting to his feet. "But wouldn't you rather take the glass with you?"

"Well, yes—if you don't mind." I was shamed by his readiness to trust my scrip.

"I'll unclip a pane for you. Wait here. It won't take long to slip it into a carrying frame." Hagan limped down the slope towards the seriate windows, through some of which the view towards Linnhe was sunny, while others were cloudy and a few pure black.

Selina drew the collar of her blouse closed at her throat. "The least he could have done was invite us inside. There can't be so many fools passing through that he can afford to neglect them."

I tried to ignore the insult and concentrated on writing the check. One of the outsize drops broke across my knuckles, splattering the pink paper.

"All right," I said, "let's move in under the eaves till he gets back." You worm, I thought as I felt the whole thing go completely wrong. I just had to be a fool to marry you. A prize fool, a fool's fool—and now that you've trapped part of me inside you I'll never ever, never ever, *never ever* get away.

Feeling my stomach clench itself painfully, I ran behind Selina to the side of the cottage. Beyond the window the neat living room, with its coal fire, was empty but the child's toys were scattered on the floor. Alphabet blocks and a wheelbarrow the exact color of freshly pared carrots. As I stared in, the boy came running from the other room and began kicking the blocks. He didn't notice me. A few moments later the young woman entered the room and lifted him, laughing easily and whole-heartedly as she swung the boy under her arm. She came to the window as she had done earlier. I smiled self-consciously, but neither she nor the child responded.

My forehead pricked icily. *Could they both be blind?* I sidled away.

Selina gave a little scream and I spun towards her.

"The rug!" she said. "It's getting soaked. "

She ran across the yard in the rain, snatched the reddish square from the dappling wall and ran back, towards the cottage door. Something heaved convulsively in my subconscious.

"Selina," I shouted. "Don't open it!"

But I was too late. She had pushed open the latched wooden door and was standing, hand over her mouth, looking into the cottage. I moved close to her and took the rug from her unresisting fingers.

As I was closing the door I let my eyes traverse the cottage's interior. The neat living room in which I had just seen the woman and child was, in reality, a sickening clutter of shabby furniture, old newspapers, cast-off clothing and smeared dishes. It was damp, stinking and utterly deserted. The only object I recognized from my view through the window was the little wheelbarrow, paintless and broken.

I latched the door firmly and ordered myself to forget what I had seen. Some men who live alone are good housekeepers; others just don't know how.

Selina's face was white. "I don't understand. I don't understand it."

"Slow glass works both ways," I said gently. "Light passes out of a house, as well as in."

"You mean . . . ?"

"I don't know. It isn't our business. Now steady up—Hagan's coming back with our glass." The churning in my stomach was beginning to subside.

Hagan came into the yard carrying an oblong, plastic-covered frame. I held the check out to him, but he was staring at Selina's face. He seemed to know immediately that our uncomprehending fingers had rummaged through his soul. Selina avoided his gaze. She was old and ill-looking, and her eyes stared determinedly towards the nearing horizon.

"I'll take the rug from you, Mr. Garland," Hagan finally said. "You shouldn't have troubled yourself over it."

"No trouble. Here's the check."

"Thank you." He was still looking at Selina with a strange kind of supplication. "It's been a pleasure to do business with you."

"The pleasure was mine," I said with equal, senseless formality. I picked up the heavy frame and guided Selina towards the path which led to the road. Just as we reached the head of the now slippery steps Hagan spoke again.

"Mr. Garland!"

I turned unwillingly.

"It wasn't my fault," he said steadily. "A hit-and-run driver got them both, down on the Oban road six years ago. My boy was only seven when it happened. I'm entitled to keep something."

I nodded wordlessly and moved down the path, holding my wife close to me, treasuring the feel of her arms locked around me. At the bend I looked back through the rain and saw Hagan sitting with squared shoulders on the wall where we had first seen him.

He was looking at the house, but I was unable to tell if there was anyone at the window.

SOMETHING TO SAY

John Berryman

I

"Fore!"

We all looked up from the subdued chatter around the breakfast tables. It was the chief's voice, hooting hollowly down the twenty-meter tube linking the Mess bubble with the Administration bubble.

There was an expectant pause at the tables. The chief seldom joined the flight crews at Mess. When he got no answer to his hail, Dr. Bellingrath dove through the tube. He came flying with lunar slowness into our bubble, hands outstretched to brake with the shock cord. The moment he got his big bulk righted and put his feet down on the floor, he began speaking rather loudly, so that all of us laid down our pushers and covered our low-G breakfast bowls.

"I'm changing assignments for this watch, gentlemen," he said in a no-nonsense tone. "Reamy," he went on, looking over at me. "I want you to fly the first one. Come to my office, will you, please?"

He started back to the tube entrance. John Yousoufian stopped him:

"Wait a minute, Chief," he said, rising carefully to his feet in the low gravity. "I drew this mission!"

Bellingrath faced Yousoufian. "I know you did, Yousoufian," he growled. "But I changed it."

"I don't like that!" Yousoufian protested. "We should fly our regular turns."

"Right," the chief agreed. "Unless I decide otherwise. You'll just have to dislike it. Reamy," he said, returning to me, "as soon as you can make it!"

"Yes, sir," I said, deciding it would be too unpleasant to stay at Mess. I stood up with the same care John Yousoufian had used. Six Beta is a tiny moon, and it's easy to fly off your feet if you move quickly, or don't keep a grip on something solid.

Bellingrath hollered "Fore!" down the tube leading to his office, put his feet in the starting blocks, leaned slowly forward in the weak pull of Six Beta's gravity, and dove with elephantine grace into the entrance. I followed him, leaving a pretty loud buzz of conjecture in the Mess behind me.

The chief didn't bother to sit behind his desk in the ten-meter bubble that was his office. He was propped against its corner when I slowed my dive on his shock cord and pulled myself erect.

I beat him to the punch. "What did I do to deserve this, Chief?" I demanded.

"Deserve what, L.C.?" he shot back.

"You know the other pilots are going to be sore about this," I told him. "They are just as interested in flight pay as I am. They'll take it out on me because you gave me this extra junket."

"Perhaps," he conceded, beginning to strip the wrapper off his morning cigar. "But that's minor compared to the problem I'm solving by having you take this flight to Six." He looked up from his work with the stogey. "Can't you figure what's gone wrong, L.C.?"

I shook my head.

"One Bloc or the other is getting desperate," he said bitterly. He paused to light his smoke. "Somebody made an illegal landing during the last watch."

"On Carina VI?" I asked, startled.

"No. Here on Six Beta. Oh, it's plain enough what's on their mind. Whether it's the Dembloc or the Sovbloc I don't know, but one Bloc has decided the only way to get preference on Six is to land some contrabands on the planet before the Federation opens it up under the Treaty. With only a standard month left before we make our first landing, they have very little time. Obviously they can't land a deep-space vehicle there without a grid, so they've got the hot idea of stealing one of our atmospheric probes."

"You mean, hijack one of our search vehicles, Chief?"

"Why not? We're wide open to that kind of attack. Well, I'm in charge of keeping this Mission neutral. No terrestrials are going to land on Six until a month from now, when the Treaty interval has elapsed! Now do you know why I want you to fly this mission?"

I did, but I shrugged.

"The devil you don't, L.C.," he growled, impatient with me. "You're the nearest thing we've got to a neutral. You're the only pilot here on Beta who wasn't born on Earth. Every other man was raised under either the Sovbloc or the Dembloc. Oh, they're supposed to be neutral, I know. But who stops rooting for the home team? Since I can't tell which Bloc landed the hijackers here on Beta, I'll play safe by putting a neutral at the controls of this mission. And if we haven't rounded up the bandits before the next mission, we'll suspend flights and deactivate all our equipment until the bandits run out of air and we can pin them. All right?"

I shrugged again. "I'm neutral," I said. "If that means anything. But you know I'm not going to put up a fight if some bandits come after my vehicle with lasguns."

"That is a hitch," he agreed. "I know you have the right, as a Nonviolent Pacifist, to refuse to carry a sidearm, but I hoped you wouldn't insist on it."

I had to shake my head. "I'm sorry, Chief. I am committed to nonviolence."

"Then you can't go alone; somebody will have to ride shotgun for you, that's all," Bellingrath said. "Whom would you like?"

"Well," I said, frowning, "John Yousoufian would be best. This was supposed to be his mission, Chief, and this way he'll get his flight pay."

Bellingrath shook his head. "He's Sovbloc," he said slowly. "Nothing doing, L.C. Pick a man from the Dembloc."

So that was how the wind blew. "I thought you said you didn't know which Bloc had put the bandits down on this moon," I protested.

"That's what I said," he admitted. "I don't *know* which Bloc has decided to go for broke. But I've got some pretty good ideas. The Federation has its own intelligence service, you know."

"O.K.," I said. "Then I'll ask for Eddie Foyt. He's a tough enough Irishman to be willing to do your shooting for you."

"I'll settle for Foyt," the chief said. "Here," he said, straightening up to walk around his desk and open a drawer. He handed me a lasgun in a holster. "Give this to Eddie."

II

A couple hours later Eddie Foyt and I sat silently side by side in our vehicle, waiting for Beta to turn enough on its axis to bring us to our launch window. Eddie had boarded first to handle the countdown, and all indicators on the panel showed green. We had nothing to do until the booster gave us a gentle kick in the pants and started us on the S-orbit that would let us make a grazing entrance into the immensely deep atmosphere of Six. The moment of pause turned my thoughts back to the situation we found ourselves in.

From the moment the flash went around the Galaxy that Carina VI had an intelligent population, the Federation had gone into action. Six was declared off-limits to all humans. A long-prepared expedition set out to assure that this new planet of intelligence would enter the family of planets in proper form.

Our Federation advance party had set up its survey base on Beta, the small second moon of Carina VI. Under the Treaty, we Federation technicians had a full standard year to study the newly discovered intelligent race from space. Only a month now remained of that standard year of survey. And once it had elapsed, the Federation had the right for still another standard year to control all contacts between the natives of Six and representatives from both Blocs. The chief's reassignment of Foyt and me to our present mission was because of an attempt to circumvent the Treaty.

Foyt and I had drawn what was my tenth or twelfth deep penetration of Six's enormous atmosphere. We were scheduled to tow behind our aircraft a drogue with several kinds of magnetometers in it. In common with most of our atmospheric searches, it was to be conducted on the dark side of Six, and so scheduled that the short blast of rocket-fire needed to get us back out of the atmosphere would readily pass for meteoric activity.

Eddie had continued to sit silently in the dimly-lit control room, hunched down beside me in his spacesuit from the moment of our unhurried blast-off from Six Beta. Only when I called off our course co-ordinates did his grunted "Check!" sound in my earphones.

I shrugged mentally and concentrated on the lighted instruments, timing our retroblast so that we would make a correctly grazing entry to Six's deep atmosphere. Just as I felt for the toggle, there was a rap on my helmet. The bottom fell out of my stomach. Eddie and I were supposed to be alone on our vehicle.

I held absolutely still. From the corner of my eye I could see the instruments' lighted dials mirrored on Foyt's helmet react as a similar rap warned him to freeze.

A gauntlet reached down beside me in the dark and pressed the release stud on my chair. I felt it swung around. I could see Eddie's chair turning, too. Then we were looking into the lasguns held by the two spacesuited figures sharing the dimness of our control room. Barely visible Cyrillic letters, stenciled on their chest plates, said they were Frol Balienkov and D. D. Stiffler. Sovbloc bandits, just as Bellingrath had guessed.

Balienkov made the gesture that means "take it off." Eddie was first, moving carefully out of his chair in the zero-gravity, and splitting his suit down the seal so that he could squeeze out of it. Balienkov oozed forward, lasgun at the ready, felt for Eddie's gun and took it from its suit holster.

A jerk of the muzzle of Balienkov's lasgun told me it was my turn next. I repeated Foyt's movements and slid from my suit like a molting crayfish.

At a gesture from Balienkov, his sidekick Stiffler moved forward, obviously searching for my lasgun.

I shook my head. "No gun," I said in English. I saw no point to giving away the fact that I spoke Russian. Both the Sovbloc bandits looked over at Eddie, twisting their heads inside the shiny bubbles of their helmets. The gleaming plastic sharply mirrored the console now behind me.

"That's right," Foyt said. "L.C. is a Nonviolent Pacifist."

"But you aren't," I said bitterly to him. "You were riding shotgun, weren't you?"

"I had no choice, L.C.," Foyt started to tell me, when I noticed that Balienkov had begun his molt. Stiffler kept us well covered as the apparent Sovbloc boss got rid of his suit. He retrieved his lasgun, and Stiffler molted.

"What do you mean, no choice, Eddie?" I said. "You must

have known since you boarded that these bandits were on board."

"Yeah," he said dispiritedly. "They were laying for me."

"He is right," Stiffler said sharply, causing me to look around. The voice had the wrong timbre. D. D. Stiffler was a woman. You can't help it. You look at them as females. So I looked at her. Dim as it was, I could see that she was quite tall, although slender. I doubted she weighed fifty kilos. Her face had a chill Nordic kind of beauty, but it was frozen with the intensity of her concentration on what she was doing. I wished there were more light in the control room.

"Mr. Foyt has been injected with a synthetic virus of Sovbloc manufacture, Mr. Reamy," Stiffler said in nearly accentless English from the near-dark. "His behavior must be understood in terms of the fact that he will not receive an immunizing injection unless he follows our orders."

I shrugged. What I might have done under the same circumstances I had no way of knowing. "Sorry I spoke as I did, Eddie," I told my co-pilot.

"Sure, L.C." he said. "Now what, Balienkov?"

"We make entry into the atmosphere of Six," the Sovbloc agent said. "Who will be in charge? Will you follow our directions, Reamy, or must we rely on the control we have over your co-pilot?"

"I'll take us in," I said. "What do you want, anyway?"

He grinned at me. "Miss Stiffler and I shall use parachutes to land on the surface, Mr. Reamy. We shall first disable the rockets of your vehicle so that it must crash on the surface of Six. We count on your loyalty to the Federation to force you to bail out near it so that you may destroy the wreckage before the natives can locate it and ponder on its significance, eh?"

"We will do that," I said.

"Then start entry as soon as we cross the terminator," Balienkov ordered, swinging my chair back to the control console. I could hear him and his female partner drawing their safety belts tight in the reserve crew seats behind us.

"Fortunately," I could hear Balienkov say from over my shoulder; "a number of the members of your Federation mission on Six Beta are loyal to their Sovbloc heritage and have kept us informed of the data you have dredged up from this newly-found planet of intelligence. Diane and I are linguists assigned to establish immediate contact for the Sovbloc with the ruling circles of Six. It was good to learn from your tapes that the indigenes use a vocal form of communication in our audible range."

I fired the retroblast and soon we were pressed hard into our seats as the deep atmosphere of Six tugged at us on our grazing entry. Because our velocity was not much more than it took to break away from the attraction of the tiny second moon of Six, we entered comparatively slowly, and the deceleration of atmospheric friction had us down to gliding speeds over the dark side of the planet within a few minutes.

Our delta-winged vehicle was capable of excellent gliding flight at Mach 3. I held her nose down and kept the Mach indicator hovering around that figure, trying to stretch our glide around to the sunlit side.

"Enough of that, Reamy," Balienkov said from behind me, tapping me on the shoulder with his lasgun. "Slow us down, Pacifist. We want to drop lower, down to where we have about one-quarter standard atmospheric pressure. And we want to stay in the dark. Diane and I will bail out when pressure hits about half a gram per square centimeter, eh?"

"Why not?" I said, raising the nose slowly and beginning to kill the speed of our big kite.

"Hey!" Foyt cried. "When do I get my immunity shot?" He swung his chair away from the console to face the armed Sovbloc agents behind us.

"Just a moment," Balienkov said, grunting. I peered around momentarily to see him tearing out a whole bank of wiring that controlled our rockets. When he was done, we were without the power to blast back into space, and our vehicle was condemned to crashing on the dark surface of Six.

Then he spoke to Foyt. "You fool," he said with relish as I concentrated on dropping our kite lower and lower into the deep atmosphere of Six. "Did you really think I would be so incautious as to bring the antidote with me, where you might be able to get it by subterfuge or stratagem? Certainly not."

"Watch it, Eddie," I said quietly from the controls, seeing my co-pilot's muscles tense. "How do you know he really pumped any synthovirus into you?"

"I checked with the med-pack, L.C.," Eddie said furiously. "He gave me the real jolt, all right!"

"Frol!" It was Diane Stiffler's turn to show emotion. The female linguist began spitting Russian at her Sovbloc companion. "You said you would give the immunizing injection! This is not right! Not fair!"

"Quiet!" Balienkov snapped at her in the same tongue.

"Murder!" she stormed at him. "I will not countenance . . . !"

I could almost feel him swing his gun toward her. "Yes, you will!" Balienkov said. "I am in command here! Follow my orders!"

She subsided. But Eddie did not. He launched himself from his contour-chair straight at Frol Balienkov behind me. The flash of the lasgun was like a bolt of lightning. The laser beam smoked hotly against the upholstery of Eddie's seat. I knew the bolt had passed clean through Eddie's body. The control room stunk of burnt flesh.

"To let you know we mean business, Mr. Reamy!" Balienkov said behind me, his accent now a little thicker. "What is our pressure?"

"Two-tenths of a gram," I said, gritting my teeth. "You said half a gram. We have a few minutes."

"Time to get into our chutes," Balienkov told Stiffler in Russian. I could hear them moving around. And then he was standing behind me. "I will go first," I could hear him telling the girl. "Wait about a minute, and then follow me. That should assure that we will land some miles apart. We can't judge the initial hostility of our reception, and by landing separately, we increase the chance that one of us will survive. After a standard day, work in my direction, and I will move in yours. Shoot this Pacifist if he so much as sneezes."

"Yes, sir," she said in surly obedience.

The lasgun barrel tapped my shoulder again. "Slow down close to stalling, Mr. Reamy," Balienkov said. "Open the escape hatch."

I touched the control and the big kite buffeted as the hatch-screen dropped open, flooding the control room with wild drafts and a lot of racket. "See you later!" I heard Balienkov yell.

A quick turn of my head assured me that he had dropped free and, if his chute had opened, was dangling beneath it as it dropped slowly through the darkness into the deep atmosphere of Six.

I closed the hatch screen.

"Open up!" Stiffler said edgily behind me. "I am jumping!"

"Don't," I said. "You'd be dead before you reached the ground."

"What!"

"Sit down in Eddie's chair," I said to her pointing to the seat beside me. "You've been tricked. Balienkov will be dead in another minute."

"Dead?" she demanded, taking the other seat, her lasgun covering me. "How?"

"Anoxemia," I told Diane Stiffler. "This is one tremendously deep atmosphere. At the surface, pressures are about six times standard. But the oxygen percentage is only one sixth of standard. While that makes it breathable *on the surface,* way up here, at a quarter standard pressure, there isn't enough equivalent oxygen to keep a flea alive."

"You knew that!"

"Sure."

"And you let Frol leap?"

"Why not?" I asked, heading our kite deeper into the dense sea of pitch-black air around us. "He killed Eddie, didn't he?"

"And you, a Pacifist!" she seethed. "Sworn to avoid violence!"

I grinned across at her in the dim light of the control room. "I never lifted a finger, Miss Stiffler," I said. "That's one thing you mustn't forget about Pacifists. We have learned to compensate for not being able to bring force to bear."

"You are a liar," she decided. "Open that hatch. I saw the transcripts of the reports made to the Federation. There is plenty of oxygen!"

"Faked," I said. "We know more about what's going on than you might expect. Do you think it was pure coincidence that there were no pilots of Sovbloc parentage scheduled for the missions this watch? Obviously the chief knew it was a Sovbloc ship that grounded on Six last watch. Your man, Yousoufian, tried to fly with me, but the chief nixed it. And if we know that much, perhaps we know your other agents, eh?"

"I'll bail out at three grams pressure," she said tightly.

"That will make up for the one-sixth-as-much oxygen concentration."

"If *that* figure was the truth," I reminded her. "You had better ride this kite all the way down with me. I think I may need an interpreter."

"No!" she said. "You are a Federation man. I would never help you!"

"You don't care *how* you die, do you?" I said, hauling back on the yoke angrily and stalling the big kite completely. A delta-wing isn't meant for aerobatics. We fell off into a flat spin at once. In about three turns our radial velocity had built up to the point where both Diane Stiffler and I were pressed helplessly into our chairs. She didn't bother to raise her lasgun to shoot. She was too dizzy to so much as see me.

The spin down into the darkness seemed endless. It only seemed that way. All things come to an end.

III

We endured a series of messy tearing thumps in the last minute or two before we struck the surface. I don't know what kind of a crash D. D. Stiffler expected, but in that soupy six-times-standard atmosphere, our final descent velocity was picayune. Still, the sudden end to our spinning gave as violent a wrench to our senses, inside the pale illumination of the control room, as the onset of the whirl had done in the first place.

In the long minutes of the spin to the surface I had done some thinking. In spite of a vertigo surpassing anything they had ever induced during space training, I crawled the short distance over to where Stiffler was trying to stop her retching in Eddie's chair, and found her lasgun. One thing about the weapon, it is easy to break. A sharp rap on any hard surface shatters the crystal, and then it is just so much junk. As my head cleared, I looked around for Eddie's weapon, but on not finding it decided that the dead Balienkov had it with him. The Sovbloc agent was still, of course, many kilometers high in the enormous atmosphere of Six.

The retching beside me came to an end. "Some merry-go-round," I said to Diane in the dark. She swore at me in Russian. My knowledge of the language was not that colloquial.

"Same to you, kid," I said, resisting a shameful impulse to smack her on the top of the head.

By then I was making my way out of the control room into the darkness of night outdoors, and letting myself cautiously down to the surface. It was firm underfoot, and felt somewhat springy, as though I had stepped on dried vegetation. The night was soundless, and the heavy air moved sluggishly against my cheeks.

A quick look into the black vault of the heavens at the position of Six's two moons revealed that we had crashed close to the dawn line, and that Carina soon would climb up over the horizon. Diane did not fight me when I came back and insisted she leave our wrecked ship. I made the routine arrangements for its destruction, set the time-fuse and led the girl slowly away by the arm. A decent cremation was the best I could do for Eddie Foyt.

"Don't you have a light, Reamy?" Diane said testily, feeling ahead of her in a fumbling fashion with first one foot and then the other.

"Federation rules permit nothing in our possession more advanced than already developed on Six," I said. "You know that. Come on, that rocket fuel gets hot when it burns."

"You are destroying the ship!" she cried. "There is food there, and medicine!"

"And a radio, and all sorts of goodies," I said. "Nothing doing."

A burst of light from behind us, growing rapidly in brightness, showed that we could walk forward quite safely. We were in a meadow or bracken, depending on how big you considered Sixian vegetation got. The ferns were nowhere more than knee-high. Our long shadows showed that the ground stretched levelly away from us for hundreds of meters, lit by the burning magnesium behind us. I was sure that the heat of the rocket fuel would be sufficient to vaporize any of the more refractory metals used in the construction of our search vehicle.

We had managed to walk a kilometer or more away from our craft by the time the light of its fire receded. Our eyes, somewhat tricked by that brightness, had failed to note the paling of the East, and Carina came redly above the horizon

more quickly than I had expected. Six had a fairly rapid rotation.

The light of the sun produced prompt activity on all sides.
In the first place, the silence of the dark gave way to a welter
of small, sharp sounds, apparently underfoot. Had I not
known better, I would have sworn all manner of mice were
squeaking and scuttling through the ferns around us.

The noises, however, were made by flying animals, who
were flapping and chattering on all sides as they ran through
the bracken before taking to the thick air in the first flush
of dawn. As if at a signal they burst from the ground like
a covey of quail.

They were headed up. And above us, I suddenly realized,
lay the forest. In the thick air, perhaps a couple thousand
meters high, floated amorphous shapes, apparently equally
made of large bladders, nearly transparent in the morning
light, and fibrous strands holding them together. There was a
good deal of greenery strung around the strands. They obviously had been the source of the rending thumps shortly
before we crashed.

"What are they?" Diane demanded, pointing up.

"Flying trees, I guess," I said. "With this thick an atmosphere, a lot of things are possible. I'm guessing that by some
inverted photosynthesis those plants separate hydrogen from
water and secrete it in those great big bladders. As the sun
comes up and they heat, I imagine they climb to some pretty
respectable heights."

Already the race between the thermal climbing of the airborne trees and the flapping zoom of the flying animals was
in force. The "birds" that had left the ground as soon as there
was a little light flapped upward strongly in flocks, and soon
fell to attacking the bladders that were supporting one of the
"trees." Pierced and leaking, it began to sag and settle, while
its companions in the forest, their bladders now well-warmed
by hothouse effect, were climbing up into the dimness and
glare above us.

The climbing disappearance of the trees focused our attention on a number of larger flying creatures. These were plainly
many times the size of the flapping animals that had attacked
the flying tree, and they soared on the morning thermal cur-
rents. Occasionally we could see a lazy, deliberate flap of a

stubby wing as one of these birds worked across from one thermal to another.

As the sun continued to climb, a search of the horizon showed a column of smoke rising fairly straight and thick above the remains of our vehicle. Even though the smoke was better than a kilometer from us, we could see a flock of still larger soaring creatures circling it, like so many stubby-winged buzzards. And then the flock peeled off and began to soar in our direction.

"Down, Diane," I said. "Here come those big buzzards. I don't know how big they are. If they go for us the way the flappers went for that tree, we've had it."

She was quick enough to throw herself belly down among the ferns, but she was female enough to stick her head up to see what was happening. This time I gave in to the impulse and rapped her sharply over the noggin, getting more Russian profanity for my trouble.

A shadow sped over us, and then a series of them. Rolling onto my back I saw that a couple of dozen of the soaring creatures had made a pass over our position in the bracken, and were turning tightly to head up-wind and land near us.

"For pity's sake!" I said, getting a good look at the last of the soarers. "Those are machines, not creatures! Look!"

We both sat up. Oh, the creature was there, all right. There was a pilot in each of the soaring things, sitting, lying, or standing, I had no way of knowing, in an open cockpit. He was steering his glider with what appeared to be two hands, and his upper end—if that's what we were looking at—was shockingly human.

Bird-like, or airplane-like, the stubby-winged gliders made a series of rough, slipping turns in a pattern and prepared to land single-file forty or fifty meters from where we sat in the bracken. As they flared out "over the fence" they wobbled in near-stalls, accentuated by the extremely low aspect ratio of their wings. At the comical last moment, the "landing gear" was extended. Just two of the most human-looking legs and feet you ever saw. Each pilot trotted a few steps and squatted down, grounding his glider.

As quickly as they landed, the pilots hopped from their machines and came running toward us. The first one to land made straight for me.

There is a lot of romantic nonsense about the first contact between intelligent populations. This native had a perfectly straightforward idea of how it was to be handled. He never stopped running. Just charged straight into me, bowling me over again, and sat on me. By the time I had started to struggle, enough of his friends had been added to the pile to make the struggle pointless. I could hear Diane gasping and crying out as she got the same treatment.

Her cries, however, had a nonhuman weirdness about them. I realized that the tapes which our disguised sound probes had yielded us had been smuggled far too effectively to the Sovbloc. Diane had some idea of how the Sixian language was constructed, and she was doing her best to produce the right sounds.

The scuffle subsided, and our captors started a considerable chatter.

In a few moments they let me sit up. Diane was already on her feet, facing one of the natives, considerably smaller than she was, but not so much smaller that he could not watch her lips and tongue closely as she rattled off some of the darnedest sounding lingo you ever heard.

I suppose the humanoid gesture of surprise is the same all over the Galaxy. These little characters were humanoid to about eight places. Outside of weighing, I suppose, no more than twenty-five or thirty kilos, and being no more than a hundred and twenty centimeters tall, they could have passed for some kind of humanity. Certainly nature had supplied eyes, ears, nose, mouth, fingers and toes in the human position and quantity.

Diane walked slowly over to my side. "Good-bye, L. C. Reamy," she said. "Too bad you aren't a linguist!"

"We should stick together, Diane," I told her. "I can't talk this stuff. They may chop my head off!"

"Too bad," she said. "If I get their drift, they are arguing over whether to kill you now or save you for a big sacrifice scene a little later. And as a Pacifist, you won't even be able to resist!"

Leaving me considerably shaken, she walked with a group of the little sky-jockeys to the largest of the gliders that rested on the bracken. Apparently it was a two or three passenger affair. With considerable care, they helped her aboard what was plainly a thing of frightening fragility.

From somewhere the gang came up with a long strand of some stretchy material, rubber or a similar natural co-polymer. Hitching it to a kind of hook on the nose of the large glider, a dozen or so of the jockeys ran forward to stretch the launch cord to the limit of its elasticity. At a cry, the big glider began to ooze forward, gathering speed only slowly. But at a ground speed of no more than two or three meters a second, it was airborne, and climbed until it passed over our heads a good five meters high, dropping at that moment the launch cord.

Already the big rig was banking, slipping toward the inside of the bank as it did, but getting around in a hitching, irregular turn as it sought to stay within the rising column of air in the first thermal it caught.

I was prepared to be taken away in the same fashion, and walked over to the grounded fleet of gliders, a flock of jockeys chattering and tagging along with me. On reaching it, I was quite suddenly knocked down again, and a squad of the jockeys surrounded me, picking me up like so many pallbearers. In a moment I realized that they were weighing me. The decision was quite plain. I was too heavy for any of the craft on the ground. After what looked like a request for volunteers, one of the small stubby-winged gliders was shot into the air by the long stretchy cord, and passed quickly away to the West, obviously hurrying rapidly from thermal to thermal.

I sat down for a wait.

IV

The sky-jockeys of Six didn't have the same idea. Several of them grouped around where I had planted my fundament amid the ferns. They wanted to talk. Diane's example explained their interest. They tried it slow. They tried it fast. They tried it loud. They tried it with elaborately exaggerated motions of their lips and tongues.

All I could do was grin at them and shake my head. *"No capish,"* I said. "I don't dig that jive, cat."

The shrug that my chief interrogator gave was human enough to be funny. I took a more careful look at him. He was dressed in a kind of cape or cloak of pale yellow that fit rather tightly about the neck and hung stiffly down almost to his ankles. So, I discovered on looking around, were the other jockeys. There was some variation in color, ranging from fawn to brown. The capes were all open down the front, which enabled me with no imagination to discover that about half of my captors were male and about half female.

From time to time my captors, for such I had to consider them, took a gander at Carina, plainly checking the passage of time. Their initial tension began to relax after half a standard hour or so. Two of the jockeys were launched by the crew on the ground, and others showed interest in leaving. Feeling my time was drawing short, if I wanted to improve on my status, I gestured trying to get across the idea that I wanted to walk around.

This called for more chatter, and started what I took to be an argument. A brown-caped jockey seemed pretty interested in keeping me off my feet. Somehow he got outvoted, but his sharp tones showed that he wasn't taking his licking lying down. When one of the other jockeys gave a show of assent, I got slowly to my feet. Quite plainly they didn't like my size, for they backed off a few paces from me as I moved slowly over to where their fleet of gliders was drawn up.

I stopped a few meters short of the nearest glider and studied it, with the brown-caped objector hopping up and down in protest.

The vehicle was a prize example of what environment can do for the most primitive of people. Without a trace of a piece of metal in it, and made, I later found out, solely of vegetable products requiring very little processing to adapt them to this use, it was as fragile as a chambered nautilus and as light as thistledown. Its frame was a kind of rattan or bamboo. Its wing and tail covering, I later discovered, was made from the bladder skins taken from the flying trees, and dyed a light gray.

As a flying machine, however, it was just plain horrible. Nothing but an atmosphere of great density, proper natural materials and relatively small humanoid stock made flight possible with the equipment. First off, the single-surfaced wings were deeply cambered. This would give good lift characteristics at low speeds, of course, a necessity with their method of shooting a landing on their own feet, which limited velocity considerably.

The wing, moreover, had a comically low aspect ratio. Span was not even twice the root chord, and, although the whole wing was roughly elliptical in shape, the low aspect ratio assured big tip losses and instability at high angles of attack, which I had noticed when the jockeys were nosing up as they slowed to land.

Walking over closer, to the tune of still shriller objections from brown-cape, I tried to get a quick idea about how the controls worked. They appeared to be only two in number, both operated by hand by the pilot, who straddled a kind of wicker saddle just forward of the wing. His feet rested in stirrups, below which were twin openings which enabled the jockey to extend his legs when landing.

Each control was a simple lever of some woodlike material, pivoted at one end, to which some thin fibers or strings were lashed. In turn the strings ran over grooved blocks of a harder appearance, which served as pulleys, to their force-points. The left-hand lever, as far as I could figure out, warped the rear of the stabilizer so as to make it act as an elevator. Apparently the right-hand lever enabled the jockey to warp the stubby wings, and served as aileron control.

Well, I reflected, wing-warping was good enough for Wilbur and Orville, and it was certainly good enough for a Bronze Age population on Carina Six, a population that seemed to find the air as much its natural habitat as the Cro-magnon human had found the surface of the sea.

There was a vertical fin of sorts making up the remainder of the empennage, but I could see no method of moving it from side to side. In other words, there was no rudder.

Now I could understand the rough slipping turns I had seen the jockeys make as they had swung around into the wind to land near Diane and me. I began to get a glimmer of hope. While I had a primary obligation to make sure the Sovbloc contraband did not tinker with the humanoid population of Six until the Treaty interval had elapsed, I figured I had a still more important obligation to keep alive in order to achieve my purpose. And the way things were shaping up, I felt I had better start to score some points with these people.

Turning to one of the less hostile jockeys who had followed me, I pointed to the strings they used for control cables and tried to show that I wanted some. That was the signal for brown-cape to burst into a wild harangue. He thumped his chest and made quite a speech of it. Funny, I could see that he was getting across to the other jockeys. Quite without visible signal, they jumped me, knocked me down and carried me a good fifty meters away from the nearest glider. My questions had got too close to the bone. So I had lost round one.

The climb of Carina to the zenith was swift, by comparison with a standard day. The forenoon passed with me sitting, painfully aware that the jockeys did not want me to move around. I was getting hungry, but whatever the diurnal pattern of my captors was, it did not appear to include food. As the sun started its downward slant, more and more time was spent studying the soupy glare of the sky. I had a pretty good idea what the little characters were seeking. And then, when irritated scowls aimed at the bracken had taken the place of their searches of the heavens, we heard a call from above us. The jockeys all jumped up, waving to a good-deal larger glider that was making the usual sloppy rudderless turns as it came drooping down from the thermal-active late afternoon air to our little covey.

The grayish-black machine swam sluggishly into the wind and oozed into a landing near at hand. Four sets of legs came out together as it grounded. Here, then, was a glider with enough lift to drag me with it, presumably in the same direction they had taken Diane. I hoped so. Unless I got to her soon, she'd be so far ahead of me with her linguistic skill that I wouldn't be able to head her off. And I still had to figure a way to compete with her for the attention of the jockeys.

A noose of the same kind of cord they used for control lines on the gliders suddenly drew tight around my left ankle. Instinctively I rolled away and drew the cord up tight in a reflective motion of escape. They came at me like little tigers and threw me flat again. I relaxed at once, unsure how much they might injure me were I to struggle.

As they slowly unpiled, Carina slipped below the horizon and the red twilight of a dense sea of atmosphere colored the whole flat landscape. The terminator, I knew from my search missions, was unusually broad because of the density of the atmosphere. Still, Six's high rotational speed meant that within minutes we would be in pitch darkness, occasionally relieved by the hurling transit of the two tiny moons. Stars there would be virtually none—the sea of air above us would screen out all but the brightest, and the slowly descending flying forest, which I gathered occurred only intermittently over the surface, would occult many that might otherwise be seen.

I've heard it said that all diurnal creatures respond to the withdrawal of light. I'll tell you that my kind of human, at any rate, gets even hungrier. It was dinner time, by my stomach. I hoped my little buddies ate my kind of grub.

V

A new kind of activity began as the light went from pink to red to magenta. One of the jockeys, a male, doffed his stiff yellow cape and withdrew from the cockpit of what I suppose was his own glider a kind of apron, which he fastened around my waist. Moving off twenty or so meters from the rest of us, he knelt down and made obeisance to the glow of the departed sun.

Taking a small article or two from the pouch of his apron, he was still for a moment or so, then suddenly moved in sharp jerks while still kneeling. The magenta light faded into darkness. Then there was a glimmer of flame from the aproned jockey, and a shriek from all the others. As the firemaker stood up, lit by the small blaze of dried ferns in front of him, the others went slowly forward, kneeling briefly a time or two as they approached the fire.

Two of my captors kept hold of my ankle leash as I walked cautiously toward the flames. Various jockeys were scrounging around for fuel, which they fed with care, keeping the fire quite small. When I reached the firemaker, I held out my hand for his fire-lighter.

He shook his head, and there was a mutter from the jockeys. Apparently I had hit another taboo. My thoughts weren't as quick as they might have been. Looking at what he held in his hand, I could see a length of bamboo-like stick, with another stick of suitable diameter fitting down into the hollow of the bamboo. He was holding a primitive form of piston and cylinder.

My stupidity, or smug superiority, made me grin in the fire-light, tap the side of my head and nod, showing that I knew how this compression-ignition fire-lighter worked. He was fearless, or completely dedicated to the priesthood he represented. His knife was in his apron, and he came for me with it without a single second's hesitation.

In a civilized world, where your associates know you are a Nonviolent Pacifist, the problem of physical assault is almost completely absent. I could not recall having to withstand it.

The animal in us is too deep, and before I had time to rationalize and permit the attack by the priest, I had leaped aside, striking him a backhanded blow over the kidneys that knocked him flat.

He was not discouraged but with a wild cry struggled to his feet. My thinker got going about that time, and I clapped my hand ostentatiously over my mouth several times, while dodging his next attacks. Then he got it. I wasn't going to spill the beans. He drew himself up to his full tiny height and gave me a stern order, pointing to the last traces of afterglow in the West.

I knelt, facing that way, and gave Carina my obeisance, too. Whether this made me a member of the priesthood occupied my waking thoughts until the sleep of fatigue claimed me, still unfed.

Morning light found me still sacked out. Small hands shook me awake. There was food. During the night the little flappers had returned to the bracken, and the jockeys had stolen around hunting for them. They were fair grub when skinned and broiled over a fern fire.

A little inspection of their skeletons convinced me the flappers were not birds in any sense, but probably were as mammalian as my captors, having developed somewhat in the manner of flying squirrels. This, at any rate, explained the low aspect ratio of the gliders' wings. The jockeys had copied nature, a nature that did not need much efficiency in so dense an atmosphere.

As the thermals built up, I was led to the large glider and carefully put aboard. They had made a few modifications of the rattan so that I could squat down substantially over the center of pressure of the wing. A doubled launch cord was used, and we were heaved droopily into the thick air when Carina was about an hour high.

The surge of the first thermal was quite plain, and our little pilot banked us around in one of those creepy rudderless turns

I had grown used to, staying within the rising cylinder of air. In no time at all we had what I took to be a thousand meters of altitude. The flying forest had risen far above us by that hour. In company with at least some of the smaller gliders, we proceeded northwest over a rather drab and featureless green landscape, pausing occasionally to circle in a strong thermal to regain altitude that had been lost by what I took was haste to complete our journey. Our flight took us in the same direction they had carried Diane. Ahead lay a confrontation.

By noon we were on the home stretch, and our pilot no longer sought any further lift. He kept the nose down, gliding in a straight line for a cluster of buildings on the horizon. He'd nose down until the structure would begin to flutter with drag stresses and then ease the nose up just enough to keep our speed from tearing the frail thing apart.

We passed over what I took to be a central airport of the town or city. That's when I got my next shock. The pilot rose in his stirrups, spoke to the jockey beside him and dove over the side. His sidekick took over the controls.

I gawked overside at the pilot who had done the Brodie, watching the poor guy fall as we swung into the landing position.

Poor guy! I had forgotten the atmosphere was nearly thick enough to swim in. The purpose of the ankle-length flying cloak, also, became apparent. With his arms extended, the pilot was using the cape to ride down the sky in big swooping curves. He was going down faster than I would have liked to, but I had a lot of confidence that he knew how to use his cloak to rear back and slow down when he got ready to land.

Once we had landed, the degree of civilization on Six became more apparent. At a good many points the combination of intelligence with a dense atmosphere produced departures from Terrestrial standards, but otherwise, they were just leaving what we would have called their Bronze Age. The wheel was there and, as I had seen, fire. There were metal instruments and doodads, supplemented to some degree with neolithic holdovers such as obsidian knives similar to the one the fire-maker had tried to use on me.

Iron and steel were not in immediate evidence, but that

iron at least existed I did not doubt, for some of the buildings in the city where we landed were of stone, and granite is hard enough to need something tougher than bronze for a chisel.

The bulk of the buildings, however, were of vegetable materials, only slightly more substantial than the gliders in their construction. The stretchy tree-bladders served as roofs, as walls and, where left undyed, as windows.

The masonry construction, I decided, was limited to structures of public or religious significance. How right I was in this idea showed up at once. I was led by my ankle leash, with a growing mob of naked jockeys following us, to the most massive of all the structures I had seen. In the time it took to shut a wooden-barred door, I was inside a cell.

The place was about five meters square, with a ceiling low enough to force me to stoop, and lit by a single barred window about chest high. In the light that came in, quite bright in the noontime glare of Carina, I made out a pallet in one corner. As I walked to the window to examine my outer surroundings, a figure rose from the pallet.

"Well, they haven't sacrificed you yet, Mr. Reamy," said Diane Stiffler.

I won't say it was a shock to run into her. My big glider had taken the same course on which I had seen Diane air-lifted the previous day, and in a sense we both posed the same problem to the jockeys. They had no way of knowing that we were not a team, a pair, a set or whatever they considered a two-unit group working together.

"They had knives out once, Stiffler," I grinned.

"And let you go? You were, of course," she sneered slightly, "incapable of offering resistance, Mr. L. C. Reamy."

My smile dwindled. "My ethics deserted me, I'm afraid, Diane," I said. "I tossed one of those jockeys on his back and got across to him that I was no danger to them."

She frowned, turning to kneel on the pallet, and eventually standing. Diane was enough shorter than I was that she did not have to stoop under the ceiling of our cell. "Danger to them?" she demanded, repeating my phrase. Then she went for the throat: "You mean, you were successful in communicating with them? How did they know you weren't a danger? What kind of danger?"

I laughed, backing away from her aggressive advance across the stone floor. A little common sense started percolating through my thick head. Our interests were adverse. She had landed on Six to grease the way for the Sovbloc, in violation of the Interplanetary Treaty. The mission I was part of on Six Beta had been recruited to prevent either Bloc from getting a preferred position.

"You want to know too much," I said, continuing to chuckle. "It's time I clammed up."

She shrugged, ramming her fists onto her hips, her feet apart. "You won't talk, eh? So I'll ask *them*." She sounded pretty smug.

I let defeat sound in my voice: "You mean you can talk with them already?" I wanted to know.

"Hah!" She leaned back to throw her words at me. "As if I should answer *your* questions! Well, there is no reason why not: Perhaps I can't exactly talk with the natives yet. But I have identified ten or twelve operators in their speech."

"Operators?" (Hollowly.)

"Oh, you know," she said with that viciousness which is peculiarly feminine. "The really important words. 'Through.' 'By.' 'Between.' 'Under.' 'Because.' That kind."

"Oh." (Grudging respect!)

She laughed softly, letting her hands fall to her sides and moving slowly toward me. "You would have been trying to identify nouns, I suppose, Mr. Reamy?" she asked lazily.

"Maybe," I agreed doubtfully. "I couldn't operate the way you are going about it, that's a cinch."

"The advantage of being a trained linguist," Diane told me. "And just to cheer you a little, L. C. Reamy, you might as well know that Sixian is a positional speech, like Chinese. But unlike Chinese, it is inflected about as much as Sanskrit."

"*Sanskrit?*" (A note of terror peeped from behind my query.)

"A forebear language of what you and I speak," she said, offhandedly, turning away to look out the barred window. She had to bend down to some extent to make it possible. "For your information," she said, coming back to me with a stride that smacked of relish, "Sanskrit had twenty-six declensions, and innumerable moods and voices. Well, Sixian makes Sanskrit look as simple as Malay, and that is as simple as you can get."

"Sure," I said, desperation beginning to show. "Everybody knows *that*."

Diane started suddenly, turning toward the barred door to our cell. Several of the jockeys were there, and a turnkey was coming up. The deputation came in.

"Listen to this," she said quietly, pushing by me to go up to our callers. Her voice was quick and urgent as she brought forth the weird sounds I had first heard her use when we were captured out on the bracken.

The most richly dressed of the jockeys raised a hand, expressed what was clearly surprise to some of the others, and moved quickly to stand before her. Two or three others tagged along at his heels.

A jerky, nervous colloquy of some kind started between them. The chief jockey gave out with plenty of nods, a smile, then a wide grin, and otherwise showed pleasure at Stiffler's accomplishment. While the two of them chattered and whined at each other, a couple of his sidekicks came over to me and tried the same song, second verse.

I shook my head. *"No capish,"* I said, trying a grin. I offered to shake hands. They never had heard of the gesture, and started back a pace or so. Their words became more urgent, obviously irritated. Then one of them threw up his hands, and they went back to the successful conversation going on between big cheese and my opponent.

She was scoring heavily. The head gazabo gestured with his palm, offering Diane the chance to leave our cell. She looked back at me over her shoulder.

"So long, stupid," she called out.

Ducking so that I wouldn't hit my head, I moved over quickly to the door, and would have gone through it right behind her except for the press of little bodies to keep me from it.

"Stiffler!" I said. "For Pete's sake, me, too!"

The big cheese laid his palm against my chest, and plainly asked a question of Diane, who was already out in the dusty street.

"Nyet!" she snapped, and repeated the negative in Sixian, while drawing her finger across her throat.

VI

Back behind the barred door once again, I tried to take stock of my situation. There weren't enough facts to go on.

Carina had passed the zenith some time before, during the business of getting me from the central airport and into the cell I had shared so briefly with Diane Stiffler. The shaft of light coming through the waist-high window crept across the floor, and the color of the light yellowed and hinted that it would soon redden. When the first ruddiness showed against the wall across from the window, I had visitors. It was a small party, dressed rather plainly in a type of apron.

One of them, from his motions, I figured out was the community firemaker. After my cell door had been opened and they all came in, he knelt and rammed his little piston home a few times in its cylinder, facing me, and got a bit of fluff glowing. A couple of females came forward, feeding the tiny glow with shreds of fern, and helping him blow the fire into life. In a few minutes they were feeding finger-sized sticks to the blaze. The smoke, of which there was plenty, eddied upward and out through a barred hole in the stone ceiling that I had not noticed earlier.

A couple more of the females came in, carrying a bowl of pottery in which were the skinned and gutted carcasses of a dozen or so of the flying mammals. While one of the males came over and pinched and prodded at me, examining just how fat I was, the cooks began roasting one of the little mammals.

They considered it cooked more quickly than I would have, but I gave them no argument, and tore the rare juicy meat from the tiny bones with my teeth. The smoky fire had given the meal plenty of taste, and I must report that I ate with relish.

As soon as I had begun to eat the first piece of meat, the cooks started roasting the second, adding more sticks to the little fire. Five or six of the animals filled me up pretty well, but they tried to press more on me. I was being fattened for the kill.

Well, it was not an altogether unpleasant idea. Any appreciable fattening, if it were not purely ritualistic, would take a number of days. And the idea of the passage of time got my thinker working a little better, I took one more piece of meat, more, really than I wanted, and munched slowly at it. At the same time, I started fishing sticks from the fire, choosing those that had burned through the middle so that I had a fairly solid piece of wood, tipped by a charred end.

There was, for a while, objection to this. But as I took care to extinguish the glow at the end of each faggot, the resistance ended. I accumulated a couple dozen writing tools in this fashion before they got tired of my dawdling over the food, packed up their remaining groceries and started to put out the fire.

I let out a holler at this, and ran over to the nearest wall, making shadow-figures with my fingers. It was the only way I could figure to ask for a light. After some moments of dumb show on my part, one of the jockeys tapped his head and left, only to return in a couple of minutes with a small lamp, consisting of a floating wick in a bowl of oil. It was strapped to a little cradle so that it could be hung to the bars of the "chimney" without the lamp's blaze kindling the fibers that supported it. I grinned and nodded enough times to make it plain I was expressing my thanks. A few shrugs said that the gift was not important. The wooden bars closed once again, and I was alone.

In my one-candlepower light, I started to work. My first question was whether to use the floor or the walls. The masonry skills of the jockeys weren't any great shakes, and none of the surfaces in the room was unusually smooth. Deciding that I had enough ideas to cover more area than the floor provided, I went to one of the side walls and began my sketching.

My resulting three-view drawing of a glider left something to be desired, but it was, from an engineering standpoint, an accurate representation of the machines the jockeys were flying.

On the opposite wall I drew with much more care. Here I laid out a better mousetrap. The improvement on their glider featured some very simple ideas. In the first place, I put some dihedral in the wings. Secondly, I increased the aspect ratio, so that span was about five times root chord, while sticking to their essentially correct idea of an elliptical planform. My biggest change, although only the engineering-minded would catch it, was in the empennage. I drew control horns on the rudder similar to those the natives had used to flex the stabilizer.

In the remaining wall space I made enlarged layouts of a couple of other thoughts. One was a more efficient wing section, employing a double-surface rather than their single-surface construction. That, I figured, was enough for one night.

It was a darned good thing I had spent the night drawing on the walls with my sticks of charcoal. Little hands shook me awake long before I would have awakened. They were ready to lead me out—and by "they" I mean some fancily-dressed characters who had the mark of priests about them.

Since my cell window faced west, there was not much brightness in the room. The moment I got the picture of what my captors were up to through my fuzzy head, I grabbed one of my drawing sticks, and pushed through the crowd to the wall, and pretended to make improvements on one of my drawings.

A couple of priests were tugging at me, and in the background I could see a third getting a noose ready to slip over my ankle, since my head was a little out of reach. But still another of the priests called for a pause. That was the first sign that I was getting to them. Knowing perfectly well that my speech meant nothing to them, I nevertheless started an explanation.

"Listen, kids. You are killing the goose that can lay the golden egg. Don't do it, little buddies. See that wing? That's got efficiency written all over it. It'll slip through the soupy air on this planet like goose grease compared to those deep-camber jobs you're flying. Like this:"

I started making hand-motions, showing the slow and the fast, and stretched out my arms, with my hands flattened to represent wings. I did some nice gliding turns around the room while they watched, half surprised, half interested.

The priest who had called for a pause went over to my better mousetrap and pointed out some of its features to the others. He tried asking me questions, and I pretended I understood him. He had enough rank, I figured out, to put the kibosh on the idea of slipping a knife into me immediately. His authoritarian voice plainly gave some orders, and a runner departed at a trot.

We continued our joint examination of the good ship Mousetrap, with his gibberish questions eliciting my gibberish answers. But that did not last long.

The jockey who came back with the runner was wearing what I would have called a carpenter's apron. Several tools hung from it in loops, among which I recognized a knife, an awl and a spokeshave. I had found a technician.

This time I was not having my hand refused. When the aproned gent came to look over the Mousetrap, I moved cautiously to his side, reached slowly for his right wrist with my left hand. With a frown, he let me take it. Slowly again, I extended my right hand, taking his palm, and went through a gentle and formalized handshake. There was some laughter at this, but the idea of joint action was not that difficult to get across.

Once again I started my explanation in English of the merits of the Mousetrap to the apron-wearer. My drawings were not clear to him, and he kept shaking his head. He pointed to the plan-view of my improvement on their glider and shook his head, gesturing to show that the high aspect ratio was no good.

But in turn I shook my head vigorously, and tapped at the side of my think-tank to indicate I knew what I was talking about. With the greatest care of all, I gingerly sought permission to remove one of his tools from the loop of his apron. He didn't think much of the idea. Whether it was because of a strong sense of personal property, or because he thought I might turn the awl on him as a weapon, he resisted at first. But I kept up a quiet insistence and finally got my way.

With the tool in my hand, I took my pigeon gently by the arm and urged him to leave the cell, pointing off into the distance. I made every kind of practical motion with the awl, showing that I knew how to use it. When that got me nothing, I returned it to him with the same careful slowness, fearful that he would interpret my movement as an attempt to harm him with its point. Still, when it was once again safely hanging in its loop, he gave me no trouble when I sought to take the spokeshave from him. This was a more illustrative tool and I got him promptly when I showed him that I knew how to use it.

Handing him one of my drawing sticks, I got it worked around to where he held it while I carefully drew shavings from it with what was, after all, a pretty sharp blade. Like the awl-point, it had the shiny glint of iron rather than the darkness of bronze.

Once again, I took him by the arm, indicating I wanted to go with him.

The chatter I had heard up to that point was nothing compared to the argument which that started. The woodworker now had a powerful yen to get me to his shop. And the priests had just as much intention to get me to the altar. It was the same bossy priest who had sent the runner away who finally gave the nod to my idea. But he took precautions. As we walked together down the path between the buildings, the technician on my right, the priest was close at my left, and a gang of his followers came along to make sure I didn't get away.

VII

Society on Six had proceeded to the point of division of labor I discovered, when they finally got me to the shop where they built their gliders. The place was of vegetable construction, but the built-up ceiling joists spanned a good ten meters. Several gliders, of various sizes, were under construction. I saw no evidence that they had the idea of mass production or standardized design. Apparently each glider was one of a kind.

What I wanted was a completed glider. I had to walk around the shop for a while, shaking my head as I came to one or another in the process of construction. At the far end I found it, a two-place machine virtually completed. Most important, the controls were installed. They let me move the two levers, and I found that my first ideas were right. The left-hand lever warped the stabilizer to change the amount of decalage. The right lever warped the stubby wings to impart aileron action. As in the first glider I had examined, there was a vertical fin, but there was no provision to flex it for rudder action.

Turning to the head mechanic, who had come to my cell, I pointed to the strings they used for control cables and tried to show that I wanted some.

It took some time, but after a while another mechanic came

forward with a good-sized roll of the cord wrapped figure-eight style around a stick, the way every kid is taught to wrap a kite cord.

I got a shock when I tried to break some of the cord. It had the natural springy tenacity of nylon and cut my knuckles sharply. Holding out a hand, I was given the head mechanic's knife. It had a good edge, and I cut the lengths of cord I needed.

Because I knew exactly what was involved, stringing the additional control line was not as hard as otherwise would have been the case. Since I was not above swiping a good idea, I took a careful gander at the way they had mounted the elevator control horn, found a piece of wood of the right size, and lashed a rudder control horn in a good approximation of the same fashion.

Plenty of jockey comment took place with each change and addition I made to the ship. Getting the knife again (he wanted it back whenever I laid it down) I used it in a little careful surgery to cut a portion of the vertical fin free of the fuselage so that it could be sprung back and forth like a rudder. As in the case of the stabilizer, the natural elasticity of the reeds used for the rudder frame was quite enough to eliminate the need for any hinges.

At last, with the rudder lines tied to the aileron control lever, I moved the handle. As the right wing was warped to a higher angle of attack, the trailing edge of the rudder was swung to the left. I worked the control a number of times, trying to judge by eye whether I had proportioned the amount of rudder control correctly to the amount of wing warp. By sliding my newly-installed control lines up and down the lever somewhat, I could alter the linkage. At last it had a "right" look, although only test would tell.

By this time the whole work force of the shop, perhaps ten or fifteen in number, had gathered around. Theoreticians among them were sounding off at a great rate on the significance of my coupled aileron and rudder. I was pretty sure none of them got it.

In the long run all of us fly-guys get down to the point where we have to explain with our hands. Since I had none of Diane Stiffler's skills with their lingo, there was no other way.

So I knelt down beside the glider I had altered and made

wings of my two palms. Showing by extending my arms palm down from my sides that I was flying, I "warped" my wings by twisting my right arm so that the little-finger side of my hand, the "trailing edge" of my wing, was lowered, and by twisting my left arm the other way, so that the thumb, or "leading edge" of my left palm was lowered. Then I "banked," leaning my body slowly to the left, and then twisted my torso to indicate that I was making a turn to the left. Neutralizing my controls, I "leveled out," and then reversed the aileron action to show how to make a turn to the right.

There was a nod or two, a quick word of explanation shot over a couple little shoulders, and the whole gang got the picture.

Clapping my hands to emphasize my point, and shaking my head in the jointly accepted symbol for the negative, I repeated the whole series of movements, but this time with a difference. As I "warped" my right wing into the added-lift position for a turn to the left, first I "banked" left and then, twisting my body *to the right* rather than around to the left in a turn, I showed that the wing with the higher angle of attack also generated more drag than the other wing, and that it twisted the glider *against* the direction of turn that the bank would otherwise have induced.

"That's called inverse yaw, kids," I told them. "And Wilbur is the guy that figured out you have to offset it with a rudder."

The idea took a while to jell. I came pretty close to popping the gussets on my sacroiliac before I did enough "inverse yaw" to get the idea across. It was the head mechanic who got the idea first. He repeated my gesture of tapping his head, and launched into rapid-fire speech, making "flying" motions with his hands to get the argument across to the others. Oh, it didn't sell easily, and finally he got to the point of shaking a fist angrily, storming around the shop while picking up materials and more tools. With a plain "come on with me" gesture, he led the whole bunch of us out into the outdoors. We were on the way to the airport.

He was a good deal more careful than I had been about attaching the rudder horn to the craft he chose for alteration. Some additional hard blocks were installed as pulleys, at points where I had rather fudged on the design. But before noon the builders, with several of them now participating, had considerably improved on my version of rudder control.

They were getting a launch cord laid out on the short greenery of the airport, a little ahead of time, for my dough. Somewhat to my surprise, their test pilot turned out to be a female. She tried to get aboard, but before I would let her take off, I showed her how the lashing of the rudder lines could be moved up and down the aileron lever, increasing or decreasing the amount of rudder action with a given amount of aileron movement. After all, too much rudder would mean that a skidding turn would have replaced their usual slipping turn, and one was about as poor as the other.

She gave a monstrous jerk of her head, and called over the chief mechanic, who I decided was also the boss designer. The test pilot operated the lever several times, craning around to get a view of the amount of rudder action, while talking in quiet, serious tones with the designer, who was standing at her side. Between them they chose a setting with more rudder action than I had thought was called for. I did not resist this change. Their race had spent a long part of its history in the air, and I had an idea it could intuitively figure the action of its own soupy atmosphere on surfaces better than I could.

Just how the word got around, I don't know. But by the time they were stretching out the launch cord for the test flight of the ruddered glider, there was a mob of several hundred standing around, yipping and hollering back and forth. I looked for Diane Stiffler, but her height was nowhere visible.

And then the altered glider was swimming sluggishly into the afternoon breeze as the shock cord slowly heaved itself back to its natural length. I held my breath. If something went wrong now, my name would be mud for however few minutes it would take my captors to finish me off with their knives.

By the time the launch cord was slack, our lady jockey was several meters high and heading into the declining sun.

The glider tossed from side to side, and for a moment I thought something had let go. But I was seeing no more than the heavy thermal activity in so dense an atmosphere after a few standard hours of sunlight.

The other end of the stick, of course, was the fact that my lady test pilot had no distance at all to go to find a thermal. In a couple minutes the stubby-winged soarplane was climbing like a homesick angel, turning in tight circles to stay within the updraft.

Then she had broken out of the thermal and came swooping down over us, nose pretty far down, and moving along, I judged, at fifteen or twenty meters a second. She took to the coupled control like a duck does to water. There was a lot to the comparison—she and her kind had been raised flying, and it came almost as naturally to them as it does to the birds. But her first really sharp turn and bank was hair-raising, as she warped the deeply cambered wings to their full extent and wrapped her eggshell craft around in a pylon turn, almost fully vertical, right over the heads of the crowd. A shrill cheer leaped from the throats around me. It took only an instant for those natural aviators to appreciate what they had just seen.

VIII

In the standard month that remained before the first legal landing would be made on Six by terrestrials, my situation changed considerably. Oh, I was still under restraint, and they locked me up every night. But I could sense there was a difference.

We spent the month, pretty largely, in designing and building the good ship Better Mousetrap. The size of wing I had drawn called for a built-up spar, something they had never fooled around with, even though the built-up ceiling joists of the glider factory said the construction idea was not foreign to them. Since there were good natural glues, and all kinds of shrinkable wrappings, after a reasonable amount of experimentation, we came up with a main spar that was the pride and joy of Tschildet's eye. In the whole time I was on Six, his was the only name I ever learned, or tried to approximate.

During the month, of course, I spent a good deal of time trying to get a lead on Diane Stiffler. For whatever reason, my little buddies had no intention of letting the two humans on their planet get back together. At first I suspected that they had done my wordy opponent in, but one time or another I saw her at a distance, usually walking along with an entourage of priests. On that basis, I decided, we were attached to opposite factions of society, she to the religious, I to the practical.

One of the design criteria of the Better Mousetrap was a cockpit designed to fit me, so that I could operate her controls. When the day came for a test-flight, there seemed to be no question in the jockeys' minds but that I would accompany the test-crew.

They probably had a variety of reasons for sending several of their race along on the first flight. Most important, I decided when I was shown a couple of knives, was their fear that I might decide to fly away in the superglider. I tried to disabuse them of the idea, shaking my head powerfully, making flying circles and showing by grounding my hand in the "grass" that I meant to return to their little city airport.

The chief test pilot was again my little female friend. She sat beside me in the nose. Tschildet and one of his chief tinkerers sat behind us, filling up the cockpit. They used four of the usual launching cord strands, and a good fifty of the jockeys stretched it out to give us a boost into the air. The launch seemed far too slow. I had visions of the Mousetrap sliding along on its skid, failing to get airborne, and coming to an ignominious halt on the "grass." But then the little gal at the controls eased the stick back. Mousetrap's nose came up and we wafted into the air. The long span gave us an unwonted stability. When the first thermal hit us, there was very little wing-waggle, and she had us climbing smoothly in no time.

Because the wing was double surfaced, and because I had insisted on considerably more streamlining than they were used to, Mousetrap flew with an unaccustomed silence. More than silent, she was *fast!* The double-surfaced wing had twice as good a lift over drag coefficient as their deeply cambered single-surface airfoil.

She let me take it away from her when we had a couple hundred meters over the field. Because I didn't want any knives sticking me in the back, I held the Mousetrap in tight turns over the airport, climbing her from one thermal to the next. At a thousand meters, by my judgment, I dropped the nose, kicked her into a straight slant, aimed at the center of town, and let the speed build up.

The design job, native and imported, had been a good one. No shimmy, no shake, just smooth, speedy penetration of the soup. Leveling out, still moving three times as fast as they had ever been able to fly, I banked the Trap into a tight turn and used elevator to help us around in a vertical bank. There was a noticeable increase in G-load, and I could see our relatively long wing flex under the strain. But everything held, and I eased her back level, headed for the airport, to the tune of excited comment from my passengers.

One thing I had not been able to sell them on was the idea of flaps or spoilers, so I had quite a time getting the efficient, clean kite back down to where I could land it. But when I hauled back and slowed the Trap down, there was none of that jittery waggle I had associated with the tipstalls caused by low aspect ratio. They got the point and were crowing with triumph when I greased her down onto her skid in as sweet a landing as you could want.

Fate lent a hand just then. Over the hollering of the big crowd, our largest to date, we could all hear a completely alien sound. Just the loudest Klaxon you could possibly imagine. And that's exactly what it was. The Federation was making its "first landing" in the specially equipped vehicle designed for grounding without a grid. In our terrifically dense atmosphere, the racket of its horn was audible for a huge distance.

"Let's go!" I cried to them. I pointed in the direction of the racket and made flying motions. The hooting continued in the distance where, beyond eyesight, the Federation's ship was slowly settling to the surface. And then the hooting became intermittent, a bellow, then a few seconds of silence, as my friends from Six Beta mooed and called for the natives to come and see what the heck was making all the racket.

After a while I got them fired up to the idea that we should take the Trap to the source of the sounds. But the idea didn't sell until they had brought Diane Stiffler to the airport and loaded her into one of their own gliders. Diane and her party took off first, but our faster ship quickly caught up with the fleet that was making for the spaceship's racketing Klaxon, and we passed them.

In less than half an hour, steering by sound, we passed over the grounded spaceship. Its length of a couple hundred meters towered up above the bracken. I could see as we circled lower that it had passed slowly through some of the flying forest, for remains of bladders and plenty of green strands were pretty well draped around the hull. About twenty terrestrials were standing around on the bracken, a good many of them pointing up to where our slick glider was circling. Somebody ran to the companionway, and the Klaxon stopped its infernal shooting.

I let my little girl friend shoot the landing, which she did with as much class as you could desire, sliding up to within twenty meters or so of the base of the spaceship.

The chief was at the head of the group that came running over to us. He recognized me the moment I stood up in the cockpit, towering over the others in the crew.

"L.C.!" he cried. "Are you all right?"

And then there was a whole gang around me as I stepped out, slapping me on the back, glad to see me alive.

"How do you like our ship, Chief?" I asked him.

"You certainly taught them a lot in a hurry, L.C.," the chief said.

I laughed at that one. "Just a better mousetrap, Chief," I explained. "They all fly things around here. Some of the local product should be arriving in a few minutes."

"Were you forced down?" he asked.

"You had it right, Chief," I said. "The Sovbloc had landed a couple linguists on Beta, and they had stowed away. I guess they had it figured that John Yousoufian would have the mission and that he would drop them by parachute without letting on what he had done."

He scowled at that one. "And Eddie?" he asked.

"They got Eddie, Chief. I'm sorry. He's dead. While his killer is dead, the other contraband got down with me. She ought to be along any minute. She had no part in Eddie's death, I have to say that."

"The linguist, eh?" he pursued me. "That Stiffler woman? Was she able to talk their lingo?"

"Right away," I said, surprised at the accuracy of the Federation's intelligence.

"And you? You can talk with them, too, L.C.?"

"Oh," I told him. "Just hand-gestures and drawings. We get along. Here, this guy coming over, the one with the apron, he's their head glider designer. His name is Tschildet. He likes to be called that. Shake hands with him."

The chief seemed to know how to handle himself on a strange planet, and Tschildet gave him full courtesy.

"I must say," the chief said out of the corner of his mouth. "You seem to be on good terms with these people."

"In like Flynn."

"And Stiffler?"

I shrugged. "Haven't seen much of her. Ask her yourself. Here she comes."

Diane was walking slowly across the bracken from her grounded glider to where the party of terrestrials stood. The natives in her fleet mostly ran over to look at the spaceship. A few were still tagging at her heels asking, I felt sure, for an explanation of the giant structure. She was shaking her head, refusing to speak.

"Well," the chief was saying, "knowing that you are a Non-violent Pacifist, I can see why she's still alive. And I suppose, if you can assure us that the Sovbloc has established no primacy because of her, she'll get away with this."

"Ask her," I suggested. "Find out how she stands."

And then Diane was before us.

"You realize you are under arrest, contraband!" the chief said, trying to sound severe.

"Not much change," she said nastily. "And the quicker you get me off this depressing planet, the better!"

The chief shook his head. "I can't understand it," he said to her. "Here you are, a prize linguist, able to talk a blue streak with the locals. And here's Reamy, making dumb-show with his hands. How does it occur that he has them in the palm of his hand, and you are still a captive?"

She shook her head. "I should have killed him when I had the chance!" she said.

"And you can't tell me how he did it?"

"No, I can't," she said angrily.

The chief turned back to me.

"She overlooked one thing," I grinned at him. "You have to have something to say!"

LETTER FROM A HIGHER CRITIC

Stewart Robb

May 5, 2415

Mark Livingstone,
25 The Standards,
Verneville, Alassippi

Dear Mark:

In your last letter you made one palpable hit, but only one: I admit that the atomic wars of the Twenty-first Century and the cataclysms of the Twenty-second Century destroyed so much of our cultural inheritance, including nearly all our Nineteenth and Twentieth Century history, that there is very little we can turn to of those times that is authentic. Apparently that is the only point we will be able to agree on.

I cannot possibly believe, for instance, as you do, that there ever did exist an Abraham Lincoln as so glowingly portrayed by our two or three surviving "history" digests; nor can I believe that there ever was a World War II, at least such as they describe. Wars, yes—there have always been wars, and a World War II may have occurred—but certainly not with such incredible concomitants.

In short, your "history" is much too fictional for me.

So pardon me if I prove my point by doing a hatchet job on this medley of stuff you seem so sure of, this "history" which is about as reliable and as imaginatively romantic as the Bible myths. My method of demolition will be identical to that of those commendably clear-headed iconoclasts of earlier days, the Higher Critics. What they did to the Bible, including the Moses and Christ legends, I shall do with our nearly equally revered American history, so called, and perhaps more thoroughly.

239

Let me begin my act of demolition by making an analogy, one that is possible thanks to the fortunate survival of that now famous Lord Chumley collection of Old English plays. In browsing through some of the playwrights of the Elizabethan, Restoration and even later periods I noticed that they had a cute habit of giving names to their characters that fitted the parts they played in the plots. For instance, Sir Giles Overreach was overreaching, Abhorson was a nasty fellow, Sir Fopling Flutter was an effeminate dandy, Wellborn was a fine young gentleman, and so on.

Now it is precisely this fictional method of applying names that dismays me when I see the obvious evidences of it in our so-called American history, and thus I am led to the inescapable conclusion that what so many of us regard as history is not history at all but pure romancing by flag-waving minstrels, though it has come down to us as sober fact. Not that this legend-building is anything new. The Song of Roland and the deeds of Arthur and the Knights of the Grail were all once considered historical. Those romances, with a little history mixed in, were simply the troubadours', skalds' or minstrels' exploitation and exaltation of their respective heroes and lands.

Now let me get down to brass tacks with my higher criticism and start in with "World War II." This terrific conflict, so the story goes, resulted in the victory of right over wrong, of decency over tyranny, of the Anglo-Saxon peoples (mainly) over the wicked Teutons! There was a big bad wolf in this fairytale named Adolph Hitler, a German ogre who burned people alive in ovens by the millions and who nearly conquered the world! Now don't you think that whoever made up this part of the yarn knew that the name Adolph in Old High German means Wolf Prince? And isn't it a coincidence that he descended like a wolf on the fold of the innocent sheep nations of Poland, Czechoslovakia and other helpless countries? This name is a fancy of the poets, surely!

Let us proceed. The great nation France is beaten to its knees by the mighty marauder, whereupon a folk-hero named De Gaulle arises who fights on against all odds, and later, with the coming of peace, assumes rule over a united Gaul. His name was beautifully tailored for his part. Note that it means "Of France" or "Of the French," indicating that he was a true patriot, French of the French.

The names of the Russian leaders in this war also indicate the poet's imaginative pen. The Wolf Prince met with real resistance in his invasion of Russia, because the opposition here was headed by Stalin, which means Steel, and his high henchman Molotov, which signifies Hammer. (Probably the names also represented the Hammer and Sickle, symbols of the Communist cause.)

This mythical invasion of Russia by the German tyrant is no doubt simply a furbishing up of the earlier yarn of the invasion of this same land by the equally fabulous Napoleon, that is, Apollyon, the Destroyer, which the name means in Greek. Both conquerors invade with mighty multitudes, and both conquerors are trounced. Justice must triumph!

Now across the Channel, at the outset of the Great War, so the story goes on, the British Empire was ruled by a mere servant-leader, fittingly named Chamberlain. But so desperate did the danger of the Wolf Prince's invasion become that the chamberlain was forced to give way to the Master Defender of the British Isles, Churchill, the Church on the Hill, of course, representing the staunch, unshakable faith of the stubborn bulldog British. This name was clearly chosen for its positive, spiritual sound.

And across the Atlantic, where the Giant Ally of the Church on the Hill was preparing for war, the names of the protagonists were equally descriptive of their functions. As America was one of the *good* nations the names were selected for their affirmative sound. The great wartime President was Roosevelt, which is Dutch for Field of Roses. A name of excellent odor! Fabled to have written the President's wartime and other speeches was Rosenman, that is, the Rose Man, the gardener who takes care of the flowers of speech of the Field of Roses. And the Secretary of the Treasury, the man who had had charge of the finances that kept the nation functioning was Morgenthau, symbolizing that he supplied the refreshing morning dew for the roses. And the Secretary of State, that is, the ship of state, was of course good old Hull.

Well, I could go on and on, for our romancing historians enjoyed the creation of such curious coincidences. Here's another obvious one: Just as they had dusted off the Napoleon Apollyon legend to re-apply it to the Wolf Prince, so in like manner they borrowed a still earlier so-called historical event, reversed it to disguise the source, and applied it to the Great War. In 1066, so it was fabled and generally believed, Normandy invaded England. At the head of the invading troops, so the minstrels reported, was a minstrel-warrior named Taillefer, a hero who struck the first blow of the war. So our latter-day minstrels fabled that just as Normandy invaded England, England and the Allies now invaded Normandy. And to the leader of the conquering forces the poet historians gave that same name of Taillefer, only this time they translated it first into German, Eisenhower. Both names, you are aware, mean Iron-Hewer, a most fitting epithet for men of war!

Now let me ask a rhetorical question. Do you really believe that these names: Adolph Hitler, De Gaulle, Molotov, Stalin, Chamberlain, Churchill, Roosevelt, Rosenman, Morgenthau, Hull and Eisenhower could have sprung up by chance? And yet if they are real historical names chance and chance alone must have operated in their selection. Therefore, I say that this history, that you and so many others credit as true history, is as legendary as the Bible stories, and for similar reasons. True history is meaningless and springs by happenstance from a meaningless world.

I note that you also mention in your letters, and frequently, that American folk-hero, Abraham Lincoln, and you actually seem to be convinced there was such a man. I, too, should certainly like to be able to believe the human race capable of producing so noble a being, but here is just another instance where the facts firmly forbid me to do so. As usual, let us first analyze the name. Abraham was well-chosen. It immediately suggests Father Abraham, the Bible patriarch. The name is Hebrew and means Father of a Multitude. All this Lincoln was. He loomed above the Civil War like a colossus, holding the nation together and keeping it one and indivisible. Preserver of nation, saviour of his people, he was veritably the father figure of a multitude, was he not? And a father figure on which the conspirators could vent their malice.

Notice, too, how so frequently he is likened to the Saviour of Mankind. Ponder that beautiful surviving pen and ink drawing, so well portraying America's conception of a vast, compassionate, Christ-like figure. Ah, that Lincoln! One of the most beautiful creations of our dreaming skalds. Would that I could accept him! Our poet-patriots made up a perfect

parallel between him and the solar myth saviour of mankind.
As follows:

> *Christ was a martyr.*
> *Lincoln was a martyr.*
> *Christ was slain on Good Friday.*
> *Lincoln was slain on Good Friday!*
> *So Lincoln joins the crucified saviours of mankind.*

Now whatever this story is, it is not history. It could not
possibly be. It stands to reason the assassins of Lincoln would
not have likened him to the All Good Man, so they could not
have martyrized him on the one and only day that would in
the minds of mankind ineffacably symbolize him as a type of
Christ. Understand the story for what it was, a sentimental,
Bible-type legend, and the creation of such a parallel is poeti-
cally, beautifully justifiable—though, of course, extremely far-
fetched even for fiction.

No, sir, Abraham Lincoln is to be added to Moses and
Christ as another myth!

Now, in conclusion, let me take care of some more wishful
thinking on your part—what you believe to be the actual name
of our country. Admittedly, many people still believe as you
do, that there was a colorful adventurer named Amerigo
Vespucci and that he gave his name to our land; but this is
simply another instance of history being written to fit the fiction required. You say the name Amerigo derives from Amel-
ric, the first Gothic king of Seville. Very neat, because if that
can be proved then the literal root-meaning of the name of
our land is Kingdom of Heaven, Amel-Ric and Himmel-
Reich being identical. Or, alternatively, if Amel be taken as
the name of the chief god of the Goths, Amel-Ric means
God's country. Either way you would win. I wish I could
believe this, because I do love this wonderful land. But sen-
timent and reason are generally mutually exclusive, and so
here.

You see, friend, a great deal of what has survived of our
American history, is in my opinion pure legend, created by
very human poet-patriots, whose burning desire was to show
our nation in the most favorable light possible. This feigning
was always typical of the minstrels of whatever realm. And
so for you this land is the golden land where the Kingdom of

Heaven—or God's Country!—is to be realized on earth. Such bosh warms my heart but it splits my head. It's beyond reason. Why, if I could be persuaded to believe this fragrant nonsense I would have to admit that in these latter days—as you call them—history is falling into some predetermined, divine plan: "towards which the whole creation moves."

But that, alas, I can never believe.

As ever,

Your friend,
Frazer Boughton

... NOT A PRISON MAKE

Joseph P. Martino

GUERRILLA WARFARE: An obsolete form of warfare practiced intermittently throughout history until the XXth Century. It was characterized by conflict between professional soldiers formally organized into regular armies, on the one side, and nonprofessional, informally organized forces on the other side. As such, it could not exist except when warfare was customarily conducted by professional armies. Its most recent appearance was during the XVIIth through the XXth Centuries. Its name, in fact, originated during that period, and means "little war" in the Spanish language—a Latin-based language formerly spoken in southeastern Europe; (see SPAIN).

It was widely practiced during the anti-colonial wars of the middle XXth Century, and received intensive theoretical and practical study by adherents of Communism (which see). This emphasis on guerrilla warfare led to a reaction on the part of the forces against which it was being used, among which were most of the industrially and technologically advanced nations of the world. The apparent paradox of poorly-trained and ill-equipped irregulars being able to defeat well-trained and well-equipped regular troops sparked an intensive program of research among these advanced nations.

The inevitable result was the development of surveillance, mobility and communication techniques which gave the regular soldier of an advanced nation considerable advantage over his guerrilla opponent.

The guerrilla, of course, could not adopt these techniques, since they required an industrial base to supply them, an organized logistics system to maintain them, and highly trained personnel to operate them. The guerrilla could not survive against an opponent who was invulnerable to surprise, and who could move over any terrain faster than the guerrilla could move. Thus after the XXth Century, only a professional army could stand against another one. This in turn led to an accelerated spiral of measure and countermeasure . . . From the *Terran Encyclopedia,* 37th Edition.

KREG WAR: One of the interstellar wars fought by the First Terran Confederation during its early period of expansion. It was named for the Kregs, a chlorine-breathing race occupying several solar systems in the vicinity of Polaris. The war climaxed a series of disputes over possession of a number of mineral-rich but airless minor planets in the region between the Terran and Kreg spheres of influence. After a number of raids and counter-raids on mining settlements, a major attack . . . The war was ended by the Treaty of Polaris, which granted to each side those planets already occupied, and provided an arbitration procedure to determine ownership of those unoccupied.

An interesting sidelight of the war was the resulting relationship between Terrans and the Kanthu, a humanoid race of oxygen-breathers. Their home planet, Kanth, occupied a strategic position outflanking several of the Kregs' advanced bases. A Terran task force landed there and set up a base which was intended to serve as a staging point for attacks against the Kregs' inner defenses. The initial policy of non-interference with the Kanthu turned out to be impossible, and . . . From the *Terran Encyclopedia,* 41st Edition.

Private Chalat Wongsuwan was growing bored. The Task Force had hit dirt three weeks ago, and at first there was plenty to keep everyone busy. The first hastily-constructed defenses had been strengthened by round-the-clock work, in anticipation of the expected Kreg counter-attack. However, no attack had come. Surely the Kregs knew the Task Force was there. What was delaying them? What were they up to? But after three weeks, even these questions lost their power to keep anyone alert. Private Chalat Wongsuwan, being an experienced combat soldier, recognized the symptoms of boredom, and knew that when on sentry duty was a poor time to get bored. He got up from the rock on which he was sitting, and reviewed his sector.

He was responsible for an area which was a rough square, one kilometer on edge, and the first one hundred meters of airspace above it. This area had been saturated with detectors of all kinds, which noticed anything out of the ordinary going on around them. The first few nights after landing, of course, had been spent finding out what was ordinary. The scents, sounds, electromagnetic radiations, seismic vibrations, and so on associated with the normal physical and animal activity of the area had been cataloged.

Now the ultrasonic pickups no longer reported the cries of an insectivorous batlike creature, but made a report only when the number of cries per minute deviated by more than a calculated percentage from what had been found to be the normal value for that time and place. The scent pickups no longer reported the mating odor of the females of a species of hard-shelled, ten-legged pseudo-beetles. The infra-red pickups no longer reported the intense emission from a small insect which, had its emission been visible, could have been called a firefly. And so on with all the other phenomena of the night in the forest.

The cataloging was not perfect yet, of course. There hadn't been time for that. Even back on Terra the detectors still pulled a few surprises now and then, and they had had centuries of refinement in the Terran environment. So several times during each watch the situation display, which portrayed the reports of all the sensors in the area in multicolored coded lights on the inside of the transparent face shield hanging from Private Chalat Wongsuwan's helmet, signaled a warning which turned out to be a false alarm when investigated.

Private Chalat Wongsuwan's boredom ended when an alarm signal appeared at a point near the center of the eastern edge of his area. He checked first with the sentry in the sector to the east.

"Ruongwit, this is Chalat. I've got a bogey at coordinates X—3917, Y—4231. Have you had anything heading my way?"

"Chalat, this is Ruongwit. Not a thing out of the ordinary in my sector. There hasn't been an alarm over your way all night, although I did have a couple on the other side earlier. When I got there, I couldn't find a thing wrong. The alarms had ceased, and everything was O.K. by then."

"Looks like the technicians are going to have to redefine

what's normal for the area again. I'd better have a look anyway. Over and out."

There was still the possibility that something might have dropped out of the sky. He should have been informed by the Sergeant of the Guard if anything had been reported by the aerial patrol, or even the off-planet patrol, but slipups did happen from time to time.

"Sergeant of the Guard, this is Private Chalat."

"Go ahead, Chalat."

"I've got a bogey which just appeared in my sector. It didn't come from the next sector. Any reports of activity upstairs?"

"No reports of anything. What kind of an alarm do you have?"

"It just about covers the spectrum. Scent, infra-red indicating a temperature near 40° Centigrade, sounds that could pass for breathing, the whole works. Only no footfalls from the seismic detectors. Wait a minute. The alarm just switched locations. The first spot is back to normal except for a reduced count on bird calls, as though the birds hadn't got over being scared. The alarm is now at a point halfway between me and the first point—exactly the same set of indications. I'd better take a look at both spots."

"Give me a report on anything, especially if it moves again."

"Roger, over and out."

He switched on his personal lifter, and reached treetop level. He drifted in the general direction of the alarm, threading his way through the treetops, getting as much concealment from them as he could without getting too close to them. His face mask display included a purple dot which was supposed to indicate his location, but he really didn't need it. The display also showed the swath of disturbance he was cutting through the night, as the many sensors reported his passage within their detection range. They couldn't be set to consider him as a normal part of the environment, without running the risk of failing to detect other humans who shouldn't be there. He reflected that, if there were any natives around who knew their way in these woods, they would have no trouble detecting him by the change in the behavior of the animal and bird life. The purpose of his multitude of sensors was to give him the equivalent of a lifetime's experience in the environment, without taking a lifetime to acquire it, and to give him more detection range than his organic sensors possessed.

The alarm was coming from a small clearing ahead of him. He hung behind a screen of branches, looked over the clearing. There was what appeared to be a man standing in the middle of it. Just before he could call the Sergeant of the Guard, the man disappeared. Had he really seen anything, or was his gear playing tricks on him? Now there appeared to be two men at opposite edges of the clearing. There was another. No, one of the two had disappeared. He ought to make a report, but what would make sense?

He switched the lifter to a high-speed attack mode, and charged down at one of the figures. The figure disappeared. He halted and altered course toward the other figure, which also disappeared. He turned around. Both were behind him, on the other side of the clearing. He drifted toward the center of the clearing, gaining altitude. A microphone near the two figures picked up the twang of bowstrings, but by the time he could interpret the sound, two crossbow bolts had struck him. As he lost consciousness, the lifter lowered him to the ground to await medical pickup.

"Sergeant of the Guard. I've got a 'man down' signal on Chalat. He's badly wounded. No, there's a change. He's dead."

"Where is he?"

"Coordinates X—3820, Y—4417."

"Squad One, head directly for Chalat's position. Squads Two through Five, seal off the borders of his sector. Squads Six and Seven, start combing the sector." Then, switching channels, "Aerial patrol, give me a tight roof over Sector 82. There's at least one hostile in it."

At this point the Officer of the Guard arrived. "Good response so far, Sergeant, but you'd better call up two or three reserve squads. We don't have enough left on duty to handle a similar attack on another sector. And warn all other sentries about what happened. I wish Chalat had given us more details as he went along."

"Sergeant of the Guard. Call from Ruongwit, in the sector next to Chalat's."

"I'll take it. Put him on."

"Sergeant, this is Ruongwit. I've got a bunch of bogeys just like the ones Chalat described. They keep jumping around.

There are about a dozen of them, as near as I can tell. They won't hold still long enough to count. Now they seem to be clustering about my position."

"Get some altitude and get out of there. Shoot at anything you see. Acknowledge, Ruongwit."

"Sergeant, I can't raise him. Now there's a 'man down' signal on him. He's dead, too."

"Sergeant, double the guard in all sectors. Call up all reserve squads. Call off the search in Sector 82. The next sector that reports some bogeys is to be saturated with all available forces."

"Yes, sir. Shall I sound a General Alert?"

"Better do that. The Kregs've clearly found some counter for our detectors. They may hit the Base next."

The Task Commander was distinctly unhappy, as any man who has been awakened at four in the morning to be told he's under attack has a right to be. "Well, Major Sakul, you were Officer of the Guard. Let's hear what happened."

"Yes, sir. Well, the first thing was Private Chalat. He was investigating a bogey that seemed to have jumped from one place to another. When we found him, he had two crossbow bolts in him, and his throat had been cut. In addition, he'd been stripped of all his loose equipment. Fortunately his recorders were still on him, so we could reconstruct what had happened. Forces had just been ordered out to comb his sector when the attackers struck the next sector. Same thing there. Ruongwit was found with three crossbow bolts in him. He must have been dead when he hit the ground, since his throat was still intact. He, too, was stripped of all his loose equipment.

"After that, bedlam broke loose. Every sector reported bogeys all over the place, all the same kind. They jumped from one place to another without seeming to be any place in between. We lost a total of eighteen guards, out of the one hundred twenty we had out. In all cases, they were stripped of their equipment. Those that weren't dead when they hit the ground had their throats cut. Next they started appearing inside the Base. They didn't seem to do any attacking there, they would just be reported somewhere, and then vanish. There were a few attempts to shoot at them, but no one hit them.

"I figured that we would do more damage to ourselves firing inside the Base than they seemed to be doing, so I ordered a halt to the firing within the boundary. After about thirty minutes the appearances seemed to peter out. There were a few reports for as long as an hour after the attack on Private Chalat, but I think they were all false alarms. I feel that the attackers first hit our guards, then penetrated the Base for reconnaissance purposes, and withdrew in order after they had what they came for. All in all, it looks like a well-coordinated attack, and if they decide to pull another one, I think they'll get away with it, too."

"Colonel Bunyarit."

The Executive Officer replied, "Yes, sir."

"What have you to report?"

"Well, our first reaction, naturally, was that the Kregs had come up with something new. Somehow they had managed to drop landing parties near our Base, without their ships being detected on the way in, and then the landing parties had managed to spoof and jam our detectors so we couldn't keep up with them."

"And it wasn't the Kregs?"

The Executive Officer replied slowly. "No, sir. When Chalat attacked one of the intruders, his action recorder went on. We got a good look at the one he went after. Then we saw the figure of the intruder disappear. The same thing happened to the next one he went after. He turned and spotted some more. However, they were the same two he started after. Despite the fact that both moons were down, there was enough starlight for the image intensifier to give us a good picture. We could identify the marking on the loincloths of the two figures, facial features, scars, and so on well enough to tell that there were only two, and they were jumping around from one spot to another. Then when they got Chalat, the recorder showed them suddenly appearing next to him, cutting his throat, stripping him of his equipment, then disappearing, equipment and all."

"Well, man," the commander burst out, "who were they?"

The Executive Officer was enjoying himself. "The natives of the planet, sir."

"But, according to the Intelligence reports of the pre-landing survey, the natives are very primitive. If I remember correctly, they practice a very destructive form of agriculture, so that they have to shift their villages every few years, and most of their protein comes from hunting. They have no cultures to speak of. How do they get the technological capability to bollix up our surveillance devices? Are the Kregs supporting them?"

"While it is possible they are getting Kreg support, sir, I think it is unlikely. If the Kregs had got another jump on us in the detection field, they would have made the attack themselves, rather than trying to work through primitive allies like the local natives. I believe that the detectors were giving us a true report of exactly what was going on. The attackers were really jumping from one place to the other without being in between. I believe they are natural teleports. And considering the way they coordinated their attack, they are telepaths, too."

"Pardon me, General."

The Task Force Commander turned to his Operations Officer. "Yes, Colonel Arun."

"As you know, sir, before I was recalled to active duty I was Professor of Military History at the University of Callisto. My period of specialization was the XXth Century. One of the more common types of military action during that period was something called 'guerrilla warfare.' It was commonly used by nations under occupation by foreign invaders, colonialists, and so forth. It is particularly adapted for use by weak and poorly organized forces against strong, well-organized forces. It seems to me that's precisely what we're up against here. It even fits the traditional pattern, since the first action of the native guerrillas was arms-gathering. They obviously carried out last night's raid in order to get their hands on some of our weapons."

"Supposing what you say is true, what do you recommend?"

"In the XXth Century, guerrillas weren't defeated until the forces opposing them learned to eliminate the genuine grievances of the people who supported the guerrillas. I recommend we use the same course of action here. We must communicate with the natives, explain our reasons for coming here, and use some of our resources in solving their more serious problems. In that way we can gain their support instead of their enmity."

"Now wait a minute," interjected Colonel Bunyarit. "Let's not go losing our sense of perspective. Our job here is to fight the Kregs, not to wipe the noses of a bunch of natives. With all due respect to Colonel Arun's academic background, I think that's precisely what his recommendations are: academic. We've got a defeatist attitude. Already we seem to think they can come in and repeat their raids as often as they feel like it. Well, last night they hit us without warning. Next time we'll be ready for them. We ought to get many more of them than they get of us. And the raiding doesn't have to be all one sided. There's nothing to stop us from going out and raiding a few of their villages. After getting their noses bloodied every time they come after us, and losing a few villages too, they'll quit bothering us. That's the way to treat them. Let's not mess around with this do-gooder attitude."

"But Colonel Bunyarit, you're making precisely the same mistake nearly every colonial power made in the XXth Century. They felt that a show of force was all that was required . . ."

"Now you look here. I've been on worlds before where the natives started trouble—caravan raiding, robbery, and so forth. You shoot up their villages a few times, and they learn who's boss. You ought to get out from behind that professor's desk of yours once in a while, and find out how the galaxy works."

"Your attitude, Colonel Bunyarit, is typically military in its obtuseness. Your suggested treatment may be quite satisfactory for handling pirates and bandits, who value their village more than they value the loot they might acquire from another raid. But it won't work against a people who are united in their opposition to the foreign invader. To them, the loss of a village is a small thing. They have their minds focused on the long pull, and are willing to make considerable sacrifices to gain ultimate victory."

"Are you trying to tell me that a bunch of half-naked savages, who haven't progressed beyond the crossbow, are going to chase us off this planet? If it even looks like they might do it, we can wipe them all out with radioactive . . ."

"Stop that talk," from the Tank Force Commander. "Don't say it. Don't even think it. If ever the rumor got out that Terra had committed genocide, we'd have every race we know about, and as many we never heard of, down on our necks. If there's anything that unites the races of the galaxy, it's their opposition to genocide. We'll hear no more talk about wiping anyone out. If we can't settle the problem some other way, we'll get off their planet and let them alone. And cut out the bickering. We've all had a hard night; there's no point in taking it out on each other." Then in a calmer voice, "We seem to have two policies proposed. One is to make friends with the natives, the other is to civilize them with a blaster.

"It's clear to me, anyway, that if we try the second policy first, and it fails, we'll never get a chance to try making friends. So we'll try the policy of making friends first.

"Colonel Bunyarit, you seem to think we can defend ourselves against any more raids. Get busy and set up the defenses. I think we're going to need them tonight. Colonel Arun, you will figure out how we're going to go about making friends with people who can vanish from our grasp before we can learn even one word of their language. That's all. Dismissed."

"Colonel Prapat," the Task Force Commander turned to the Provost Marshal.

"Yes, General?"

"Come to my office with me. There are a couple of things I want to talk over with you. Have you had breakfast yet?"

"No, sir."

"Neither have I. I'll have some sent in. I don't think any of us are going to have time for regular meals for a while."

"You know, General, there are times when I wonder how much more I can take of Arun and his professional attitude. He seems to think none of us ever read a book. I admit I've never heard the word 'guerrilla' before today, but, if these are guerrillas, their tactics don't seem to be much different from those of a lot of bandits I've fought on a number of worlds."

"Yes, I know Arun gets on a lot of people's nerves. First of all, Reserve officers who are called up at the outbreak of a war often have a low opinion of us Regulars. The fact that we had to call them up seems to be proof that we weren't competent to win the war without them. In addition, college professors seem to have a firmly fixed opinion that a military officer is a wooden-headed dunce. And when you combine both in the same man, as we have with Arun, he sometimes gets hard to live with. However, don't forget he has a good point. Although the tactics may be similar, there is considerable difference between a bandit and a guerrilla.

"The motivation of the guerrilla makes him willing to put

up with a lot of punishment. Even a long series of defeats won't dishearten him, and severe repression actually provides him with recruits from people who figure they have nothing to lose. As long as things are going to be tough anyway, they might as well be doing some fighting, and getting in a few licks at the people who are making things tough. At the moment I'm more concerned about Bunyarit. If there's anything I've learned in my career, it's that you should never underestimate an opponent. Treating an opponent with anything other than respect is a good way to get whipped in a hurry. If we don't treat them with respect, we'll try to beat them with half-measures, and get bogged down in a messy, indecisive war just like what happened to the XXth Century colonialists."

"That scared me, too, while I was listening to Arun. To a bandit a gun is a means to money. He gets one so he can use it to commit banditry, or to sell it to someone else who will use it to commit banditry. From Arun's description, a guerrilla considers a gun a means to more guns. He uses it to get another gun, to give to a friend, so they can both go out and get more guns, to give to more friends, until they have a big enough force to wipe you out. I don't see how you can beat a thing like that."

"Don't be too shaken by the idea. Despite Arun's air of authority, he's not the only one around here who's read some history. He wasn't quite correct on one point. Historically the guerrilla was whipped when surveillance devices were developed to the point where he couldn't surprise you, when mechanized armies quit being roadbound and learned to move over any territory a man on foot could move over, and do it faster too, and when communications were developed to the point where you could coordinate the actions of a lot of scattered units.

"The trouble with whipping him is that it isn't enough. He won't stay whipped. You can't relax your guard. Even in supposedly pacified towns, troops have to go around in pairs, or they'll end up in an alley with their heads caved in. And you can't bring in civilians as tradesmen, miners, and so on. They'll be murdered as soon as you turn your back. As Arun pointed out, if you want them to stay whipped, you've got to eliminate their legitimate grievances. It's important that you be able to whip them, of course. If you simply do things for them after they attack you, you merely whet their appetite for more. But if you do whip them, you can afford to take the attitude that they have been done an injustice, and deserve better treatment. If you neglect either half of the program, however, you're in for trouble.

"That's the sort of thing we've got to avoid here. In the long run we'll have to come to some agreement with these people or get off their planet. But in the short run, maybe we can hold our own against their banditlike tactics by using the tactics that work against bandits. That's what I want to talk to you about."

"Well, as a Provost Marshal, I've had considerable experience with bandits on various worlds. I've found that by and large bandits have a good sense of economics. If their gain from banditry is less than their loss from your reprisal for the banditry, they soon take up some other line of business, like fleecing tourists legally. But your reprisals, if they are going to be effective, have to be quick and precise. The bandits have to see the justice in your reprisal. If a small gang in a village engages in a raid, and you bomb the whole village, all you've done is get a lot of people mad at you. You've provided the bandit with allies. You have to identify the bandits and conduct your reprisals against them alone."

"That sounds reasonable. Now how do you find out who the bandits are?"

"I think of that part of the work as nothing but conventional police procedures, just patient collection and sifting of facts. To get the facts, you have to know the area and the people. You have to build up nets of informers and agents in the villages. You have to keep watch over roads, and such natural convergence points as bridges, fords and mountain passes. If you suspect anyone, you arrange to have them watched constantly. You offer open rewards for information, and secret bribes and offers of reduced sentences for members of the gang who provide evidence. In extreme cases, you can take a few squads of police or troops and seal off a whole village. Then you arrange to interview each and every person in the village, separately. You arrange so that all the interviews are approximately the same length, so that no one stands out as particularly suspect for having spent a lot of time with you.

"In the meantime, while the others are standing around,

you might have a doctor giving shots, passing out pills, giving a health lecture, or something, so you don't antagonize the innocent. Sometimes in these interviews you actually get information; other times you can only recruit agents who will later pay off for you. But that's the sort of thing you have to do. It's just patient, detailed police investigation, putting together small scraps of information, and trying to get more information."

"How would you apply your techniques here?"

"Frankly, I'm baffled. Even if I could get one of them to stand still, I don't know how to talk to them. I don't know what they value, so can't offer rewards. And even if I did know what to use as a reward, they could steal it from me more easily than they could earn it anyway. It seems to be a circular proposition. If we could stop them from attacking us, I could probably build up a net of agents who could tell me who did the attacking. But, then I wouldn't need to, since they wouldn't be attacking any more. And until I can get information out of them, I can't do anything to stop their attacks."

"I can see the vicious circle clearly enough. I had hoped your methods might help us to break out of it. All right, thanks for the information. Now I'd better go see what kind of defenses Colonel Bunyarit is working out."

The Task Force Commander sat at his console in the Battle Control Center. All the other Duty Officers and NCOs were seated at their own consoles, all wearing battle armor. The consoles were tightly packed against one side of the long room, instead of being spread throughout the room, as was usual. A freshly-painted white stripe marked off the now-empty remainder of the room from the consoles. Coils of barbed wire hung from the ceiling, festooned the walls, and draped over the sides of the consoles, filling every possible cubic centimeter of the space between the white stripe and the wall, leaving the men at the consoles just barely room to move. At the far end of the room, the end wall was covered with a newly-installed bank of electronic apparatus.

The room below, containing the computer complex and auxiliary power supply, was also crammed with barbed wire. The Center itself was, of course, underground, and reasonably safe from any ordinary attack. However, the commander scanned the interior of the room carefully, wondering if any additional improvements would make it better protected against attack by teleports. Then he caught his first glimpse of one of the natives, standing in the cleared portion of the room.

This particular native had spent the day practicing a particular tactic. He would choose a target, and a spot near it, teleport to the desired spot, attempting to arrive facing the target and with his gun pointed at it, fire quickly, and return to his starting point. He had, in fact, become quite proficient at it. Now, moving with the speed of thought, he appeared in the Battle Control Center just behind one of the consoles, corrected his aim on the duty officer slightly, and squeezed the trigger.

Unfortunately for him, the speed of thought can be measured in milliseconds. In the newly-installed bank of equipment at the end of the room an electronic circuit, operating in microseconds, reacted to a sensor which had detected his presence and closed the circuit on a blast rifle which happened to be pointed through the volume of space he was occupying. Long before the nerve impulses arrived at his trigger finger, he was dead and falling to the floor, receiving more blaster bolts as he activated other sensors during his fall. A second native, attempting to retrieve his fallen weapon, was likewise cut down. After that, there were no more attacks on the Battle Control Center.

Sergeant Sawang Nakvirote drifted slowly across the base, at an altitude of slightly less than fifty meters. His squad, in diamond formation, followed him. Just below him stood a row of obviously fresh pyramids of the earth. All the hand-weapons on the Base, except those actually issued to someone, were buried under those pyramids. It had been explained that this would keep the natives from raiding the armory. They would have to fight for each weapon they captured. Ahead of him stood the vast parking area of the space field, normally crowded with ships, but now empty. All spaceships had been moved well away from the planet, as a precaution against attack or sabotage.

He was beginning to wonder whether the natives were going to attack this night, or give it up as a bad job, when the crackle of blaster fire reached his ears. Almost simultaneously, a voice from the Battle Control Center blared from his communicator. "Attacking force in Barracks 34-D. Squad 17 counter-attack."

Sergeant Sawang led his squad in a high-speed, swooping dive for the front entrance of Barracks 34-D. It was a long, low, one-story structure, with a door in the center of each of the two long sides. Inside were two rows of cots, with a footlocker at the foot of each cot. A separate room at one end contained the precise number and kind of sanitary facilities specified by regulations for thirty-two men. Sergeant Sawang led the front vee of the diamond as it merged into a single line, passed through the door, and spread out again. The rear vee of the diamond swung up over the roof of the barracks, turned, and opened fire on the figures who had suddenly appeared in front of the barracks, firing at the rest of the squad as it entered.

One of the figures dropped, and immediately another one appeared beside it, retrieved its fallen weapon, and disappeared. The rest of the figures had by this time also disappeared, although not without drawing blood in turn. The last of the squad members entering the barracks stopped short in mid-flight, as he was hit. His personal lifter, instead of lowering him to the ground, took him up to an altitude of a hundred meters, and hovered there. His body could be recovered later for proper burial. In the meantime, his weapons were safe from capture.

Inside the barracks, Sergeant Sawang found considerable damage, and some smoke from several cots which had been set on fire. However, there was no sign of the attackers. Half the men immediately took up positions at the front windows, to cover the entry of the rest of the squad. The others tried to cover the interior of the barracks, but without success. A native suddenly appeared in line with the doorway, fired once, and disappeared. A man just inside the doorway flung his arms out in a spasmodic jerk, then drifted toward the ceiling as his lifter attempted to raise him to the programmed hundred-meter altitude. A native appeared on the floor below him, grasped vainly for his feet, and died on the spot as someone realized what was going on and fired. The dead man was unceremoniously hauled out the door by two of his comrades, and allowed to float upwards out of reach.

At this point Sergeant Sawang's communicator spoke up

again. "We're sending Squad 32 to reinforce you. As long as the natives want to fight in Barracks 34-D, we might as well accommodate them. Try to capture a few of their weapons, if you possibly can."

Squad 32 was led by Sergeant Jirote Phranakorn. Switching channels, Sergeant Sawang spoke. "Jirote, this is Sawang. Since your squad's still at full strength, you take the main bay of the barracks, I'll take the 'fresher."

The reply came back. "Fine by me, Sawang. Cover me as I come in the door, then I'm going to have my squad sweep up and down the length of the barracks, in line abreast, so we'll provide poorer targets."

Sergeant Sawang hovered in the doorway of the 'fresher, and watched Jirote's squad sweep through the barracks in precise formation, half the men facing ahead, half to the rear. Again with a suddenness which defied belief, a group of natives appeared. Sawang noted that these seemed to have different markings on their loincloths than the two he had seen earlier. There were eight of the natives, one for each member of Jirote's squad, and each native seemed to have placed himself directly in the path of one of the squad members. In a time-span so short that Sawang still hadn't reacted, there was the crackle of blasters, and the natives were gone again. Six of the squad members drifted toward the ceiling. The remaining two stopped, confused and uncertain. Their uncertainty was brought to an end as four more natives appeared at the far end of the barracks and sent their blaster bolts into the two remaining soldiers.

Sawang flung himself out of the doorway just in time, as more attackers appeared and fired at him. At the end of the crackling barrage of blaster bolts, he swung past the doorway again, glancing into the main bay as he passed. It seemed to be full of natives, all attempting to form gymnastic pyramids in order to reach the men floating against the ceiling.

Sawang zipped past the door again, flinging a grenade into the main bay as he went by. He led his squad into the main bay immediately after the blast, to find nearly a dozen of the natives crumpled on the floor, and several patches of blood evidently left by others who had escaped. He put his men to work immediately, getting Jirote's men and their weapons out of the barracks. No sooner was that task completed when he heard another voice from his communicator. This one was flat and metallic, and he knew he was being addressed directly by the Battle Computer, not by any of the humans at the Battle Control Center.

"Switch your lifter to Remote Control." Sawang did so. "Your direction of motion and velocity will be altered at random intervals, to make your motion as unpredictable as possible. From time to time you will be ordered to look and point your weapons in a specific direction. Fire immediately if you see an attacker, and fire anyway if ordered to do so."

Sawang watched his men move around the interior of the barracks in a mysterious, seemingly pointless dance. They moved up, down, right, left, forward, backward, without apparent reason. Suddenly he heard a blaster bolt crackle past him, just after he had felt a sudden change in motion. He glanced briefly in the direction from which the shot had come, to see no one, then returned his gaze to his assigned direction. He spotted one of the natives, fired quickly, and missed. The attacker disappeared before he had another chance to fire.

The next few minutes were a confused, whirling nightmare. Sawang's men danced around inside the barracks at what would have been an insanely dangerous speed, if they had had to depend on human reaction times to keep them from colliding with the barracks walls and each other. Attackers appeared, fired, disappeared. Sawang's men returned the fire as best they could. Neither side seemed to be able to draw blood.

Then Sawang noticed a subtle change in the pattern of the dance. All the changes in direction seemed to be nearly at right angles now, and they came at greater intervals. Furthermore, the direction he was ordered to look no longer coincided with his direction of motion. The flat voice of the computer came to him again.

"Look thirty-seven degrees." He did so, the direction being slightly to the left of his course. "Fire, and keep firing." He fired once, at nothing. He fired again, and just as he squeezed the trigger, a native appeared in the path of his aim. He was so surprised he hesitated before firing the third shot, which turned out to be unnecessary, as it passed over the dead native.

The next few minutes were another confused whirl. "Look forty-five degrees. Fire and keep firing." And another native down. "Look ten degrees. Fire. Look ninety degrees. Fire.

Look. Fire. Look. Fire. Look. Fire." It was clear what had happened. The computer had deduced the habits of this particular group of natives, and their reaction times. It kept each human on a single course long enough for a native to track him and decide to attack. It then predicted where the native would appear, and had someone else fire at the predicted point of arrival. That way the native was never alerted by a hostile move on the part of the human he was tracking.

Finally the crackle of blasters ceased. There was another human floating near the ceiling, and another dozen natives dead on the floor. The important fact was that this time all the dead natives were armed, except two who had died in the act of trying to retrieve weapons from their fallen comrades. The computer had caught on to that practice, too.

Before anything else could happen, Sergeant Sawang ordered his men to recover all the loose weapons, and then go back on remote control. However, apparently someone had decided that the Battle of Barracks 34-D was over. Another voice, this time a human one, came from his communicator.

"Squad 17, proceed to the Electronics Repair Shop. It is under attack."

The Electronics Repair Shop was a single-story structure consisting of a long, narrow central building with a number of shorter but equally narrow wings branching out on either side. Both the central building and the wings consisted of a hallway lined on both sides with small cubicles, each closed off by a door. The building was entirely windowless, but there were doors at the end of each of the wings.

As Sergeant Sawang's squad circled around the Electronics Repair Shop, in a now somewhat ragged diamond formation, another message reached them.

"Sawang, this is Major Prasert." That would be Major Prasert Tanwong, Sawang's Battalion Commander. "The attackers are apparently trying to draw us into a fight. They've been appearing in the test cubicles, smashing some equipment, and leaving. By the time we get there, they're somewhere else causing more trouble. In order to keep them from wrecking everything, I'm going to have to put a man in every cubicle, with more men patrolling the halls as a backup. I've already got all the rooms in the northern-most wing manned. I want your squad to patrol the hall in that wing. As I get more men, I'll extend our control into the other wings."

Sawang decided that on the face of it the plan sounded good, but the natives might have some other surprises they hadn't revealed yet. Before he committed the remainder of his squad to a particular tactic, he wanted to reconnoiter the territory he was going to have to fight in. He left the squad to circle the building, and dove through the doorway at the end of the hall he was going to patrol. He came to the door of a cubicle, knocked, and opened the door. The soldier guarding the room was floating back and forth across one end of the room, with his back to the end wall and his head brushing the ceiling. His gun was pointed toward the center of the room, ready to fire. While the man's course was fairly predictable, he still presented a moving target instead of a sitting one. Sawang nodded his head in satisfaction, waved at the man, and left the room.

He then studied the hallway thoughtfully. After his experience in the barracks, he didn't like the idea of his men moving up and down the length of the hallway, where they could be picked off easily by enfilade fire. Nor was he happy about the hallway down the central portion of the building. It was uncontrolled, and his men would be subject to flank attacks as they crossed the entrance to the hallway, at the center of the wing. He decided the alternatives regarding the central hallway were to attempt to control it, or to abandon it to the attackers and accept that his squad would be split into two halves, on either end of the wing.

The first alternative would be difficult to achieve, but the second went against all his training and experience. He decided to station himself at the juncture of the central hallway and his wing, keeping near the ceiling and partially protected by a corner, so that he could watch the hallway and fire if anyone appeared. He could then put two men in each wing, and his central position would give him better control over the action as it developed.

He called the squad in and told off two men for each end of the wing. They were to stay abreast of each other, and facing in opposite directions. They would move in a corkscrew spiral along the length of the hallway, reversing direction as they reached the end, or middle, of the wing. He then took up his position at the middle of the wing.

Hardly had Sergeant Sawang gotten into position when a series of explosions rocked the building. He glanced around, and saw the door of one of the cubicles sag open, and smoke drift out. He called to his squad to maintain the patrol, and swooped for the nearest cubicle. He yanked the door open and swept inside, to find a native standing on a test bench and removing a blaster from the unresisting hand of the soldier now floating lifelessly against the ceiling of the cubicle. Before Sawang could fire, the native was gone, gun and all. He ordered his squad to stop patrolling and check the cubicles. He then tried the next door, to find it bolted from the inside. He blasted the lock and hurtled inside, to find the room empty and its guard dead and stripped of weapons. In the next room the guard was still alive, and the badly mangled body of a native lay on the floor.

"He appeared right in front of me, Sergeant, and dropped a grenade on the floor. My gun was pointed at him, and I must have fired by reflex. He fell over the grenade and soaked up the force of the burst."

"Reflex or not, that's nice shooting. Keep up the good work."

Sawang returned to the hallway, to find it filling up with guards from the rooms which had not been attacked. He was in the process of sorting his squad out from the strays when a volley of blaster fire erupted from the central hallway. He turned to see a group of natives standing in the middle of the wing, having a field day firing at the troops in both ends of the wing. In the confusion, no one seemed to be able to organize any counter-fire.

Someone yelled "Out the doors! Let's get out of here," and a rush started for the doorway at the end of the wing. This escape route was closed by more blaster fire from natives stationed outside the doorway. An incredible jam formed at the door as men milled about, fired on from front and rear. Sawang and the other NCOs started herding the men out of the hallway into the cubicles, where they started returning the fire of the natives, who were now rapidly shifting their positions along the length of the hallway.

Suddenly a voice roared over the emergency communicator channel. "All troops in the Electronics Repair Shop. Take cover. Get under something quickly."

Sawang and his men had just ducked under a workbench

in one of the cubicles when a shattering explosion sounded in the hall outside, followed by the earsplitting shriek of a one-man scout fighter as it whipped over the building at low altitude and high speed, then headed back for the stratosphere. There was now a gaping hole in the roof over the hallway, through which an orderly flow of men was escaping, while others still in the cubicles provided covering fire for them. Sawang led his men out in their turn, then circled back over the building. When all the men appeared to be out, he received permission to lead his squad back to look for wounded and retrieve weapons.

The fire from the scout had been aimed with precision, and had taken out the roof right over the hallway. This, of course, meant that the beams supporting the roof had been cut through at the center, allowing a portion of the roof to collapse into the hallway. They found a number of bodies, both human and native, under the wreckage. They dragged the humans free and let their lifters carry them out through the roof. The natives, they simply disarmed. As Sawang pulled a blaster away from one of the figures on the floor, he saw it stir slightly. He took a step away, then the significance of the event struck him.

"Battle Control Center, this is Sergeant Sawang, Squad 17. We've got a prisoner. He's been knocked out, temporarily anyway. What do we do with him?"

"Good work, Sawang. Hoist him up to a hundred meters and hold him there so his friends don't try to rescue him, while we figure out what to do with him."

"Sorry I'm late for the meeting, General. I had an experiment in progress, and I wanted to be able to include the results in my report."

"That's all right, Doctor, we were just getting started. Sit down and catch your breath, and we'll hear from you in a few minutes. Now, Colonel Bunyarit, will you give your report?"

"Yes, General. First I'd like to describe some of the thinking that went into the defense planning for last night, then describe how it worked out. To begin with, we had to accept that the natives were teleports. It became clear that the ability to teleport also implied some sort of clairvoyance. If a person is going to teleport himself to some distant point, he has to be sure that there are no objects in the way where he wants to go. Simply remembering the place is not enough. Someone could easily have moved an obstacle into a place remembered as being clear of obstructions. Thus the question became one of how good their clairvoyance was. Did it, in effect, make them omniscient about all events anywhere? If so, we had no hope of defeating them.

"On the other hand, they all have eyes, and on the first night they attacked, it's worth noting that their victims were shot while silhouetted against a fairly bright starry background. Thus they still depend heavily on their eyes, despite the existence of clairvoyance.

"So I decided to assume that their clairvoyance was not much better than the minimum required for successful teleportation; that they could observe only a small area at a time, as through a peephole, but that they could scan the 'peephole' around to investigate a large area or track a specific target of interest. I assumed also that their ability to inspect some complex object would not necessarily tell them how it worked or what it did, if it depended on principles beyond their level of technological development.

"On the basis of these assumptions, I planned the defense. First, there were certain areas like the Battle Control Center, the Power Plant, and so forth, which had to be made into traps which even teleports could not invade successfully. Limits on time and equipment, of course, meant that the rest of the Base could not be so protected. So all weapons not being carried by someone were buried. All spaceships and other vehicles were moved out of the way to prevent attack or sabotage. Since any soldier standing in a fixed position could be attacked and disarmed before he could react, fixed guard posts had to be abandoned. The simplest solution was to put all the troops up in the air and keep them moving.

"The obvious counter to this was to attack our unprotected installations, forcing us to move troops into them. However, I felt safe in assuming that the natives would be fairly unsophisticated. If they found a tactic that worked, they'd keep trying it. Nor would they be organized to detect our responses to their tactics, and change them as necessary. So I felt that the Battle Computer, with its ability to handle large amounts of data and deduce patterns from it, would give us an edge which might make up for the enemy's ability to teleport, if our troops were drawn into a battle.

"I feel that the defense was quite successful. Certain points were defended with complete success. In those places where our men had room to maneuver, we put up a good defense, inflicting more losses than we took. In other areas, the battle was more nearly even. However, overall we lost forty-two men, while they lost one hundred eighty. I could say that is a very favorable ratio. I expect that we can make further improvements in the defenses before tonight, and if they attack again, we should be able to force an even more favorable exchange ratio."

"Thank you, Colonel Bunyarit. Now Colonel Arun, you look like you want to say something."

"Yes, sir. I beg to differ with the optimistic conclusions just voiced. First of all, the actions of guerrillas tend to be limited by the number of weapons available, not their manpower. And their chief source of weapons is capture from their opponents. Thus in combating guerrillas the measure of success is not the casualty ratio of the forces, but the ratio of weapons lost by each side. The attackers started the battle last night with what weapons they had seized the previous night, namely eighteen blasters, eighteen blast rifles, and fifty-four grenades. Last night they expended twenty grenades, and we recaptured twenty-five other weapons. However, they captured twenty-two blasters, twenty blast rifles, and sixty grenades. In last night's attack, then, they essentially doubled their supply of weapons.

"Furthermore, much of last night's defense was based on the assumption that they cannot teleport themselves into a position in space, say a hundred meters off the ground. It may be that they had never had to do it, but that is no reason to assume they can't learn to do it.

"In short, I consider last night a defeat for us. Without any change in tactics, they can come back and double their weapons supply again. And they may be able to change their tactics in such a way as to nullify most of our defenses."

"Thank you, Colonel. You have some good points. However, things are not all black. We did manage to get a prisoner, so the night wasn't a total loss. Doctor, may we have your report now?"

The Staff Surgeon slid his chair back and stood up. "The

most important news, of course, is the prisoner. When he was delivered to us last night, he was still unconscious from having a roof fall on him. Our first check, naturally, was to see if he had suffered any serious injury. A hasty examination showed that there were no bones broken, or anything like that. Next we made some rapid checks to see if any anesthettics we had would be safe and effective on him. We had to keep him unconscious, or he would have simply left us.

"It turned out that one of our standard anesthetics would work on him, and as far as we could tell it would be safe. Naturally we started with light doses, and monitored his heart and lung action. However, we, of course, had no idea what his normal pulse and respiration rate should be. The anesthetic seemed to do the trick, so we started sampling everything we could without doing him any permanent damage, as well as taking electrocardiograms, encephalograms, and so on.

"After about an hour, we observed that his pulse and respiration seemed to be weakening, so we cut down on the dose of anesthetic. This helped, but after a while he started to get worse again, so we cut out the anesthetic entirely. In short order he returned to consciousness, and did the expected thing. He vanished right off the table. It was quite a surprise, even after having been told it could happen.

"In all, we spent about two hours examining the prisoner. We have a great deal of useful data, although most of it is still in raw form, and can't be used for anything yet. It must be remembered that we never examined him under normal conditions. He was knocked out when we got him, and was anesthetized in addition. So we are still not completely satisfied with our data. And in any case, we would like to have a lot more. We are performing autopsies on the attacker corpses. These, in conjunction with the data from the prisoner, are telling us quite a bit about their nature."

"If we managed to get another prisoner, could you do better with a new anesthetic?"

"Yes, General, we now know enough about them to be able to synthesize an anesthetic which would be both safe and effective."

"Do you have enough information to design a knockout gas sufficiently effective to have military utility, and with no serious side effects?"

"Oh, yes. That would present no serious problem. We could even design one which would be absorbed rapidly through the skin, so they couldn't avoid it by holding their breath. We could even design it to have no effect on humans. I would say we could have a sample synthesized by noon. Any larger quantities, of course, would have to come from the Materiel Officer."

"All right, Doctor, you get your staff busy on the synthesis. Have them work closely with the Materiel and Armament Officers. I want a reasonable quantity of gas bombs available by no later than midafternoon. In the meantime, Colonel Bunyarit, get some high altitude patrols out, and locate a few villages. Then get a strike force organized. As soon as the gas bombs are ready, we're going to get us a few prisoners."

"But General, there's not much more I can learn from an anesthetized prisoner. What good will capturing a few more do?"

"I've got an idea about how to hang onto an unanesthetized prisoner. Now let's get busy. Meeting's dismissed."

"Another drink, Commissioner?"

"Thank you, General, I will. It's not the sort of luxury one normally expects at a forward base like this."

"I believe in being comfortable, Commissioner. Any fool can be uncomfortable. And besides, one doesn't normally expect to find a Commissioner for Native Affairs at a forward base, either. You realize, I hope, that we've already had one Kreg attack, and there may be more."

"Yes, but I've been under fire before. The Kregs can't possibly be any worse than some of the natives I've had responsibility for. But tell me, how did you manage to work out an agreement with the natives? I've read your report, of course, but it's so blasted brief. I mean, how did you learn their language, how did you analyze their culture, how did you learn what would induce them to behave? And for that matter, how did you manage to get them to hold still for you?"

"Commissioner, as you are aware, the basic problem was holding one, voluntarily or involuntarily, and getting the information out of him. By a stroke of good luck, we acquired a prisoner. Naturally we couldn't hold him permanently, but from a study of him we learned enough to enable us to capture some more. It turned out that the ones we worked with had no inhibitions about telling us what we wanted to know, after we learned a bit of the language. After all, learning an alien language is a pretty well-developed technique, nowadays, and these people don't have a very complicated one.

"We confirmed earlier reports that they move around a lot. They farm by burning off a stretch of forest, thus fertilizing the soil. They farm it for a few years, by which time it's worn out, and they move on. Naturally they can't come back to the same site until the forest is regrown. This means that each tribe has to have a pretty large area it can call its own. Naturally there's a lot of jockeying between tribes for particularly choice areas, such as those with good rivers, and so on. The social structure, as between tribes, approaches anarchy. Their Golden Rule is 'Do unto others before they have a chance to do unto you.'

"We learned that about fifty years ago a spaceship crashed on this continent, and one tribe managed to get some modern weapons from it. They cut quite a swath for a while, until they ran out of power packs. None of the tribes, however, forgot what energy weapons were, or how they could be used. When we landed, a few of the nearby tribes viewed us as their golden opportunity. They gave each other the bare minimum of co-operation which would enable each to get some weapons. They then were each going to grab themselves some more territory. Eventually, I suppose, they would have fought each other for the best land, but it never came to that stage.

"Once we understood the situation, we simply flew over their villages and broadcast to them that if they didn't let us alone, we'd supply weapons and instructors to their most deadly enemies. That was the stick. For the carrot, we recognized that in their chaotic situation, they would be willing to follow anyone who could offer them protection from each other. We offered them that protection, if they would help us in enforcing it. That's where you come in. They quickly saw the good sense of our offer, and came to terms. The only problem was to prevent ourselves from being robbed blind by teleporting thieves, and we solved that by sealing all the buildings, putting on double-door air locks, and flooding them with anesthetic."

"But, blast it, General, you still haven't told me . . ."

"How we managed to hold a conscious prisoner? That

turned out to be fairly simple. We realized that their teleporting range had to be limited, since it was we who found them, and not vice versa. So we loaded our unconscious captives into a scout cruiser, and took them several planetary diameters off-world. It turned out we guessed right the first time, and we had them far enough out they couldn't teleport back. When they realized they weren't going anywhere, we had no further trouble with them. They were model prisoners."

10:01 A.M.

Alexander B. Malec

At 10:01 A.M. the accident occurred, setting off a triple concurrence of actions; the first of which was the following dialogue:

"What was it?" asked Slick when the vehicle pulled over and stopped.

"I dunno," said the driver as he hopped down, looked at the object on the mall and returned; the other vehicles whistling above him. "Looks just like a rag doll. You know, no frame, no nuthin'."

"Did you see it coming?" asked Slick, reclining back with his stogie.

"Naw," said Poxie, who was the driver, as he energized the vehicle and headed it into the mainstream. "Don't hardly look real or nuthin'. All covered with catsup it looks like."

"Yeah," said Slick, observing a stream of smoke issuing from his O-shaped lips, feeling rough and "with it" in his brand-new black leather boots, his black leather trousers and his black zippered pockets. "These things happen." He slicked back his bushy mop of black hair with a comb.

"Yeah," said Poxie, who was called so due to his moon-crater like complexion, that is, pock marks. He passed the other vehicles to get into the top speed lane; passed them vertically, that is.

The second and third concurrence of action took place also at 10:01 A.M. When a particular section of the roadway, with all its sensors, noted that something untoward had occurred and dispatched onward the time and location of occurrence, the course of involved machine, and due to the type of signal transmitted, caused to home in on two separate locales, two special and very different from each other vehicles.

273

At 10:03 A.M., the first vehicle, called simply a "Patroller," arrived on the scene, dropped to ground level, found the "Rag Doll" and carefully placed her within the Patroller.

Officer John Cramdon, never really insular from his job, wept slightly taking a Retina Identification Check, while the information automatically traveled via Pulsed Carrier to a building known only as "Center" some fifty kilometers away.

At 10:07 A.M., the information arrived from Center and stated that her name was Cynthia Marie DeSantis, red hair, blue eyes, weight: twenty kilograms, height: one hundred and two centimeters, age: eight years old, residence: 10D, 4th quadrant, Lloyd Wright Gardens, Churchill City, Kansas, mother's name: Eva Marie, father's name: Lawrence Joseph, occupation: Machinist.

This information appeared on the scope of Sergeant John Cramdon's Patroller; the visual display which, before facing out, automatically etched this information onto a blank transparent sheet of lucite, with the time and code letters to identify same, and dropped into a file.

The same information also appeared on the scope of the second larger vehicle now homing in on its moving target.

Also at 10:07 A.M., at the Traffic Division of Center, Captain Roland Reese, for the nth time, drew his courage together—which was parcel of his job of police captaincy—and pressed the studs on the telephone which would connect him to a residence at 10D, 4th quadrant, Lloyd Wright Gardens, Churchill City, Kansas; which would connect him to Eva Marie, mother of Cynthia Marie DeSantis.

At 10:09 A.M., Officer John Cramdon was already vectoring on a building in Churchill City, near Lloyd Wright Gardens with his cargo.

Fully twenty-seven kilometers away, where first alerted of the "occurrence," the larger vehicle took fully six minutes to overtake the top lane carrier of Poxie and Slick, which was hurtling at 200 k.p.h. This was at 10:07 A.M.

Slick noticed it first. "Poxie. You see what's in back of us?" he yelled in dismay.

Poxie looked back and gulped, "Agh! A Fetcher!"

"Hit it," hollered Slick.

Poxie jammed the accelerator fully to its limit.

At 10:08 A.M., the "Fetcher" enclosed the smaller vehicle

of Slick and Poxie, and at that instant the Fetcher made a turn unauthorized to ordinary drivers, re-routed and, at top speed, homed in on Center which was now, due to the In-line chase, some one hundred thirty-three kilometers distant. The journey would take approximately seventeen minutes.

If being enveloped by a Fetcher is a chilling experience, it is not an oft-repeated one; an off-shoot doctrine of the civilization that could produce a Fetcher and a need for one.

Perhaps if Poxie were to resist incarceration by a Fetcher —as some did—by initiating a sudden turn; left, right, up, down, in the hope of at least wrecking the machine that swallowed them in an "I'll-take-one-of-them-with-me bravado," he couldn't have done so. For the reason that his reaction was in the realm of the highly probable and therefore implemented against; another way of saying a de-gaussing network on the inside walls of the Fetcher canceled out his control and driving field so that Poxie's machine was as inert and immobile—and about as useful—as a large rock of equal mass.

The sudden switch from sunlight to artificial light alone is enough to induce goose flesh; the sudden change in noise level and acoustics will again produce the same sensation as the front aperture of the Fetcher closed much as a camera lens. Clamps thumped their device securely to the deck, and electromagnetic shoes, as a double precaution, held them fast.

There were no officers in sight; just the white-painted, brightly-illuminated walls and the moire pattern of the closed aperture ahead.

Suddenly, a Public Address System sounded. "Leave your vehicle. Enter the doorway to the rear." The PA system then added an emotion-tinged, "Come on, you birds. Move!!"

Poxie and Slick did so. In passing through, Poxie noticed the glowing nodes placed about ten centimeters apart vertically in the door jamb. He knew it was a frisking mechanism of some kind.

They entered a small, brightly-lit room which contained a functional metal desk and stools fastened to the deck, an assortment of "Black Box" electronic gadgetry, scopes and switches on the bulkheads and two officers of the law who looked the picture of hard, well-oiled efficiency as if they had been turned out by the same machine. They wore gray uniforms, blue leather boots, triple-ridged white helmets, and to add to their anonymity and authority, they wore translucent masks.

The officer who was standing relieved Poxie of the screwdriver in his right knee pocket.

"For adjustments," said Poxie with a sly grin.

"Shaddap," said the standing officer. At that, the officer who was seated, waved at the other to ease off. Poxie knew that the "shaddap" was rare, and unauthorized, he knew these men were fighting to keep a closed lid on their emotions.

"Sit here, please," said the seated officer, indicating two stools which had two optical gadgets, about where eye-level would be. In the meantime, the other officer consulted a plastic sheet index which was in fine print. Slick noticed the title on the plastic sheet. It read: Accumulator, Location of . . . As they sat down, they could hear the other officer stomp out of the small cubicle through the glowing node doorway, in front to where their machine sat captive.

"Look through the eyepieces, keep both eyes open. Focus on the cross you see there."

As Poxie and Slick did so, they knew the officer had depressed some kind of stud, for this was a Retina Identification Check.

"All right," said the officer, and caused the optical gadgets to swivel on their brackets and nestle each in their own niche in the bulkhead.

"Where were you fellows headed?" he asked.

"Albuquerque," said Poxie. The interrogating officer had both hands flat on the desk, writing nothing down, so Poxie knew something, somewhere, was taking a permanent record of this conversation.

"Where were you coming from?"

"Chicago," offered Slick. The officer depressed no stud or toggle to differentiate between the two young men talking. Apparently, then, the recording device had no difficulty in separating and tagging the voices. At that moment, Poxie looked at the wall clock. It said 10:10 A.M.

"At what level?"

"Ah," Poxie stammered, "low level. You know that."

The tone of the officer's voice seemed to contort the inscrutable translucent mask into hardness, if that were possible. "Oh, I know that, all right. But, what is low level?" Poxie looked at him blankly. "Come on," said the officer with irritation. "What is low level?" The "come on" prodding of the officer surprised Poxie; very seldom these people showed any emotion.

"Eight meters," said Poxie.

"All right, that's the upper limit," said the hard officer of the Traffic Division. "Now, what's the lower limit . . . of the low level?" he added.

"Four meters," said Poxie. He was beginning to feel very nervous with the line the questioning was taking.

The inflections of the interrogating officer made Poxie think of the old-time Prosecuting Attorneys as he had seen them on the re-constituted "movies." The question he heard now was, "Four meters, huh? You sure you weren't going any lower?"

"How could we?" asked Slick. He was becoming nervous, too. "You can't go lower!"

Poxie wasn't sure the line of questioning was not part of police procedure. But the man asking the questions had a curiosity and an "In" for the two young men before him. He was literally venting off his spleen.

"Why can't you go lower?" asked the lawman. He pointed to Slick. "You."

Slick stammered, "Because the controls are, well, you know, governed; if you go any lower than twelve feet, I mean four meters, well, you might hit somebody."

"A lot of fun, wasn't it?" said the officer. This taunting was *really* unauthorized, thought Poxie. "Knocking off the tops of trees, scaring the daylights out of people."

"We didn't," said Slick lamely.

"You didn't?" said the officer. "Then how is it you struck a little girl at a cross mall? A little girl who was hardly a meter high."

Slick didn't answer. Poxie gulped and stared at the wall clock: 10:12 A.M.

At this lull in conversation, the other officer returned; the one who had gone to where the enclosed, captured vehicle of Poxie's was. He held in one grimy hand what looked like a battery-operated cutting tool. In the other he held what appeared to be on one side a weathered hexnut, but on the inner side, protected from the weather, looking like something else again; a shiny micro-electronic-looking something else.

Slick stared at it bug-eyed. Poxie was somewhat fascinated, too.

The seated officer spoke, "Surprise, huh?" Slick, the one who was being addressed, didn't speak. "Thought you had found the Accumulator on your vehicle and put a pin through it, didn't you?" The seated officer looked inquiringly at the other officer, who took his cue and spoke.

"The other one has been found—and damaged. But this one is all right," he said and held up the Accumulator.

Slick stared at the untouched, unfound, undamaged Accumulator as one hypnotized by a twirling vest pocket watch. He stared at this undamaged, but oh so easily reciprocally damaging, Accumulator.

"How come there were two?" asked Poxie of the standing officer who held the cutting tool in one hand and that murderous piece of evidence in the other. The addressed officer didn't answer right away but handed the hexnut-disguised Accumulator to the seated officer, whereupon that one got up, entered behind a partition that half cut him off from view and performed some kind of act to the Accumulator; an act as yet unknown to the young captives.

"There's no law that says there can't be two," said the officer with the grimy hands and the cutting tool, "Or even three." Slick did a take on that "three." "The law only says there must be one." He held up one finger for emphasis, "One." Poxie and Slick followed the officer's soliloquy with no little entrancement. "So many times it happens, the vehicle's Accumulator when it leaves the factory—the one in plain sight—gets somewhat damaged." He looked at Slick with bland, tongue-in-cheek, saying, "Ordinary, routine damage. Can happen to anybody." Slick turned his eyes down on that one and Poxie looked away to the wall clock. It read: 10:15 A.M.

"So you see," said the soliloquizing officer; he was obviously the talkative one of the bunch, "Why we do what we do. In time of collision between two vehicles and in the ensuing investigation, it is necessary to fix the blame; either driver or both drivers. Or, as happens sometimes, the fact of mechanical failure on the part of the vehicle. In that case the involved driver is not held. We learn all the data surrounding and contributing to the accident from playing back the Accumulator attached to each car. I guess you know that in the event of accident with a vehicle containing a . . . ah . . . pre-damaged Accumulator, we would then have to rely on the testimony of drivers, passengers and other eyewitnesses to the scene. And human testimony"—he said "human" as if it were a dirty word—"is so prejudiced and . . . so inaccurate."

"Oh," said Poxie, wondering if these officers of the law were married; would they have stooped to something as commonly human as marriage.

"So," the seated officer said. "We rely on the Accumulator. It gives us a lifetime record of the car's behavior. And, in case of accident, of any kind"—he emphasized the "of any kind"—"we have an unbiased record of the vehicle's height, lane, speed, attitude at time of impact and the performance of the driver prior to that impact."

"And," took up the standing officer, arms at his sides, who looked as deadly as a viper, "the performance of the driver"— he looked at Poxie—"after the impact."

Poxie had been reasoning that a man who could stand thus, arms at sides, without any emotional crutches such as a cigarette, must be very sure of himself. When the officer stopped talking, Poxie said, "Oh," coloring in embarrassment and took in the reading on the wall clock. It read: 10:17 A.M.

"That's what is happening now," said the standing officer.

"What is?" asked Slick.

"What happens when we put the Accumulator in the Acceptor mechanism."

"What does that do?" asked Slick.

"It relays the information upon the Accumulator," said the seated officer. "Ahead. To Center."

Poxie didn't know why but he chilled when the man said "Center." The wall clock still read: 10:17 A.M.

"Just like happened," asked Slick, "when you had us look into that glass thing? It went on to Center?"

"That is correct," said the standing officer.

At this point Poxie wondered if it wouldn't be wiser to try to overpower the two officers of the law; these officers appeared to be unworried about such a thing happening and carried their sidearms outside and accessible, much as officers have always done. Poxie knew they were in deep enough trouble to make such a try worthwhile.

His notions were inadvertently replied to in the next few minutes.

The seated officer arose, and said to the other, "Are there, ah, marks?"

"Yes," said the other.

"I'm going to have a look," he said.

"I'll go with you," said the other, making Poxie's ears perk up almost a rabbit's length. As the officer went through the doorway, his hand flipped something on the right of the doorway and he said, "Sit tight. Don't move." And he was gone.

Poxie and Slick were all alone in the interrogating cubicle of a police Fetcher vehicle, with its gadgets, meters, toggles, rheostats and scopes that were fauna of modern-day traffic misdemeanor and felony control. Poxie would have been confused as to what gadget to grab hold of first, except that the decision had been made for him when the officer had flipped that something.

"Look," said Slick, crestfallen.

"Yeah," said Poxie, also crestfallen.

"Laser bars," said Slick.

"Yeah."

All around them in an oval, to encompass them and the two stools they sat on and not much more, was a cage of vertical laser beams.

"This kind gives you a shock, I think," said Slick. "An electric shock."

"Some other kinds burn you," said Poxie.

"Yeah. And there's another kind. They use it in mining and in war, I guess. It vaporizes things."

The officers returned. The first one through flicked that toggle something on the right wall of the doorway and the laser cage disappeared. The second officer coming through said, "It's there, all right." Poxie reasoned he was speaking for the benefit of the audio pick-up device somewhere in the cubicle, for use as further evidence. "Blood," was the officer's follow-through comment. Poxie wondered how many times you can kill a dead ox; how much evidence did they need? He looked at the wall clock. It read 10:22 A.M.

The first officer through, continued through the cubicle and exited through a rearward passageway. "We're getting close," he said before he disappeared.

The second officer sat down behind the desk though the detained young men couldn't know if this one was the original who had been seated or had they switched.

"He went to bring it in," said Slick.

"Yeah," said Poxie.

"The thing was running by itself," said Slick.

"Yeah."

The second officer had his head down, both hands on the desk, reading, as best as Slick could divine upside down: "An Abstract of Codes and Decrees As Applied To Civilian-Commercial Null-Vehicles Traversing The Alpha Roadway System." This must be, thought Poxie, how they gotta spend their free time; reading law. No novels, no nuthin'. Then Poxie had a question. And the answer, by reflection of what prompted it, pointed out the guilt of the questioner. "What," asked the pock-marked incarcerate not quite into his twenties, "are you going to do with the machine once we get to Center?"

The seated officer looked up, his mask chilling in its inscrutability, and said, "We're going to analyze it." He said this slowly. "No null-vehicle can possibly dip below four meters except . . ." Then he explained: "There are fail-safe circuits and auxiliary servomechanisms that make it possible to alight slowly and safely in case of power failure. But in no case is it possible for a civilian null-vehicle to dip below four meters . . . over a cross mall . . . and still retain power. There are built-in governors. But you know about that, don't you? And there are built-in power cancellors should the factory-sealed governor mechanism be tampered with. As far as we know, there is no way for a layman to tamper with a vehicle in such a manner and still manage to run that vehicle. We are very curious"—he was looking at Slick when he said this—"to see how this was done." The inscrutable impartiality mask of the law paused a few seconds before it spoke again. "It would seem . . . that we have a mechanical genius in our midst." It was a backhanded compliment with a lot of left hand to it. Slick reacted by reddening his ears a little.

While Poxie, sensing his friend's discomfiture, prodded him to give him a cigarette. He looked at the wall clock. It read: 10:24 A.M. We're almost there, he thought, and sure enough, he sensed a subtle change in the almost inaudible whining tone that is a police "Fetcher" vehicle in motion.

At 10:26 A.M., after the awesome whines and clicks outside had ceased, a final sound made itself apparent; that of the vehicle's camera aperture doors opening. It was a whirring sound. The officer who had rated Slick a moment ago as a "mechanical genius" remained seated. However, another officer made the scene. He was standing on the platform, in front of the yawning aperture opening. He was dressed in every detail as the mobile officers had been except for the green helmet and the clipboard which he held in front of him, from which he spoke loudly, "Mr. James Smith. Mr. Rodney Cooper." Poxie and Slick respectively responded to their names with a start for they had not told the two vehicle police their names. "Please follow me." They meekly complied.

They were in a huge auditorium-like building with a lacquered floor and large enough for noises to reverberate. The roof was a dome through which the brilliant late morning sun shone through some transparent building material; and behind them, the two awestruck young men saw the platform upon which similar police Fetcher and Patroller vehicles were in a constant state of arrival and departure on a loading platform so long that it dwindled, perspectivewise, into infinity. "Big business," said Slick.

They were escorted across the shining acreage of the Center's interior into a small lounge-like room.

"Wow," said Slick, impressed by the luxurious interior of the room which was done up in hues of green, abstract art and subdued lighting.

"Make yourself comfortable," said the green-helmeted officer through the translucent mask.

"Sure will," said Slick and plopped on a foam rubber sofa.

"What's all this for?" asked Poxie.

"You are to wait here," said the officer, "for your trial."

"Agh," said Poxie making a face of distaste. He now decided to sit.

But the officer didn't leave. He still had some business to attend to. Holding the clipboard stiffly, he said, "Mr. Rodney Cooper." Slick looked up with a "huh" expression.

"You are to answer one question."

"Go ahead," said Slick.

"I'm not finished," said the officer. "After I ask the question and the answer is in the negative, I must inform you that you will then be subject to a polygraph test. Is that understood?"

"Yeah," said Slick.

"Speak louder."

"Yeah," said Slick, knowing now there was an audio pick-up somewhere in this ultra-comfortable lounge.

"Here is the question," said the officer with the clipboard. "Did you, Rodney Cooper, knowingly tamper with the controls of your Mark Nine Phaeton null-vehicle so as to enable that same vehicle to traverse below the legal minimum allowable height on the Alpha-type Roadway when crossing a pedestrian mall?"

"Yes," said Slick. Then he yelled to the hidden pick-up, "Yes!"

The officer now turned to Poxie. "Mr. James Smith."

"Yeah."

"After I ask the question and the answer is in the negative, I must inform you that you will then be subject to a polygraph test. Is that understood?

"Here is the question," said the officer. "Were you a party to this tampering, either by actual aid, sanction or knowledge, of this same Mark Nine Phaeton null-vehicle along with the aforementioned Mr. Rodney Cooper?"

"Yes!"

The officer all but clicked his heels when he said, "That is all." As he made to leave, he had one more thing to say. "To your left is a Menu Selection Board. You may eat if you wish. You have a choice of four main courses."

"Specialty of the house," jeered Slick.

The officer made to leave once more, but Poxie ran up to him and asked, "Hey, Mac. Got a cigarette?"

The police officer lifted an arm, reached into a pocket and gave Mr. James (Poxie) Smith a cigarette. He left.

"What'd you do that for?" asked Slick. "You got cigarettes."

"Wanted to see," said Poxie, lighting up, "if that guy was human."

"Smart," said Slick. "Let's go eat." And he rushed to the Menu Selector. Poxie made to follow him, but not before he noticed the two doors on the far end of the room. Between the doors was a wall chronometer. It read 10:31 A.M.

At 10:33 A.M. the meals came, and the young incarcerates turned to them with gusto.

At 10:36 A.M. the same officer who read the questions to them returned. He had with him two thin plaques.

"What's this?" asked Slick between bites of beef pot roast, as he was handed his plaque.

"An extract of the Criminal Code," said the inscrutable mask of the officer as he handed the other plaque to Poxie. "As it applies to you during the trial." Again, he did an about-face and left.

Said Slick, munching loudly, scanning the plaque given him, "Wow, room service and all. Now they give us reading material with our food." He munched on. "Hey," he said, as if coming upon a gem, "did you know, Friend Poxie, it ain't against the law to mess around with the innards of a null-vehicle?"

"No?" said Poxie, tearing at a chicken drumstick, scanning his reading material. "Why not?"

"Because," said Slick. Then he stopped to chew some more. "Nobody ain't ever done it before. So how are you going to make a law about a crime that can't be committed?"

"I dunno. How?"

"Except it's been committed, Nit!" said Slick with a grin. "Don't you see? Me, Slick, I'm the first one that ever messed with the innards of a null-vehicle. Me."

Poxie was sugaring his coffee as he said: "Then how is it," he took a sip, "that you're here?"

Slick's face dropped a couple of notches. "Oh, they're getting me on an old, old law, statute they call it." He read ". . . Contributing to a felony or being a party to a felony." He looked up. "See, they got ya one way or another. Hey, how about yours? What's yours say?"

Poxie pursed his whole face in reading the thin plaque. "I dunno. Whole bunch of mish mash. Words I never saw, like, ah, well, like eugenics. What's eugenics?"

"I dunno."

Poxie read for a few more minutes. "Well, how about"—scanning his plaque hard and sipping his coffee—"genetics."

"Genetics?" asked Slick brightly. He lay full length on the divan, his meal finished.

"Yeah."

"That's your folks, your mother, father, your grandmother, grandfather, all the way down the line."

"Oh," said Poxie and pushed his plate away; he couldn't finish. He was looking at the wall chronometer which read 10:46 A.M. when the same officer who had visited before entered with the announcement.

"Your trial," he said to both of them, "is over."

When Poxie and Slick had absorbed this news, he continued. "The Tribunal of the State of Kansas . . . finds you Guilty!"

Then came the long reading-out by the officer, as per procedure, ample material for this having been brought along.

"You, Mr. James Smith, First Defendant, according to the criminal code of this State, Article 29, are convicted of, due to criminal negligence, the manslaughter of Cynthia Marie DeSantis, a minor of eight years of age, on May the 8th, ten-oh-one A.M., at Churchill City, Kansas.

"And you, Mr. Rodney Cooper, Second Defendant, are convicted of a lesser count of contributory manslaughter of the same Cynthia Marie DeSantis, in that you, by your own voiced admission, caused—by mechanical manipulation of Drive and Control systems of a null-vehicle, Mark Nine Phaeton, License number EV 30899, Chicago, Illinois, owned and operated by Mr. James Smith, First Defendant—and enabled this same vehicle to dip below the authorized height for civilian vehicles of this type traversing Alpha Roadways and thereupon bringing about the demise of the said Cynthia Marie DeSantis."

The green-helmeted officer took a couple of breaths and continued. "The accumulation of evidence leading to the conviction of First and Second Defendants, Mr. James Smith and Mr. Rodney Cooper, is as follows:

"An indication of occurrence from triangulation sensors at east-west, Route One Hundred and Three Roadway, Co-ordinate B-Four-One-One, which is at Churchill City, Kansas, and accordingly tracked by these same sensors until apprehension was accomplished. It must be stated now to present Defendants, an indication of occurrence by triangulation sensors does not, by itself, constitute evidence. Only a tributary to such evidence.

"The fact of blood found on the seized vehicle of Mr. James Smith did, indeed, match that of the decedent, Cynthia Marie DeSantis.

"A playback from the Accumulator of the vehicle of Mr. James Smith showed that indeed there had been a traversing at heights below that authorized, namely one half a meter from the ground, at point of impact, at a time coinciding with that recorded by the Roadway triangulation sensors, at a time of ten-oh-one A.M., 8th of May.

"The fact of a brief stop immediately following time of occurrence, as recorded by triangulation sensors.

"The fact of traveling at an excessive rate of speed following this recorded impact and stopped by Police Retriever Vehicle oh-oh-nine.

"As further substantiation of the guilt and a proof of lessened probability that this may have been a freak occurrence, a playback of the Accumulator on the vehicle of James Smith shows many such below-authorized-height travels, besides other dangerous practices: overspeeding, too rapid level changes and illegal mid-roadway stops.

"The hypothesis of whether James Smith and Rodney Cooper, the occupants of involved vehicle when seized, were the same occupants of involved vehicle during time of occurrence, ten-oh-one A.M., May 8th; becomes highly substantiated theory. One: when seen that the post-occurrence speed of involved vehicle was too high to permit disembarkation and changeover of occupants. Two: the fact that involved Police Retriever Vehicle oh-oh-nine noted no such change on its scope. Three: an unseized-upon opportunity to deny involvement in the occurrence by the First and Second Defendants in a playback of conversation from Police Retriever Vehicle oh-oh-nine."

The green-helmeted, translucent-masked officer lowered his clipboard. "That," he said, "sums up all the evidence toward you, Mr. Rodney Cooper." Slick seemed to relax.

"Oh, you mean that's all," said Slick facetiously.

The officer directed this next to Poxie. "However, there's additional evidence against you, Mr. James Smith." He raised the clipboard. "In that James Smith, Personal Identification Ex-I-Ex, residence eight-one-one Church Street, Chicago, Illinois, had been operating his vehicle on an Option License, due to a history of the grandfather of James Smith, Beauregard Smith, by name, who was adjudged mentally incompetent and insane, post-occurrence to a driving mishap that took two lives. The case of Beauregard Smith had been relegated to the Authority of the Federal Eugenics Program and an apt notation officially made in regard to the offspring of Beauregard Smith." He lowered the clipboard and asked, "Your father wasn't allowed to drive, right?"

"Right," said Poxie.

"And you were only allowed to drive under an Option?" A question which Poxie did not answer.

"Is that it?" asked Slick, laying back on a divan, chewing on a toothpick. The officer nodded.

"What's next?"

"Sentence," said the green-helmeted officer. Slick sat up in one piece suddenly, and Poxie looked at the chronometer. It read 10:49 A.M.

"Of course you do know," said the officer, "that a complete rundown of all this goes to your immediate relatives. Also, a notification to employers, lodges and associations, debtors and creditors."

"Mostly creditors," said Slick. And Poxie had to grin. Then, Slick snapped his fingers impatiently. "Come on, sentence."

The officer dutifully took to his clipboard and began to read. "Due to the involvement of Rodney Cooper in a fatal accident, his driver's license is hereby revoked . . . forever."

Slick didn't seem fazed. "How about him, Poxie here? His license revoked?" The officer presented a blank mask and didn't answer. "Well," admonished Slick, "how about him? His license revoked?"

The officer answered, "Yes, it's revoked." He resumed reading. "It is the contention of the Tribunal that brilliance of any kind be allowed to perpetuate and that Rodney Cooper, showing proof of a high degree of mechanical aptitude, be allowed to serve where he may be most useful; the Lunar Observation Laboratory . . . for a period of one year."

Poxie winced at the "year on the moon" bit, but Slick went, "Yeow, the moon! I drew the moon!" He actually jumped up.

The officer pointed to one of the doors. "Would you leave now, please," he said to Slick. The addressee looked confused. "The left door," said the officer.

Slick dashed out, yelling, "Be good, Poxie. Take care of yourself, Bo. See you now," and he was gone.

The chronometer read 10:50 A.M.

"And you, my lad, go through the right doorway," said the inscrutable mask of the green-helmeted officer.

As Poxie made to comply, the officer called after him. "Oh, you will be allowed one phone call."

Poxie didn't answer, just kept right on walking.

"You will also be given counsel."

Poxie stopped, puzzled. "Counsel?" He looked at the officer. "Counsel? Now?" He made a face.

"Just go through the right doorway."

Poxie went through the indicated doorway at 10:51 A.M.

At 10:59 A.M. he kissed the crucifix.

At 11:00 A.M. James (Poxie) Smith was vaporized.